W9-CMI-410

Library of Congress
Cataloging-in-Publication Data

Nadelson, Scott.
Aftermath : stories / by Scott Nadelson.
p. cm.
ISBN 978-0-9790188-6-2
(alk. paper)

1. Life change events – Fiction.
I. Title

PS3614.A34A69 2011

813'.6 – DC22

2011002625

Hawthorne Books
& Literary Arts

9 2201 Northeast 23rd Avenue
8 3rd Floor
7 Portland, Oregon 97212
6 hawthornebooks.com
5 *Form:*
4 Adam McIsaac, Bklyn, NY
3
2 Printed in China
1 Set in Paperback

For Alexandra

Acknowledgements

I AM DEEPLY GRATEFUL TO THE OREGON ARTS COMMISSION for an Individual Artist Fellowship, which aided in the completion of this book. I would also like to thank the Foundation for Jewish Culture, the Union of Reform Judaism, Ledig House International Writers Residency, Peter Turchi, Grace Dane Mazur, Adam O'Connor Rodriguez, Rhonda Hughes, Kate Sage, the former big cats – Jay, Van, Jesse, Natalie, Willa, and Erin – and the editors of the publications in which the following stories originally appeared:

"Dolph Schayes's Broken Arm": *Ploughshares*
"Oslo": *upstreet*
"Aftermath": *Glimmer Train Stories*
"The Old Uniform": *American Literary Review*
"If You Needed Me": *Alaska Quarterly Review*
"Backfill": *Camera Obscura*
"Saab": *Cimarron Review*

Stories

AFTERMATH

Scott Nadelson

HAWTHORNE BOOKS & LITERARY ARTS
Portland, Oregon | MMXI

When the summer fields are mown,
When the birds are fledged and flown,
    And the dry leaves strew the path;
With the falling of the snow,
With the cawing of the crow,
Once again the fields we mow
    And gather in the aftermath.

HENRY WADSWORTH LONGFELLOW
Aftermath (Birds of Passage. Flight the Third), 1873

It's over. It's time for loss to build
its tower in the yard where you
are merely a spectator now.

Admit you'd like to find something
discarded or damaged, even gone,
and lift it back into the world.

STEPHEN DUNN
Dismantling the House, 2003

AFTERMATH

Dolph Schayes's Broken Arm

THE SUMMER I FIRST DISCOVERED HOW IT FEELS TO suffer in love, I worked for a local newspaper, selling subscriptions over the phone. It was a miserable job, and I was lousy at it. I stumbled through my script, apologizing too often, agreeing with people on the other end of the line that it was rude to call during dinner, that the paper wasn't well-written, that no one needed so much recycling to haul out to the curb every week. Occasionally I'd convince some mostly deaf grandma to sign up for a trial subscription, free for two weeks, failing to mention that the subscription would continue past the trial period if she didn't call to cancel. I sold one daily to a thirteen-year-old whose father later threatened to sue the company. The job paid minimum wage plus commission. Some of my co-workers made upwards of twenty bucks an hour. Most weeks I put in forty hours and took home less than $180.

I was twenty years old, just finished with my junior year of college, and the previous semester I'd spent in the bed of a girl who'd marked me in a way I now recognize. I wish there were adequate words to describe this sort of thing. The best I can manage is to say that she'd moved something inside me, as if her touch had rearranged my organs. I've experienced the feeling again from time to time, but then it was entirely new and left me in pain even before we'd separated for the summer, she to her parents' house on the south shore of Long Island, me to my parents' in north central New Jersey. The real pain, though, started only when I made it home. The girl – I'll call her Kara – took a day or two to return my calls, and when we did talk there was a distance in her voice I didn't want to admit to. She put off making plans to visit, talking instead about all the old friends with whom she'd reconnected, all the parties to which she'd been invited. One name – Darren, I think – came up too frequently. I pretended not to hear it. She told me about going, on a whim, to a psychic, who'd told her she had all sorts of adventures ahead of her before she settled down. Adventures sounded fun, I said. We could go on one together. Did she want me to drive out to the Island to see her this weekend? She'd check her schedule, she said, and get back to me.

I don't blame her for any of this. I was young and uncommunicative, she was whimsical and self-involved, and I can see now that by the end of the semester my mooning over her must have become oppressive. We were just kids, and our relationship was brief and trivial and fumbling, and I'm sure she's forgotten me long since. I might have forgotten her, too, if not for the suffering she caused me, which didn't feel trivial at all, not then. Not now, either, in part because I've experienced similar suffering since, and its accumulation, I have to believe, accounts at least somewhat for the way I've lived my life, with the expectation that joy will always be tempered by deprivation or longing or loss.

The pain then was physical, located just beneath the arch of my lowest ribs. It was anxiety, I suppose, that wrenched my insides. For most of that summer I couldn't eat without afterwards running to the bathroom, sitting hunched in agony as love scoured my bowels. I'd always been slim, and by mid-June, after dropping five pounds, my face looked gaunt, my eyes and cheeks sunken.

At work I didn't eat at all, for fear of embarrassing myself by running out in the middle of a call, and this is likely what kept me from getting fired. At the beginning and end of the dinner break my supervisor saw me sitting at my station, dialing numbers – the paper didn't have money for automated dialers, or headsets, for that matter – and must have decided I was motivated, if not competent. My co-workers might have begun to resent me, an overachiever, if my commission didn't stay flat from one week to the next. Instead they gave me pep talks, assuring me that when they'd started they'd averaged only four or five subscriptions a week. They were kind not to point out my average was one and a half.

I didn't actually make any calls during the dinner break, instead keeping my finger on the receiver button as I dialed, running through my pitch to customers who didn't exist. It was disconcerting to hear my voice alone in the call room, stammering, apologizing, blowing even imaginary sales. When the others were there my voice was lost in a chorus of aggressive hustling, and it was easier to forget how awkward I sounded, to imagine I was part of a team that was accomplishing something, even if I contributed nothing. My co-workers' sales invigorated me, and I listened to their calls with a measure of hope, a hand pressed to my aching middle.

One voice always stood out from the rest. It belonged to Stanley Davidson, a broad, well-dressed man in his late sixties, the only person to come to work in a jacket and tie. The other men, including me, wore jeans and T-shirts, and some of the women came in sweats. Most of us ran through our scripts as fast as possible, hoping to ambush potential customers into signing up out of sheer bewilderment. Stanley spoke slowly, carefully, enunciating every word. He detailed the merits of *The Daily Record*, from its thorough coverage of local high school sports to its comic strips for children and adults – his grandkids loved *Peanuts*, he'd say, and as for himself, he never missed *Doonesbury* – to the reams of coupons on Sunday. "My wife saved nearly two hundred dollars last week at the Pathmark. That's no small chunk of change." Whether he made a sale or not, he always ended his calls by saying, "I do thank you for your time, sir, and wish you a pleasant evening." As far as I could tell, no one ever hung up on him.

At first I thought Stanley was simply indifferent to his commission, as I was trying to be, but when I sat next to him during a shift and peeked around the divider that separated our stations, I quickly discovered this wasn't true. When he hung up the phone, he'd respond in one of two ways. If he'd sold a subscription he'd raise his hands over his head and toss an invisible ball toward an invisible rim, catching, I imagined, nothing but net. But if the call went badly he'd curse under his breath, bounce a fist softly on his desk, and then say, louder, in his deep, calm, salesman's voice, "Easy, Stanley." Unlike the others in the call room he never offered me any advice or encouragement, but after overhearing me flub four calls in a row, he stuck his head around the divider and said, "No need to be so nervous. We aren't selling warheads, last I checked."

"Maybe I should start reading the paper," I said. "If I knew it as well as you do – "

"I wouldn't use it to wipe my ass," he said. "Not even if it was wrapped in silk."

When I asked how long he'd been working at the *Record*, he glared at me, his face too narrow for its length, I thought, as if his skull had been pinched in a vice, his nose a pitted blotch in its center, eyes heavily hooded. After a moment he said, firmly, "If I don't work, I drink."

The safest subject to approach with Stanley, I soon found out, was basketball, which he'd played in the schoolyards of The Bronx as a teenager, alongside the great Dolph Schayes. I'd never heard of Dolph Schayes but gave an impressed nod anyway, and then looked him up when I got home. "He'd still be the best player in the league," Stanley said, "even with all these big shines and their slam dunks. The man knew how to pass." Stanley and I were both Knicks fans, and this season – 1993-94 – was the most promising we'd had since I was old enough to watch. Our star center, Patrick Ewing, was getting old for the game, and his knees were fragile. Before they gave out, we had one last chance to come away with a championship. Stanley brought a little transistor radio to work, one he must have had for the past twenty years, with a single flesh-colored plug he'd slip into his left ear when our supervisor was out of the room. Between calls he'd lean around our divider and update me on games in progress, giving more detail than I needed – not just who'd scored, but who'd taken down rebounds or made steals and assists. "It's all about passing," he said whenever the Knicks blew an offensive possession. "That's what these people don't understand. Pass, pass, pass. And always keep moving. No one should ever stand still."

That year the Knickerbockers – Stanley always called them by their full name – were tough, scrappy underdogs, strong on defense, and even if I hadn't grown up rooting for them, I would have admired them now. Their roughness appealed to me, their ability to come from behind and squeak out improbable victories. Those evenings I wasn't working I watched every game, hunched forward on my parents' couch to take pressure off my tortured insides. Not quite consciously, I'd begun to pin my hopes on the feisty Knicks, believing that my fortunes were tied up with theirs. The hazy superstition took on real shape after they won the first round of the playoffs, beating the Nets in four games. Kara called a few minutes later, sounding cheerful, pleased to hear my voice. She wasn't a fan, didn't watch sports at all, but still I took it as a sign. I didn't talk to her about basketball, except to mention what I was doing with my free nights, and she couldn't talk long anyway. She was heading out with friends. I didn't ask which friends, but she told me anyway – Melissa, Jamie, Darren.

The rest of the playoffs were agonizing. Both the conference semifinals and finals went to seven games, with the Knicks just barely scraping out enough wins to advance to the championship series. After a loss I was in such pain and so agitated that I couldn't sit still, and even if it was close to midnight I'd head out into my parents' quiet neighborhood, the neighborhood in which I'd spent a simple, placid childhood, and run feverish laps around the block. Some nights I sat on the toilet, doubled up in a cold sweat, until after dawn.

That Stanley, too, was tormented by the Knicks made me feel close to him. We were in this together. A championship was a matter of life and death. Those days following a loss, he looked as if he hadn't slept any more than I had, his blazer rumpled, his face puffy. "Flat-footed," he'd say. "No one wins without moving and passing."

During the championship series he could hardly work. He sat hunched over his phone, hands cupped over his ears to hide his earplug, making calls only during timeouts and commercial breaks. Our supervisor couldn't have failed to notice, but she let it go. And in any case, even making just a few calls an hour, Stanley still sold four times as many subscriptions as I did. For their part, the Knicks seemed outmatched. They lost two of the first three games, Patrick Ewing's height countered by that of Houston's star center, Hakeem Olajuwon. "Dolph could have beat either of them," Stanley said. "I don't care how tall they are."

When the series came home to Madison Square Garden, Stanley took two nights off from work. A friend had tickets to the games, all the way up in the last row of the blue seats, the very top of the arena, but he wouldn't miss this chance for anything. "I didn't make it in '73," he said. "You don't let history pass you by twice, right?" I was born in '73, and had the feeling that history had passed me by altogether, but I agreed with Stanley and told him to cheer extra loud for me. He lent me his radio, with the pink earplug, and for those two nights I suffered alone, imagining Stanley saying, "Pass, pass, move, move!" while I stumbled through my awkward sales pitch, telling people who'd probably never read a newspaper in their lives how much they could save off the newsstand price. At times the pain in my guts made me close my eyes. When the Knicks were down I was nearly in tears. But against all odds they pulled out wins both nights. One more, and they'd be champs. When I came home after the second night, there was a message waiting for me from Kara, her voice on my parents' answering machine warmer than I'd heard it since we'd left campus in early May. She missed me, she said, and hoped we could find a time to visit soon.

Stanley came to work the next evening looking dapper and composed, though there was something manic in his smile and the way he slapped my back and said, "Did you see how they were moving?" I didn't bother reminding him that I'd listened to the game on his radio and couldn't have seen anything. "Just like Dolph and me. Never take a shot without first looking to pass." His calls that night were manic, too, his pitch hastier than usual, some of his words slurred. Whether he made a sale or not he raised his hands and tossed his invisible ball into its invisible net. When we broke for dinner he pulled me out of my chair. "Come and eat," he said. "You're practically skeletal."

I tried to make an excuse, saying I didn't have any money for dinner, that I needed to keep making calls to boost my commission. "Face it," he said. "You're not making any more money until you get a new job. And anyway, I'm buying."

I followed him out of the call center, but instead of heading into the break room, he led me outside, down to the parking lot. He popped the trunk on a huge silver Lincoln, recently washed and waxed, and pulled out a pair of deli sandwiches and bags of potato chips. I was touched that he'd have thought of me when he stopped at the deli, but my mouth was so unused to food that the roast beef tasted burnt to me, its texture slick and heavy and hard to swallow.

He reached into the trunk again, and only now, as he brought out a pair of plastic cups and a half-gallon bottle of gin, did I understand his sloppy smile and slurred speech. "Two more games, and all we need is one win," he said, handing me a cup and pouring generously. "Sometimes you've got to celebrate along the way." I took a few sips and then stopped, waiting to see if the booze would loosen the knot inside me or yank it tighter.

It was a warm night, and we were close enough to the freeway to hear trucks roaring east toward Long Island, or west away from the girl I loved. Stanley downed his gin and refilled his cup. Because I had nothing else to say, I asked him about playing with Dolph Schayes, whose record I now knew almost by heart, from his college days at NYU to his championship season with the Syracuse Nationals in 1955. Stanley set down his cup on the Lincoln's roof. He dribbled an invisible ball, spun, passed, cut across the parking lot, and made a slow but surprisingly graceful lay-up. He came back breathing hard, stepping gingerly with his right foot. "He was better than most people give him credit for," he said, "and most people say he was one of the best ever. He was *the* best ever. Not even a question. When I played with him he was good, and then he broke his arm and got even better. Can you imagine, playing a whole season with a broken arm? His *shooting* arm, for Godsakes. He didn't sit on the bench like one of these big pansy shines. Played the whole time. Learned to shoot lefty. Can you imagine? Not even Mr. tongue-wagger Jordan could do something like that."

He took another shot, this one lazy and half-hearted, and then picked up his cup. He drained it and filled it again. "I was pretty good, too," he said. "Not like Dolph – no one was. But I wasn't bad. Baseline shot, that was my specialty. But nine times out of ten I'd pass. I wasn't selfish, not like these show-boats, rather bounce the ball under their crotch than get it in the bucket." He could have gone on to play college ball, he said. He'd gotten an offer, not from a big-shot program like NYU, but some school in Ohio he'd never heard of. But that was in late '44, and the war was on. As soon as he was eighteen he signed up. He'd just shipped out of San Diego, a few hundred miles into the Pacific, when the bomb fell on Hiroshima. "It was all over by the time I got there."

He said it sadly, as if this were the great disappointment in his life, much worse than working a terrible job selling newspapers to keep himself from drinking. He drank now, another long gulp, and I handed him the second half of my sandwich. He finished it without a word. He looked rumpled again, his blazer sagging on his shoulders. My bowels churned, and even though we had another fifteen minutes before the break was over, I had to excuse myself and run for the bathroom. I was glad to get away from him, from the images he'd put in my mind, of Dolph Schayes playing ball with a broken arm, of a young man on the deck of a ship, yearning for a war that was over before he could join it. Both things added to the weight inside me, to the faint, fading hope that grew more painful with every passing day, with every feat of Patrick Ewing and his small band of scrappy underdogs. I told myself I'd never eat again.

When I came back from the bathroom, empty and sweating, Stanley was at his station, leaning back in his chair, eyes closed. I spent the rest of the shift with my finger on the receiver button, pretending to dial, running through my script more fluently than ever, offering huge savings to people who weren't there.

THE KNICKS, OF course, lost the series. The sixth game was a heartbreaker, close until the final moments. I watched the seventh on my day off, alone, in agony, imagining that my appendix had burst. The next day, Stanley and I didn't talk. He sat morosely in his station, making calls in his old, calm, steady voice, racking up sales, raising his commission. I wanted him to comfort me, to say that our Knickerbockers would be back next year, a stronger team, with more experience. I wanted him to tell me that Ewing still had a few good years left in his knees. Kara hadn't returned my most recent call, and by now I was mostly certain she wouldn't, except to let me know that she'd met someone else, that she was sorry to hurt me, that I was a great guy who was certain to make some lucky girl happy, that her psychic had told her so.

That call did come, eventually, at the end of the summer, long after I'd lost the job at the newspaper and found a better one at a screenprinting shop, where I hosed off squeegees and folded T-shirts and ducked behind the building with my co-workers to smoke joints two or three times a day. By then my appetite had returned – helped by the joints, I'm sure – and I even found myself interested in another girl, the shop's shy receptionist. I slept with her before the summer was over and then didn't call her, as I promised I would, when I went back to school in the fall.

But that day after the Knicks' defeat, I couldn't have imagined any of this. I still held onto the smallest measure of hope, and the pain inside me was unbearable. I'd given up making calls altogether and was beginning to catch looks from my supervisor, whose compassion, I knew, would extend only so far. It unnerved me that Stanley's voice was so calm and assured, betraying nothing. Toward the end of the shift I peeked around the divider, and then I could see what his words didn't let on. After he logged a subscription, he just went on to the next call without shooting a hoop. And when he blew an easy sale, his fist pounded the desk. Then he picked up the receiver and clocked himself, hard, across the temple. Hard enough to make him wince and grunt and close his eyes.

Somehow it was the worst thing I'd ever seen, and even now I wish I hadn't looked. Wasn't life already disappointing enough? Why add willingly to your own pain? My eyes burned with threatening tears, and I turned my chair away.

I wanted to tell Stanley something, but what could I say? That not everyone could be as good as Dolph? That for most people it was pointless to play ball with a broken arm? That he should have felt lucky to have missed the war and all its dangers, the likelihood that he wouldn't have survived?

When our shift ended, the supervisor asked me to stay behind. I said goodbye to Stanley, knowing I wouldn't see him again. He only muttered, "Another day, another dollar lost for you," and brushed past me. I imagined I saw a lump rising on his forehead. I kept picturing it as I drove away, growing larger and purple, spreading across his receding hairline, and wondered how he'd explain it to his wife when he got home, to his co-workers when he returned in the morning. The sky had turned that same shade of purple, the whole world become an enormous, tender bruise. By the time I made it to my parents' house, the noose around my guts had loosened the slightest bit, and I knew I no longer had hope for anything.

Oslo

Jerusalem, August 1995

THE ORANGE SODA WAS TOO GASSY FOR JOEL TO GULP.
He'd wanted orange juice but had made the mistake of letting
his grandfather order for him. His grandmother had made the
same mistake, and now the waitress brought out coffee in
tiny ceramic cups. His grandfather took one sip, said, "Awful,"
and pushed the entire saucer away.

His grandmother winced but managed to swallow. "It's
Turkish," she said. "If we want regular, I think we have to order
'filtered.'"

"Awful," his grandfather repeated. His white hair stuck up
an inch from his scalp all around, so thick it was hard to see
how a brush could make its way through. His skin seemed thick,
too, but darker and leathery from the Florida sun, the wrinkles
circling his eyes like cracks in a punctured windshield. Joel knew
something about windshield cracks, having shot a BB at his
mother's boyfriend's Mustang a week before they'd left on this
trip. His grandfather wore a white golf shirt, white linen slacks,
white socks and tennis shoes, and in his back pocket was a white
cloth hat he'd put on when he started to overheat. He flipped
through the guidebook he hadn't let go of once in the last two days,
holding it at arm's length to read. "The tour starts at ten-thirty."

"You told us already," Joel said. "You told us yesterday."

"Why don't you put your glasses on," his grandmother said.
"You'll strain your eyes."

"We should get going," his grandfather said.

"We've got half an hour," his grandmother said.

"We're always early," Joel said.

His grandmother lifted her cup to her lips, balancing it between both thumbs and forefingers. "I'd like to finish my coffee. It's lovely once you get used to the grit."

The café was on Ben Yehuda Street, their table so far out into the pedestrian lane that twice now, a passing tourist had bumped Joel's arm. "Good for people watching," his grandmother had said, but Joel watched only his fingers in the mesh of the wrought iron table top, his pinkie able to wriggle through one of the holes. He was thirteen, three months past his bar mitzvah, a sunken-chested boy with long twig arms that suggested he might, one day, grow taller than his grandfather, who claimed to be five-foot-nine but couldn't have been more than five-seven, Joel was sure. Joel's father was five-nine, but since Joel hadn't seen him since his bar mitzvah reception three months ago, it was hard to remember exactly how tall that looked. His mother's boyfriend was six-three, too tall for his mother, Joel thought. Too loud for his mother, too, with a booming voice that bubbled up from his round belly. His mother had been going out with Dennis for nearly a year now, her soft words drowned out by Dennis's constant yammering, his snorting laugh. Dennis knew something about everything and didn't let anyone else talk, ever. You could say, "I ate a yeti for lunch today," and Dennis would twist the end of his mustache and answer, "Funny story about yetis. When I was backpacking through Nepal and Pakistan—" And then he'd be off, talking for an hour straight about climbing to base camp at K2, about how he thought his ear was frostbitten and ready to fall off, about his friend who went snowblind and nearly dropped into a crevasse, but not another word about yetis.

It was impossible not to hate him, and all summer Joel had tried to make Dennis hate him back. He'd hidden his wallet for a whole week, returning it only when Dennis said, "Look,

pal, I'm about to run out of gas. You let me have my Visa, I'll buy
you a guitar. I started playing when I was about your age. First
guitar I had was a beat-up Les Paul – " Then he was off again, talking about his band, the time he'd gotten thrown off the stage
at the Fillmore, and to shut him up, Joel brought him his wallet.
Later, he let the air out of all the Mustang's tires. After his mother
lectured him for half an hour, Joel shook Dennis's hand and
muttered an apology. "A truce, huh?" Dennis said. "Just like Grant
and Lee at Appomattox. 'The Gentlemen's Agreement.' Most
people think that was the end of the war, but it wasn't. Did you
know the last Confederate general to surrender was the Cherokee
Stand White – "

Truces were made to be broken, though he knew the BB
had been going too far. He'd borrowed the gun from a neighbor
kid and then swore he'd had nothing to do with the hole in the
windshield. His mother had promised to punish him as soon as
she had enough evidence. It was only a matter of time before
she found out where he'd gotten the gun, one of the few things
that made him thankful to be spending the next three weeks
halfway around the world. The windshield would be fixed by the
time he got home, the whole thing, with luck, forgotten.

This trip was his bar mitzvah present from his grandparents, though he'd asked for a computer or cash. His grandmother
had kept it secret until after the reception, when only a few
family members were left at his mother's house. Joel had already
been in a lousy mood by then, because his father had just left,
on his way back to Seattle, where he sold medical equipment and
lived in a converted warehouse. Joel hadn't been out to see
him yet, and could only imagine him walking around in an open,
echoing space, cardboard boxes stacked in one corner, a fork-
lift in another. Before he drove to the airport, his father had
clapped him on the back and said, "Way to go, kiddo. You really
nailed that *haftarah*." But Dennis had been close by, and though
he wasn't even Jewish, started talking about the origins of
the Kabbalah. Joel wanted to pull his father away, talk to him in

private, ask him about the warehouse and when he might visit, but his father seemed interested in what Dennis was saying, nodding often and encouraging him with a mumbled, "Is that so?" and "I had no idea." Didn't he know better than to humor the guy? Didn't he want to knock him on his ass for the nerve of dating his ex-wife? Soon his father checked his watch and said, "I'd love to hear more, but it'll have to wait till next time. Come give me a hug, JoJo. Have fun opening your presents."

Then his grandmother came to him with an envelope, smiling in a tense, close-lipped way that tried to hide her excitement but couldn't. She looked much younger than his grandfather, partly because she dyed her hair a reddish brown and kept it up in a wispy sort of perm, partly because her skin, though slack over cheeks and chin, was the softest he'd ever felt. When she kissed him he smelled baby oil. The envelope wasn't heavy, which meant most likely there was a check inside, not cash. A check would go straight into his bank account, not to be seen again until college, but he'd already pocketed three hundred-dollar bills his Uncle Ron, a dentist, had slipped him on the sly. But now, instead of a check, he pulled out a plane ticket. Seattle, he thought, and got ready to hug his grandmother. But then he saw the airline: El Al. "We leave on August first!" his grandmother squealed, and his grandfather said to people around him, "It nearly killed the woman to keep a secret this long. It's all I've heard about for six months." Joel missed his father already and wanted to cry, but his grandmother was smiling so brightly, the relatives saying what a wonderful gift it was, especially now with all the recent developments, peace finally within reach, that he did hug her and said thanks to his grandfather, who took the ticket from him, saying he'd keep it safe until they left. "The thing about Israel," Dennis said. "It's not just the history that's complicated, or the politics, but the people who live there –"

And that's when Joel had had it, heading up to his room, leaving the rest of his presents for another day.

NOW HE FINISHED his orange soda and tried to belch, but the gas just rattled around his chest and leaked out silently. His grandmother smiled at him, black grounds caught between her front teeth, top and bottom. It was still morning and already too hot, hotter even than Fort Lauderdale, where his grandparents lived between a golf course and a pond shared by exotic birds and an alligator. Already his grandfather had the scowling, impatient look that for the past three days hadn't shown up until afternoon. All around them were air-conditioned buildings, but here they were, sitting under the broiling sun like morons. Across the street was McDavid's, a name Joel found less funny than curious, wondering what the Jewish version of the Big Mac would taste like, whether there was a Ronald McDavid with a beard and sidelocks. Twice so far he'd asked if they could eat there, but his grandfather said fast food would clog your arteries whether it was kosher or not.

Joel had never thought much about coming to Israel, though his Hebrew school teacher, Mrs. Nachman, had talked about it constantly, closing her eyes and saying wistfully, "Next year in Jerusalem," even when it was six months until Passover. The walls of her classrooms were covered in maps made between 1967 and 1978, none with the Green Line printed in, just a solid mass from the Golan to Sinai. "If we give up land for peace, the six million die in vain," she told the class. "When the next Holocaust comes, you'll be glad there's enough room for all of us." Another time she said, "The Arabs, they breed like vermin. That's why you have to have as many children as you can." She called Rabin a traitor, Clinton a fool, Arafat the spawn of demons. Joel didn't question what she said, didn't care one way or another, until she started talking about intermarriage. "If you want to get divorced, go ahead, marry a gentile. If you want to destroy three thousand years of history. If you want to spit on the graves of the six million." The Jewish girls Joel knew were all flat-chested and loudmouthed, and he had no intention of marrying any of them. At his bar mitzvah he'd danced with three girls from his middle school, all blonde, all Christian, all giggling at the blessings over the wine and bread. Afterward, Dennis said, "You've got an eye for the *shiksas*, huh, pal? You know about Portnoy's complaint?" Before he could go on, Joel said, "I'm not complaining," and all the adults around him laughed.

He knew he should be grateful to his grandparents for bringing him here, knew he should feel a connection to the land Mrs. Nachman called his birthright. But all they did was take tours of one part of the city or another, and it was like being around Dennis for hours on end, getting piled with dates and details when all he wanted was to let his head be empty for a change. It was a hundred degrees and he had to wear long pants everywhere or else get turned away from the churches and synagogues and mosques. They had three weeks of tours planned, to the Galilee, to the Negev, to the Mediterranean coast, and he thought he'd go crazy. The only place he wanted to go was the Dead Sea, to find out if he really could float because of all the salt, but that trip wasn't planned until their last week, and by then he'd just want to stay at the hotel, floating in the pool.

All he liked so far were the shops, the ones here on Ben Yehuda Street with silver and ceramic menorahs, the ones in the Arab bazaar that sold spices and pungent meat and strangely shaped pipes. He'd already gotten his grandfather to buy him a pair of sandals and a T-shirt: The Grateful Dead play the Dead Sea. He wore the shirt now. Last summer he'd had a camp counselor who'd worn Grateful Dead T-shirts every day, and though he'd never heard the music, Joel mimicked the lazy way the counselor had walked, swinging his arms loosely from the shoulders. He liked the picture on the front, a skeleton wrapped in robes, riding a camel. His grandfather hadn't wanted to buy it and peered at it disdainfully now. "You look like the Grim Reaper," he said.

"The Grim Reaper doesn't ride a camel," Joel said.

"How do you know? Ever seen him?"

"He carries a scythe," Joel said.

"Maybe he's got it hidden under his robes," his grandfather said.

"I think it's an interesting shirt," his grandmother said. Now, along with coffee grounds, lipstick had smeared on her teeth. "It's clever."

"It doesn't make any sense," his grandfather said. "Why would a dead person be grateful?"

"How would you know?" Joel asked. "Ever met one?"

"Drink up already," his grandfather said. "It's time to go."

A group of soldiers was passing as they stood, his grandfather puzzling over the bill, holding each coin up to one eye before laying it on the tray. There were five of them, and two were girls. Joel's grandfather had said he could never get used to seeing guns everywhere he turned, but Joel couldn't get over the sight of girls carrying them, the rifles almost half their size, their green uniforms calling attention to tan skin and big dark eyes. If he lived here, he thought, maybe he'd change his mind about intermarriage. His grandmother turned her smile on them, and Joel flinched at the sight of her stained teeth. She held up her camera and said, "Would you mind?" They gathered together and grinned patiently, one of the boys making a face, another holding two fingers over one of the girls' heads. "No, no," his grandmother said. "Be serious. I want you to look like soldiers."

The tallest of the boys winked at Joel and said, "Yes, yes, be serious. No time for jokes." He called out a command in Hebrew, and all of them stood at attention.

"Couldn't one of you hold your gun in front?" his grandmother asked. The two girls unslung their rifles, gripping black metal in tiny brown hands. "Joel, go stand with them." He shook his head. "Go on."

"Yes, come," one of the girls said.

The tall boy said, "Come, Mr. Grateful Dead. We'll make a soldier of you."

His face burned. His grandmother's teeth were repulsive, her eyebrows arched over the top of the camera. His grandfather

was looking at his watch. One of the girls put a hand on his shoulder, and he tried to smile. "You couldn't give him a gun to
hold, could you?" his grandmother asked. "No, of course not.
Just another second. Okay. Now smile. Wait, no, don't smile. Be
serious."

"Just take it already," Joel said. The camera snapped while
his mouth was open.

One of the girls squeezed his chin between two fingers,
the other tugged his ear. "Have a nice day, Captain Groovy," the
darker of the two said. "Watch out for the brown acid."

"A souvenir," the prettier one said, and handed him a
golden rifle shell, the length and width of his forefinger.

"Let's go," his grandfather said. "If we're late, I'm not talking to either of you for the rest of the day."

YESTERDAY'S TOUR HAD been called "Archaeological Wonders of
the Old City." Today's was "Religious Communities of Jerusalem,"
and they looked at the same stone walls, the same churches
and synagogues and mosques. But Joel liked today's tour guide
better than yesterday's, a mumbly woman with a thick accent
he could hardly understand. Today's guide was Lou, a man as old
as his grandfather, only taller, almost as tall as Dennis, with a
limp and a nasal voice like that of Joel's Uncle Ron, who lived in
the Bronx. "I came over in '48," Lou said. "Wanted to be a
big-shot hero." He patted his thigh. "Careful what you ask for."

Lou asked Joel his name, and for the rest of the tour
called him, "Mr. Schreiber." He talked about history, and just as
Joel's head began to swim with facts, with images of Dennis's
mustache, of the Mustang and the hole in its windshield, said,
"It's not boring at all, is it, Mr. Schreiber. It's the reason you're
here." And Joel nodded.

Half the people on the tour were European, and they
squinted and strained to understand what Lou was saying. Three
young men from Nicaragua fingered crucifixes hanging around
their necks and asked every few minutes, "Via Dolorosa?"

"Not yet," Lou said. "First, we're going to visit – " He lowered his voice and finished dramatically, "The Armenian Quarter!" The Nicaraguans shrugged and shuffled their feet. Lou pointed out bullet holes above the Zion Gate – some as wide around as Joel's wrist and deep enough for him to put his whole fist in – and said, "The last ones we'll ever have here, right, Mr. Schreiber?"

"How come you didn't come over in '48?" Joel asked his grandfather. "Didn't you want to be a hero?"

His grandfather forced his hat down over his springy hair. "I had a family to take care of."

"Big deal," Joel said.

"I'm not like some people – "

"Charlie," his grandmother said, and his grandfather shoved his hands in his pockets and looked away.

At the Western Wall, Joel thought about sticking a note between the cracks as he saw others doing, something like "Get rid of Dennis," but he knew God didn't make things so easy. If anything He'd make Joel suffer through another year of Dennis just for asking. Instead he tried to measure how big each stone block was – his whole arm span, plus half another. He spent some time staring up at pigeons roosting on the stones above, and wondered whether it would be a secret blessing or an omen of disaster to get crapped on at the holiest place in the world. When he rejoined the group, Lou said, "You're quite the mystic, huh, Mr. Schreiber?" Joel didn't know how to answer, so he shrugged. "I know what you mean," Lou said. "I don't have a religious bone in my body, but when I saw that wall for the first time in '67, man, I fell down on my knees and cried. Okay, everybody. Now we're about to enter – " Again the pause, the lowering of his voice. "The Muslim Quarter!"

"I still can't believe where we are," his grandmother said for the third time today, and maybe the twentieth since their plane had landed.

"Believe it already," his grandfather said. "Because there's nowhere else we could possibly be."

But Joel couldn't, either. Even after three days, he couldn't. In his mind he pictured a globe, the little strip of land no more than half the size of his thumbnail. He pictured his trajectory, from New Jersey to the JFK Airport, and then out over the ocean, but where did they go from there? Across Europe? Straight down the length of the Mediterranean? He pictured Mrs. Nachman's maps, but in no way could he connect them with the crowded bazaar, the racks of rugs and leather purses, the strange smells of spices and rotting meat, the sound of a kitten crying soon drowned out by a boy shouting, "Alo, alo, alo!" before barreling past them with an oversized wheelbarrow. He had the same trouble when he located Seattle on the globe in his bedroom and tried to link the word with his father. He had to spread his thumb and forefinger as far apart as they would stretch to bridge the distance between them. The only time he ever listened to Dennis was when Dennis described Seattle, which of course he'd been to a dozen times. Occasionally Joel would even prompt him, asking how tall was the Space Needle, how far away was Mount Rainier. "Your dad picked one of the prettiest places in the world to live," Dennis said, and for a minute Joel thought maybe he could actually like the man, that they could be something short of friends. But then Dennis went on, "When you go visit him, you'll have to take the ferry to the San Juans. You might see some Orcas. Did you know that Orcas are probably the smartest animals in the world? Some people think dolphins are smarter, but–"

Joel had called his father the night before he'd left and asked if he could come visit when he got home. "Doesn't school start right after?" his father asked.

"I don't care," Joel said.

"I'm sure your teachers care. We'll get you out here some-time soon."

"Thanksgiving?"

"Maybe," his father said. "I'll check out my schedule, and we'll talk about it when you get back. I gotta go now, JoJo. You have a great time with all the zealots. Send me some postcards. And don't let your grandparents drive you too nuts."

That night at dinner he spilled a full glass of Coke on Dennis's lap. His mother lectured him in the same tired voice she used to use with his father those late nights Joel stayed up listening at the door of his room, the words lost to him, the tone clear and hopeless. Her eyes were full of tears. He would have taken it back then if he could have. "It was an accident," he said when she told him to apologize. He repeated it enough times that he began to believe it himself. Tears formed in his own eyes. "I swear."

From the sink, where he was mopping up his crotch with a dishtowel, Dennis said, "If he says it was an accident, then I believe him." His voice was softer than usual, almost as tired as Joel's mother's, with a little tremble to it that made Joel furious. The last thing in the world he wanted was to feel sorry for the man. Dennis kept his back to them, fanning the wet spot with a pot lid. "No need to apologize. We'll just let it go, okay, pal?"

It was lunchtime now, and his grandmother handed him a pita stuffed with falafel. He'd eaten falafel three days in a row now and didn't see how it was any better for his arteries than McDavid's. This one tasted sour, maybe because he was eating it standing up, staring at a row of hanging goat heads, no skin but eyes intact. Beneath the sound of sizzling oil he heard the kitten still but couldn't spot it. His own sweat stunk worse than the rotting meat, and he knew he wouldn't be able to wear the Grateful Dead T-shirt again until after he'd gotten home and washed it, and then only when Dennis wasn't around to see it and start in about rock concerts and the Fillmore. The soda can his grandmother handed him had a lemon on its side, but what came out of it tasted like licorice.

"It's really remarkable," his grandmother said. "Don't you think? That they can all live together like this?"

"Anyone can live together when soldiers are walking around with machine guns," his grandfather said. "I don't see how you can trust these people. Doesn't anyone remember the Olympics? The whole team, slaughtered."

"These are our friends," Lou said, and just then, as if to prove it, a shopkeeper stepped out of a stone alcove choked with shelves of silver trinkets, grabbed Lou's hand, and pumped it vigorously.

"My friend!" the shopkeeper said. "My friend! It's too long, too long. When are you coming to see us?" He was as short as Joel, mostly bald, with a patchy mustache that seemed to grow straight out of his wide nostrils. He turned to the group and said, "You like Mr. Lou's tour? The best tour. The best man. Yes."

"Get outta here," Lou said, brushing away the compliment with a backhanded wave.

The shopkeeper's smile, surprisingly white teeth fringed by the gray hairs of his mustache, turned toward Joel. "You are Jew?" he asked. Joel blinked. Was he supposed to answer? He glanced at Lou, at his grandparents, looking for a sign, but found none. He thought of Mrs. Nachman, who warned that anti-Semitism lurked around every corner, who told the class over and over, "Never apologize for who you are." He nodded. The shopkeeper threw open his arms, hugged him, and said, "I am Arab! We are brothers!" Then he fixed a *kufiya* on Joel's head, borrowed his grandmother's camera, and took a picture of him standing next to Lou. Joel wondered what Mrs. Nachman would think when she saw it – spawn of demons! – and felt some kind of pleasure at the thought of her horror. When Joel tried to return the cloth, the shopkeeper shook his head. "For you, for you." To Joel's grandfather he said, "Twenty shekels."

Lou herded them out of the bazaar and announced, finally, "Via Dolorosa!" The three Nicaraguans dropped to their knees and crawled. Lou greeted a monk in a brown robe and rope sandals, who was renting man-sized crosses for Christians to carry. Joel's grandfather tugged on his hat and said, "I don't trust any of them."

"So?" Joel said. "Why didn't you come do something about it in '48?"

"I told you already," his grandfather said. "I had a family to take care of."

"Charlie," his grandmother warned again, but this time his grandfather went on.

"I'm not like some people. Move to Seattle. Abandon their families. Try to forget they ever had kids. I always knew he was a louse, from the first time I met him."

"Charlie, please," his grandmother said.

"You think he paid a dime for that fancy reception of yours, for that awful D.J. with the music so loud?" His grandfather took off his hat and smacked it against a thigh. "You think he sends the checks for support like he's required by law? If it weren't for me and that big doofus who loves your mother so much you'd both be in the poorhouse. No grim reaper T-shirts or anything else to wear."

Now it was Joel's turn to shove his hands in his pockets. He fingered the bullet the girl soldier had given him, along with a pair of loose shekels. He tasted the sour falafel again, and his stomach gave a sudden roll. Above him was a stone arch bridging the street, a window in the middle from which tinny dance music trickled down, the beat unexpectedly in rhythm with the sound of a power drill he could hear but couldn't see. He could already picture the hole the rifle cartridge would make in the Mustang's windshield, gaping next to the BBs. There were no such things as truces.

Lou said, "All right, folks. Now it's on to – the Christian Quarter!"

THE LAST STOP on the tour was Mea She'arim. It was a relief to get out of the Old City, the dusty air held in by dusty walls, but outside Joel didn't have any easier time breathing. His insides felt shaky, with anger, he guessed, though it bothered him that being angry made him want to cry. He hung back from the group, as far away from his grandfather as he could get. The Nicaraguans had stayed behind at the Holy Sepulchre, and somehow this, too, bothered him – everything, it seemed, was falling apart. Lou called, "Mr. Schreiber, you're missing out back there. I've got important stuff to tell you."

His grandmother said, "Joel, honey, your grandfather didn't mean it."

"Let him pout," his grandfather said.

They crossed a busy arterial clogged with traffic, drivers honking and shouting as Lou waved the group across. Out here he couldn't tell Jews from Arabs – everyone looked dark and enraged, and without clothes to distinguish them they might as well have been the same people. "Better cover your shoulders before we go in," Lou told a pair of European women, who draped themselves with silk scarves. "They take modesty pretty seriously." He talked about the different sects of Haredim and pointed out more synagogues and yeshivas. Rickety balconies sagged from the back of a crumbling tenement. An ultra-Orthodox man in a long coat and wide felt hat saw them, turned, and hurried off in another direction. Mrs. Nachman didn't think any better of these people than she did the Arabs. She called them "the black hats," and said they were traitors for refusing to join the army. Some didn't even believe in the state of Israel, she told the class, preferring instead to wait for the Messiah to come and give them their homeland. "They can wait all they want," she said. "In the meantime, we have to defend ourselves against the next Hitler."

In a courtyard strung with flapping laundry, a pair of women bald beneath headscarves shouted at them and made angry gestures. "They don't approve of women wearing trousers," Lou said. He tried to pacify them, but before long another tour group followed them in, blocking the way out. Pebbles rained down from a nearby rooftop. Joel had seen enough images on TV

to think of them now, dirty children hurling fist-sized rocks
and Molotov cocktails at soldiers who responded with rubber
bullets and live rounds. His grandfather was right – they
shouldn't have trusted anyone. Shading his eyes he could see
half a dozen boys on the roof, with wispy sidelocks and yarmul-
kes, wiping their dusty hands on white dress shirts, then picking
up more pebbles and tossing. "Get back!" Lou cried, but with
the other group behind them, there was nowhere to go. Several
of the European women had taken refuge in a doorway, but
Joel and his grandparents were left exposed against a bare wall.
A few larger stones pinged against the roof of a parked car, its
windshield clouding with chips.

"Animals," Joel's grandfather said.

"They're Jewish!" his grandmother cried.

The pebbles kept coming. Two or three hit Lou around the
face and neck. Joel's grandfather tried to edge into the doorway
behind the European women. His grandmother stood her ground,
spreading her arms in front of Joel, her back to the falling
stones. She whispered in a strange, exhilarated voice, "I can't
believe where we are!" The women in headscarves yelled louder.
And Lou was yelling now, too, not at the boys on the roof but at
the other tour guide, a bewildered looking woman Joel's mother's
age, wearing a floppy yellow sun hat. "She should know better,"
Lou said. "Bringing them in here wearing shorts and tank tops."

Something ugly was happening in Joel's stomach. He had
the rifle cartridge out of his pocket, gripped in a fist, the metal
slick in his sweaty palm. Why couldn't he be in Seattle, or at home,
or anywhere other than here? Why couldn't there be a war, so
he wouldn't have had to come? He cursed the peace accords the
way Mrs. Nachman did – to hell with Arafat and Rabin and
Clinton, to hell with Dennis, his mother, his father. He was going
to be sick. The falafel was poison. The shopkeeper's grin, his
patchy mustache, had hidden malicious intentions. The skeleton
on his T-shirt was laughing. Everyone hated him, Arabs, Jews,
it didn't matter. And his father hated him most. "As soon as I'm

settled," he'd told Joel the day he'd moved, and that night his mother had said in her tired, tear-filled voice, "Don't hold your breath." For his bar mitzvah present his father had given him a savings bond, a hundred dollars that wouldn't mature until Joel was twenty-three.

Everyone hated him except his grandmother, whose eyes were wild now as pebbles drummed her back, and Dennis, who'd given him the guitar he'd promised, a Les Paul like the one he'd played at the Fillmore. Joel would never forgive him for it. He dropped to his knees and heaved, splattering the cuffs of his grandfather's pants and the thighs of his own.

"I THINK HE'LL be all right now," his grandmother said.

"Just make sure he gets lots of water," Lou said, and ruffled Joel's hair.

They were back on Jaffa Street, the whizzing traffic making Joel dizzy. The sun reflecting from sand-colored buildings stung his eyes. His grandmother had a welt on her neck where a pebble had struck, but her face was shining, her teeth clean and bright now, free of coffee grounds and lipstick when she smiled. His grandfather looked stricken, gaze darting about the street, shoulders flinching at every sound, his cloth hat missing.

"Sorry about the ruckus," Lou said and patted his bad leg. "I guess you got the full Israel experience."

"It was the best tour I've ever been on," Joel's grandmother said.

"Get outta here," Lou said, with another backhanded wave. "You take care of yourself, Mr. Schreiber. Stick with hamburgers for a while."

The thought of hamburgers nearly made him retch again, but he managed to breathe and settle his guts. Lou hobbled onto a bus and disappeared. "I don't see why anyone would want to come here," his grandfather said hoarsely. "It's a third-world country. They're all barbarians." It was strange to see him looking so jittery and embarrassed, his clothes so bright in the crowd of dark faces. That he was a coward wasn't a surprise, but Joel didn't feel up to reveling in it now. He'd lost the bullet the pretty soldier had given him. All that was left in his pockets were a pair of shekels and the *kufiya* from the bazaar, which he'd used to wipe vomit from his mouth and chin. He didn't know if he would have come in '48, either.

They were all the way back to Ben Yehuda Street before his stomach rebelled, and he had to run into the bathroom at McDavid's. There was no bearded Ronald McDavid in here, nothing to distinguish the place from any fast-food joint at home. The air-conditioning and the familiar smell of burgers and fries calmed him, and he sat on the toilet looking at graffiti in three languages. He could read only two lines: "I like kosher meat," in black print, and beneath, in slanting red cursive, "Jewish faggot."

The night before they'd left, Dennis had told him about the joys of traveling, the strange experiences that were what made life worth living. Joel had pretended to read a magazine, trying not to listen. "I've told you about that hike up K2," Dennis said. "About halfway to base camp I got so cold I thought I was finished. But then I looked behind me, to see how far I'd come. Right then the fog lifted, and the whole range opened up. Mountains peaks in all directions, and I was higher than any of them. Suddenly I didn't care anymore if I made it to the top. Didn't care if I made it home. Didn't care if I lived or died. That's when I knew I'd done something worthwhile."

"What's taking so long?" his grandfather called from outside the stall. "Are you sick?" Joel didn't answer. As long as he didn't move, he thought, his insides would keep from surging. Through his thin pants, the ceramic cooled his legs. The illegible writing on the door might have told important secrets if only he could read it. He could sound out some familiar letters but couldn't put meaning to any of the words. He had the feeling that he shouldn't leave until he knew what they said. His grandfather knocked. "Did you fall in or what?"

Aftermath

I.

TRIAL SEPARATION. IT SOUNDED LIKE AN APPROPRIATE step, though far from permanent, and that's what Richard and Alana Weintraub agreed to, not quite seven years into their marriage. They'd give themselves some time, see how things felt, and then there was always the possibility of counseling. They wouldn't do anything rash, like filing papers, until all other options had been exhausted. A few weeks before the start of the school year, Richard found an apartment two miles from their house and signed a six-month lease that started on September first. The next day Alana came with him to look it over. She didn't want him to be miserable, she said. There was no reason either of them should suffer. They agreed that the place was too small and potentially noisy, with neighbors above and below and on both sides, but Richard insisted it was only temporary – no matter what finally happened between them – and it would suit him just fine. She helped him pick out some furniture, an armchair, a kitchen table, a desk. He bought the bed himself, debating between a double and a queen, finally deciding on the smaller to save money, though he liked the idea of extra room to stretch his legs after so many years of being confined to half a mattress. He booked a small U-Haul for Labor Day weekend and started boxing his winter clothes, a spare set of dishes, a stack of LPs he hadn't listened to for nearly a decade, camping gear that had never been used. The last he could have left in the garage, but the apartment came with a storage unit, and the thought of having nothing to put inside made him uneasy for reasons he couldn't explain.

A week before he left, Alana's mother sent him a house-warming gift, a frosted crystal vase from a boutique in Santa Barbara; once poor, she now couldn't spend her new husband's money fast enough. Alana's father, still poor, offered to help with the move, and to make him feel needed, Richard accepted. Larry rode the train out from Brooklyn, spent the night on the hide-a-bed, and helped pack the truck the next morning. Only when the rear door was closed and locked did he offer, looking down at his shoes and rubbing the back of his neck, to return the rig to U-Haul when they were through. He just had a few things to pick up from a friend in Syosset, and he'd have it back before noon the next day. "I'll save you the extra hassle," Larry said. "You did book it overnight, didn't you?"

Richard shouldn't have been surprised but was furious anyway. Why couldn't the man just ask to borrow it? Why did he have to act as if he were doing Richard a favor, making it nearly impossible to turn him down? "Be a pain for you, wouldn't it?" Richard said. "Not much parking in your neighborhood."

"I can manage," Larry said. "You could give me a few bucks to stick it in a garage."

"Be more than a few bucks."

"Safer that way."

"Dad," Alana said, coming out of the house with a few shirts Richard had forgotten, left months ago in the laundry room. He'd meant to iron them, but now he thought he'd just take them to the dry cleaner's. Or else he'd chuck them and buy new shirts, start everything fresh. "We're not giving you any money. You can leave it on the street."

"It'd be safer in my parking lot," Richard said.

"You don't want to deal with it tomorrow. You've got all this stuff to unpack."

"How do you know what I want?"

"I'll park it on Henry," Larry said. "No one'll mess with it there."

"If it's late they'll charge me for an extra day."

"It'll be there."

"I can't go looking all over Brooklyn for it. I've got to finish my lesson plans."

"Rich," Alana said, shoving the shirts at him. "He said he'd have it there."

She didn't trust her father any more than Richard did, but he knew she didn't want them arguing today. She didn't want to think too much about the truck or the new apartment or the way the house would feel the first few hours after he was gone, and he didn't blame her – he wanted to be done with this part as quickly as possible and get on with the new phase of their lives. She'd already been irritated to have her father in the house last night. Who knows why it mattered, but the idea of spending their final evening together in some kind of communion, mentally preparing for what was to come, had seemed important to her. Richard had wanted to make love one last time, had managed to get her excited in the way he knew he could when he put his mind to it, running his fingernails along the backs of her thighs, patiently but not too gently, the perfect balance of indifference and insistence. If he'd always concentrated like this, would they have avoided all their problems? It felt that way as she arched her back against his chest, as she let her legs open. But then there were her father's footsteps clunking beneath them, the kitchen faucet running, wet coughing. She stopped his fingers as they rounded her hipbone. "Let's save it," she said. "We can christen the new apartment." He kissed her ear and rubbed her shoulder and did his best to hide his frustration, but he knew she could feel it anyway, a solid presence in the bed, his body a stiff bundle beside her. Neither of them slept much. Larry looked well-rested in the morning, or as well-rested as he ever looked, with his unruly curls, stubbled cheeks, smoke-yellowed eyes.

And now those eyes were set on Richard, heavy gray brows

leaning together, questioning, he thought, full of either concern or suspicion or accusation. "You can take the damn truck," he said. "Let's just get this done."

"I'll drive," Larry said.

Richard handed him the keys. Alana followed in Richard's Camry. He watched her in the side mirror, fiddling with the radio as she pulled onto Route 10, flicking hair out of her face. He couldn't tell if her eyes had reddened or not. She didn't smile when he waved a finger in the mirror, but he couldn't be sure she'd seen it. "So?" Larry said. "Go ahead. Let it out."

"Let what out?"

"Don't bullshit me. You just got kicked out of your house."

"I didn't get kicked out. We told you, it's just a trial—"

"Bullshit. Shout a little. It'll make you feel better."

Those hooded eyes were set on him again, and they stayed on him too long. The truck was speeding down an incline, and up ahead shone the red of brake lights. Now Richard did try to shout, but all he could manage was a choked, "Whoa! Larry! Whoa!"

He fell forward against the seatbelt, and its recoil knocked him back again. "I got it under control," Larry said. "Whoa. What am I, a horse?"

"Just pay attention to the road."

In the mirror, Alana was gesturing in confusion and anger, her mouth moving, and this time Richard pretended he didn't see her. Larry had both hands on the wheel now, eyes on the car ahead. "I don't see why you're staying out here," he said. "Now's your chance to move into the city."

"It's close to school. I can't give up my job."

"New fucking York," Larry said, and whistled. "The only place in the world to live. Everywhere I've been, nothing like it. The people, the energy—"

"I'll take the train in every weekend."

"It's not the same."

"I'll move in someday," Richard said. "When it's the right time."

"Sure you will," Larry said, lifting one shoulder and letting it drop.

Chastised – that was the way Richard felt around Alana's father, despite the man's shabby clothes, his threadbare sport coat with a flake of dried lettuce on the lapel, his second-hand jeans with cuffs rolled three times, his battered tennis shoes and mismatched socks, one solid navy, the other tan with fine maroon stripes. Despite everything, Richard respected him, valued his opinions, was partly in awe of him, someone who, against all odds, had never compromised what was most important to him. Larry Fessler would never get rich from his artwork, but he'd go on making full-room installations – "after-maths," he called them – in which viewers came upon scenes of unfamiliar rituals, with no explanations, only artifacts: an arrangement of floor pillows, a wooden chair with leather arm straps, a bucket filled with human hair, coils of rubber tubing. He didn't have gallery representation and didn't sell to collectors. He lived from one grant to the next, and when grants didn't come through, he painted apartments of friends and admirers who took pity on him. Critics loved him; one dubbed him "the most neglected major artist in America," but the magazine the phrase appeared in soon went out of print, and Larry continued to be neglected.

Richard had called him one night during the last month, just before he'd found the apartment, wanting advice, or comfort, or simply a connection to a world he feared he was about to lose forever. He was alone in the house, Alana out at a fundraiser for the Howard Dean campaign. He turned on all the lights, put on music, made himself dinner. House projects called to him wherever he turned. The tub needed to be re-caulked, the kitchen re-painted, a broken light fixture in the bathroom replaced. He expected Larry to tell him to give up on Alana, to move on quickly, as he had when her mother had walked out. Was this what

Richard wanted to hear? That he'd find other women who'd understand him better, who'd accept him as he was? Maybe. But Larry was drunk when he answered and said he didn't know any Richards. "Plenty of Dicks," he said. "Are you that fucker with the harelip?" Richard hung up then and in a panic tried Alana's cell phone, and after hearing her recorded voice considered getting drunk himself, imagining waking up in the morning with the phone hugged to his chest, nose pressed against a baseboard. Instead he was in bed when she came home, struggling to focus on the opening page of a massive biography of Giacometti. "How go the king-makers?" he asked.

She dropped her coat to the floor. Her hair was crinkled where she'd been clutching it. "I can't believe we're really doing this," she said.

He couldn't help feeling relieved. To see her struggling made him calmer. "We don't have to do anything," he said, laying the heavy book on his chest. "Nothing's written in stone."

"Don't do that," she said. "Don't put it all on me."

"I'm not putting anything on you. I'm just saying. We could talk about it more if you want."

"What do *you* want?"

He could have tried to back out of it then. He could have said it was all a mistake. Why didn't he? Curiosity, maybe. Pride. Or maybe he really believed his own words: "It'll be good for us one way or another. It'll help clarify things. We agreed it would."

He shivered now, despite the heat pouring in through the open windows. The sun seemed too small and far away in the hazy blue sky. Dead grass lined the road on both sides. Up ahead, the Pathmark parking lot was choked with cars. "Take a left at the light," he said.

"This place?"

"It's not so bad."

"It's not the city," Larry said.

The complex had shallowly pitched roofs and gray wooden siding, splintering in places, in others replaced by aluminum.

The pool was covered by a tarp scattered with last year's dead leaves. A chain-link fence had been flattened in one spot, two posts bent all the way to the ground. "Maybe next year I'll get into the city," Richard said. "Maybe I can get a job in a private school."

Alana was already pulling boxes out of the Camry's trunk. Her face had the same shape as Larry's, a broad forehead and narrow chin, a sharp nose sunburned at the end, the skin around her eyes puffy even when she wasn't tired or crying. "Did you hear?" she said. "Another suicide bomber. Right outside the big mosque in Najaf."

"Terrible," Richard said.

"The world died twenty-five years before you were born," Larry said.

"We've got to get these criminals out of office," Alana said.

"Did everyone forget Hiroshima?" Larry said. "Auschwitz?"

She was trying to get her short arms around a box that was too big for her and waved Richard away when he tried to take it. He opened the back of the truck expecting everything he owned to have collapsed in a jumble, nothing intact, and was strangely deflated to find that the cords had held.

"A year from now," Alana said. "We'll be getting ready to celebrate. Can you imagine it? President Howard Dean."

He heard the catch in her throat and knew her eyes must be misting over. The first of the primaries was still months away, but already the prospect of the election moved her to tears. All summer she'd spent her evenings on the campaign, hosting house parties and making phone calls, once driving up to Vermont to hear the former governor speak. She strove for optimism, though it wasn't necessarily in her nature – she needed it in order to do her job as a counselor at a drug rehab center in Morristown. Richard had wanted to share her enthusiasm, but instead it worried him – he'd never have told her so, but he was sure she was setting herself up for a fall. Better to remain skeptical, he thought, expecting nothing, rather than suffer constant disappointment.

"Still a long way to go," he said, pulling out the ramp from the back of the truck, the sickening groan of metal on metal.

"Of course it is," she said, her voice taking a sudden hard, defensive turn. "But the fact that he's even in the race – "

"You're right," he said quickly. "It's incredible. It really is." But she'd already turned her back, starting up the stairs to the second floor, pausing once to get a better grip on the box. "The truck handle okay?" he asked Larry. "It'll make it out to the Island?"

Larry didn't answer. He lit a cigarette and grabbed a single folding chair, carrying it up to the apartment slung over one shoulder. Richard followed with an armful of clothes, trying to be careful with his suit and slacks so he wouldn't have to press them. In the apartment Alana was already unloading the box she'd brought up, arranging his dishes in a pressboard cabinet laminated to look like hardwood. "You don't have to do that now," he said. "I can take care of it later."

But she didn't stop. The apartment manager had promised to clean the stove, but it was still sticky on top, charred bits stuck between the coils of two burners. Larry blew smoke at the ceiling and let ashes fall to the linoleum. He flicked a fingernail against the edge of the new crystal vase, making a dull ping. "Your mother never did have any taste," he said.

"I'd love to move into the city," Richard said. "Maybe next year we'll both move in. To celebrate the election."

False optimism would annoy Alana even more than cynicism, he knew, and he wished he would just stop talking. Her father didn't care where they lived or what they did – he only wanted his ideas and opinions affirmed. *No one ever listens to me*, he'd said dozens of times in the ten years Richard had known him, though on visits to his studio, Richard was always conscious of hanging on to the merest grumble, swearing he'd remember every word. The purpose of art, Larry had once told him, was the same as that of dreams – to broaden the scope of experience, to let people live lives they'd otherwise never be able to imagine. Richard had packed the thought away, treasuring it, but Larry had been drunk then, too, and a month later, when Richard brought it back up, commenting on the newest installation, Larry squinted at him and grunted, his hair dusted with plaster, a bit of sawdust caught in his stubble. "Kid, I don't know what the hell you're talking about," he said. "I just make what I see."

After they'd emptied the truck, they lingered in the parking lot, Larry smoking another cigarette, Alana shuffling her feet, avoiding Richard's eyes. She'd worn flip-flops, and there were band-aids on both her ankles. Why did he notice only now? If he were a better husband, he would have scolded her, told her to wear shoes that would protect her toes from falling boxes or dropped furniture.

"I'm sorry we'll miss your opening," Alana said. "I want to see the pictures. Is Martin documenting?"

"He's in Peru," Larry said. Then, with a grunt and a shrug, he added, "No one'll be there."

"It's a tricky time for it. People are just coming back from the long weekend."

"There was a nice write-up in the *Voice*," Richard said.

"The *Voice*," Larry said, and made a scoffing sound through his nose. "No one reads that rag."

"I do," Richard said.

Larry only shrugged again. "That's because you live in Jersey."

He finished his cigarette and stubbed it out on the pavement. Seagulls squawked on the edge of the dumpster. The sky filled with the faint roar of a jet engine, but even without any clouds Richard couldn't spot it. When he looked down, Alana was watching him, waiting, her eyes puffier, he thought, arms crossed. A giddy panic pricked him, a feeling of being cut loose from everything, and he reminded himself that this was what he wanted, or at least what part of him wanted, at least part of the time. "Well," Alana said. "I guess we'd better go and let you get settled. You've got everything you need?"

She opened her arms, and he stepped into a hug. Her cheek against his neck, the warmth of it, the softness, made him close his eyes. "Remember, it's just a trial," he whispered. "Nothing's set in–"

She pushed away. "I know. I'll call you later, okay?"

"I'm only two miles down the road," he said. "We can have dinner some night soon."

All of Larry's sullenness suddenly dropped away. He smiled his crooked smile and patted Richard's arm. "Listen, kid," he said. "Don't be a stranger, all right? Come out and take a look at the new piece. I could use another set of eyes."

And then they were both in the truck, the engine hacking and grumbling to life. He could see Alana in the side mirror, hair tucked behind her ear, the tint of the window making her skin look sickly. She didn't glance at him. She didn't wave. Larry put the truck in gear, and Richard determined to stand his ground, to watch with dignity until they were out of the parking lot and well on their way. But when the truck started moving, he suddenly remembered and cried out: "Make sure you fill up the tank before you return it!" But it was too late: the U-Haul and his wife were speeding away.

2.

RICHARD'S PARENTS DIDN'T send a housewarming gift. They didn't offer words of encouragement. A few days before he moved out, he got separate emails from each of them. From his mother: *I've got extra blankets and pillows here. Don't waste your money on new ones.* And from his father: *Did you see that game yesterday? These people need to learn how to swing.* They didn't believe in trial separations. They didn't believe a break-up could be anything other than final. But what did they know about break-ups? In their forty years together they'd never once, as far as Richard knew, questioned their need for each other. They could admire themselves all they wanted, talk about their conviction and commitment, but to him this was their marriage's deepest flaw: they'd valued security over fulfillment, fear over truth. He and Alana had their problems, true, but they were also willing to take risks, to challenge themselves and their bond, and they would be stronger for it. He tried to explain this when he called his parents to let them know he'd found an apartment, that he and Alana were really going through with their plan. But his mother said only, "People who love each other don't run away from their troubles." His father said, "I'm sure you know what's best," and then started talking about baseball scores.

How different it had been when he'd shown up at their house to announce the separation three weeks earlier. He and Alana lived only twenty minutes from where he'd grown up, and the sight of his childhood home with a For Sale sign out front had made his throat go suddenly dry. His mother had retired from selling real estate last spring, and his father was leaving his patent law practice in two weeks. Just before Thanksgiving they were moving to West Palm Beach, and only now was Richard distraught to see them go. He took a moment on the front lawn, studying the beige siding, the bay window with his mother's collection of Peruvian ceramics on display, the scrawny hedges his father had put in last April, after the old ones, growing for twenty years, had suddenly wilted. He wondered briefly if his parents would let him stay here for six months, put off the closing on the new house, put off the move. Wouldn't his mother want to take care of him?

She was chopping onions in the kitchen when he went inside, her mascara running, and for a moment he worried, irrationally, that Alana had called already and told them horrible things about him – or worse, that his mother knew him so well that she could predict his disasters before they happened. But when he told her the news, she wiped her face with a dishtowel and stared at him, dry-eyed. "What did you do?"

"Why do you assume it's my fault?"

"Just tell me."

He tried to explain. He heard the words – *We've been growing apart, we need to see if we'll be happier this way* – but they didn't illuminate anything, not for his mother, not for himself. He couldn't put what had happened into words. He couldn't quite understand it himself. They hadn't fought. They hadn't been miserable, but after being married six and a half years, something strange had grown between them, a thickness in the air, an unpleasant odor, as if the pipes in their house were slowly leaking gas. Everything they said was muffled, distorted, hard to comprehend. Maybe they'd gotten together too young. Maybe their relationship had run its course. It wouldn't be the end of the world, would it, if they'd had a solid, loving marriage for a time and then decided to go their separate ways? There were worse things, weren't there?

"So it's too late to go back and apologize?" his mother said. She was shorter than him by five inches, her hair dyed a coppery red and thinning, the skin around her neck and jaw gone slack in the last few years, but as always she had a way of making him feel as big as a bug, and as smart.

"Apologize for what? I didn't do anything wrong."

"If you had kids by now, you'd stay together," she said. "You've got nothing to keep you grounded."

"It's just a separation," he said. "We're not filing papers or anything. We'll keep talking every week. We'll re-assess after a few months."

But his mother heard nothing now. Her face had lost its rigid set, eyebrows falling, cheeks, chin. The composure that came and went in him like the tide was now receding, replaced by the nauseated, jittery feeling that made him want to run laps around the block, shadowboxing, kicking at dead leaves. "Oh God," she said. "I always knew this would happen."

Always? Why hadn't she told him? At the wedding she'd been flushed and giggling, tipsy on a glass and a half of champagne.

When they'd danced together, she told him he'd made the best choice in the world – she couldn't have dreamed up a better daughter-in-law if she'd tried. But now she stuck her head out the kitchen door and called up the stairs, "Hal! Come down, please. Richie's got something to tell you."

His father's eyes reddened right away. He opened his mouth but couldn't speak. He scratched the bushy bristles of hair above his ear, waved a hand in front of his face, and left the room. When he came back he tried to talk about the Mets, but Richard's mother wouldn't let him. "This is important, Hal. If you can't listen, go back upstairs." To Richard she said, "I don't understand."

"Of course you don't. I didn't expect you to."

He'd gotten used to them not understanding years ago. He was a couple months shy of thirty-three, but in their eyes he was still a child and would always be. They talked to him now the same way they'd talked to him as a teenager, when they'd tried to dissuade him from going to art school. When he announced his intention late in his junior year at Parsippany High, they immediately questioned his dedication, his drive. Sure, he'd been doodling since first grade, and a teacher told him he had talent – but he'd also done well in history and civics classes. They were certain he'd make a wonderful lawyer. Didn't he want to leave his options open? Until then Richard had had his own misgivings, but their doubts made him determined. They talked him into sending an application to Rutgers, but he swore he wouldn't go, not even if he got turned down everywhere else. "I'd rather join the army," he said.

"You can do your art on the side," his mother said. "There are plenty of, I don't know, heart surgeons who paint in their free time."

"Heart surgeons?" he said. "Are you kidding me?"

"You know what I mean."

"What kind of artist has a name like Richard Weintraub?"

his father said, looking up from his crossword puzzle. "Jews aren't supposed to be artists. Musicians, maybe. Or writers."

"What about Chagall?"

"Sure, Chagall. There's always an exception."

"Modigliani. Pissarro."

"Sephardim. That's not the same thing."

"Man Ray."

"Maybe if you change your name to Rick Wine."

"Jacques Lipchitz. Louise Nevelson. Jacob Epstein."

"Never heard of them," his father said.

"Exactly," Richard said.

"Exactly," his father agreed, returning his attention to the squares of his puzzle, half already filled in with his meticulous letters, first in pencil, and then when he was certain of them, covered over in ink.

"That's all beside the point," his mother said. "I'm sure you'll be a household name one day. In the meantime, it wouldn't hurt to be able to get a job."

Despite their concerns, they paid his tuition at University of the Arts in Philadelphia. He came home after his junior year talking about another Jewish artist, whose daughter he'd met at one of the ubiquitous pizza and cheesesteak joints within walking distance of his apartment, this one run by a Pakistani only too happy to serve beer to underage college students. He'd stood behind her in line one night, waiting to order. She swayed as she counted change, holding each coin up to one eye before slapping it onto the counter. When the pile of coins was big enough, she shouted, "Another Schlitz!" The forty-ounce bottle was absurdly large in her tiny hands, fingers as delicate as bird bones. Her hair, dyed blue a month before, maybe two, was fading back to brown. She turned abruptly, her jutting chin knocking straight into Richard's chest. She looked up at him, blinking, then took his arm and said, "Help me finish this. If I do it myself I'll probably die."

He abandoned his friends and squeezed in beside her at

an already overcrowded booth of sour-faced girls watching hookers pass before the adjacent window, commenting on their clothes and make-up. "That skirt's all wrong for her ass," one said. "She should go looser, give it a chance to sashay."

"I'd go for that one," another said. "That is, if I were a creepy, hard-up old dude."

"You're reasonably cute," Alana told him. Her eyebrows were her best feature, he decided, expressive lines over ruddy eyes, carefully plucked but still just the slightest bit lopsided. She handed him the bottle. "Drink up, and I bet I'll get cute, too."

He learned about her between fits of giggling. She was a psych major at Penn, had come downtown to avoid an ex-boyfriend who showed up every place she went.

"Are you celebrating something?" he asked.

"The end of the world," she said. Her parents were splitting up. "Should have happened a long time ago, but still, you know, it's pretty much the worst thing ever." She went from giggling to crying and back. "Don't tell me you go to art school," she said. "Fucking artists. I should have known." But by then their hands were locked under the table, their thighs pressed together. In the street her friends tried to drag her away. "I'd kiss you," she said. "But I'm afraid I might puke."

She did puke, and so did he, but not before getting her to write her number on his arm. When he called two days later and asked if she wanted to get coffee, she said she remembered who he was but not what he looked like. "You might have been the Elephant Man for all I know."

"You said I was cute. Reasonably."

"That might have been the Schlitz talking."

"Schlitz is never reasonable."

"Okay," she said. "But you've got to come out to West Philly. I'm not going anywhere near the scene of the crime. I'm still queasy." Before hanging up, she added, "You should know right away, I don't trust artists."

By then he no longer thought of himself as an artist, at

least not the way he'd wanted to three years earlier. He'd switched majors twice, from painting to illustration to animation. He studied the conceptualists but could come up with no concepts himself, instead using what turned out to be moderate skill, but never more than moderate, to imitate what he saw in museums and books. His teachers praised him, but only for being a good student, for following instructions, never for his talent or vision. He'd already begun to think about graduation and what he'd do afterward, looking into teaching programs in the area, considering going abroad. To his parents he kept insisting he was going to live in a hovel, covered in paint and charcoal and plaster dust, but even the idea of a hovel had lost its appeal – he was uncomfortable enough in the apartment he shared with a pair of musicians, the sink always full of soiled dishes, the shower curtain clouded with soap scum and mildew, the toilet seat dribbled with piss. When he showed up at the café, he couldn't shut himself up, speaking at length about the myth of the mad artist, how it was all bullshit, how a person could be creative and still live a healthy life, keep a clean apartment, stay sober six days out of seven.

Alana's face was drawn and pale, eyes swollen and half-lidded, those wonderful eyebrows arched. "You don't know what you're talking about," she said. That's when she told him about her father, the years of shuffling from one apartment to another, the overdue rent notices, the stoic or stupid way her mother had made excuses for him for so many years, apologizing for him and then defending him, calling him her genius. "When she said she was leaving he hardly looked up," Alana said. "He was hammering a plank onto some two-by-fours. He didn't even shrug. 'We all do what we have to do,' he said. After twenty-one years. Asshole. I hate him." She cried then, and Richard did his best to comfort her, glad for the opportunity to put a hand on her shoulder, to feel the bone beneath the rough fabric of her sweater, the place where bone gave way to muscle, feeling only slightly guilty for taking advantage of the moment. He would have been more ashamed, maybe, if he didn't find her so beautiful just then, the faded blue ends of her hair falling across one cheek, her long nose wrinkled, lips pursed and wet, and wondered how someone could be beautiful when she was in so much pain. It was a profound thing to have seen, he thought, and admired himself a little for having noticed. Then he did feel ashamed and took his hand from her shoulder, instead sliding her his unused napkin. She wiped her eyes and said, "This is ridiculous. I can't believe I'm doing this. I don't even know you."

"You will," he said, as insistently as he'd ever said anything in his life. "You'll know me."

What had she seen on his face then? Not the confidence he'd hoped to project, or the passion, but something comical and absurd that made her burst out laughing and made him want to crawl under the table, slink out of the room. But as he leaned away, she reached out and took his hand. "Thank you," she said, when she'd caught her breath. "That's exactly what I needed. I haven't laughed in two weeks. Not without forty ounces of Schlitz." Later he would wish he could have seen himself through her eyes, to know what it was on his face that made her so suddenly happy, or at least lighthearted – how many times would he want to recapture that look, to use it in difficult moments. He would have bottled it if he could have.

Soon she had to go to class. Richard had already skipped one of his and decided he wouldn't go to any more today. "I'm going to take you out this weekend," he said, but this time the insistence was forced, self-conscious, and only made her smile.

"You do that," she said, and hugged him. A hug wouldn't ordinarily have struck him as special, only somehow this one was. Their ears pressed together like the ends of two plungers, and his head filled with a soft, liquid roar, not so different than that found in seashells, only deeper and rumbling. This is the sound of her, he thought, and held on for a moment longer than he should have, when he could already feel her beginning to pull away. This is the sound of us. Their ears came apart with a faint, heartbreaking pop.

AT LEAST THAT was how he remembered it the first night alone in the new apartment, when he finally broke down and called her, after having resisted all day. By then he'd realized he'd forgotten to buy a shower curtain. He'd discovered the closet pole was missing so he couldn't hang his suit and slacks, instead laying them out over a pair of empty boxes turned upside down. He'd failed to remove the sticky spot on the stove with any of the cleaners he'd brought, not even with steel wool. He'd rearranged the dishes Alana had put away, determined to put his own stamp on every inch of the apartment. For once in his life, everything would be exactly the way he wanted it. He dragged the armchair to three different spots before deciding he liked it best where it had started, backlit by the living room's one large window, which looked out onto a concrete walkway suspended above the parking lot. He put the stereo in the hallway, with speakers facing opposite directions, so he could listen to music in either of the two rooms. Alana would have hated it there, would have said it was ugly and in the way – and maybe it was, but that's how he preferred it, and that's where it would stay.

When all the boxes were unpacked and flattened, the place looked as small as ever, but still partly vacant, too, the walls bare, only the empty vase decorating the kitchen table, no nightstand for his bed. He wished he had bought the queen-sized. If he'd been able he would have crammed the place full, leaving himself just enough room to maneuver through, just enough air to breathe. From the apartment below came the sound of clattering pots and pans. A TV anchorman's voice came through the kitchen wall, far too clearly, talking about the bombing Alana had mentioned earlier, and he pictured the way her eyes would lower, her shoulders slump, head shaking, that posture he knew so well, the sadness in her bearing he'd once had no trouble teasing back from the brink of despair. But then the channel changed next door, the anchorman's voice replaced by a crowd's laughter and applause.

Soon he raised the blinds and opened the door a crack to let in air, and if his new neighbors wanted to stop by and say hello, he wouldn't have minded. He did have lesson plans to finish, but he had an excuse not to do them now. So many of his colleagues got away with shoddy teaching by saying the words, "personal problems," and coming to school disheveled and bleary-eyed. How could he be expected to worry about his classes when all his energy was going into keeping himself healthy and sane? Though in fact, energy was something he had in abundance, running through him in giddy waves, making him jump up from the chair every time he sat down to read the newspaper or the Giacometti biography, propelling him to move the crystal vase from the table to the windowsill and back again, adjusting it each time so the engraved flower on its side caught the light from the ceiling fixture.

But even with the door open, none of his neighbors introduced themselves, much less brought him welcome baskets as his mother used to do whenever a house sold in their neighborhood – as she'd done, that is, until a few years ago, when a half-dressed man with hairy shoulders barked at her, "I'm not buying," and slammed the door before she could explain herself. While Richard scanned the sports pages, memorizing a few stats for his next conversation with his father, a fit, sweaty man in jogging clothes passed his window without looking in. Later, a heavyset girl with two black-haired toddlers in tow met his eyes and quickly turned away. In the evening a woman in a nurse's uniform, carrying an overstuffed bag of groceries in each arm, smiled at him, or he thought she did, though it was hard to tell as the light outside was beginning to fade. She was too old for him, pushing forty, he guessed, or even forty-five, but her body was trim and her neck gracefully long, and he listened carefully to determine how many doors down she lived. He strained to hear her soft shoes, the swish of her tights, and then did hear a rustle, a thud, a muttered, "Shit," and he ran out to help her. But the nurse was nowhere in sight. Instead the heavyset girl was dragging a crate down the walkway, her dimpled arms straining, her breath coming out hard. "Can I give you a hand with that?" Richard offered, but the girl only shook her head and continued to strain, taking a step backward and yanking the crate – a baby in a crib pictured on its front – several inches toward her. The girl's face was sweaty, hair plastered to her forehead. She was barefoot, and one of her big toenails was purple. From the door at the end of the walkway, one of the black-haired toddlers appeared – Richard couldn't tell if it was a boy or girl – and cried, "Go 'way!"

"Are you sure I can't – "

"Go 'way! Go 'way!"

He ducked back inside. He picked up the phone and put it down. He returned the vase to the windowsill. It was just after eight, and even on weekdays he never went to bed before eleven. He hadn't bought a TV, deciding he was going to try to live without one, to spend his time more productively. But on what? Of course he planned to start painting again, but he didn't have an easel yet, or brushes, or paint. He was going to stretch a canvas at school, as soon as he had time. Time. What else did he have? He closed the shades and went back to work on the stove's sticky spot, attacking it again with steel wool and two solvents at the same time, not caring if the mixture kicked off dangerous fumes.

He wasn't surprised Alana hadn't called first. It was part of her new stubbornness, her refusal to show weakness. But that was weakness in itself. There was strength, he decided, in reaching out. He waited until almost ten before dialing. He had a message prepared for her voicemail, something confident and compassionate, just calling to make sure she was holding up okay. But when she answered, he said, "The place is all ready for christening. Whenever you want to drop by."

There was a long pause. He heard her breathing. Finally, she said, "You left your briefcase over here."

"I was just kidding, you know. About the christening. I just wanted to talk."

"This is so fucked up," she said.

"I wanted to make sure you're doing okay."

"Do I sound okay?"

"I can come over if you want."

"I'll leave the briefcase in the front hall," she said.

"I can't believe how much I miss you already."

"That's the problem, Rich. You can't believe it."

"I could make us dinner here this week," he said. "Are you free Tuesday?"

"I don't know," she said. "I don't know anything." A few more mumbled words, and she was off the phone. The cackle of TV voices was louder than ever through his kitchen wall. He went into the bedroom and lay diagonally across the bed, trying to take up as much space as possible. Overhead the ceiling creaked under heavy footsteps. This is the sound of us, he thought, and mashed his mother's pillows against his ears.

3.

THE TRUTH WAS, as soon as he and Alana started talking about separation, Richard knew he wanted to sleep with someone else. They'd dated for four years before getting married. They'd been having sex for nearly eleven. He'd never seriously considered cheating since the wedding, but suddenly the idea of a body other than Alana's obsessed him. Later he'd wonder if this was why they'd considered splitting in the first place, so they could test the boundaries of faithfulness, find its proper shape in their marriage. At the moment he thought he simply craved change, the thrill of novelty. The last time he'd been with someone else was nine years ago, while Alana was traveling in Europe with college friends. A brief fling with a co-worker at a hotel where he'd been bartending. He recalled the exhilaration of that summer, or

thought he did, though not as well as he remembered Alana's
return, the sweaty week they'd spent in bed.

Now he set his sights on a new teacher in the English
department at Union Knoll High School, where he taught art in
a makeshift studio sandwiched between the auto shop and the
welding room. He didn't want to mix his work and his personal
life, but what other choice did he have? All his own college
friends were married now, or close to married; several had moved
out west, to San Francisco, Seattle, Portland; only two were
practicing artists, neither terribly successful, both still in Philly,
supported by their families. For several nights he tried
haunting local bars but always found himself alone on a stool,
surrounded by swirling smoke and inane conversation. The
personal ads made him cringe – every time he read, "tall, beautiful woman searching for …," he imagined a cackling troll
scribbling furiously in a room full of bones.

Becky Block had been a student teacher the year before in
Bobbi Henderson's classes, and he'd already gotten to know
her a little, had even taken her out to lunch to celebrate her being
hired. She was older than most of the student teachers to come
through Union Knoll, twenty-seven or eight, attractive, Richard
had thought from the first time he'd met her, sexy, even, though
he'd never have called her beautiful. Her round face was taken up
by enormous eyes, the irises nearly as dark as the pupils. Short
hair suited her, he thought, hers cropped in a stylish way, with
little flares over the ears. Her body was strangely proportioned,
hips wider than her frame called for, or shoulders narrower,
and it was made more awkward by the way she walked, never
swinging her arms, feet seeming to step gingerly, deliberately,
coming down too squarely on the heels.

Most of the time she was soft-spoken, polite, but in the
faculty lounge she sometimes broke into raucous laughter, and
had a way of slipping profanities unexpectedly into her speech.
"I told the little shithead this was his last chance," she'd say,
sitting between Bobbi, a devout Presbyterian – fundamentalist

crazy, Richard thought – and Art Cushing, the vice-principal. "You're really fucking funny, Mr. Weintraub," she once said, after Richard had told a story about his father-in-law, the time Larry had cut off the tip of his pinkie on a table saw and kept working, afraid he'd lose his momentum on a project if he went to the hospital. When he finally called the ambulance, he was in shock and so lightheaded he was delusional, having an argument with Alana's mother, who'd left seven years earlier. Richard told the story often, spinning it differently for different audiences, sometimes telling it reverentially, other times with an edge of slapstick. The teachers wouldn't appreciate an artist willing to sacrifice his body, even his life, for his work, Richard knew – so he told it comically, playing up his own role of cleaning the table saw so Larry could get back to work as soon as he was released. Most of the teachers chuckled, but Becky snorted, closed her eyes, laughed breathlessly. And then: *you're really fucking funny*. He felt the heat in his cheeks. "Richard," he said. "Please, call me Richard."

Over the course of the semester he learned that Becky had lived in Manhattan for five years, most recently in a walk-up on the border between SoHo and Little Italy, working in the magazine business, first as an editorial assistant at *Woman's Day*, eventually climbing her way to managing editor of a feminist start-up called *One Voice*. But the magazine folded after four issues, and then Becky ended a three-year relationship. She moved back to her parents' house in West Caldwell – just for a year, she swore – and enrolled in the Master of Arts in Teaching program at Montclair State. Teaching had always been in her mind as a fallback, though now, she confessed only to Richard, she didn't know if she was any good at it, didn't think she liked kids, wasn't inspired by the material. "I'm telling myself I'll give it a year after I graduate, and then decide."

"I hated it my first year," he said. "That's normal."

"What made you stick with it?"

Lack of imagination, he thought. Lack of courage. He said,

"I knew I was making a difference. I could see it in a few of the kids' eyes when they really got into something. Skate punks making psychedelic T-shirt designs. I had this linebacker a few years ago, drew still-lifes as delicate as Audubon's. After a while that's all you see. The other stuff fades into the background. Your perspective shifts. Like those 3-D posters. They look like random squiggles, until you adjust your focus, and suddenly there's a pirate ship, or sharks, or something."

"So teaching's like a 3-D poster," Becky said, and laughed her raucous laugh. "That's fucking ridiculous."

By then he and Alana were in trouble. He knew it even if they hadn't spoken of it yet. They still talked about their day, and laughed, and made love, but there was something labored and slow about all of it. Alana had just turned thirty-one, and her looks hadn't faded in the least – if anything, she was more attractive than ever, her Converse high-tops and Fugazi T-shirts traded for skirts and fitted blouses, her hair grown out to her shoulders. Her posture had improved, her shoulders forced down and back to keep from getting knots. Most mornings she woke with them anyway, wincing, rolling her head, struggling to reach the spot between her shoulder blades and rub away the source of her suffering. She wouldn't let Richard touch her, saying his fingers were too clumsy, that he didn't know how much pressure to apply. And he let her writhe, mostly indifferent to her pain, though he knew it was something meant to be shared between them. It was hard to believe how far he felt from her – there was a time when he couldn't watch her nick herself shaving without wanting to attack the offending blade, to throw himself on her ankle and suck away the hurt, the impulse shuddering through him even as he restrained himself, standing silently as she washed the blood away.

As on the day he moved, band-aids covered both her Achilles tendons when they went for a walk in Morristown one Sunday in early summer, the week after Becky Block had been hired on for next year and Richard had taken her to lunch. They were idly window shopping, stopping occasionally to finger the fabric on silk throw pillows, testing out wicker chairs they might put on their patio to replace cracking plastic ones. The day was warm and pleasant, the air tinged with the smell of grass clippings and freshly laid asphalt. They held hands, their hips occasionally brushing, and though there was a comfortable intimacy about the stroll, there was also something forced, and Richard couldn't help feeling irritated by the lazy way Alana swung her arm, by the clicking of her sandals on the cement, by the falsely exasperated, satisfied note in her voice as she said, "How did we turn into such dull suburbanites?"

They'd had this conversation too many times already, reminiscing about what wild kids they'd once been, talking about how one day they'd drop everything and move into the city, or to Spain, where they'd gone on their honeymoon. Richard had never wanted to move back to Jersey, especially not fifteen minutes from his parents, but Union Knoll was the only school that offered him a job straight out of his teaching program, and Alana had encouraged him to accept. She'd been miserable those first two years here, working first in a florist's shop, then as a receptionist for a marketing agency, and though she never said so, he knew she blamed him for her boredom, for her aimlessness and lack of purpose. He was used to coming home to find her crying, and if he talked about his students, the progress one of his skate punks was making on an acid-inspired logo, she'd say, "Don't rub it in. I'm wasting away here."

But he didn't mind her misery then. He knew exactly how to handle it. He let her cry for a few minutes, making affirming noises, and then held her shoulders, looked her in the eye, and said, "Enough of this. If you're unhappy, let's fix it." They should be practical, he said. They should think about all their possibilities. She could go back to school. They could think seriously about having kids. They could always move. "I'm married to you, not to my job." Of course he didn't really want to move again or look for another job, and he didn't feel ready for kids, but saying these things calmed her, and soon she'd quit crying. Her eyes would be nearly swollen shut, and she'd stifle a yawn. "Let's figure it out tomorrow," she'd say, and instead they'd watch a video and go to bed.

But eventually she did go back to school, getting her MSW at Kean, and soon after found the job she loved, counseling housewives hooked on Valium, businessmen who snuck into the bathroom to shoot up before lunch meetings, teenagers who cleared out their parents' liquor cabinets every weekend. She made friends. She joined a book club. She no longer cried when he came home – in fact, she rarely came home before he did. And now that she'd started working on the Dean campaign, some days he saw her only in passing, for the few minutes before getting in bed and falling asleep, and the frenzied hour in the morning as she rushed to get out the door on time. Richard's own summer days stretched out endlessly in front of him, and though he told himself he needed the recovery time, to rejuvenate after the long school year, he felt his own aimlessness take hold. He started house projects but didn't finish them. He thought about painting but couldn't bring himself to work until he'd converted half the garage into a studio, as he'd been planning for years. Now when he talked about moving into the city, or taking another trip to Spain, Alana only sighed and said, "Someday." When he brought up having kids, she said, "I don't see how anyone could have kids right now, with the world the way it is. Maybe next year, after the election."

He was useless to her now. Even as she held his hand and let her hip brush against his, even as she pointed out frilly placemats and said, "What do you think? We could just give in and make our house look like your mother's," he knew she didn't need him here – it could have been anybody's hand in hers, anybody's hip she brushed against. Sunglasses covered the part of her face he used to be able to read so easily. He'd forgotten his own sunglasses, and the reflection from the windshields of parked cars made him squint. His khakis stuck to his thighs, and his shirtsleeves chafed the insides of his wrists. An absurd self-pity took hold of him, along with resentment, and he slowed his pace, even as she pulled him along. She pointed to a shop full of Asian antiques, or replicas of Asian antiques, and said, "Maybe we can find something for Carlie's wedding." He didn't feel like going in the shop. He didn't feel like going to her cousin's wedding, didn't feel like buying a gift for people he hardly knew. He tried to ignore what she'd said, the same way he tried to ignore his resentment, his boredom and anxiety, his desire to take off running down the street. He kept walking, pretending to gaze at trees in a nearby park, the people lounging on benches, pretending not to notice the resistance on his arm. "Rich?"

"Huh?"

She stopped short and turned to him. Her dark glasses covered the most important lines of her face, but he could see the anger plainly in the set of her mouth. Her shoulders had risen toward her ears, and by the time they got home she'd have knots in her neck, and most likely, a headache. "You heard me," she said.

Why couldn't she talk to him in the understanding, indulgent voice she used with her clients, those hopeless junkies who showed up again at the clinic two weeks after they'd been released? Why was she always so hard on him? "I was thinking about Spain," he said, a safe topic, he thought, one that held nostalgia for both of them. It would have been the right thing to say if she bought it, but she didn't. She took off her sunglasses, and it was so much worse now that he could see the way her eyes narrowed and hardened in the light. Part of one tooth appeared where she bit the edge of her lower lip.

"Can't you just say what you want for a change? How hard is it, really?"

"Come on, Lani. I wasn't paying attention. I was daydreaming. What's the big deal."

"No, really. Say it. 'I don't want to go in the stupid shop and look at fake, ugly Japanese crap.'"

"We were having a perfectly nice day–"

"So now I've ruined our day," she said.

He let go of her hand and hugged himself. The smell of his sweat was ripe and pleasant, something that was all his. "I didn't say that," he said. "Can't we just let it go? I'll come in the store with you, all right?"

He wished she would waver then, that she'd suddenly start crying. Then he could comfort her, apologize even, and go back to pretending nothing was wrong. But she only put her sunglasses back on, turned, and walked into the shop. He followed. They came out with a pair of ceramic candlesticks for her cousin.

When they finally did discuss the change, they were perfectly rational, polite, analytical. "It's weird, isn't it?" Richard said. They were at the kitchen table, just finished with breakfast, the Sunday paper spread between them, their second cups of coffee growing cold. "I know I love you. That's not a question. I just feel, I don't know, a little numb."

"I guess that's about how I feel," Alana said, tearing out an article she wanted to keep, the sound of the ripping paper making it hard for him to tell if he detected uncertainty in her voice or only imagined he did.

"Is there something we can do about it?"

"I'm sure it's just normal," she said. "It'll pass."

But it didn't feel normal, and it didn't pass, not in the next week or month. When they made the decision to separate, this discussion was almost as rational as the others, though they did both cry afterward, and then had better sex than they'd had in months, charged by pain, he supposed, and anger. In its wake Alana looked sickened and drained, as if his fluids had poisoned her. When he began to rub her back, she flinched and rolled away.

"Maybe we should have done this three years ago," he said. "All this time, what a waste."

BECKY BLOCK WAS sympathetic during the first few weeks of the new school year, listening to him during the prep period they shared, agreeing that it was unfair for Alana to make him feel guilty when the decision had been mutual, when he was the one who'd had to move out, when all she had to do was say the word and he'd be more than willing to try to talk things through or make an appointment to see a counselor. "She expects me to read her mind," he said.

In the faculty lounge Becky was able to carry on a conversation and work at the same time, which gave Richard the opportunity to study her jawline, the flutter of her eyelashes, the little flares over her ears that had grown out a bit over the last two months, with reddish highlights coaxed by the sun. Adorable, he told himself, though she'd gained a pound or two over the summer, and a tan didn't complement her complexion, bringing out an orange undertone to her skin. She had a textbook open in front of her and a notebook beside it, and after scratching across the page for a minute, her pen would find its way between her pursed lips. "Sounds like a bad sign," she said.

"What do you mean a bad sign?"

"Like she's already made up her mind."

"I don't think so."

"Well," Becky said, glancing up from her notebook with a pitying little smile. "I don't really know what I'm talking about. You've got a better sense of it than I do."

Of course he did, but that didn't keep a cold shudder from running through him. Made up her mind about what? "I appreciate your insight," he said.

Becky told stories of her own break-up, about how she thought she knew her boyfriend as well as she possibly could have, and then one day he was a stranger. "The whole prospect's fucked from the start," she said, the profanity jumping from her mouth, her entire face seeming to alter as she said it, her features darkening, her eyes at their widest. "You're supposed to meld your life with someone else's, but no matter what, you're still individuals. There's no getting around your own fucking skin."

She cackled when he told her about Larry and the moving truck, and the phone call he'd gotten from U-Haul the next day, asking him to please come in and settle the bill. He laughed with her, though he didn't find it funny at all, neither at the time nor now. Not only had the truck come in late, with its gas tank nearly empty, but its rear bumper was dented, and on its side, covering half the U-Haul logo, were huge, spray-painted bubble letters, black with a white outline. SPUR, it said, only the R was upside down and backward. Insurance covered the damage, but the gas cost him an extra $250. He called Larry in a rage, for once not holding back at all, telling him how irresponsible he was, how he'd never trust him again. He sounded like the parent of a teenager, which depressed him, now that he might never have the chance to be a parent at all. "Do you think I need this right now? Don't you think things are hard enough for me already?" Larry took it with surprising calm, waiting until Richard finished before saying, "Hey, you're right. And I'm sorry, okay? I'll make it up to you. Fuck those U-Haul people. SPUR. That kid's a genius. He's the best thing going right now. They should be honored to have their ugly-ass truck tagged by a master." When Richard didn't respond, he said, "You come on out here, and I'll make it up to you, I swear. I'll show you this kid's work. It's inspiring."

Becky shook her head, more amused than incredulous, amused most, it seemed, by Richard's outrage. "I've got to meet this guy," she said. "He's got no conscience at all. What a great way to live."

"You should come with me when I go out to visit him," Richard said in an offhand way, pretending to scan his attendance roster. "We could grab some dinner downtown."

"Great," she said. "And on the way we can go egg my ex-boyfriend's apartment."

They had drinks after school one afternoon and then

dinner a week later. In the restaurant parking lot, Richard kissed her, and she kissed back without reluctance. "Oh my, Mr. Weintraub!" she said when their lips came apart, fanning herself with both hands, faking a swoon. But when he suggested going to his apartment, she opened her car door and said, "That was a nice kiss, Richard. But no way I'm going to be your comfort fuck."

"That's not what I want," he said. "I like you. We could start something."

"Come on," she said. "Don't kid yourself." Those big eyes blinked, wide hips folding awkwardly as she slid behind the wheel. Her engine revved and she rolled down her window. "I'll see you in school, Mr. W."

He pursued her, casually at first, agreeing it was best not to rush into anything. Two or three afternoons a week he timed his walk to his car so he'd run into her coming out of her classroom and be able to escort her to the parking lot. In the faculty lounge he was often ready with some piece of news he'd seen on TV the night before, something he knew would interest her, the plight of women in Afghanistan, the doomed campaign of Carol Moseley Braun.

He did the same thing with Alana on the phone, and when they finally met for dinner, almost a month after he'd moved out. She insisted they get together somewhere other than his apartment or their house, so they went to The Hunan in Morris Plains, a place he'd never have taken Becky, far too busy and brightly lit to be romantic. He talked to Alana about the Dean campaign, which he was following more closely now than he ever had before, but even as he encouraged her, he was aware of the note of condescension in his voice, and a new power he had over her that she didn't know about. He leaned back in his chair, listening intently to her stories about work and fundraising, thinking he had no stake in any of it anymore, or if he had a stake, it was only a partial one, one he might give up altogether if things went his way. He could see the sadness in her face and acknowledged it with sincere questions and gestures of affection. "How are you holding up?" he asked, brushing two fingers across her wrist. "Anything need fixing in the house?" When they said goodbye he hugged her generously, proud of himself for his strength, reveling in the reluctant way she clung to him before checking herself and easing away.

He and Becky had more drinks, more dinners. Sometimes she let him kiss her, other times she didn't. One night in mid-October, at a corner booth in a dimly lit tavern, she cut him off mid-sentence, leaned across the table, and bit the end of his nose. Didn't this have to mean something? Again that night he invited her to come home with him, no pressure, no expectation, just to sample the premium bourbon he happened to have, bought that day during his lunch hour. She was suddenly stern. "I thought we went through this already," she said. "Isn't this good enough?"

"Of course it's good enough," he said, though in his voice the word "enough" sounded like gibberish, a made-up word, two random syllables put together. Even "good" rang strangely in his ears. What he and Alana had had was "good," but that didn't keep him from feeling bored by it, or oppressed by it, or confused by it from one day to the next. "Good" and "enough" didn't belong in the same sentence, he was convinced. "What's wrong with wanting more?"

"You want it from anyone," she said. "I just happen to be the lucky girl in your way."

"That's not true," he said, and for lack of any argument, blurted, "I'm in love with you."

He expected her to laugh at him, as she had so many times before, but instead her face grew serious, lips tightened, chin tucked, eyes narrowing and then growing red. Her tears surprised him so much he was slow trying to comfort her. "You asshole," she said, and ran out of the bar.

He told her he loved her again the next day, and for several days after, sometimes believing it himself. But she started avoiding him, going to the library during her prep period, taking lunch off-campus, heading straight for her car after school. He called her parents' house, out of which she still hadn't moved after more than a year, and said, "You're killing me. You're breaking my heart."

"If you had a heart, I might listen," she said, and hung up. He couldn't help thinking about the Tin Man, the silly silver hat he wore, his pasty make-up, and almost immediately felt sorry for himself. He had a heart, he knew that, only it felt flaccid and numb and full of shameful feelings, nothing he could be proud of. He paced the apartment, waiting for Becky to call back and apologize, sipping on a gin and tonic he didn't want – but he thought he *ought* to drink in a situation like this, that drunkenness was called for. He didn't even like gin, but it seemed the proper drink for a man separated from his wife, living alone. When the phone did ring, he was already muttering, "You're right, I'm sorry, I'm really sorry."

"No, *I'm* sorry." It wasn't Becky's voice. It was Alana's. She was hysterical. He could make out only half of what she said. "It was stupid. It didn't mean anything."

"What didn't?"

"I didn't do it to hurt you," she said. "At least not consciously. Maybe I did. I don't know."

"Did what?"

It took him a minute to piece together what she was telling him. An affair. A man she met through the campaign. It didn't mean anything. It was over now. "I'm so ashamed," she said.

"There's no need," he said. "We're separated. You're allowed." Any guilt he might have felt about pursuing Becky dissolved instantly, but the relief that might have replaced it was overtaken by an envy so piercing he nearly doubled over. An ulcer, he thought. Appendicitis. "I can't deal with this right now," he said. "I'm not feeling well. Let me call you later."

"Don't hate me," Alana said.

"I'll try."

"I wasn't planning this. You know that."

"We all do what we have to do."

He didn't call her back that night or the next. He spent the
weekend imagining Becky with other men – teachers at school,
students from her master's program, the ex-boyfriend she'd once
described as tall and scruffy, with the nicest arms she'd ever
seen. He looked at his own arms in the mirror, wiry, lightly haired,
cut with bulging veins, biceps rounded well enough, but wrists
so slender he could wrap his fingers around with nearly an inch
to spare. No one would call his the nicest arms, not even Alana.
How could anyone possibly love him when he had arms like
these? He pictured Becky covered by arms of various shapes and
sizes, all thicker than his, with denser hair, and by Saturday
night he'd convinced himself he'd lost something precious, that
she really had broken his heart. He wanted to punch something.
He paced the shabby apartment, swinging his fists, clapping his
hands, shouting, "Fucking Becky. Fucking life. Fucking fuck
fuck fuck."

He was exhausted by Monday morning, his nerves frayed.
He saw Becky's car in the parking lot, and his breath left him.
But the person who stepped out from behind the wheel wasn't
the one he'd been imagining all weekend. She was just an awkward girl with narrow shoulders and wide hips, nothing seductive
about the way she moved, nothing erotic in her clunky shoes
and the loose skirt meant to hide her heavy thighs.

Where had his desire gone? How could it disappear in an
instant? What took its place were Alana's sputtered words,
her weeping, the little jump in her voice when she said the word
"affair." The image of her naked body was more familiar to him
than his own, and he saw it now, so much nicer than Becky's,
everything in proportion except for her feet, which were nearly
as big as his. There was a scar on her back the size of a dime,
where a suspicious mole had been removed the year after they'd
met. After sex, he always rested his forefinger there and felt
as if he were touching something far beneath her skin. Only now

was he struck by the horror of someone else's finger there, touching that place that was meant for him alone.

He couldn't get out of the car. He wanted to throw up. Becky made her way inside, waddling, he thought, and he suddenly hated her, for confusing him, for making him forget the scar on Alana's back, for tricking him into thinking he could exchange it for something else. His head rested against the steering wheel when the morning bell rang, and he had to sprint to make it to his classroom before the first students arrived.

4.

GRIEF SHARPENED HIS memory, when all he wanted was amnesia. He suddenly recalled the flavor of their wedding cake – rum-soaked, with a raspberry glaze – and its texture against his tongue. The ceremony played over in his mind, the vows they'd written for the sole purpose of shocking his parents and making their friends laugh – "I promise to clean the lint from between your toes, to comb your back hair, to check your head for lice" – and then the reception, when Larry surprised everyone by insisting on an impromptu dancing of the horah, Alana's whoops of delight as she wobbled on a chair her father pumped drunkenly at the ceiling.

More than anything he kept remembering their honeymoon to Spain, the sudden shock he'd experienced as it dawned on him that he'd pledged himself to someone for the rest of his life. Their first night in Barcelona he'd been groggy with jet lag, stumbling through the narrow, cobbled streets of the Gothic Quarter, unable to find his way back to their hotel, and Alana pretended not to notice his growing anxiety, instead remarking on the architecture, on the same three tapas bars they'd passed half a dozen times on their way through the maze. During those first few days she ignored his nervousness, his eagerness in bed, his jittery talk, acknowledging how much she'd recognized only after he'd begun to calm down. "You feel better now?" she asked as they came out of the Sagrada Familia, his head swirling with Gaudí's impossible vision and nerve. "Being married to me's not so bad, is it?"

Later, in a park by the zoo, they sat on a bench watching small green parrots making a nest in a nearby tree. He felt some kind of movement beside him, or heard a sound, and when he pulled his gaze away from the birds, saw that Alana's purse was gone. Her passport was in there, two credit cards, all their traveler's checks. He was off the bench in a second, running before Alana even knew what had happened. The thief was only a hundred yards up the path, squatting by a bush, rummaging through the purse, and in that moment Richard thought he could have killed the man, happily pummeling and kicking until he'd knocked the life out of him. Instead he tore the purse out of the thief's hands and stood trembling in front of him, his empty fist clenched, heat and hatred mixing in some kind of tingling feeling all over his skin. Only when the man straightened did Richard realize how much taller he was, how much broader, his face stony and surprisingly handsome, his features almost noble, his mouth pouty and sensitive – only then did it occur to him how easily he might have been hurt himself, killed even, if the man pulled a knife or gun. But the thief only muttered, "Lo siento," and walked off slowly, hands in his pockets, as if he'd done nothing more than accidentally bumped into Richard on the path, or stepped on his foot. It all happened in under a minute, and when he came back Alana was still gathering herself from the bench. He held up the purse triumphantly, the tingling feeling now complemented by his racing heart. "Oh, thank God," she said, and hugged him, giving an uneasy laugh. "My hero." Then she shook her head, blinked, and said, "My husband. That's so weird. I guess you are, aren't you." I'd kill for you, he thought, though now that his anger was fading, so was his thirst for violence, and he had a hard time believing it. By then Alana's own anger had taken hold. "We should go find him," she said. "We should get the police."

"He took off running," Richard said over the hollow beat of

his pulse, imagining what the handsome thief might have done to him if he'd decided not to walk away. "He's long gone." And then came the overnight train to Granada, the two of them clinging to each other on the narrow berth, in hysterics every time the car careened around a curve so fast they were sure it would jump the tracks. Nothing could touch them now, nothing. The last full day of their honeymoon they visited Alhambra just before sunset, the angled light making crystalline patterns of shadows on the walls, on the floors, dancing in his vision, and on their way back to the hotel a gypsy woman grabbed Alana's arm and wouldn't let go. She forced open Alana's palm and said, "Long life, happy love, many children." Then she grabbed Richard's hand, and he let her open it without resistance. "Long life, happy love, many children." She waved a sprig of rosemary in front of them and then demanded eight hundred pesetas. Her face was grooved, her front teeth chipped to points. Richard didn't believe her words, didn't believe she'd even looked at the lines on his hand, but he was sure she had the power to curse them if she chose to. He handed over the money despite Alana's objections, and when she hounded him about it afterward he didn't tell her he'd done it out of sheer terror, desperate to protect the happiness that felt so fragile, that was threatened on all sides. "How could I not pay her when she got our future exactly right?" he said. "You ready to get started on those many children?"

Had she cursed them after all? He wished he could believe it, wished he could blame anything other than his own stupidity and selfishness. It was November now. His parents moved to Florida. His father developed a sudden fear of hurricanes, and his mother waged war against the fire ants in her new backyard. Strangers were living in his childhood home. For his birthday, he went to a nearby diner and ordered cheesecake, taking grim pleasure in stabbing each of the strawberries on top, those little red hearts. On Thanksgiving he was sure the laughter coming from the apartment downstairs was directed at him, a pathetic man eating a turkey and cranberry sandwich alone.

The next day he took the train into the city to see Larry's new piece, at a temporary arts space in Greenpoint, housed in a turn-of-the-century public bath. He didn't know why the installation troubled him, smaller in scale than much of Larry's work, and less elaborate. He didn't understand the piece exactly and also knew understanding was beside the point. Piled on a wooden desk and spilling over its sides were dozens of fleshtone pin-cushions, some with the cotton stuffing spilling out, some soiled as if they'd been handled with grease-covered fingers. Scattered on the floor were notebook pages that had been dunked in water, the writing illegible. Richard read loss in it, the same way he read loss in the gathering clouds, the stiff wind, the roar of traffic when he broke away and stepped out into the street.

Larry was supposed to have met him an hour earlier, but of course he didn't show. On the phone the week before Richard had told him he'd had it with Jersey, that he was moving into the city for real, to hell with the job, to hell with everything. Could he really live here? Against the gray sky he saw sharp things, cranes and church spires. The screeching hydraulics of a garbage truck made him wince. Across the street a warehouse door was tagged with SPUR, the upside down and backward R, no skill to it at all, he thought, something one of his least promising students might have done. He left a message for Larry, saying how much he liked the new piece, how he'd decided to wait until spring to look for an apartment. On his way back to the train he spotted SPUR six more times, the entire city claimed and spoken for.

The following night he drove to Philadelphia to visit a college friend, one of the two working artists left from a group of more than a dozen who'd taken a solemn pledge a decade ago to fight the forces of conformity forever, under penalty of a slow, monotonous death. Dawn had been the wildest of them all, experimenting with substances Richard wouldn't touch – things that

could have killed her – covering her arms and back in tattoos,
once showing up at a student exhibition wearing nothing
but green body paint, her pubic hair dyed silver. Her sculpture
was fairly tame by comparison, abstract, Brancusi-inspired
forms cast in white plastic, like plumbing parts for toilets in an
alternate universe. She was represented by a gallery in Philly
and another in Denver, and if she sold three pieces a year she
considered it a success. She was only too happy to have Richard
come out. "It's about time, you suburban prick," she said on
the phone. Her apartment was small, but tidy, in a brownstone
near Drexel, the walls decorated with prints of Mapplethorpe
flowers, real flowers in a vase on the counter, fruit in a bowl on
the kitchen table. Dawn had gotten unambiguously fat in the
last five years, growing a second chin, the tattoos on her arms
stretching into faded blobs. Her girlfriend was even fatter, with
spiky black hair and a ring through her septum, and when he
saw her Richard immediately pictured a bullfight, a matador's
red cape.

They offered him green tea and kiwi fruit and talked about
Dawn's last show in Denver, the terrible write-up she'd gotten
in the local paper. "Those stupid hicks," Dawn said. "They only
like statues of elk and buffalo."

"She sold a piece," her girlfriend said. "That's all that
matters."

Dawn knew about his separation, knew that he and Alana
were taking a break from seeing each other or speaking at all
until they decided what to do next. She must have been able to
see the pain in his face, but she made no effort to comfort him,
not even when her girlfriend got up to go to the bathroom.
Instead she kept up a steady stream of gossip about their old
friends, most of whom had lives even duller than Richard's – one
was an investment broker, another a public relations manager
for a gas utility. When the girlfriend came back, Dawn took her
hand into her lap and said, "We've got something to tell you,
Rich." The girlfriend smiled shyly, nostrils flaring. Dawn let out

a little squeal and cried, "I'm pregnant!" The baby was due in
May. The donor was one of the girlfriend's best friends, a
gorgeous boy from Baltimore. Richard hugged them both and
told them they'd make wonderful parents. The salty burning in
his throat made it difficult to speak. Dawn said, "Life is so strange,
isn't it? I never thought I'd be a mom."

It was the girlfriend who put a hand on Richard's arm
and said, "Things'll get better soon. Two years ago my life was a
disaster. It's all about cycles." He hugged her a second time.

After his third cup of green tea he drove downtown and
wandered familiar streets, the ones he'd stumbled through as a
drunk twenty-year-old in love as much with his own recklessly
beating heart as with the girl on his arm. There was the apartment
he'd shared with the two musicians – one of whom was making
a name for himself in experimental electronica, the last Richard
had heard – the one Alana had spent so many nights in that
year before he graduated, the one where they'd first had sex. He
wished he could remember the act itself, the way she'd touched
him, whether there had been the promise of joy in it or of
catastrophe, but now he was passing the Pakistani's cheesesteak
joint, packed with college kids, half a dozen hookers lined up
around the corner on Broad Street.

He made eye contact with one of them, a brown-skinned
girl of some indefinite ethnicity, with hair unnaturally straightened, eye make-up that was supposed to evoke an Egyptian
princess or a refugee from one of Warhol's long-gone parties. She
wore spandex shorts and a matching sports bra, nothing else
but heels and a chunky silver necklace. What would it take for
him to sink even lower? No one was holding him back, not Alana,
not Becky Block, not his parents or Larry or Dawn. He gave
the girl the slightest nod. She stepped forward from the group.
He kept walking. "Hey," she called, her voice sweeter sounding
than he'd expected, a singer's voice, perfectly pitched. He picked
up his pace. "Hey, motherfucker!" He heard her heels on the

sidewalk behind him and took off running, not stopping until he reached his car, a block from Independence Hall.

FOR WEEKS HE'D been imagining a reconciliation, a long night of negotiation and tears, when he and Alana would discuss the things they could live without, the things they couldn't, when they would ask over and over that one unanswerable question – "Where did we go wrong?" – Richard refusing to believe they'd been wrong from the start, refusing even to consider the possibility, though the possibility nagged at him day after day.

He started following the Dean campaign in earnest, taking an interest not so much in the candidate's agenda as his personality, his boyish charm and bumbling straight-talk, his lack of polish and obvious love of attention. His surge of momentum was so unexpected that Richard clung to it desperately – if this man stood even a chance of becoming President, there might be hope for him as well.

When he finally called to arrange a meeting, the day after he visited Dawn in Philadelphia, Alana sighed and said, "Okay. I guess so," as if he were asking her to help with some tedious chore, taking plastic bottles to the recycling center or scrubbing mold from his bathroom wall. Our Versailles, he called the meeting as they were making arrangements, and instantly regretted it. It was a stupid comparison, making him the defeated German, ready to accept all blame, all responsibility. He took on the role too easily when he showed up at the house, smiling nervously, kissing her politely on the cheek, his pressed shirt and slacks a façade of respectability, hiding nothing. Why did he feel like the wrongdoer, the one who deserved punishment? Maybe because Alana was the one who'd stayed put – she had territorial control, leaving him the interloper, treading on unfamiliar ground. But he'd been wronged as much as anyone. Alana, after all, was the one who'd managed to have a fling. Shouldn't she be the one torn apart by guilt, begging for forgiveness?

Instead she greeted him coolly, smiling without parting her

lips, her posture stiff, hair up in back and pinned, not a strand loose. She'd prepared for him. The house was spotless, or at least what Richard could see – she'd shut the bedroom door, the door to the office they'd once shared, the one to the garage, half of which he should have converted into a studio when they'd first moved in, so he could have been painting all this time. On the kitchen table was a bottle of wine, two glasses, their wedding album. In front of Alana's seat was a notepad and pen. "I don't get to take notes, too?" he said, not seriously, but she only shrugged and answered, "You know where everything is. Help yourself." Part of him wanted to give in to all her demands right away, to be done with this as quickly as possible, but the thought immediately triggered his stubbornness, his determination to stand his ground. He opened the wine and poured. The chair was the same one he'd sat in for four years, eating hundreds of breakfasts and dinners, but now the wooden slats dug into his back, the cushion felt lumpy, the legs unsteady. Had he gained weight in the last three months? He hadn't thought so. He felt gaunt, emaciated. He imagined himself wasting away in his lone-liness, though in the mirror each morning he was surprised to find himself looking no different than he had the night before. He shifted on the chair but couldn't, for the life of him, get comfortable. "Where do we start?" he asked.

"Don't do that," she said. "Don't put it all in my lap. We're in this together."

He took a deep breath and had a hard time letting it out. "I meant the question for both of us," he said. "I suppose we should start by saying what we want. And maybe what we're afraid of."

"I think that's premature," she said. "You're talking as if it's a done deal, like we're really getting back together. First we need to figure out if it's even feasible. If we can really do it at all."

Would he ever be on solid ground? She talked as if she could take him or leave him, and either way life would go on. He hadn't felt that way for quite some time. He'd come to the end of a long road, one that kept narrowing and getting bleaker the farther he went, and there was only one way off, back the way he'd come. He was living for the moment when they both recognized how much they needed each other, how impossible it would be for them to stay apart – he pictured an embrace that erased everything, that obliterated all practical obstacles and past mistakes. It took all his restraint to keep from throwing himself on her mercy, slobbering on her feet and pleading to come home. "I think anything's feasible, if we both really want it to be. That's the real question. Don't you want it?" He paused only a second. He wasn't ready for her answer. He went on, with all the insistence he could muster, the strength he barely remembered from their early days together. "I want it. I know that for sure. I want it more than I've ever wanted anything in my life."

It worked – he could see her resolve weaken, the stern set of her eyes softening, breaking contact with his own. "It's not simply a matter of wanting. I wish it was. But it's not."

This was the biggest difference between them, he thought. For him, wanting was everything. But he braced himself and said, "Okay. What else? What are your concerns?"

"*My* concerns? Don't *you* have any concerns? We nearly got *divorced*. I *fucked* someone else, remember?"

She didn't say it to seek absolution – it was a dagger, thrust into his open wound. He pushed away from the table. "I'm concerned that you're not even going to give this a chance. That you've already decided against it."

"I haven't decided anything."

"Maybe not consciously."

"Okay, Dr. Freud."

"I don't care who you fucked," he said, though this was an outright lie. He'd already heard more details about her lover than he wanted to know – that he was married, that they'd slept together only twice, that he was gruff and inattentive in bed. But the one detail Richard wanted she wouldn't provide – a name to go with the faceless, roving prick, a focus for his rage and hatred. Instead he was left with nothing but envy, and disappointment in his failure to have an affair of his own. "I don't care about any of it. I just want you to have hope for us. Otherwise all this is pointless."

She was silent. He let his eyes wander, to give her time, maybe to make her wonder if she was losing him. He missed the walls of the house they'd bought together, hung with some of his favorite reproductions, Klees and Hartleys, with the artwork of people he'd known in college, with her father's sketches. "I want to hope," she said, softly. "I just don't know if I can." He made a move to stand. Would he really have gotten up all the way? "Don't go," she said, and there was a break in her voice, the signal he'd been praying for. Soon she'd be sobbing, unable to catch her breath. He felt ashamed for wanting it but knew he could make her end up in his arms. "Give me hope," she said, as the first tears fell. "Show me how."

He took her to bed. The scar on her back was smaller than he remembered, a good fit for his pinkie, not his forefinger. She hadn't shaved her legs, and their stubble chafed his shins. The smell of their sex made him nostalgic even as he breathed it in. After they finished, she propped herself against the headboard, with the notepad she'd fetched on her way back from the bathroom, and started making lists. Separate columns for fears, desires, dreams, needs. She cross-referenced, ranked, traded, eliminated. She asked him questions, and he gave answers he thought she wanted to hear. "So you won't freak out if I go up to New Hampshire for the primary? Even if I'm gone for a week?"

"Of course not. Go for two, if that's what you need to do."

After an hour he no longer knew which were his dreams or her needs. He'd compromised everything, or nothing. Did he really want to do this for the rest of his life? Finally he took the notepad from her and drew a picture, the two of them shaking hands in front of the palace at Versailles. Only he couldn't remember what the palace looked like, so he drew the Louvre instead. Sparrows cackled the approach of dawn. Alana rolled on top of him. "Let's do more than shake on it," she said.

He didn't know what he'd agreed to. He didn't know what deal they were sealing. He didn't care. He didn't care.

5.

HE RENTED ANOTHER truck for mid-December, from a different U-Haul outlet all the way out in Ledgewood, an extra twenty-minute drive. While they waited for the moving day, he and Alana made hasty plans for a trip to celebrate their seventh wedding anniversary, coming up on New Year's Eve. If they'd had more time, they both agreed, they might have tried for something exotic, an adventure to the Costa Rican rainforest, or to the Mayan ruins in Guatemala, or else a quick European jaunt, to Sicily, or the Greek Isles, or back to Spain. But on such short notice the best they could do was a package deal to the Bahamas, four nights at a resort between a golf course and the beach, with tickets to a New Year's ball at a nearby casino included. "In another seven years," Richard said. "All this will seem like just a bump in the road."

Alana's mother sent a set of leather suitcases from another Santa Barbara boutique. Richard's parents sent emails. They didn't trust reconciliation any more than they did trial separations. *I just want you to be happy*, his mother wrote. And his father, *Our bridge game's improving. By spring we'll be pros*. A month ago he'd booked a flight to Fort Lauderdale for Christmas week, desperate at the thought of spending his vacation alone, and his father had immediately called a plumber to fix the hot tub they never would have used themselves. When he canceled, his mother said simply, "I understand. You'll come when you can." But it was clear from her muted voice that she understood nothing beyond her own disappointment and hurt feelings.

Again Larry offered to give a hand with the move, and this time Alana invited him, over Richard's objections. "He can help with the heavier things," she said. "It's bad for my back."

Larry looked as if he hadn't slept in weeks when he showed up, wearing a coat that was too thin for the frigid day, a shirt that was stained with varnish, his beard grown out a quarter of an inch. He'd taken an early train this time, instead of staying the night. He yawned and stretched his arms over his head and seemed generally put out to be here, as if he'd come only because they'd begged him. "I wish you two would make up your minds, already. I'm not coming out here a third time."

"Don't even think about borrowing the truck again," Richard said. "It's not going to happen."

"Jesus, are you still on that?"

"I'm serious."

"One little mistake and you'll hound me to my grave."

"And beyond."

"I don't want your damn truck anyway," Larry said.

This time all three of them rode in the cab together, Richard driving, Alana wedged between him and her father. Heat poured out of the dashboard. Grimy snowbanks lined Route 10. Larry stared out the window, sulking, and to bring him around, Richard said, "I think the new piece is your best yet. I can't stop thinking about it."

"So all the others were crap, huh?"

"You know that's not what he means," Alana said.

"It's really haunting," Richard said.

"Nobody cares," Larry said.

Alana started talking about their trip, the pictures they'd seen of white sand beaches, blue water, red coral beds they could snorkel around. "I think I convinced Rich to give it a try. I promised him there wouldn't be any sharks."

"A shame if you don't get to Havana," Larry said. "You'll be so close."

"I told you already. We're not going to Cuba."

"Havana," Larry said, and clucked his tongue. "Most incredible place I've ever been. The people, the cars –"

"That's what you said about New York," Richard said.

"We've seen *Buena Vista Social Club*," Alana said.

"It's not the same."

"We'll get there someday," Richard said. "Another trip."

"Sure you will," Larry said.

Richard kept his eyes on the road so he didn't have to see Larry's disgusted shrug. The Pathmark came into view, and then the apartment complex, the roofs piled with snow, the tarp covering the pool sagging with its weight. A familiar shiver of panic ran through him. They really were together again. For the next month, the next year, they'd be stripped down, exposed, in each other's presence more intensely than they'd ever been before. Were they ready for it? He wished they could ease into the transition, to test their resolve – they could date for a few months, sleep together three or four nights a week, ensure they were making the right decision. Why couldn't he be settled on anything, ever? Already he was pulling into the parking spot nearest the stairs, turning off the truck's ignition. Suddenly Alana's cheek was against his neck, the heat of her skin making his own prickle. "Here we go!" she whispered, and then a quick nibble on the edge of his ear. They were ready for anything, he told himself.

"You should be paying me for this," Larry said.

"As soon as we get these criminals out of office," Richard said, as he opened the back of the truck. "Then it'll be easy to go to Cuba. A year from now we'll be getting ready for the inauguration."

"President Dean," Alana said, wistfully.

Richard didn't believe his optimism any more now than he had three months ago, but Alana didn't seem bothered by it today. He'd put a Dean for America sticker on his Camry, causing trouble with the union representative at school, who was pushing for Gephardt. If she was setting herself up for disappointment, what else could he do but prepare to console her in its wake?

Larry had a cigarette lit and was already on the second floor walkway, peering into the window of the apartment on the end. The door opened, and one of the black-haired toddlers poked his head out. Richard braced himself for screaming, but it didn't come. Larry knelt on the concrete, his cigarette behind his back. The toddler – a boy? a girl? – stuck a thumb in its mouth and turned partly away, flirtatiously. The heavyset girl came out, hugely pregnant now, both arms resting on the shelf of her belly. Larry said something that made her laugh.

But in the apartment he was no less sullen than before. "Let's get this done quick," he said. "I've got better things to do with my time."

Alana wore practical shoes, clunky Doc Martens that must have been holdovers from college or the few years after. She grabbed Richard's suit and slacks, still draped over a cardboard box, bunching them in her arms. He'd have to take them in for pressing if she wasn't careful, but he didn't stop her. "There's an artist colony on Abaco," he told Larry as they hauled the first boxes down the stairs. "It's not in any guidebook, but a college friend told me about it."

"It's not Havana," Larry said, breathing hard.

"You can only get there by boat. This sculptor was supposed to have gotten shipwrecked there in the fifties. He lived in a cave for a year. Eventually built a bronze foundry. Some of the best casting in the world. At least that's what Dawn said."

"Sculpture's dead," Larry said. "And I still say it's not Havana."

When everything was in the truck, including the unused camping gear from his storage space, Richard went back up alone, just to make sure he hadn't forgotten anything. Whether he had or not, he needed to see the place one last time, what was supposed to have been the launching pad for a new life. If he'd been a different person, he might have set up an easel and splashed paint on canvases. He might have bedded women. He might have brewed up methamphetamines, as one of the tenants in a nearby complex had done, creating a big scandal covered by the local paper. Without his furniture and clothes, the rooms seemed to have shrunk and brightened. He had forgotten things after all. The crystal vase was still on the counter, the Giacometti biography on the windowsill in the bathroom, fewer than fifty pages read. And elsewhere, the detritus of those disastrous months, a balled-up piece of packing tape on the bedroom floor, a rubber band on the kitchen counter, a brown stain on the living room carpet, where he'd spilled half a cup of coffee. All of it evidence of his failure, so complete and predictable. He considered smashing the vase on the concrete walkway, as a symbol of something, or simply as a release, but then thought of the toddlers walking over the shards, and decided instead to leave it for the new tenants or the manager when she came to inspect for damage. The biography he tucked under his arm and turned to leave.

Larry was in the doorway. He was smiling now, clapping his hands, saying, "Need a hand with anything else?"

"I said you didn't have to come up. We got it all."

Larry didn't seem to hear him. He wandered into the kitchen, and then poked his head into the bathroom. "I'm sorry you won't be in the city, but I'm glad you two got your shit together. You belong with each other. I've always known that."

Richard had a hard time answering. His throat swelled up and so did his sinuses. It was the kindest thing he'd heard in months. "Me, too."

"Look, kid. I want to ask you something."

He wiped his eyes. "You can't have the truck."

"Did I say anything about the truck?"

"I'm serious."

"I don't want your goddamn truck, okay? This place. The lease. You've got it for another three months, right?"

"Two and a half," Richard said.

"I could use some extra space," Larry said. "For a big piece I'm working on."

"Are you gonna pay the rent?"

"You've got to pay it anyway, don't you?"

He could have argued but knew he'd eventually give in. He handed over the keys. "Just don't graffiti the walls, okay?"

"Can't you let that go already? Do I have to hear it for the rest of my life?"

"In the afterlife, too," Richard said.

In the parking lot Alana had the truck running, and when they came close she rolled down the window and called, "You won't believe it." Richard could hear the radio on, a newscaster's voice blaring. He expected her to tell them about another bombing, about more bloodshed. But that wasn't news, it was daily routine. "They caught him. Saddam. They found him hiding in a hole."

They listened to the report on the way to the house, and again on the way to the train station in Richard's Camry, Alana in the backseat now, Larry beside him. Richard found himself strangely dispirited by the description of the fallen dictator, haggard after living underground for so long, disoriented and begging for his life.

"It's good, I guess," Alana said. "The guy's a monster. I'm glad he'll be held accountable. Not so good for Dean, though."

"The world died a long time ago," Larry said. "None of this really matters."

"He'll still win," Richard said. Hope was pointless, he knew, but hope was all he had. He met Alana's eyes in the rearview mirror, and she gave a little nod, shoving all doubt away. "I know he'll win."

On the platform, Larry hugged them both. "Thanks, kid," he whispered in Richard's ear. "I owe you one." He had a cigarette lit as the train pulled up and kept smoking it on his way to the doors. But he stopped halfway, turned, and said, "I almost forgot. For your trip." With his free hand he reached into his jacket pocket, pulled out two small packages wrapped in newspaper, tossed one to Alana, one to Richard. Alana caught hers with an agile swipe, but Richard's slipped through his fingers and skittered across the cement. He chased it down, more embarrassed than he needed to be, burning with a shame that was so familiar by now he didn't try to fight it.

"Take care of yourself while we're away, okay Dad?" Alana called. "Moderation, remember?"

"Give my regards to the barracudas," Larry said, tossing his smoldering butt onto the tracks.

Then he was in the car, the doors shut. Richard watched the train pull away, off toward the city he knew he'd never call home. When he turned around, Alana was unwrapping her present: a bottle of Coppertone, already opened, a dollop of old cream crusted on the spigot. He tore away the paper from his and found a felt sketching pen, the kind Larry used for his installation studies, half the ink gone. "He put a lot of thought into these," Richard said, as they made their way to the parking lot, to his Camry with the Howard Dean sticker on its bumper.

"He could have given me the pen and you the sunscreen."

He held up his arm, let his sleeve slide down to reveal a pasty, bony wrist, scattered here and there with light brown moles. "I could probably use it more than the pen."

"Who knows," she said. "You might get inspired and draw all the sharks we see when we go snorkeling."

"I thought you promised no sharks."

"Only the kind that eat people."

"I think I'll stay on the beach and draw girls in bikinis."

"Girls in bikinis aren't allowed at this resort. Only fat guys in Speedos."

"Then I'll just have to draw you," he said. "No bikini."

"All these years, and only now does he ask me to be his model."

"I've been waiting for the right pen," he said, and for the first time all day she kissed him, a sloppy, moving jab on the jaw. It was the best he'd get right now, and for now it was good enough.

The Old Uniform

THREE NIGHTS AFTER HE CALLED OFF THE WEDDING
and moved out of Stacey's condo, Adam put on the old uniform:
black high-top Chuck Taylors, dark jeans with the cuffs rolled
once, a maroon T-shirt printed with the faded logo of a trucking
company, a battered leather jacket with a crumpled pack of
stale cigarettes stuffed into the front pocket. Everything still fit,
the jeans a little stiff, the sleeves of the jacket crackling when he
stretched out his arms, and for the first time all week he
believed, momentarily, that his life wasn't over, that he might not
have to suffer as deeply as he'd first imagined. These clothes
had once felt like a second skin, one he'd shed happily enough
during his time with Stacey, and slipping back into them now,
he wished he could forget he'd ever had them off.

It took him an hour to find it all, rummaging through boxes
he'd stacked in his parents' basement, between the dusty ping-
pong table that hadn't been touched since he'd graduated high
school and the toy chest that still held his childhood treasures,
Lego sets and Lincoln Logs, Matchbox cars with windshields he'd
smashed to make them look like victims of a horrific freeway
pile-up. In the process he discovered other things he didn't want
to come across just yet – a sweater Stacey had bought him last
Hanukkah, a robe that still held her scent, a deck of cards they'd
taken on their one overseas trip together, to Ireland, just over a
year ago. Their second trip was supposed to be coming up in
less than a month, following the ceremony and reception down

in Fairfax – four nights in Rome and three in Venice, at small, family-run hotels recommended by a travel agent cousin of his father's. The tickets were non-refundable. He'd paid a deposit on the hotels. He hadn't yet called the cousin to find out about cancellations. He didn't know if he'd bother.

What did money matter to him now?

His parents were waiting for him in the kitchen when he came upstairs, his father wearing a brittle smile, confused, maybe, to see him in his old clothes, his mother unable to keep herself from reaching out and touching an elbow, quickly pulling her hand away – afraid, he guessed, that he'd shrug her off, or else infect her with his misfortune. "Are you sure you don't want to eat something before you go?" she asked. "I made a nice chicken. And I've got that eggplant sauce you like. Just a few bites?"

"Ma," he said, and gave what he hoped was a reassuring smile, though his face felt awkward doing so, his cheeks resisting. "Thanks, really. I'll eat in the city. I'm fine for now."

"But you won't be there for another hour."

"Let him be, Rita," his father said from the kitchen table, one of the massive popular histories he loved to read spread in front of him, an account of the spice trade during the Renaissance or a biography of Grover Cleveland. His eyes scanned the page too fast, Adam thought, to be taking in any words. "If he says he doesn't want to eat, he doesn't want to eat. He's a grown man."

"You need to keep up your strength."

"I don't have the flu," Adam said, and tried to laugh, but his mother only blinked a few times and turned away, pulling out the silverware drawer. In the glare of the kitchen lights her dyed hair had a brass tint to it, so far from her natural dark brown, the color of his own hair. It didn't look right paired with his father's thick white waves. Adam was always surprised to discover how much they'd aged, even when he saw them every few weeks. Part of him still expected to see them as they'd been when he was a boy, lively, confident people in their late thirties – his mother a force on the PTA board, president of the local Hadassah chapter, a mahjong shark; his father climbing up the ranks at AT&T, playing tennis three nights a week, hosting a cocktail party for his colleagues every winter and a barbecue every Labor Day. Now all they talked about was their coming retirement, the move they'd make within the next five years to a gated community in Boca, the outrageous cost of a dual golf membership.

In three days they hadn't once asked what had happened between him and Stacey, though he was sure they were dying to – they were respecting his privacy, he supposed, waiting until he was ready to share. He wanted to comfort them, to tell them he was going to be okay, eventually. No one died, he could have reminded them. This wasn't the end of the world. But as soon as he thought so his knees felt rubbery, and he had to fight hard to keep them from buckling. Neither of them was looking at him, his mother reaching into a high cabinet, his father rubbing at something on his fingers. The gleaming counters hurt his eyes. Go ahead, he thought. Just ask already.

But his mother was on her way to the fridge, plate in hand. "As soon as you get a whiff of that sauce, you'll want some," she said. "I remember how much you liked it last – " She stopped herself, rustling a plastic bag in the crisper. He knew what she was thinking: that the last time he'd eaten the sauce he was supposed to have liked so much he'd been here with Stacey. He might have liked anything then. How could you trust your senses when they were distorted, made gluey by love and hope and thoughts of the future? How could he trust them now, soured as they were, making everything his mother offered sound nauseating? They were as suspect as anything, a source of constant betrayal.

"Really, Ma," he said. "I've got to go. I'll miss my train."

"I'll take you to the station," his father said, closing his book and rising.

"I've got my car."

"Costs a fortune to leave it overnight."

"And there've been all those break-ins, haven't there?" his mother said. "People's windows smashed, stereos stolen. You've got such a nice stereo in your car. A shame to have some jerk take it."

"They're not after stereos anymore," his father said. "They want receipts, credit card slips. It's all about identity theft these days. The worst kind of criminals – "

"Well, whatever they take," his mother said. "It isn't safe."

"Can you imagine it?" his father said. "These people get all your information, they open accounts, they ruin your whole life – "

"Okay," Adam said, knowing they could go on this way all night, as they'd done when he was a boy. Over dinner they'd argue about brands of margarine or which route was fastest to the Rockaway Mall, which was best to avoid traffic, and he'd listen, silently, with the half-formed notion they were speaking some other language, a code that concealed the true content of their conversation. Back then the sound of their nonsense had somehow comforted him – he didn't want to know what was really on their minds, what actual troubles they might be facing – but now he found it maddening. "Drive me if you want. But we'd better get going."

"I'd rather be robbed at gunpoint," his father said, shaking his head, still picturing, Adam knew, those thieves scouring his glove compartment for credit card and social security numbers.

"Wait," his mother said. "Take this." She shoved a plate into his hand, heaped with chicken and chunks of tomato and eggplant. "Just eat a few bites on the way. I know you'll like it." She stuck a fork in his jacket pocket and found the ancient cigarettes. His heart gave a little jump, an aftershock of the first time she'd caught him smoking at sixteen, when she'd raged for an hour, threatening to send him to boarding school – did she think they didn't smoke there? – before breaking down in hysterics, asking if he hated her, if he had a death wish, if he wanted to talk to a psychiatrist. "Oh, Adam," she said now, softly, only a shadow of the dynamo she'd been then. "You're not going to start smoking again."

"Ma," he said, and checked the anger he heard rising in his voice, the tremble he felt at the back of his throat. Her eyes were watery behind her glasses, and she shrank from him, expecting a scolding. This isn't about you, he wanted to say. I'm the one who's supposed to be crying. "Don't worry so much, okay?"

"Promise me you won't," she said.

"If he ever deserved a smoke, this would be the time," his father said.

"You've seen those terrible pictures. The lungs, all black and—"

"Ma."

"Rita," his father said. "Lay off already."

"Promise me," she said again.

"Okay," Adam said. Hadn't she learned by now that promises didn't mean anything? "I've got to go."

AT THE END of the driveway his father turned the car too soon, nearly clipping the mailbox, and rolled over the curb. Adam grabbed the dashboard with one hand and balanced the plate with the other, the eggplant nearly sliding into his lap. As soon as the car settled, he pulled on his seatbelt. His father, oblivious, adjusted the rearview mirror, then turned on his headlights, though it was still an hour before dusk.

Only in the last few years had his driving begun to frighten Adam, though it had been this way all his life. His father would get distracted by anything the slightest bit out of the ordinary—daffodils blooming in a drainage ditch, a biplane taking off from the local airstrip, a prison crew picking up trash from the median—and for a few seconds he'd lose track of the road. But that wasn't the scariest part. Worse was when he remembered he was driving and jerked the wheel to correct his drifting, the car heaving all over the pavement. It was less than five miles to the train station, but even by the time they made it to the end of the block,

Adam's hand was tense on the armrest, one leg straightened, braced against the floorboard.

Until this week he'd believed he wouldn't care about his own life if he lost Stacey, that the idea of death wouldn't trouble him at all. He'd once told her as much, when she was planning to go skydiving to celebrate her twenty-ninth birthday. They'd been together almost a year then, and he'd decided they had a long future together. "I don't mean to go all mother-hen on you," he said. "It's just that ... if something happened ... I don't, like ... I couldn't handle it. I couldn't go on." She hugged him and told him he was sweet and only after he'd begun breathing easier, let him know she was going to do it anyway. It was important to her, she said. She was sorry it made him uncomfortable, but wasn't that how relationships worked? Weren't they always full of risks, every moment of every day? "What's the difference between jumping out of a plane and crossing Seventh Avenue?" He didn't argue, but he couldn't bring himself to go watch, either, instead waiting at home for a devastating phone call, waiting to find out his future had been shattered. When a call did come, Stacey's voice squealing with exhilaration, he swore, silently, that from then on he'd keep his worries to himself.

But now that he had lost her he was as afraid as ever that his father, distracted by a butterfly, would jump the divider and slam headfirst into an oncoming semi, or jerk the car into a ravine. He gripped the armrest and studied the airbag sign on the dashboard. The smell of his sweat along with that of the chicken and eggplant in his lap made him queasy. He'd hardly eaten anything in the past few days, his mother's worst fear. But he didn't need food for strength right now. Since he'd moved home he had a strange abundance of energy, adrenaline jitters that kept his eyes from closing at night, that made it hard to sit still. He considered forking the chicken out the window, bit by bit, as he'd once dropped the carrot sticks his mother had always buried in his lunch bags behind school bus seat cushions. Instead he let go of the armrest reluctantly and set the plate on the backseat.

"I'll forget it if you leave it there," his father said.

"I'm really not hungry."

"I'll come out in the morning, and the whole car'll smell like garlic."

"I can't eat it."

"She means well."

"I know that," Adam said. His father was waiting for him to go on, to broach the subject of Stacey and the wedding, to spill his guts. Adam knew what reaction he'd get – sympathy followed by silent judgment and even a hint of accusation. How could he have been so blind? his father would have thought. How could he have let things go so far?

For years his parents had looked at him skeptically. Not only when he'd been hanging around musicians and heroin addicts in Brooklyn, living a mildly bohemian existence, the kind that came with a steady salary, a working shower, a moderately balanced diet. They didn't understand how alive he'd felt then – the most alive he'd ever been, he thought now, feeling a swell of anticipation, hoping he could step back into that life the way he'd stepped back into his jeans. When he was in college, too, they'd second-guessed his choices. They didn't think he should major in business administration – it wasn't intellectual enough, they said; it didn't give him a well-rounded enough education; it didn't offer broad opportunities. He should have studied history or philosophy and then gone to law school, as his father had. Insurance underwriting wasn't much of a job in their eyes, and it was true that the work was tedious, that most days getting through eight hours was a trial. But he made decent money, and there were moments when he truly enjoyed what he did, the little puzzle of it, scanning medical records and credit history, finding that perfect crossroads of risk and profit. His boss had recently praised him, saying he had the team's sharpest eye for fraudulent applications, but his parents wouldn't have understood the pleasure that gave him, and he didn't tell them about it. He'd learned a long time ago to tell them as little as possible.

But with Stacey there'd been no questions. They'd approved of her from the start. They'd treated her like a daughter-in-law long before she and Adam had gotten engaged, though she, too, had lived a wild life in her single days and had a business degree, with an emphasis on marketing. She never apologized for who she was, and his parents never asked her to – she talked about her job in front of them, and about ex-boyfriends, more of them than Adam wanted to acknowledge. The wedding was his parents' favorite topic of conversation, and for the past six months they kept remembering more people they wanted to invite. They'd already started talking about grandchildren.

And once again he'd disappointed them. The fact weighed heavily on his father's face, which Adam struggled to picture as it had once been, framed by black hair and mustache, eyes brighter than they were now, skin less slack around the jaws. At one time, his father's presence – solid, predictable, caring, if a little distant – might have been enough to set him at ease, to reassure him that the ground wouldn't always drop out from underneath his feet, that those things he put his faith in without a second thought wouldn't always turn to shit. But now his father's eyes left the road and settled on him, as if he were some mysterious object that didn't belong in the car, and in his tight-lipped expression Adam saw only frustration, a recognition of how little encouragement he had to offer. "Did I tell you?" his father asked. "They're making me downsize the department again. Another five people. I've got to decide who by next week."

"Dad, the road," Adam said.

His father jerked the wheel, and the car ricocheted from double yellow to single white. "That's twelve this year."

"Terrible."

"There's nothing worse than letting someone know they're out of a job. All I can say is how sorry I am. And tell them a year from now they'll be in a completely different place, they'll have a new job, a better one, and the whole thing won't seem like such a tragedy." He glanced at Adam again, but this time his eyes quickly returned to the road. "It's hard," he said. "Knowing nothing can help them. Nothing but time." He nodded to himself. "Time. That's the only thing you can count on."

"Sure," Adam said, and looked out the window. He knew his father was trying to help and knew, too, that this was the best he could do. But if there was something similar about getting canned and having your fiancée leave you for someone else, he didn't want to think about it now. He didn't want to think about time, either. It did strange things – to his father's face, to the streets they drove through, so familiar from the years he'd spent here as a child but altered in ways that confused him. The trees, once saplings, towering now. The houses he'd watched being built now growing weathered, their contemporary style – irregularly shaped floorplans, with strangely angled roofs and multiple skylights – so unusual then, now not only ordinary but dated. The town had grown up around the train station, reflecting the area's new wealth. Here were storefronts he hadn't seen before or hadn't noticed. An upscale salon where there'd once been a tobacconist, a shop that sold decorations for children's bedrooms where he used to get sub sandwiches and his favorite fountain drink, a squirt of every flavor of soda mixed together in one cup.

There'd been a seedy quality to the neighborhood when he was eleven, twelve years old, and it had always felt like an adventure to ride his bike over the tracks, to sip his soda on a bench outside the store, where a crowd of long-haired teenagers in denim jackets and fringed leather boots smoked and talked about music and about how they'd score acid or mushrooms if they could get some money. Mostly they ignored him, but once, a girl with terrible acne, a long nose, and an innocent, dreamy smile turned to him and said, "Little dude looks like a pilot to me. You gonna come fly with us, little dude?" They all laughed and cheered and hooted and said they'd see him on the dark side of the moon. He liked the attention, the sense of camaraderie, and agreed that he'd make a good pilot or astronaut. But when the girl held out her hand, a little tinfoil square between the chapped and split knuckles of her first two fingers, he abandoned his drink, hopped on his bike, and pedaled away.

To think about time meant thinking about the three years he and Stacey had been together, and the odd blurring that occurred whenever he tried to make sense of it. He could remember their first date as if it had just happened, with almost perfect clarity – the taste of the gyros at the Greek deli around the corner from his old office; the way he'd told her at the end of the night, in determined, if halting, terms, how much he wanted to kiss her; the way she'd laughed and said, "Good for you," and then, while heat rose to his face, a chill in his groin, added, "Well? Are you going to or not?" – but he couldn't remember what life had been like before they'd met. Time had a funny way of collapsing or expanding or turning circles on you, elusive in all ways but the one that kept you moving forward. In three days he'd turn thirty.

"Dad," he said, as they pulled into the station's parking lot, thinking now that he needed to offer some kind of explanation, something to convince his father that what had happened wasn't his doing, that some things were out of his control. "I know you're – you and Mom – I know how much – "

"The chicken," his father said, jerking a thumb at the backseat, eyes turned away. "At least dump it in the trash before you go. If I bring home a full plate, your mother won't sleep at all tonight."

ON THE TRAIN his body felt strange. Lack of sleep, he guessed, and lack of food. But he'd been tired before, and hungry. The strangeness seemed more profound than hunger or exhaustion, as if some part of him had loosened, come unhinged. What came to mind was a car engine, a belt slipping from an important gear, or a piston misfiring, or lubricant gumming up and sticking between moving parts. He knew almost nothing about cars, and somehow this seemed appropriate, his body so foreign to him now, so separate from his senses, which wavered in and out of focus, the noise of the wheels rushing over tracks, of screeching brakes, of passengers navigating the aisles and listening to music on leaky headphones at moments deafening and other times distant, muddled, as if passing through water. His sight, too, would suddenly go hazy, and then out of nowhere an object came into view beyond the window and froze in front of him – a towel flapping on a clothesline, so close he might have reached out to grab it. And then he wished he could, to grab onto something, anything the slightest bit solid, though by the time he thought so the towel was far behind, sucked back into the liquid landscape.

The train stayed far enough south of Montclair that he didn't risk glimpsing Stacey's building, or any of the buildings nearby, and the towns it did pass through were ones he didn't know well, though he'd lived in close proximity most of his life: Madison, Millburn, Orange, Brick Church. The houses that faced the rails were uniformly run-down, constantly shaken by passing freights, gawked at by bored commuters. A miserable existence, he thought, though it didn't stop people from putting lawn chairs and planters full of geraniums on their balconies, from pretending that they had a view of something other than trash-strewn tracks.

It didn't matter that he couldn't see Stacey's building. He knew it well enough that he could picture it, against his will, superimposed over any structure he laid eyes on. Of course it had been his building, too, for the past two years, and he'd been present in it almost from the start. Stacey had bought the condo only a month before they'd gotten together, and on their second date he'd helped carry the last of her boxes from the storage unit in the basement.

If not for the condo, they might not have met at all. Stacey and her roommates had been out celebrating their last week together, first at a bar on East Third, then at a party one of their friends had heard about, on the rooftop of a building on Mott. Adam was at the same party with his own roommates, Marcus and Will, who'd heard about it from another friend, who'd heard about it from a co-worker. None of them knew whose party it was. Adam had already made it up to the roof by the time Stacey and her roommates arrived. He was wearing the same Chuck Taylors, the same leather jacket, smoking a cigarette that wasn't yet stale, staring out across the old water tanks of Little Italy, at the sun setting over Jersey. It was one of those magical nights in the city, early summer, before the heat and garbage stench made people bitter, when everyone was tipsy and ready to hug each other. Adam was unusually conscious of the figure he cut on the rooftop, the way the breeze ruffled his hair, the way his profile would look to people coming out of the stairwell, backlit by the pink flare of the horizon. He still wore his hair long then, which suited his face, he thought, and made his sideburns look more natural, and the little square patch of beard under his lower lip, which he finally shaved off a year ago, sick of being teased about it at work. Without it, Stacey said, his mouth looked strange, older somehow, more serious.

At the party he didn't remember having first spotted her, or even their first words to each other. Afterward neither of them could remember how they'd fallen into conversation, only that they had, swapping stories for hours in a corner of that rooftop, leaving it only to refresh their drinks, ignoring both sets of roommates. What Adam did remember now was how much he was drawn to her voice, deeper than he'd have expected for someone so small, with a whispery quality that set something off in him, speeding his pulse. She wore her hair in two braids and kept flicking them off her shoulders, and whenever she finished a drink, she tossed the ice over the railing, nine floors down onto the street.

He heard about the condo then, and Stacey's reasons for

moving out of Manhattan. She was tired of pouring money into rent. She was tired of feeling cramped all the time. She loved the girls, but to be honest, she was sick of their noise, their house rules, their need to have "together time." Staying here meant never growing up, in a way. In the city you could be a kid forever, and sure, there was something appealing about it, but not for her, not anymore. The New Jersey stigma was bullshit, she said. The commute was no longer than from most of Brooklyn. She was tired of worrying about whether or not she was hip enough, tired of people judging her. "I just want to do my own thing," she said. "Fuck everybody else."

It turned out she was a year older than Adam, and he admired her maturity, and also the way she hinted at the adventurous life she'd been living since moving here from northern Virginia five years ago. She mentioned a friend who'd overdosed and another who'd spent six months on Riker's Island. She talked about an asshole ex-boyfriend who played keyboards in a band Adam had seen half a dozen times. He took note of the hole in her bottom lip where it had once been pierced and the spider tattoo that peeked out at her waistline whenever she shifted her body enough that her shirt pulled away. He'd taken his jacket off, and now every time she touched his bare arm to emphasize a point he wanted to pick her up and swing her around. Instead he played it cool, keeping a respectful distance, holding his drink between them, blowing smoke over his shoulder to keep it out of her face. Then, on their way to the bar, someone bumped into him, and to keep his balance he put a hand against her side. His thumb accidentally slipped down into her jeans, just touching the band of her underwear, taut over her hipbone. Shit, he thought, he'd blown it, and started to apologize. But she only leaned into him, laughed, and said, "Now you know I don't wear g-strings. In case you were wondering."

At the end of the night he asked for her number, and she wrote it on his elbow, because, she said, there it was less likely to get smeared if he started to sweat. "That way you don't have an excuse," she said, and her voice went suddenly suspicious, as if she'd just discovered something about him that gave her pause. She was good and drunk by then, and one of her roommates, a heavy girl with a squeaky voice, was trying to drag her away. He'd caught glimpses of Marcus and Will in the background throughout the night, giving thumbs-up signs, making obscene gestures. "No excuses, motherfucker," she said, suspicion turning to accusation. But she touched his arm again, high up, just under the sleeve of his T-shirt. "You better call. I'm tired of scared little boys, only make a move when they're hammered."

Even if she hadn't said it he would have called. Of course he would have. He'd always believed that. But her words put him on edge. They gave him something to live up to. And hadn't he tried? After they'd dated across the river for six months, he took a job at Prudential's headquarters in Newark, less than a mile from where the train was now passing, on its way to Penn Station. It was a lateral move with an insignificant pay raise, but he told Stacey it was a career break, something he couldn't possibly turn down. And it wouldn't make sense for him to stay in Brooklyn. If she wasn't ready for him to move in so soon, he'd understand. He'd find a place nearby, in Nutley, maybe, or Bloomfield. "Shut up and go get your stuff," she said, and that night, after they'd made love first on the living room couch, and then on the bed Stacey had brought from her old apartment, the bed she'd slept in with who knew how many other men, the bed she might be in right now with someone else, he'd fallen into the deepest, most secure sleep he thought he'd ever have.

And now, as the train slid across the Meadowlands, he didn't know if he'd ever sleep again. Out the window the tall grass rushed by, some of it just beginning to brown, seed pods lifting their heads. In the freight yards stacked containers awaited idle trucks. Then an abandoned brick factory, all its windows broken, and a concrete one behind it, spewing white smoke into the arriving dusk. He was heading in the right direction, at least, and again he felt that comforting swell of anticipation, that tentative hope. The sights lulled him, and so did the feel of worn leather against his neck. Maybe he'd sleep after all. But then the conductor slammed into the car, calling out, "Tickets. Tickets, please," and frantically clicked his hole puncher. Adam handed his ticket over without glancing up, but the conductor lingered beside his seat, the hole puncher silent.

"Since when you a senior?"

"Excuse me?" Adam said.

"You a lot older than you look." The conductor himself couldn't have been older than twenty-five or twenty-six, his short-brimmed New Jersey Transit hat pulled down over cornrows.

"I don't know what you're talking about."

"This a senior ticket."

"It's a mistake. They must have given me ... I'll show you the receipt." But he'd lost the receipt or thrown it away. It wasn't in any of his pockets, not there beside the old cigarettes, one of which, he decided now, he'd smoke as soon as he stepped off the train.

"Three bucks," the conductor said. He stood in the aisle facing Adam squarely, dug in for a fight, and Adam felt himself rising to it, a sudden indignation at a world that could treat him so badly, that could toss him one humiliation after another. Other people were staring at them now, a pair of eight- or nine-year-old boys on their knees peering over the back of the seat ahead, an older couple across the aisle who likely had senior tickets themselves. He was suddenly self-conscious about his clothes, wondering if he looked like someone who'd raided his younger brother's wardrobe. The train heaved forward and took a sharp curve, and somehow the smell of eggplant came back to him. He grabbed hold of the seat in front, just under one of the boys' chins, bracing himself as he had in his father's car. Did he look like someone who'd try to cheat a few dollars off his ticket? Did he look like someone whose fiancée would fuck someone else a month before their wedding, just a few days after the invitations had gone out, and then confess, eyes dry and locked on him, as if he were the one who had something to answer for? He reached for his wallet and handed over a five. The conductor made change in quarters. "Thanks, grandpa," he said, and gave Adam's ticket three quick clicks, a spine of diamond holes down its middle.

HE MADE IT to Williamsburg by eight. Marcus opened the door and hugged him right there in the hallway, whispering, "You're with us now, bro. You don't have to worry about anything."

Will clapped him on the back and sang out, "Mr. Grossman. The grossest man I know."

They had food waiting for him, a huge pot of spaghetti with sauce straight from a jar and cut up pieces of hot dog. He took two bites and laid his fork down. Marcus handed him a shot of Maker's. Will gave him a Heineken to wash it down.

He'd hesitated before calling to tell them the news, saying little more than he'd said to his parents – adding only that Stacey had gotten together with a co-worker, that he hadn't seen it coming – leaving out all the details. He hadn't been such a good friend for the past three years. As soon as Stacey entered the picture he'd been too busy for them. He forgot to return their calls. He missed one of Will's birthday parties. He didn't ask either to be in his wedding because Stacey wanted only two bridesmaids and he felt obliged to make his father and brother groomsmen. But when he did call they offered to do whatever they could to help, whatever he needed. How could he have expected anything else? Their lease was up next month, and already they'd started looking for a three-bedroom, so he wouldn't have to crash with his parents for long. "That fucking bitch," Marcus had said over the phone, and Adam had answered, "Yeah," though he wasn't yet ready to link those words with the woman he'd loved for three years, the woman he'd intended to marry. Will had said, "Get your ass out here, Jersey boy, and we'll take care of you."

He was sorry he'd neglected them. He'd forgotten how

comfortable it felt to plop on the couch between them, gulping his beer, staring at some bullshit documentary on VH1, the history of punk music in twenty-eight minutes. The feeling was so familiar, a blurry sort of forgetfulness, as if he had no past, no distant future, only the moment he was in and the one approaching, and again he thought that maybe he'd come through this easier than he'd feared, maybe he'd survive mostly unscathed. Marcus was dressed in plaid slacks and fuzzy green slippers, Will in a mod suit he'd found two years ago in the Flushing Salvation Army. Neither of them had shaved in at least two days. The couch smelled of burnt popcorn and yeast. Will sang along with Johnny Rotten and Joe Strummer, making up new lyrics as he went. *God save the bean, its farting regime. The onion's browning, and I want to eat the liver.* Marcus wondered out loud what it would be like to have sex with Siouxsie Sioux. "Think you'd turn into a zombie?"

"Vampire," Will said.

"Even if she didn't bite you?"

"British vampires, you know, they don't have such good teeth. They've adapted, though. All she's got to do is breathe in your direction, and you're toast."

"Worth it," Marcus said.

"One lay and you're undead for eternity," Will said.

"I stand by my decision," Marcus said, and gave Adam a nudge. "What do you think?"

"I don't know," Adam said. "I suppose if you got tired of drinking blood you could always jab a wooden stake through your heart and end it all."

He'd meant it as a joke, but Marcus looked at him seriously, then ruffled his hair and dropped an arm over his shoulder. Will sang along with Blondie, *Sundae or a burger, I'm gonna order, I want some ketchup, ketchup, ketchup.*

Until this week, Adam had had a hard time understanding how they could go on this way, living right on top of each other, with no room to move. It was hard enough to live with someone you wanted to be close to all the time and not occasionally feel claustrophobic, worrying that dirty dishes and strewn magazines might set off a sour mood, wondering each day if you'd wake up to face someone who was happy to see you, who'd shower you with affection, who'd say no one had ever let her be herself before, or someone who'd push you away and say she needed alone time, who'd say she needed to catch up with the girlfriends who knew her better than anyone, who'd say she was afraid of losing her identity.

Maybe it helped that Marcus was on the small side, a compact guy with bushy hair and heavy scruff, hardly taller than Stacey, though broad-chested, with the first hint of a gut. Will was taller and willowy, with a prominent Adam's apple and gangly arms and fine, rust-colored hair. Both of them made enough money now that they could have afforded their own places, Marcus as an account manager for an ad agency, Will as a techie for a financial firm. They'd changed apartments three times since Adam had moved out, and this was the smallest by far, the kitchen big enough for no more than one person standing, the bedrooms hardly more than closets. They were constantly on the hunt for better neighborhoods and easier commutes, and here they were surrounded by bars and restaurants, a subway station just down the street with an easy line into midtown.

It was a far cry from their first place, the entire top floor of a rickety building down in Carroll Gardens, in what had once been a loft, now carved up with sloppily erected drywall. To get to the bathroom from the living room you had to walk through all three bedrooms. Across the street was a private club straight out of a mob movie, a sign above the door reading, "The Society for Citizens Palazzo." In the afternoons, when the door was open, they could see a dozen overweight Italian men drinking and smoking cigars and playing poker. The apartment was always full of people, friends visiting from out of town, women who'd followed Marcus home from a bar, the drummer of some band they liked who'd gotten evicted from his place in Queens. Empty liquor bottles lined the counters, and occasionally Adam would find used hypodermic needles in the bathroom trash. He was proud of himself for living so close to the edge, though far enough from it that he never came close to pitching over, never did more than glance from a safe distance down into the abyss.

One winter night, late, their cab had a flat just over the Brooklyn Bridge, and they walked the rest of the way down Henry, shouting into the frigid air, dancing in the middle of the street, laughing until they couldn't breathe. Marcus took off his jacket and shirt and swung them over his head, and when they finally made it back he was blue and trembling. A ridiculous night, at the end of a ridiculous year, and even while he was in the middle of it Adam began to miss it, knowing this wasn't something he'd be able to hold onto forever, knowing that someday he'd remember it fondly, an important passage of youth, a moment of freedom he'd never manage to repeat.

But the feeling didn't last long. On the way up the stairs, they heard the noise. A moan, building to a wail, and then trailing off in whimpers. It grew louder when they opened the door, and they followed it to the bathroom. Inside a girl was on hands and knees in the tub, naked from the waist down, her skin pale and slick with sweat, her small buttocks puckered, short hair soaked and plastered to her scalp. She acknowledged them with a glance and turned away, the moaning starting again, then the wail. She crouched down and closed her eyes, arms trembling, the muscles in her neck tensing and then going slack. Adam had no idea who she was or what she was doing, but he did know he shouldn't have felt the desire that crept up unbidden, with the image of himself tangled in her skinny limbs. "Coming off the junk," Will said. "She probably hasn't shit in a month." Adam asked why she wasn't on the toilet, but no one answered him. Marcus stayed with her, coaxing her as an expectant father would, "One more time. Okay. Come on. Push. Push." Adam listened to her screams for most of the morning, groggy, spinning

in his bed, thinking there were some things you didn't need
to see, some experiences you didn't need to have. At dawn, after
masturbating, hating himself for what he'd pictured while doing
so, he finally fell asleep, and when he woke after noon, the girl
was gone. She'd left a log in the tub. She'd stolen Will's amp and
speakers.

On TV, Henry Rollins and Debbie Harry were making pro-
clamations about the importance of the punk revolution.
Marcus took off a slipper and threw it at the screen. "Fucking
has-beens," he said, and then turned to Adam. "We're thinking
we'll hit The Oak and then head over to Krakow. Danny and
Tim's band's playing. You remember them. Cosmatic?" If Adam
did he couldn't bring them to mind, and for some reason this
unnerved him. He nodded anyway. "I think you saw them when
they were still Astrojack. Or maybe back when they were The
Inquisitive. Anyway, they're on at eleven, maybe eleven-thirty.
We're on the list. We'll get some drinks into you in the meantime. You won't even remember your name by the time we're
through."

"You ever call Becca and tell her you're not meeting her?"
Will asked.

"I'm starting to get ready," Marcus said, "to think about
being able to deal with it."

"You were supposed to be there five minutes ago."

"Is she the one with the poodle?" Adam asked.

"Nah. That was Becca Tomlinson. This is Becca Daley. And
it was a sheltie, not a poodle."

"Yippy fucker," Will said.

"Whatever happened to her?" Adam asked, casually, as if
he didn't care. But he did, so much that it startled him. Not
about Becca, necessarily, but about what became of people when
they disappeared from your life, when you didn't think about
them anymore. "She still around?"

"I heard she split," Marcus said. "Back to Minnesota, or
wherever the fuck she came from."

"Wisconsin," Will said. "Outside Madison."

"How do you always remember shit like that?"

"We talked about cheese," Will said. "And Old Milwaukee."

"She smelled like cheese," Marcus said. "Stilton."

"She'll be pissed," Will said. "Daley, not Tomlinson."

Marcus stood and retrieved his slipper. He switched off the TV.

"You should call her," Will said.

"Let's get the fuck outta here," Marcus said.

THE SECOND BOURBON went down easier than the first, but Adam didn't feel it yet. Maybe he was immune to alcohol now. Or maybe it did the opposite of what he'd hoped, what it had always done for him in the past, numbing his mind, muddling his thoughts. His nerves still tingled, his ears buzzed. The promise he'd felt earlier, in his parents' basement, in Marcus's and Will's apartment, had faded, replaced by a new kind of cold, suspicious scrutiny. The Oak had had a different name the last time he'd been here, but it was the same narrow room with a single pool table at the back, the same crowd of scruffy boys and girls in tight tattered clothes clamoring at the bar. Adam had probably sat in the same booth maybe five, six years ago, and he'd over-heard the same snippets of conversation. "I mean it's totally out of line, don't you think?" someone said at his back, and a girl answered, "Depends what side of the line you're on." Why hadn't it seemed so inane back then, people drinking and talking about nothing? Why did it strike him that way only now?

"I started checking out apartments," Will said, and took a sip of cognac. He always drank cognac when he went out, and always listened for women with European accents. Unlike Marcus, who met someone every few months, spent a week or two crazy in love, and then another three weeks trying to get out of the situation with the least amount of hassle, Will always fell for the unattainable ones, the ones who were more fantasy than reality. Most recently it had been a Slovakian graduate student, in

New York for a year to study urban planning. Now she was back in Bratislava, and last Adam had heard they were exchanging letters and e-mail, and Will was thinking about a visit in the fall. He was the most well-read of Adam's friends, the one who watched the most obscure movies, and in all these years Adam had never once seen him upset or angry, nothing more than mildly irritated or mildly depressed. All those books and movies kept him isolated from the world, separate from the messiness of real emotions. Now he gave Adam a look similar to his father's, sympathetic but remote. He wanted to know only as much as Adam wanted to tell, hoping, most likely, that that wouldn't be much. "There's one place on Berry. Not bad. Only it's weird, there no sink in the bathroom."

"Weird?" Marcus said. "That's fucking dysfunctional."

"Somebody rip it out?" Adam asked.

"No, it's like there never was one. Shower, toilet, that's it."

"*Hey, Jimmy, looks like we forgot something in the john,*" Marcus said, trying to layer a Brooklyn accent over his Boston one. He had a dark pint in front of him and wore a straw cowboy hat, more scarecrow than redneck. His expression was impatient, his eyes drifting down the narrow bar toward the door. "*No big deal, let 'em shave in the kitchen.*"

"I don't want you shaving in the kitchen," Will said. "Your nasty hair all over our food?"

"Then why'd you bring it up?" Marcus said. "It's out."

"We might be better off in Greenpoint," Will said. "The places are bigger and – "

"Forget Greenpoint," Marcus said. "You'll end up falling for some Polish teenager."

"It's not all Polish anymore," Will said. "A lot of Hondurans have been moving in."

"Honduran, then," Marcus said. "Maybe preteen."

"I'll keep looking," Will said.

Marcus drummed the table, and his impatient look came to rest on Adam. "I'm proud of you, man," he said. "You're taking care of yourself. You're doing what you've got to do." Adam shrugged and raised his glass to his lips. What else did he have to do but drink himself into a stupor? "It takes courage to walk away and not look back. Some guys would stick around and torture themselves."

"Why are you looking at me?" Will said.

"Really," Marcus said. "I admire you. I mean it." Adam started to shrug again but then stopped himself. It was easier to agree with everything. "So? Out with it."

"Out with what?"

"Come on, man. Now's the time. We're listening."

"Leave him be," Will said. "If he doesn't want to talk he shouldn't have to."

"He wants to talk," Marcus said. "Of course he wants to talk."

"There'll be new listings in tomorrow's *Times*," Will said. "In the morning we can –"

"Don't change the subject," Marcus said. "This is important. He's got to get everything on the table. He can't keep it all inside."

"I'm going to a shrink," Adam said, and decided on the spot that he would.

"Doesn't matter," Marcus said. "Shrink's not your friend."

"That's the whole point of a shrink," Will said. "They're supposed to be neutral. Objective."

"Fuck objective," Marcus said. "What he needs is someone on his goddamn side."

"He'll talk when he's ready," Will said.

"He's ready," Marcus said.

Adam emptied the last of his bourbon and took a sip of watery beer. He wiped his mouth with the back of a hand. The night she'd confessed, Stacey had told him she'd already made an appointment with a therapist. "If I've been fooling myself all this time," she said, "thinking I can really do this whole conventional get married thing…" Her hair was tied back, but she kept tossing her head as if it blocked her view. Only then did she start crying. "It's humbling," she said, "realizing how little you can know your own mind."

What right did she have telling some stranger the details of their life? Shouldn't he be in the room to defend himself?

"Well," he said, raising his eyes to meet Marcus's. "I guess – "

"Oh man," Marcus said, glancing over Adam's shoulder, half-standing, squinting in the direction of the front door. "Look who just walked in."

"Did you tell her where we were going?" Will asked.

"Nah, man. This is boys' night."

"She sniffed you out then."

"Who is it?" Adam's voice was thin in his ears. He'd been holding his breath. He let it out now, relieved not to have to go on.

"True love," Will said. "For at least three more days."

"Another Becca?" Adam finished his beer and ran a finger along the rim of the glass. He wanted one of his stale cigarettes, but here was one thing that had changed about the city since he'd left – no more smoking in bars. This was as hard to believe as anything, the place gone soft in his absence, one further disappointment.

"Nah, man," Marcus said. "This one's not a total dipshit. She's an artist."

"Maybe only two days," Will said.

"Look who she's got with her," Marcus said, and raised a hand, casually, one finger extended, and then touched the brim of his hat. "Her crazy Belgian friend. Right up your alley."

"I'm taken," Will said.

"When's the last time you heard from the Slovenian princess?"

"Slovakian."

"How long?"

"Two weeks. She's been traveling – "

"She's ten thousand miles away."

"I'll hear from her any day."

"You haven't seen this chick in five months, and right in front of you's a live crazy Belgian – "

"I love Irena," Will said.

"Help me out here, Grossman."

"I need another drink," Adam said.

"Hell yeah you do," Marcus said, slapping the table with both hands and standing abruptly. "Coming right up."

Adam watched him move through the crowded room, not stopping at the bar. He opened his arms wide to hug someone Adam couldn't see. Then he was talking, gesturing broadly. "I better get the drinks," Will said. "Otherwise we'll be waiting all night." He gave Adam another sympathetic smile, a smile that said he was glad not to be in Adam's place. Again he clapped him on the shoulder. "Just like you never left, huh? Welcome home."

HE'D NEVER BEEN to Krakow. He'd never heard Cosmatic. He once knew all the clubs and kept track of all the local bands, even ones he didn't like. He could do it again if he wanted, learn the names of drummers and bass players so he could raise his chin or wave when he passed them on the street or strike up a conversation when he stood in line behind them at a coffee shop. Easy enough to fall into the routines of the person he'd been at twenty-five, and maybe everyone would overlook the first gray hairs that had cropped up over his ears. Back in the city he could be whoever he wanted to be. He could be nobody, and nobody would give it a second thought. But now the idea only depressed him. The booze clarified his vision even as it made his steps wobbly, causing him to apologize twice already to people he'd jostled on his way in the door.

The club was a single open room, completely unadorned, the walls and exposed rafters painted black. There was a bar in the back corner, where Adam got himself another double and listened to Will trying to talk to the Belgian girl about European health care. Will swirled his cognac, warring with himself, Adam thought, between the fantasy of a Slovakian girl thousands of miles away and that of a Belgian within inches. There was no point in being faithful, Adam could have told them. A waste of energy. But the Belgian didn't seem interested in Will or his conversation. She was almost as tall as him and seemed embarrassed by it, shoulders hunched forward, neck bent, chest concave. When Will asked how long she'd been in New York, she shrugged and said, "Too long. Forever, forever." Her clothes were baggy and odd-looking, the sleeves of her sweater too short, her feet in scuffed men's oxfords. Will swirled his drink again and introduced her to Adam. Her name was Els. She gave a little bow and backed away. Her teeth were crooked, her breath sour. "I really shouldn't be here," she said. "I should go."

Marcus brought over his new love interest, Summer, a sweet-faced girl with a tiny, upturned nose, a Midwestern accent, a short, stylish haircut, part punk, part fashion magazine. She had on a frilly vintage dress that showed off lines tattooed up the backs of her legs, made to look like seams in old-fashioned stockings. She couldn't have been older than twenty-four. Adam shook her hand and felt himself smile too broadly, a moment too late. His face felt stiffly elastic. On the walk over from The Oak he'd finally smoked one of his old cigarettes – thinking without wanting to of his mother's fragile, disappointed face – and now his throat was scratchy. Marcus whispered in Summer's ear, and she gave Adam a sad, condescending look, a look meant for a hurt child. When Adam released her hand, she took his wrist and squeezed it. Her fingers were small and gentle, warm on his skin. It was an intimate gesture, but casual, meaning nothing. "You've never seen Cos?" she said. "Oh, they're great. You'll love them."

"Danny finally learned how to play guitar," Marcus said. "Makes a big difference."

"You're so mean," Summer said, giving him a playful smack, showing all her cards. She'd go home with him tonight, and in a week he'd break her heart, and a week later she'd go home with someone else. On and on it went.

The Belgian, Els, pulled at Summer's elbow. Will hovered behind her, always present, always aloof, always alone. "We shouldn't be here," Els said. "We should go."

Summer ignored her. "I saw them last month at Ferraro's," she said. "They were, you know, just ... I can't even describe it. I'm telling you ..."

"My man here used to see shows five nights a week," Marcus said, and threw an arm around Adam's shoulder. "He had more stamina than any of us." Adam couldn't help leaning into him, woozy and embarrassed, more drunk than he'd realized. He could stand on his own, but the truth was he didn't want to. He wished Marcus would prop him up the rest of the night.

"I'm worried," Els said.

This time Summer turned on her, that pretty face even prettier with a flash of anger, the punk haircut looking momentarily authentic. "Just relax, okay?"

"I'm going," Els said, and stood there, arms crossed.

"I'll get you a drink," Will said.

"She's just freaking out over nothing," Summer said.

"It's not nothing," Els said. "It's Anya."

"She's fine," Summer said.

"We haven't seen her for three days," Els said, looking straight at Adam, her eyes big and imploring in that awkward, elongated face. Why him? What made her think he gave a shit about her problems? "She hasn't answered her phone."

"She's done this before," Summer said. "She just met some girl. I'm sure she's fine."

"Two girls together, huh?" Marcus said. "Sounds exciting."

"You're such a pig," Summer said, and smacked him again, harder this time, on the chest.

"We can all go back to our place later," Will said. "I picked up some really nice wine last week. A guy I know works for an Australian distributor—"

"She's into the Oxy," Els said. "She doesn't know what she's doing. She needs people to look after her."

"We'll go when the show's over," Summer said, and before anyone could say more, four skinny boys took the stage, all of them in worn jeans and tight T-shirts with faded logos. Adam recognized the guitar player, Danny, but he couldn't remember how he knew him or whether or not he liked him. The drummer mumbled thanks into his microphone, and the four of them shuffled around for a minute, the bass player asking for more keyboards in his monitor, the keyboard player holding down a single chord to test. Then they all looked at each other, and Danny counted. A quiet drone drifted out of the speakers. Suddenly a hand was on Adam's upper arm. Summer's. Her lips were close to his ear. "A year from now," she said. "You won't believe how much better you'll feel." Then Marcus pulled her away, bumping her hip with his. He spilled some of his beer, just missing her feet, delicate things in single-strap sandals, toenails painted a deep red bordering on violet. Adam finished his drink and told himself that was the last, but then Will handed him another. He turned and offered it to Els, who had her eyes closed, her hunched torso bobbing the same as Danny's and his bandmates'. What had happened to all her fretting? She opened one eye, shook her head, and closed it. The drone slowly gained volume and speed, and Adam felt himself swaying, too, but not in rhythm, his legs unsteady, the taste of bourbon clinging all the way down his throat.

What would he have told them – his parents, Marcus and Will – if they'd given him the chance? That he wasn't entirely surprised by what Stacey had done? That the moment she confessed his first thought was that he'd driven her into the arms of this other man, that she'd done only what she had to do, that he should have expected it all along? Would he have told them what he'd become convinced of in the last three days, what she hadn't admitted to him but what he imagined her saying in a therapist's office or in the arms of her new lover – thick, hairy arms, he thought, like Marcus's: that she'd slept with someone else because Adam had been too tentative for her, intimidated in bed, worried that he wouldn't satisfy her, paralyzed by the possibility that she'd say she was too tired, that she'd turn him down? Would he tell them how often she'd had to make the first move, how ashamed it made him?

"Hold on," Marcus said, his arms suddenly around Adam's middle. "On your feet." He hadn't realized he'd been falling. The clear vision he'd had twenty minutes ago was gone, the bodies in front of him a blur, the drone of the band somehow making it hard to see. He took a gulp of his drink to regain his balance, to get everything back in focus. "We got you. You're okay."

Beside him Els still had her eyes closed, but she wasn't bobbing anymore, her arms crossed again beneath her hollow chest. Will had moved away from her, talking now to a girl whose accent sounded English, or maybe Australian, when she shouted over the music. Marcus cupped his hands around one of Summer's ears and whispered something that made her laugh and touch his arm, just above the elbow. He'd given her his cowboy hat, which was too big for her head, coming down to the arches of her plucked eyebrows. Without it, Marcus looked haggard, his scruff darkened in the last hour. Adam was tired of the leather jacket. It was too hot, too tight, and somehow got stuck on one of his wrists as he tried to strip it off. He lost his balance again, this time stumbling backward and to the side, his heel coming down on Summer's foot. Fucking bitch, he thought, his own flash of anger weaker than he'd hoped, the words still sounding false, someone else's words, about someone he didn't know. He felt her toes beneath the worn rubber sole of his old shoe, kept it there a moment too long, until she pushed him away. "Motherfucker," Summer said. "That hurt."

"I'm sorry," he said, and grabbed her bare shoulders, pulling her close, spilling some of his bourbon down her back.

When she shoved him away again, her fist raised, her girlish face furious and lovely and formidable, he kept moving. Through the wall of bodies he pushed in the direction he hoped he'd find the door, his jacket trailing from one arm. He didn't know where he was heading, or why. He felt as if he'd known a moment ago, but now the idea was lost to him, and he just pushed for the sake of pushing. Behind him, Marcus said to leave him alone, he knew how to take care of himself. Summer asked if he was going to puke, her voice sweet again, all her fierceness gone. "Likely," Will said. "No one's grosser than the Grossman."

He didn't get far before someone was pulling him in a different direction, and he smelled Els's sour breath before he lifted his head to see her crooked teeth, her bent neck, her pleading eyes. "We'll go check her apartment, yes?" she said. "We'll see if she's back." Stacey's apartment? No, he thought, they couldn't go there. They'd find her in bed with someone else. That was the last place he wanted to be. "It's not far," Els said, and took his drink from him, setting it on a nearby table. Then she clamped both hands around his wrist and maneuvered backward through the crowd, guiding him along. "If we can just see her I'll stop worrying. That's all I need. Just one look. It's always worse when you don't know." They reached the door, and Els pushed it open with her heel, those big horrified eyes never leaving his face. She dragged him out, into the night.

THEY'D WALKED TWENTY blocks, maybe twenty-five. Adam concentrated on the sidewalk, where his feet had trouble coordinating with one another, one moving forward, the other lurching to the side. It was warm on the street and crowded, and he managed to get his jacket all the way off, carrying it over a shoulder. He tried to pull another cigarette from the crumpled pack but dropped it, the pack, the lighter, all of it gone now, somewhere behind him. His mother could stop worrying. He kept bumping into people, mailboxes, light poles, muttering apologies. He apologized to Els, too, and to Summer. "Tell her I'm sorry I stepped on her foot," he said. "Tell her I'm sorry I made her fuck someone else."

"Come," Els said, and Adam followed. Marcus had called her crazy, but there was authority in her voice, the sound of someone who knew what she was doing. "It's not far. Not too much. We have to hurry."

She walked fast, arms crossed, long legs moving strangely in those baggy pants. She'd get a block or two ahead, and whenever Adam thought she'd left him behind – a pang of loneliness blotting out any panic he might have felt at the prospect of being lost – there were her scuffed shoes on the sidewalk in front of him, waiting. "Hurry," she'd say. "It's not much farther."

The night he'd walked with Marcus and Will all the way down Henry from the bridge, Adam had whooped and shouted louder than either of them. He didn't worry about the cold or his tired legs or the job that bored him senseless, about the future that would never feel as open as this moment, that would never hold as much promise. He just cupped his hands around his mouth and let loose, and he tried it again now, swinging his jacket over his head, making sounds that were meant to erase the facts of his life: that he was thirty, that he was single, that he lived with his parents. But he couldn't get his breath behind it, and the shouting was half-hearted, not loud enough to make more than a few people turn to stare. Els grabbed his arm again and pulled him forward. "I told her to stay away from the Oxy," she said. "It's a stupid drug. I always told her so. Why do you want to do something so stupid?"

The longer they walked, the more half-hearted his drunkenness, too. He felt it draining away, replaced by a weariness heavier than any he'd felt in the last three days, a despair different from the one that set him crying in his parents' shower, that made him pour shots of bourbon down his throat. Different because he could already sense its limit. He skirted a trashcan and thought of his father's words of advice in the car. "I just got canned, that's all," he told Els. "It's not the end of the world." He did feel sorry for his father, having to fire twelve people, having to tell all of them they'd be fine in a year, that only time would help. But his father was probably right, and so was Summer. He wouldn't live with his parents for long. He likely wouldn't be single for long, either. In a year he'd feel better, maybe, but what good did that do him now? Time stretched out ahead of him, as murky as what had come before. "I don't want to find a new job," he told Els.

Without warning, she ducked into a corner shop. This time it was Adam who waited. Latin music was blasting inside, the smell of grease and meat billowing from the door. She came out with a bottle of water, took a sip, and handed it to him. "You're thirsty," she said. "It's good for you." And then she was on the move again, pushing through a group of men in sleeveless T-shirts gathered around a car with the hood up, the engine revving. "Such a stupid, dirty place," she said when they'd passed. "Who wants to live here?"

There were other smells, too – from a kebab stand across the street, from a pizza joint on the next corner. Here were the first stirrings of appetite again, unexpected, unwelcome. He tried to drown it with the water Els had given him. He wasn't ready to be hungry yet. He wanted to shout and cry and stomp on feet. That was what he deserved.

"Everyone says it's such a fabulous place," Els said. "Everyone says you have to go live there, it's so fabulous. There's the music, it's true. If there were only the music, it might be worth it. But the rest of it isn't fabulous, it's dirty and ugly and stupid."

What he really wanted right now was to be able to talk to Stacey, to tell her about this strange night, how he'd gotten drunk and followed a Belgian girl all over Brooklyn, looking for someone named Anya who might be on Oxy or might be with another girl. She would have appreciated how absurd it was, how odd. On the rooftop downtown, he'd told her the story of that other night, when he and Marcus and Will had come upstairs to find the half-naked girl in the bathtub, howling, pleading with her bowels to move. He'd left out the desire he'd felt, and also the fear. In that version he was the one who'd stayed with the girl all night, encouraging her, letting her squeeze his hand to relieve her pain. He saw how impressed Stacey was when he told it, just as he was impressed when she talked about the friend who'd overdosed and the one in prison. Had it really taken her this long to figure out he wasn't the person she'd imagined, the one he'd invented for her that night, the one who'd slipped his thumb into her pants? How long after she'd realized it before she started to drift away?

"Here," Els said, stopping at an unmarked door in a sooty brick building, no names legible on the intercom box. Around them the shop signs were mostly in Polish. They'd walked all the way to Greenpoint. Els pressed the buzzer for apartment 3B. "If something happened," she said. She shivered and hugged herself and without asking took his jacket from his shoulder and put it on, its sleeves just as short as her sweater's. She pressed the buzzer again. "If something happened, I'm going home," she said. "I should have gone last year, when everything got so crazy. But I thought it couldn't get any worse, so I stayed. I should have known better."

She pressed the buzzer once more. He'd let her keep the jacket, he thought. He didn't want to wear it anymore, or the T-shirt, either, whose logo was unreadable now, the trucker who'd first worn it retired most likely, or in the ground. He glanced up at the zigzag grid of fire escapes, at the orange glow of the overcast sky, and pictured Stacey's squealing, exhilarated face as she jumped out of an airplane, so different from the face that was mild, sweet, affectionate as she handed him a lambs-wool sweater for Hanukkah. If he'd told her the real story, how he'd cowered in his room, wishing the girl would quit screaming, wishing he lived somewhere quieter, safer, more predictable, maybe she wouldn't have bothered to write her number on his elbow. Maybe they would have saved themselves all this trouble.

"I keep thinking it's all going to be different now," Els said. "No one's going to do anything stupid. But it's always the same, more stupid things, one after another, and no one wants to make it stop. I don't know why I'm still here. The music isn't worth it." Her voice caught, and Adam saw that she'd started crying. "If something happened, I'll never forgive myself."

"She might be somewhere else," Adam said, knowing it wasn't true, knowing that the worst, the stupidest thing always happened. Had she been crying all along, and only now did he notice? "She might be with a girl, right?"

"I can't stand it," Els said, and before he knew what was happening, she'd crumpled against him, shaking, the worn leather soft against his neck and arms. "I want to go home."

He was hungry. He was tired. He was a mile or more from where he was supposed to spend the night. But he knew he would stay here holding this woman as long as she needed, until dawn if necessary. The thought did something strange to him, made him giddy. It suddenly amazed him, the things people could stand, the things they could live through. You could scream in pain for hours and then in the morning be well enough to steal a stereo, to carry it off in broad daylight down a busy street.

"I'm being so stupid," Els said, and pulled away, wiping her eyes with a sleeve of his jacket. "If I could just see her, I wouldn't have to worry." She turned toward the street, made a move as if she were about to hurry away, and Adam quickly pressed the buzzer. This time there was a hum over the intercom, a click as the latch released. "Oh God," she said. "Please."

She pushed the door open, and he followed her inside, the giddiness gone. The stairwell was musty, industrial green paint flaking from the railing. He hesitated at the bottom as Els's heavy shoes clumped their way up. He didn't know what they'd find and doubted he wanted to know. He could stay down here, or he could leave. He didn't have to face it. But even if he did, it was too late to tell Stacey how he'd react, not the truth, not another lie. He no longer had to work at being someone other than he was. She no longer had to pretend to be committed, content with their life together. They were done telling each other stories.

"Come," Els called, her frightened voice echoing down the shaft. "Please."

If You Needed Me

I.

ONE SATURDAY MORNING IN EARLY MARCH, WHEN AMANDA
Horenstein was eleven and her brother Donald nine, their
grandfather drove his Cadillac into the side of their house. If the
car made a noise on its way toward them, the children didn't
hear it. They were watching cartoons, Amanda on the couch,
Donald on his belly only inches from the TV. Amanda's bare feet
were cold, and she was waiting for a commercial to get up and
put on socks. In the meantime she had them tucked under the
dog, Harvey, a fawn-colored collie-mix with the first signs of
old age in the gray hairs of his muzzle. Sometimes Donald lifted
his head, his fluffy brown curls blocking part of the screen,
and Amanda said, "Duck, Dorko," to which he replied, "I'm not
a duck, I'm a goose," and made a farting noise with his lips.

There was no blare of a horn, no screech of brakes, because
the old man touched neither. He was visiting for the weekend,
on the way from his home in Queens to a gathering of Navy
friends in Atlantic City, and had gone out to pick up the paper
and a quart of milk for his cereal – whole milk, since all his daughter kept in the house was skim. The errand took less than twenty
minutes. He'd left the children in front of the same Bugs Bunny
cartoons he and his own children had watched on the big screen
thirty years ago, preparing the way for the Jerry Lewis pictures
that had made them laugh so hard they couldn't breathe.

He hadn't worried about leaving the kids alone – they
spent most weekday afternoons that way, finishing school hours

before their mother came home from work. Latchkey kids, they were called. He didn't approve of letting kids run free, but neither did he approve of a woman with young children working full-time, sometimes as many as fifty hours a week. He also knew he was old-fashioned and out-of-date and had long ago determined to keep his opinions to himself. His own wife – his Sylvia, God bless – had worked part-time in a secretary pool for only two years during the war. And when she was dying she'd thanked him for the life he'd given her. "For everything," she whispered brokenly, each syllable spoken only after a new breath, all she could manage with lungs destroyed by emphysema. He couldn't have stopped her from smoking, though if he'd known what was coming maybe he would have tried harder. "For everything," she said again. He gave a dismissive wave and said, as he had when she'd first told him she knew she wouldn't survive, when she'd first told him she'd never remarry if he didn't make it back from the South Pacific, when she'd first told him she loved him, "What's this crazy you're talking?" Before she closed her eyes for the last time he planted a dry kiss on the dry skin of her forehead.

Later, the old man would explain that his foot had slipped only momentarily from the brake to the gas pedal, that the car jolted forward and wouldn't respond to his attempt to turn it, that the steering wheel had locked. But from the expressions on the faces of the policemen who came to the scene, on the face of his son-in-law who was called out of surgery, of his daughter when she came home from shul, it was obvious that no one believed him. They saw confusion, the onset of senility. The truth was, the driveway had always been tricky for him, the entrance cut at an awkward angle, the slope too steep, pitched in a way that often made him nervous. It was necessary to accelerate over the hump at the curb and then turn sharply left to aim toward the garage. Too many steps – gas, turn, brake – and he got stuck on the first.

Maybe he'd been thinking of Sylvia still, though he knew he tended to blame her, poor woman, for too many things.

Because of her illness and early death, he hadn't traveled as much as he'd intended; he'd gone on working out of loneliness and to pay off medical bills; he'd cut himself off from old friends to avoid painful memories. But he'd also blamed her in life, and the kids, too, for making him work so hard, for never allowing him to think about himself. He'd never wanted to be a pharmacist. Given a choice, he might have tried his hand at politics. His own mother used to joke, when he was a boy, that he'd be the first Jewish mayor of New York. That was when she still didn't speak a word of English.

He saw it all coming: the azalea bushes, the bay window, the recently finished stucco on which his daughter had spent a fortune, replacing the weathered wooden siding he'd found more attractive. He saw it the way he'd seen Sylvia's death, something that couldn't be stopped or even slowed, and he was overcome with self-pity. He was staring at his hands at the moment of impact, veiny and arthritic, the nails he used to have manicured when it was still fashionable for men to do so, the small scar on his thumb from a shipboard knife trick gone awry, these hands that since the war had done little other than pour powders and liquids and pills from one vial into another. Useless, he thought, as glass shattered, as stucco and wood splintered around him, one beam falling onto the Cadillac's hood, inches short of where it might have killed him. Useless, these hands that gripped the wheel, trembling, even after the car had stopped and dust settled around him, along with the first terrible dawning that his grandchildren were nowhere to be seen.

He held those same hands up to show the policemen, to show his son-in-law the surgeon, to show his daughter. "They're no good anymore," he said. "No good for anything." He kept saying it, for the rest of the day, for the rest of the week, and only much later did his daughter imitate his dismissive wave, the phrase he'd spoken so often, her accent sounding more like Bugs Bunny's, he thought, than his own: "What's this crazy you're talking?"

But by then it didn't matter what she said. He knew. Useless.

2.

BARBARA HORENSTEIN, THE children's mother, was far from devout, but when she turned the corner onto Crescent Ridge and saw an ambulance in her driveway, police cars in the street, her husband in blood-stained scrubs running to her across the lawn, she let out the beginning of a prayer, "Please, God," and then stopped herself. She could have asked for her children's safety, for her father's health – or, if it was his time to go, for a pain-less death – but to ask for such things seemed to invite disaster. She didn't trust prayer or piety, though she knew she should have, being surrounded by it all week, having just come from services. But she went to services only as part of her job, alternating between Friday night and Saturday morning, this week deciding on Saturday because her father's visit was brief. Last night she'd made him a special dinner for his seventy-seventh birthday, which had passed nearly a month ago. At the time she'd been too busy to get away from work, and during the weeks since had been plagued by a relentless, needling guilt.

For six years now she'd been development director for Temple Emek Shalom in Chatwin, New Jersey, an old, established Reform congregation just over the ridge from Union Knoll, where she and her family lived. During that time she'd led a cap-ital campaign to refurbish the synagogue's ballroom and gym, to tear out asbestos ceilings in the Hebrew school classrooms, to purchase a modern heating system that replaced the turn-of-the-century boiler. She'd also increased the endowments by fifty percent and helped raise the annual operating budget by half a million dollars. She was good at her job, though being good, she told colleagues at fundraising colloquia, was mostly a matter of persistence, stubbornness, a willingness to give up Friday nights and Saturday mornings, to drive all over the county, to sit in plush living rooms and listen to the complaints of people far wealthier than she, who was herself wealthier than she'd ever dreamed of being.

She'd fallen into the job accidentally, or at least without much forethought. After college, she'd committed herself to volunteer work, partly out of a sense of responsibility, partly out of frustration. That was the late sixties, when so many of her friends spent their time protesting against the war, against poverty, against the mistreatment of women and minorities; but the war went on, as did poverty and mistreatment. She was against the war, too – but it was so big and so far away that to think about it too much brought on feelings of futility and despair that often ended as migraines. Instead she tried to look closer to home, helping in a women's shelter in Boston, where Jerry had begun medical school. At first she made beds and set tables for dinner, but later she organized bake sales, auctions, a charity sack race. She found herself talking to donors with a passion that surprised her, describing the lives of women who'd been beaten by husbands and boyfriends and fathers, women who'd spent months sleeping on sidewalks or in parks, women who'd sold their bodies for food, for drugs. She managed to bring herself to the edge of tears and then hold back, though many of the people she spoke to couldn't. They wrote larger checks than they'd intended and thanked her for her work. The shelter's director put her on his payroll at the end of the year.

After that she found jobs easily, with a food bank, with a children's hospital, with an organization that provided jobs for the mentally disabled. When Amanda was born and they moved to Jersey – less than twenty miles from where Jerry had grown up – she worked part-time for a theater company in Morristown. The productions were amateurish and sparsely attended, and for years the company had been in the red. The manager talked often of bankruptcy. Barbara enjoyed theater, but not in any crucial way, and not the plays this company produced. But she needed to get out of the house for a few hours a week, and a few hours was all the company could afford to pay her for. She felt no passion as she spoke to potential donors, only the challenge of her fundraising goals, the impossibility of her bottom line. But by then she no longer needed passion in order to raise money, and in two years the theater was thriving, or at least stable, its productions as poorly directed as ever, though its sets were now designed by professionals, its programs printed in two colors rather than photocopied.

When the kids started school, she went on the market and got nearly a dozen offers almost immediately. Some were with organizations whose mission truly moved her – one that promoted harmony between the races, one that fought disease in Africa, another homeless shelter. But the first had a ramshackle office, no cubicles even, just an open cluttered space jammed with desks and people shouting into phones; the second couldn't offer any benefits, not even paid vacation; and the shelter would have meant a forty-five minute commute. Emek Shalom was only ten minutes away. The job came with a private office and a month off in summer. "How can I work for a synagogue?" she asked Jerry. "I don't even believe in God." Except for the bar and bat mitzvahs of nephews and nieces, she hadn't been to services since she was a girl. She and Jerry had been married by a rabbi, but only to appease their parents. But Jerry shrugged and said, "You didn't believe in bad theater, either. And God pays better."

And now she was a pro. She researched her prospects and knew exactly how to speak to each of them, whether to focus on education, or social activities, or spiritual matters. She could quote from the Torah when necessary, and had memorized a few lines of Talmud, of Maimonides, of Woody Allen when she needed a joke. She gave talks to the Men's Club, to the Temple Sisterhood, about the importance of tradition and the history of the Reform movement. She had two assistants working for her, setting up meetings, processing gifts, organizing events. She'd perfected her pitch, knowing exactly when to speak a number – always a larger one than expected – and then fall silent, letting the request hang heavily in the air. The rabbi, the synagogue's president, the board of directors all praised her and called her a Godsend.

And still she didn't believe in God. Or didn't think she did. But her reasons for not believing, coming mostly from her reading during college, her brief membership in the Socialist Party, seemed less logical than they once had – or else logic itself seemed less essential than it once had. And it was true, at times, that she felt something like spiritual comfort during services. Her real work didn't come until afterward, at the kiddush, when she would seek out members who hadn't yet made their annual pledge, or thank those who had. During the rabbi's sermons, which always made predictable parallels between the mistakes of the Reagan administration and those of Biblical rulers who'd come to ruin, she often went over shopping lists in her mind, or thought about ongoing house projects. But then certain prayers, sung by the whole congregation, led by the young cantor's rich alto, made her glad to escape momentarily from the concerns of job and family, to wonder at the possibility of divine purpose and benevolence. It was an idle wondering, without any real conviction behind it, or even a desire for conviction, but it gave her genuine pleasure, and she didn't fight it.

But now she'd crossed a line, done what she'd never allowed herself to do before: "Please, God." She'd said it as if she did believe, and maybe in that moment she did. She couldn't finish the prayer because there was too much to ask for.

Please, God, let everything be okay, always.

And as she pulled to the curb and got out of her car, she felt she'd asked too much already. Disaster. Her father's Caddy in her den. A gaping hole in the side of her house. Her children nowhere in sight. She'd unleashed something terrible on her family, divine injustice and malice. She was crying by the time Jerry reached her, the calm face she'd always relied on looking frightened and haggard, his heavy brow creased, his eyes wide, his trimmed hair mussed, and what he said made no sense.

"Everything's okay. Everyone's fine." These words, too, sounded like prayer, and she wanted him to stop talking. His mustache prickled her ear. She cried harder. "Your daughter's a hero," he said. "She saved Donny's life."

Even when she saw her father, taking his slow, rickety steps beside a policeman, when she saw Donald come running out the front door with nothing but a bandage over his left eye, when she saw Amanda carried by a paramedic, her feet wrapped in gauze, her arm in a sling, she couldn't stop crying. The flashing light of the ambulance refracted through her tears, the entire world gone red. Plaster dust lifted in a sudden breeze. She'd been blessed with so much more than those women in the shelter where she'd once made beds and set tables. Did she deserve this, too? She didn't know if her prayer had been answered, or if she'd been spared in spite of it. She'd never know, could never know, whether it had done any good or not.

3.

ONLY ON THE way back from the hospital did Donny remember the dog. By then it was a relief not to have to think anymore about the way his sister had grabbed him around the waist this morning, yanking him off the floor before he could begin to struggle, tossing him toward the open door to the basement, where he'd slid headfirst down the stairs. In that brief, confusing moment he'd thought she was angry at him for blocking the TV – she had a temper, which he often tried to provoke by making her tell him at least three times to stop doing whatever it was that drove her crazy. Sometimes she threw a pillow at him, and once, when he wouldn't pass the ketchup at dinner, pretending not to hear her repeated requests, a butterknife. But he'd never expected real violence, and as he bumped down the stairs he shouted out apologies and begged silently for mercy. Then came the blunt smack of his forehead against the railing and with it a terrible noise, a crash, a screech, a groan of metal, a squawk of rubber and wood, all the result of Mandy's rage, he believed, the rage for which he was responsible.

The sounds seemed to have lodged somewhere deep in his ear and kept replaying one after another even now as he rode in the back of his mother's car. He wished he could turn them off. Mandy was beside him, but he didn't dare look at her for fear – though he knew it couldn't be true – that the sounds were coming from her. He hadn't looked at her once since coming out of the basement and finding the hood of his grandfather's car where the TV had been. Not when he heard her voice coming from the kitchen, saying the word "emergency" so calmly that he forgot for a moment what the word meant. Not when she dabbed at the cut on his forehead with a cottonball and covered it with a bandage, doing both with one hand, the other hanging limply at her side. Not now, when she pushed his fingers away from his new stitches, her cast scraping his arm, and whispered, "Don't mess with it, Dorko. You'll make it worse."

Instead he put his head between the two front seats and said, "What happened to Harv? Who's taking care of him?"

From the way his parents hesitated, he knew they'd forgotten the dog, too. His father scratched his mustache and said, "I'm sure he's fine, pal. He's a tough old guy."

"He might have got out."

"He knows his way back."

His mother didn't say anything. Usually she drove with only her left hand on the wheel, the other on the armrest, but now both hands steered carefully, her body stiff, eyes forward. A tremor passed through her jaws every few minutes, making Donny want to reach out and touch her but at the same time making him too nervous to move. They'd left his grandfather behind at the hospital, just for the night, just to make sure everything was okay, and Donny felt a twinge of envy that he didn't get to do the same. He was envious of Mandy's cast, too, which would last longer than his stitches. His father had sewn up the cut himself, and the nurse in the room told him Dr. Horenstein was the best, that he'd hardly have a scar. But he wanted a scar, wanted something to mark the day. He imagined people asking him years later where it had come from, and he'd say casually, gauging the awe and pity in his listeners' expressions, "My sister threw me down the stairs when I was nine." It was easier to picture an act of cruelty than an act of love, though either way he had to be amazed all over again at the way he'd flopped in Mandy's arms and flown through the air. Her arms were twigs, hardly thicker than his own, one of them entirely swallowed by white plaster now, the fingers swollen and red when he let himself peek at them. Her feet, too, were red, still bare except for the paper booties she'd gotten at the hospital, stitched on their soles because she'd stepped on glass. He started to lift his eyes toward her face, but then his mother let out a gasp and said, "My God."

He looked up in time to see the tremor pass through her jaw again, but this time his father put a hand on her shoulder. Through the windshield he saw the tow truck pulling his grand-father's Cadillac out of the hole in the house, bits of stucco and wood falling in its wake, and again he wished he could have stayed behind at the hospital with his grandfather. "It's just a wall," his father said, in the same way he said, "It's just money," whenever he bought a new car or a piece of furniture or a Persian rug.

"We need a new TV," Mandy said.

"First things first," his father said.

He waited for Harvey to come bounding out of the hole, with a two-by-four between his jaws. Whenever they took him for a walk in the woods, the dog always found the biggest stick he could carry, so big it made him lean to one side, and when he tried to run he tripped everyone in his path. Harvey was older than Donny by a year and two months, his hips creaky whenever he stood from a long nap, but he still came running when Donny and Mandy came home from school, still chased rabbits in the backyard.

But now the hole stayed empty, even when they slammed the car doors. "He got out," Donny said, but no one answered. His mother was talking to the tow truck driver, a kid in a denim jacket, with hair longer than Mandy's, smoking a cigarette and shaking his head in what seemed like a sympathetic way. His father carried Mandy so she didn't have to walk on her stitches. Tomorrow they'd have a wheelchair for her, and after a few days, crutches. The wind blew one of the paper booties off her feet, and before Donny could catch it, it skittered across the driveway, across the lawn, into the street. "Forget it," Mandy said, when he started to chase it. "I don't need it anymore."

"Stay out of the den, okay?" his father said.

He touched the stitches again, four of them, a sticky ridge with little canyons on either side. The pain was mostly gone, unless he pressed down hard, which he did now, feeling something ooze onto his fingertips. "Harv!" he called, again expecting the dog to come running from a neighbor's yard, carrying the carcass of a chicken found in the trash, his breath ripe and steaming. "Harvey!"

He searched the yard, and when he got cold, searched inside, the kitchen, the bedrooms, his father's office, the basement. At the bottom of the stairs he saw the railing where he'd hit his head, a bit of blood dried on the varnished wood, and he decided not to tell anyone about it, to leave it for as long as he could. He whispered now, "Harv," not willing to disturb the strange silence in the house, the quiet tension he still associated with the coming sounds of the crash. He checked behind the furnace, behind the water heater, but no dog. Above him he heard his father's voice, no more than a rumble, and then Mandy's, clearer than he expected, "I don't know. I just did." He recalled her arms around his waist, recalled the rush of air, the bump of stairs, and tried to believe her throwing him was done out of love, as it must have been, though in his memory he could feel only the terrible force of anger, which he was sure must have canceled out any love.

Water flushed through a pipe overhead. He moved boxes and old clothes and toys, releasing a musty smell. He didn't call for the dog now, because he knew Harvey wasn't here. But he didn't want to go to the one place he guessed the dog might be, afraid of what he'd find. He waited as long as he could, sifting through shirts he'd worn as a baby, through Mandy's abandoned dolls, and only when he heard his father rummaging in the garage did he go upstairs.

His mother was sitting at the kitchen table with her head in both hands, and she didn't look up when he passed. Mandy called to him from the living room, where his father had laid her out on the sofa, but he didn't answer. Everything in the den was covered in white dust, the couch, the coffee table, the bookshelves, the rug that used to be blue. Where the TV had been was a jagged view of grass and asphalt, his grandfather's car and the tow truck gone now, and Donny had an urge to take up his old spot on the floor and watch the hole as he'd watched the morning cartoons. But that spot was where the hutch had landed, where the TV had smashed. He tried to imagine himself underneath the rubble but couldn't. He didn't know what time it was now but knew his mother would have come home from services hours ago and told them to turn off the boob tube before their eyes went square.

His parents had tried to prepare him for Harvey's death, telling him most dogs didn't live much past twelve or thirteen. It was easier to picture the dog's crushed body than his own, a relief, in fact, one that made him dizzy. "Poor Harv," he said, thinking of the way kids at school would say, "Poor Donny," when they saw his stitches and heard about his dog.

But in answer came a muffled whimper, and he was only momentarily disappointed to have his vision of pity shaken, and then ashamed of his disappointment. Harvey wasn't under the rubble. He'd squeezed into the space between the couch and the wall. He whimpered again when Donny slapped his palms against his knees and whispered, "Come on out, dummy."

Harvey's graying muzzle was flat on the floor. His tail didn't wag. "Poor Harv," Donny said again, and meant it this time, seeing fear in the dog's eyes, a trembling in his flank that didn't seem so different than the one in his mother's jaw. "It's all over now," he said, and reached a hand in to scratch the dog behind the ear. But instead of whimpering, this time Harvey growled. "It's me," he said. "It's Donny."

Harvey's yellow teeth were bared, the fur on his neck bristling, making him look nothing like Harvey, and Donny wondered if he, too, looked nothing like himself, now that he was someone who'd almost died. I almost got killed, he'd tell kids at school, inspiring awe, which was even better than pity. I almost got killed, he thought, and now he did picture himself under the rubble, an arm sticking out from beneath the smashed TV, a leg twitching and then stopping. "I almost got killed," he told Harvey, and reached out a hand again, but Harvey's growl grew louder, and his jaws snapped, just missing Donny's fingers.

"Move over." Mandy's cast was beside him, the white plaster that would soon be covered in signatures and well-wishes and funny pictures. She'd crawled on her knees and one hand, making a trail in the dust from the hallway to the couch.

"Something's wrong with Harv," he said.

"He's scared."

"He tried to bite me."

Now he did want to see her face, to know if it, too, had changed, as Harvey's had, but it was screened by her hair. She made a clicking noise with her tongue, and the dog's growl turned back into a whimper. Another click of the tongue, and then came the thump of Harvey's tail. "I found him," Donny said.

"Big deal."

He wouldn't have been able to lift her from the ground if he'd wanted to. He wouldn't have been able to throw her into the basement. He couldn't even make Harvey come out from behind the couch. "I almost got killed," he said.

"I know, Dorko. Get out of the way." She snapped the

fingers of her good hand, and Harvey's muzzle appeared, then his eyes, ears, front paws. He slipped past them, head low, and ran up the stairs. "Get out of here before Dad sees you," she said, and finally he did catch her look, no different than ordinary, her sleepy, half-lidded eyes, her freckled cheeks, her droopy lips that kids in school made fun of, all of it normal, no extra anger, no extra love. She crawled away, shuffling to keep from putting pressure on her cast. The soles of her feet were both bandaged, so he couldn't count her stitches, though he knew there were far more than four. Outside, his father was shaking out an old black tarp to cover the hole, and Donny imagined it draped over a mangled body, the canvas hardly rising over a shapeless lump.

He whispered this time, only now hearing what the words meant, the sounds of them so much uglier than the sounds of the crash they made his chest ache. "I almost got killed."

4.

THE PATIENT DR. Horenstein had run out on the morning of the accident was Jolene Carson, a pretty sophomore at Drew with a gumball-sized cyst on her jaw. A biopsy had come up negative, so by the time she came to see him, Jolene was concerned above all about her face and how the scar would look. Young girls and attractive women were often referred to Jerry, who was known for the delicacy of his incisions. He scorned cosmetic surgeons, people who tried to create beauty where there'd been none before, or at least not for years – but he had no qualms with preserving beauty when threatened by an unfortunate mutation of cells. He knew how to cut with the skin's natural creases, often going out of his way to avoid unsightly marks. He felt good about his work, even though the surgery he performed wasn't technically difficult, mostly dealing with growths just under the skin or in surface tissue. He didn't have the pressure that some of his colleagues had, the immediacy of life and death, though he often prolonged lives that might have been cut short and was thanked in letters, and occasionally with gifts. Of course there was always the possibility of something going wrong, of unexpected reactions to anesthesia, of shock, but he'd never yet lost a patient, had never faced even the threat of malpractice. The thought of cutting into hearts, into brains, made his hands – ordinarily so steady, admired by his colleagues for their competence and grace – tremble and sweat.

Jolene had first come to see him a month ago, accompanied by her mother, who'd breezed into his office in a fitted sweatsuit and flirted with him shamelessly, tugging the rings on her slender fingers, gazing at him through severe black bangs, saying, "She has such a lovely jaw. Whatever you can do to keep it that way."

He was scheduling six months out at that point but agreed to fit Jolene in on a Saturday morning, as he did sometimes for pretty girls who needn't walk around for half a year with an unnecessary blemish. Jolene looked stricken and nauseated, her whole head unbalanced by the gumball bulging below her cheek. Her hair was lighter than her mother's, all one length, pulled back and twisted into a knot at the base of her neck. She had a small nose, full lips, round hazel eyes, and Jerry felt a shameful pang, knowing his own daughter wouldn't grow up to have such unambiguous good looks. People would say Amanda had an interesting face, that she had exotic qualities, but really they would be expressing what a shame it was that she'd turned out to be homely.

Jolene hadn't declared a major yet, her mother said, but she was thinking about international relations. She might want to be a diplomat. She'd need to be able to make a good impression. "I wish I had a jaw like that," her mother said. "I did once."

He'd make the incision just under the jawline, he told them, and come up around the side of the bone. It would take a bit longer to heal that way, but in the end the line would be almost invisible, impossible to see from more than a few inches away.

"Only by dashing young men coming in for a kiss," Jolene's mother said, giving her head a shake that ruffled her bangs.

Jolene spoke for the first time then, her voice deeper than he'd expected, husky and exasperated. "Keep it in your pants, will you?" Her mother blinked and bit her lip and didn't look at Jerry for the rest of the consultation.

But now, a week after Jolene's surgery, her mother's eyes were locked on his, all trace of flirtation gone. She had on a black suit, the collar open at the neck to reveal puckered, sun-wrecked skin, her lipstick dark and unsexy, hair pinned tightly in back. "We're not happy about this at all," she said.

"I understand."

"Not one bit."

"If I could change it I would," Jerry said. "Believe me, this isn't a situation I would have chosen."

Jolene was silent again, sitting with her legs crossed beneath the silky fabric of a long skirt, her feet in sandals though it was still brisk outside, another week until the start of spring. She had two slim braids framing her face, the rest of her hair loose and thick to her shoulderblades. A hippie girl, that was the look she was going for, a look she'd never fully achieve – even now her toes were too clean, their nails closely clipped. It was a look his own wife had been toying with the year they'd met, when Jerry himself was working on a patchy beard and talking about his dreams of healing people in a remote African village. That was before medical school, before he'd understood what it meant to be in debt, before he'd known how many different ways there were for a person to die. Barbara's toenails had been just as neatly filed as Jolene's, though the soles of her feet were nearly black, having gone almost two weeks without shoes of any kind. But the look hadn't suited Barbara any better than it did Jolene, nor any better than a beard had suited him – though unlike Jolene, he hated to admit, Barbara hadn't had the advantage of high cheekbones and lovely round eyes to make up for the ugly clothes and dirty feet.

Today Jolene was as pretty as ever, the swelling in her jaw gone, only a bandage covering the wound. He'd made the incision before the duty nurse came into the operating room and told him he was needed at home. It had been a good cut, as clean as anyone might have asked for, and the rest he left in the hands of an intern, Kelly Edwards, a competent young surgeon, who one day might be as sought after as Jerry himself. But Dr. Edwards was more concerned with accuracy than aesthetics, and to get to the cyst from the awkward angle Jerry had provided she'd had to stretch the incision, and hadn't stitched it as finely as Jerry would have. It was a functional job, impressive for an intern put on the spot, but now Jolene would be left with the scar Jerry had promised she wouldn't have, seen by more than those young men who'd bend close to kiss her. The scar wouldn't affect her beauty in the least; it wouldn't cause anyone to hesitate in his pursuit of her. If anything, he thought, it would add to her appeal, roughening up the perfection of her look, giving her character.

But her mother wasn't interested in his thoughts on beauty and character. She was here with an agenda. She wanted him to re-cut, to re-stitch, to do what he'd promised to do. Cosmetic surgery. She insisted that he schedule it as soon as possible. She wouldn't pay another dime. She'd already talked to a lawyer. "We paid for *your* hands," she said. "Not for some orderly's."

"It was an emergency," he said. "I wouldn't have chosen it."

The eyes that had previously observed him coyly through bangs now conveyed nothing but anger and indifference. The lips that had smiled at him, that he'd briefly, against his will, imagined touching with his own, were set and unfriendly, lipstick bleeding into the creases at the seams of her mouth. "Your emergency doesn't concern me. My daughter's face does."

He explained what the procedure would involve. A skin graft. General anesthesia. A painful recovery, several more weeks of healing. "I'll be glad to do it," he said, turning to Jolene, who seemed to be studying him, her tongue working behind her lower lip, prodding the spot where the cyst had once been. No matter how many scars she had on her neck, she'd always be more beautiful than his wife, his daughter, and he suddenly wished he could have given Amanda a better chance in life, providing her a more attractive combination of genes. "But I need to be sure this is something you really want."

"Of course it is," her mother said.

"Is your daughter okay?" Jolene asked, flinging one of the braids out of her face. "I saw her on the news."

"Just broke her arm," he said, surprised to find himself choking on the words, his nose suddenly clogged.

He was on call until eleven that night – occasionally he was asked to oversee an emergency procedure, never to participate – and then drove home in the rain, thinking about Jolene and her mother, who'd gone back to smiling by the time she left the office, saying she was glad she'd be seeing him again. She apologized for being so hard on him, she'd just do anything for her daughter, she was sure he understood. He despised her then but couldn't stop himself from imagining unbuttoning her blouse the rest of the way, taking off that ugly suit, seeing the whole of her tanned, wrecked skin, and now tried to shake away the image and the disgust it brought. He remembered the way Jolene's shapely legs had shifted beneath her skirt, her toes flexing in the nylon sandals, her husky voice answering slowly when he asked again if she wanted the extra surgery, "I guess I can handle it." If he'd been stronger, more determined, he might have tried to talk her out of it, but with her mother glaring at him, he'd only shrugged and said, "A week from Saturday."

The black tarp flapped in the wind, its edges beating against the house, rain seeping in. He spent twenty minutes pinning it down further with industrial tacks, making more holes in the stucco, his wool coat, warm enough but useless against the heavy drizzle, quickly soaking through. The contractors had postponed once already but were supposed to begin next week. During the day he worried about burglars, and last weekend he'd put a sign on the garage, another in the lawn, "Beware of Dog." A burglar would have something to worry about with Harvey, no question – the dog had grown jumpy, growling around anyone but Amanda, something in his mind snapped by the accident. He wondered about the mind of a dog, if it would suddenly believe the world was falling apart when a car crashed into a house. If so, Harvey was like Barbara, who seemed to expect more walls to crumble at any moment. A harried look had settled into her face over the past week, and she'd stopped laughing in her usual way about people at work, the rich donors out of whose pockets she wheedled enormous checks. She'd stopped going to services on Friday night or Saturday morning, saying she already worked hard enough during the week. In the last two days she'd begun talking about going back on the job market.

She was in bed now, and so were both the kids. Only the lights in the kitchen were on, where Jerry's father-in-law, Ivan Zacheim, sat drinking coffee at the counter, the newspaper folded beside him. Twice now Ivan had said he was ready to go back to Queens, where he couldn't cause any more trouble, and twice Barbara had talked him into staying longer. Jerry was ready for the house to return to normal, for the wall to be fixed, for the old man to leave. The two things seemed bound together, and sometimes Jerry wondered if Ivan couldn't go until the evidence of what he'd done was gone as well. The old man spent a good bit of his time staring at the wall, or at the kids, imagining, maybe, what might have happened if Amanda hadn't acted as she had. Jerry imagined it, too, at unexpected times, the thought of burying his children making all the spit dry up in his mouth, pains shooting through his legs and arms. It happened once during surgery, requiring all his effort to keep his hands steady, the one part of him he'd almost always been able to control, unlike his thoughts.

Ivan didn't glance up when he came into the room, just lifted the cup to his lips, no steam rising, nearly as much milk in it as coffee. The cup shuddered on its way back down, sloshing brown liquid into the saucer. The old man's hair was oiled, still thick where it hadn't receded, and he wore a sport coat and tie, as he did everywhere except in bed. Outside he wore a fedora, too, refusing the believe that hats had gone out of style. Jerry had always admired the dignified way he carried himself, his erect posture, his careful enunciation, his slow stride that managed to hide stiffness and pain behind a façade of unhurried thoughtfulness. His confidence made up for his sagging face, a worn version of Barbara's, whose own face was a weathered version of Amanda's, all three sharing the shapeless mouth, the wide nostrils, the small, deep-set eyes that kept them on the verge of ugliness.

"It's late," Jerry said, because he was tired of silence and could think of nothing else worth saying.

"Sleep is a luxury I seem to have given up," Ivan said, flexing the fingers on his right hand, his arthritis worse since the accident.

"The coffee isn't going to help."

"There comes a time when it's better not to fight anymore."

"Look," Jerry said, trying to keep the irritation out of his voice, an irritation he didn't entirely understand. "It's just a wall. No real harm done."

"I'm not much good to anybody these days. Not for a long time."

"Donny's stitches come out tomorrow. Mandy has the cast for a month, and then she'll be back to normal."

"I could have been mayor of New York," the old man said.

There was no sense trying to reason with him, but Jerry couldn't stop himself. "The contractors come next week. Why does everyone act like it's the end of the world?" From the living room came a slapping sound, the tarp loose again, his tacks useless against a sudden wind gust. "Why can't everyone just relax?"

The old man ignored him, taking another sip of coffee. Why couldn't he go back to feeling normal himself? Why was he so uneasy walking through his own house, coming from the job he'd had for long enough now that even a difficult meeting with

Jolene Carson and her mother should have felt routine? He didn't expect cars to come plunging through walls at any moment, for his roof to collapse without warning. He knew that what had happened was an aberration, not to be repeated. It wasn't the accident that had surprised him so much as how it had played out, his daughter, often difficult and whiny, complaining whenever she was given a chore, sulky when she didn't get a gift she was hoping for, now shocking everyone with her selflessness, her simple courage and the stoic way she carried it afterward. He'd never expected much from Amanda, he was ashamed to admit – her grades were average, her behavior in school often eliciting ambivalent remarks from teachers. And now he was even more ashamed to realize he wanted her to return to the way she'd been, to go back to being difficult and predictable, something he didn't have to wonder about, though now wonder was all he did. How could she have risked her life to save her brother? Where did she find the strength, when her own father passed up on performing any surgery with the slightest hint of urgency?

He left Ivan in the kitchen, climbed the stairs, walked past the closed door of his own bedroom, past the kids' bathroom, past Donny's door. Rain splattered the skylight above him, a hollow sound, and he knew he should re-tack the tarp before any more water leaked into the ruined den. But instead he stood outside Amanda's door, as he had every night for the past week. He tried to make out the sound of her breathing but couldn't over the drumming of the rain. He wanted to open the door and stand over her bed as he had when she was an infant, watching her sleep, amazed at what he and Barbara had produced. He was amazed again, but amazement was something he thought he'd given up years ago, an emotion too worrisome to indulge in middle age, one he had no time for. His hand was on the knob, as it had been every night for a week, the minty smell of toothpaste coming from the bathroom, Donny never remembering to rinse the basin when he finished brushing.

The rain came harder. He couldn't let go of the image of

Jolene Carson probing the inside of her mouth with her tongue, flinging her braid out of her face. He couldn't stop imagining her mother unbuttoning her blouse. For years he'd been undressing women with his eyes, twice with his hands, but until now he'd always been able to push their faces out of his mind when he came home from work, to go through the motions of family life without lingering on the regret he felt, having married a woman he'd never been more than mildly attracted to, and now not at all.

He turned the knob and pushed the door open. One bark, and Harvey's paws were against his chest, jaws snapping at his face. Over the dog's head he saw his own reflection in Amanda's mirror, his trimmed mustache, his salt and pepper hair, his distinguished jawline, a face that was unquestionably handsome, more so than it had ever been as a young man's face. He'd settled for a near-homely woman, had loved her genuinely, but only, he'd always known, because at the time he believed he couldn't have done any better.

The dog's breath was sour and fishy as Jerry struggled to keep his teeth away. Not the face, he thought, hearing the words in Jolene Carson's mother's voice, not the face. "Dad?" Amanda asked groggily, sitting up in bed, her matted hair silhouetted against the window, her own features in shadow. "Harv?"

The dog lunged again, and Jerry put a hand in front of his chin, a hand that should have been saved for surgery, that was his life, his purpose. Before he could take it away, the dog's jaws closed over it, teeth crunching through bone.

5.

WHENEVER AMANDA WATCHED the news clip – not just in the weeks after the accident but in the months and years that followed – she was always shocked to recognize the strange expression on her face, a look of pity and understanding that seemed beyond the grasp of her eleven years, her wide mouth sorrowful and dignified on the shaky recording, the tape's poor quality making her skin look sallow. She tried not to watch very often, but sometimes, without understanding why, she was drawn to it, playing it only when no one else was in the house.

The clip had been recorded by a neighbor, the one other family on the block with a VCR – the only one after the Horensteins' had been shattered by the Cadillac's grill. The local anchor, a boyish, wavy-haired heartthrob from the station in Chatwin, locked eyes with the camera and said, "And now we have a special story this evening, the story of an eleven-year-old girl's incredible courage." A graphic, "Young Heroine," flashed across the screen, before the camera cut away to a pan of Crescent Ridge, of the house with its gaping hole, the tarp taken away for the sake of the news story.

The interview was shot the day after the accident, while Amanda's mother was picking her grandfather up from the hospital. The reporter asked silly questions: "Do you love your brother?" and "How do the kids at school feel about having a bonafide hero in their class?" The Amanda on screen answered sincerely, ignoring the emaciated woman's patronizing tone, while the one who watched thought, Give me a break. The Amanda on screen said, "I feel bad for my grandpa. He didn't mean it." She sat in a wheelchair in front of the hole, her posture upright despite the sling around her neck. "I hope my dog didn't get too scared."

This wasn't Mandy, the undersized girl who was a loudmouth at school, pushy with other kids, always talking back to teachers, the one who didn't do her homework, who once slapped another girl on the playground, bloodying her nose, because she wouldn't give up her turn at jump rope. The Amanda who watched herself on screen couldn't fit the two images together, and neither could her schoolmates, nor her teacher, Mrs. Travers, who up till now would have ignored any attempts she'd made at reforming. They spoke to her hesitantly, with a hint of reverence, while she wheeled around the hallways, and then hobbled on crutches. Her class gave her a standing ovation her first day back in school. Kids who'd never before had a kind word for her asked if they could sign her cast. Mrs. Travers' way of talking to her changed from one of defeat and derision to a wary, uncertain respect.

The face of the girl on TV somehow overshadowed that of the girl who'd been loudmouthed and belligerent, even for Amanda – afterward she couldn't go back to being Mandy, giving the nickname up at the beginning of the following school year. She'd never dreamed of being able to start over, of becoming a different person, but given the chance, she was happy to find herself quieter and milder mannered, easier on herself and others. This person had been inside her all along, she guessed later, held back from the surface by distrust or fear or doubt or any number of things she didn't understand or whose source she didn't remember. The new Amanda turned in most of her homework, not always on time and not always carefully done, but regularly and proficiently enough to keep her from standing out. She talked back to teachers only when they were being unreasonable, and even then in a softer, sterner voice, a voice of authority. At recess she watched games of jumprope and kickball from the sidelines, and even after her cast was off, her arm and feet healed, she declined to join in, sitting instead with the more demure fifth-grade girls, the ones who wore makeup and skirts and leg warmers, the ones for whom playing sports and getting sweaty was something remembered only vaguely from the distant, childish days of third or fourth grade. To her surprise, no one told her she belonged elsewhere.

Even her parents treated her differently, as if she'd aged a dozen years overnight. Or maybe it was they who'd changed so abruptly, becoming younger in those hours after the accident, less sure of themselves, less interested in being parental. They no longer sent her out of the room when they discussed finances or problems at work, no longer lowered their voices when they had a disagreement. "I'm not arguing," her father said, a few weeks later, his hand bandaged where Harvey had bitten him.

"I just want you to really think this through."

"That *is* arguing," her mother said. "And who says I haven't thought it through?"

"I just don't think you should be impulsive about it. I think you should take more time. This has been such a crazy month."

"Another week isn't going to make any difference."

"You can't make rash decisions in the heat of the moment."

"*You* can't," her mother said. "*I* can."

Later, when her father went up to bed, and Amanda was trying to read about the ratification of the Constitution and answer questions on Mrs. Travers' worksheet, her mother made a racket loading the dishwasher and then said, out of the blue, "He's never liked it that I'm independent. That I can think for myself. All his talk about women's rights in the seventies. Bullshit. What he really wants is a nice traditional wife. Someone to do all the housework and keep her mouth shut." She slammed the dishwasher closed and shook her head. "I don't know. That's probably not true at all." She let out a heavy breath and examined a few hairs for split ends. "I don't know what he wants. I never have."

Amanda watched the tape that night, in the dark of her bedroom, on the TV and VCR her parents had given her as a surprise the day Harvey was put to sleep. She'd watched it that day as well, and watched it again eight months later, on the day of her grandfather's funeral. She watched it when her parents announced their separation the following year, and after coming home from her first disastrous date in high school. She watched it when Donny wrecked their mother's Jeep, out joy-riding with a friend before he'd even gotten his learner's permit.

She watched it once more her first year in college, but this time she wasn't alone. Beside her was a broad-shouldered boy with perfect teeth who, along with the rest of his lacrosse teammates, shaved his head and wore a T-shirt with the sleeves rolled up, to show off muscles and a fresh tattoo, a Chinese character symbolizing something to do with honor or bravery or enduring pain. She'd asked him about the tattoo at a party, but his answer had been drowned out by booming bass and drums. Instead of asking again she stayed close to his muscles, close to the tattoo, drinking cups of punch he offered, topped with chunks of fruit marinated in vodka, and when the party wound down she brought him back to her dorm room, empty for the weekend, her roommate gone home to visit a high school boyfriend.

He was her second lover since she'd started school, but despite his muscles he wasn't any better than the first had been, a tall boy with impressive stubble, who claimed she'd broken his heart when she stopped returning his calls, who now looked the other way whenever they crossed paths on campus. The lacrosse player, Bennett, rolled off her, yanked off his condom, and said, "I'll be able to go again in a minute. I got more stamina the second time."

The vodka-soaked fruit had begun to wear off by then. Her head hurt, and she wanted to sleep. But Bennett sat up at the end of the bed, back against the wall, feet hanging off the mattress, hand on his crotch, waiting. She traced the tattoo on his arm with a bare toe. He ignored her for a moment, then grabbed her foot, and ran a finger down the scar. She pulled it away. "That tickles."

"How'd it happen?"

"I'll show you."

She said it without thinking, and without thinking she walked across the room to her closet and began digging through piles of clothes, through shoe boxes full of old photographs and journals, until she found the tape. She was aware of her skin lit by a streetlamp through the window's flimsy shade, of the hips that had taken on weight over the first three months of college, as everyone had warned her they would.

If she had a reason for showing Bennett the tape, it was at least partly out of spite, for his being such a bad lover, for thinking he had courage just because he wrote it on his arm in a language he didn't understand, because he threw a ball around with a stick and hurled himself against other boys with his helmet and shoulder pads. His erection was coming back by the time she returned to bed, and she was relieved to be able to press play on the remote control, to see the heartthrob news anchor's sincere look into the camera, to hear his confident voice speak her name. And there she was, an awkward, stoic-looking girl in a wheelchair, saying of course she loved her brother, saying she felt sorry for her grandfather, saying she was worried about her dog.

Was she any less awkward now? Her teeth were straighter, her hair darker and styled. She had breasts now, and thighs shaped by running on a treadmill, shoulders strengthened by swimming. Her lips still drooped, her eyes were still deep-set and prone to getting bags beneath them, her chin weak, but none of that stopped muscled lacrosse players from wanting to come home with her and push themselves between her legs. Seven years later she still carried that pose of dignity she'd discovered during the TV interview, her head held up despite the sling, shoulders squared, eyes steady. It was the same pose she'd held at the party a few hours earlier, when she'd gone straight up to Bennett and asked what his tattoo meant. She'd seen how impressed he was, breaking off from talking to another girl, quickly claiming her for the night. And now she watched him watching her, the Amanda who'd been a hero, who'd saved her brother's life. She was glad to see he'd stopped rubbing himself, that his erection had gone away. His eyebrows lifted, the only hair on his entire head. "Damn," he said. "Bad ass."

"There was glass everywhere," she said, and wedged her feet under his leg. "That's how I got the scars."

"How'd you do it?"

How. That was the one question the emaciated reporter never asked, the one question Amanda had never been able to answer herself. One minute she was watching cartoons, annoyed with Donny for blocking the TV; the next she had him in her arms, tossing him toward the basement door. She guessed now that Harvey had heard the car even if she hadn't, that the dog had jumped from the couch and startled her, that somehow she'd realized what was coming. The feeling she recalled wasn't fear or anger or panic, but only purpose and power. In that moment and in the few hours following, she'd felt herself capable of anything that might be asked of her, that she could bear whatever came her way. The pain of her broken arm, of the glass in her feet, was nothing next to Donny's safety, her parents' alarm, her grandfather's sorrow. It was recalling that feeling that allowed her to pose for the camera the next morning, that allowed her to approach a muscled lacrosse player while he was talking to another girl – though she'd never felt it again directly, not once since that day.

And sometimes she wished she'd never felt it at all. After her grandfather's funeral, she'd considered getting rid of the tape. Until then it had been sitting on the shelf above her desk, with the two halves of the cast she'd worn, every inch of plaster covered in signatures. They came home from the cemetery on Long Island to find the contractors at work again in the den, the sound of saws and drills and filing. The first contractors had done a shoddy job, leaving stucco that cracked and a window that leaked.

The front door was open, but they didn't have to worry about Harvey getting out anymore. Her mother had driven the whole way, with that new careful posture, her hands tight on the wheel, eyes never leaving the road, and now she went straight to her bedroom and closed the door. She still hadn't found a new job since quitting the synagogue eight months earlier, saying she couldn't raise money for something she didn't believe in. Her father hadn't driven because his hand was still bandaged. His doctors had set the bone without realizing there was an infection, and now, after several surgeries, he could close his fingers only halfway. He was in physical therapy twice a week and didn't know if he'd ever make it back to the operating room.

Donny had cried through the whole service, wailing when Amanda hugged him and whispered, "What's this crazy you're talking?" He was still crying now, following her upstairs to her bedroom, throwing himself face down on the bed. "I want Grandpa," he said. "I want Harv."

What she wanted was to get her dress off and her itchy tights, to put on sweats and slippers. To have the contractors gone so she could watch TV without the noise of power tools and hammers. To have her father healed, her mother back to work, Donny out of her room. She listened to his whimpering and recalled Harvey's from the nights he'd spent beside her bed, the dog calming down only when she clicked her tongue. She saw her grandfather's stunned face, her mother's bewildered, her father's in pain, Donny's streaked with tears. They all wanted her to be strong, to make things better, to ease their distress, but she'd already done everything she could. What power she'd had that Saturday in March was long gone. Instead she was left with the fear she hadn't felt that day, and the sadness, and an anger she didn't understand as she watched Donny's curls bounce on her pillow in rhythm with his sobs. "I want my dog," he said.

"I don't care what you want, Dorko. Enough already. I don't care."

He didn't look at her. He didn't say another word as he left the room. She took off her dress and tights, put on sweats and slippers, grabbed the tape and cast from the shelf and held them above the trash can beside her desk. She'd go back to being Mandy, back to being the loudmouthed girl who'd made up for being ugly and teased with backtalk to teachers, with cruel gossip and pushiness. She wondered if now she, too, might be able to cry for her grandfather, to cry for Harvey, for her mother's and father's careers, for the hole in the house.

But no tears came. Downstairs her father was arguing with the contractors. A table saw whined through wood. Donny passed her door and made a farting noise, a sound she hadn't heard since last March. Water was running in her parents' bathroom, her mother filling the tub. Through her window she saw a black sports car take the sharp turn onto Crescent Ridge, kicking up fallen leaves, and speed off down the street. Her breath was as shallow as it had been for months, her muscles as tightly clenched. She set the tape and cast on the desk, thinking she'd throw them away tomorrow, maybe, or the next day.

Now she crossed the dorm room, popped the tape out of her roommate's VCR, and tossed it back into the closet, not watching to see where it landed. She could feel Bennett's eyes following her bare body, the breasts she was proud of, that she knew how to make prominent by pulling her shoulders back.

"Bad ass," he said again, and whistled. He'd gone back to rubbing his crotch, his erection returned to full strength.

"I'm tired," Amanda said. She climbed into bed and turned her back to him. She felt his breath on her neck, his warm skin, his surprisingly soft hands, but she closed her eyes and braced herself against his desire, his ache, giving not the slightest sign that she was moved by it. She kept in mind the image of the girl on TV, this person who was her and not her, who she'd been once and would never be again.

"Come on," Bennett whispered, his hands making their way over her hips. She pressed her knees together with a strength that dwindled with each passing year, that now seemed to waver with each hot breath against her neck. It would have been so much easier, she knew, to let him flop around on top of her a second time, and not have to do a thing.

Backfill

THE PLAN FOR THE DEVELOPMENT WAS STRAIGHTFORWARD
enough. A hundred and thirty-seven houses on two parallel
streets ending in cul-de-sacs, with two cross-streets connecting
them. But nothing was ever as straightforward as it should
have been. The site had been a rock quarry in the '50s, filled in as
most quarries were with whatever happened to be on hand:
tree trunks, chunks of concrete, old tires. A nightmare for excavation, and no better for new construction. Half a million dollar
homes, and in three, four years, Robert had no doubt, they'd start
to sink. Without foundations ten feet thick they weren't worth a
dime.

He'd been on worse job sites in seven years with Boonton
Excavation, or at least worse on a first glance. The rim of a ridge
below Pyramid Mountain, with two yards of leeway before a
thirty-foot drop-off, and rock that crumbled to bits after blasting.
A floodplain in Denville, with the Rockaway River swelling,
and mud so saturated you couldn't dig six inches without water
seeping through. And his all-time favorite, the grounds of an
abandoned chemical warehouse in Troy Hills, where the track
hoe turned up barrels of chlorine buried illegally and nearly
poisoned the entire crew.

He'd still been down in the ditch then, laying pipe in driving rain or choking heat, doing whatever he was told. When
he started he wasn't much older than Walsh, but he never complained about the weather the way Walsh did, just kept his head

down and fit one end of pipe to the next. It was a summer job at first, just after he graduated from Rutgers, a few months after he'd met Lisa. A friend's father did business with the owners of Boonton Ex, who needed bodies for a big sewer project in Parsippany. June through August, and then, if he listened to his parents, he was supposed to find a job vaguely related to his major – anthropology – or start applying to graduate programs.

But he was tired of school by then, and happy to have money in his wallet, and when his superintendent offered to keep him on, he hardly hesitated. The classes he'd taken over the past four years – Language of Social Diversity, Prehistoric Archaeology, Gender and Power in Asia – seemed frivolous next to steady wages and a clear purpose to his days. The simplicity of the job appealed to him. Nothing but numbers: how many hours logged, how many feet of pipe, how much profit for the company. Lisa joked that he was already working in his field, digging in the dirt, studying primitive cultures. She encouraged him to keep the job. It was more real than some bullshit academic or corporate life, she said, more honest. She was a political science major, writing an honors thesis on Hegel's *Philosophy of Right*. When she graduated she wanted to find a job as a labor organizer. It was sexy to go out with a working man, she said. When he drove down to New Brunswick straight from the job site on Friday afternoons, still in his Carhartts and dusty shirt, pockets full of dirt and pebbles, she'd pull him into the bedroom before he could get in the shower. Sweat turned her on, she told him.

He stayed with the job through the fall and in winter helped with maintenance in the company shop. He never talked back to the foreman or tried to make jokes or ragged on any of the crew. He worked hard to prove he was one of them, never talking about college friends or classes, never mentioning his parents, both teachers, or the house he'd grown up in, a four-bedroom Colonial in Randolph. Even when the mainline digger punched through a gas line and tried to blame it on him, even when his foreman docked him two days for staying out with the flu, even when someone dropped a spool of wire on him and knocked out three of his teeth, even when he hated the job so much he wanted to lie down in the ditch and let the backfill man pour gravel over him, he kept his mouth shut and worked. And if nothing else, he earned a measure of self-respect, something Walsh had probably never heard of.

Now he spent his days above ground, handing down pipe, ordering gravel and sand, mapping out grade, calling in progress reports. Two years ago he'd made foreman, and since then he'd driven the one-ton truck with the Boonton Ex logo to the job site every morning and doled out the day's gear. He ran safety checks and made sure every inch of pipe was up to code. He called for breaks and kept the crew from slacking when they were behind schedule. He took pleasure in telling them when they'd done a good job and whenever possible let them off an hour early on Friday. He was younger than two of his three crew members, but at times he felt fatherly toward them, the responsible head of a family – a little stern, maybe, but always compassionate and always fair. And for two years they'd been the most efficient in the company, hands down, with a profit margin over ten percent. Even these past two months – distracted as he was since Lisa, without warning, had asked him to move out – they'd always come in under budget and hadn't once finished a job late.

But some things you couldn't anticipate or control or even try to understand. How the developer suckered the county planning commission into letting him build on a former quarry, for example, or why Robert's super, Gordon Millbrook, bid so low, or what made people so stupid as to want houses where they didn't belong. No one else could have made the job pay, and Gordon knew it. Robert bitched him out when he saw the site, but only to himself. "Anybody can handle it, you can," Gordon said. Robert knew false flattery when he heard it, but he thought anyway: Damn right. "We need fifty yards a day," Gordon said.

LATELY, WHEN A job was running smoothly, Robert would end up sifting through memories, searching for the moment when his marriage took its recent turn. If he could find it, he could fix it, he thought, the same as a faulty engine belt or a section of broken pipe. But the memories that most often sprang to mind were ones that didn't do him any good – all of them ending with Lisa taking off his clothes and then her own – and after a while he'd think of them less as memory than speculation, imagining how things would be different in a week or a month or a year, after he'd made all necessary repairs, after Lisa asked him to come back.

But now it was a relief not to think about the past or future. The present required all his attention. In good dirt fifty yards was nothing, but the first day in this pit they made less than twenty. Not more than an hour into the job, the shovel hit metal – twisted-up rusted siding that screeched and groaned and, to Robert's delight, sent Walsh ducking for cover. Al eased it out of the ground with the bucket and dropped it at Walsh's feet. "Jesus fucking Christ," Walsh said. "What are we, garbage men?"

"Archeologists," Al shouted over the noise of his track hoe, giving Robert a wink as he swung the bucket back into the ditch. "Another couple feet and we find *T. Rex*."

"And Bluebeard's treasure," Robert said.

"Yeah," Walsh said. "And Jimmy fucking What's-His-Name."

"You end up in here too, you're not careful," Al said.

"Don't you know Rob's connected? The Syndicate, you know?"

"The what?"

"Meyer Lansky. That's his great-uncle."

"Who?"

"Guy that owned Vegas. Didn't you ever see *Bugsy*?"

"If his uncle owns Vegas, what the fuck's he doing running a sewer crew?"

"Careful you don't piss him off," Al said.

"Too late for that," Robert said.

"Wake up one morning in one of these pipes," Al said.

"Drowning in rich people's shit," Robert said.

Al was the best mainline digger in the company. He had a feel for the shovel's teeth, as if his own nerves extended out of the cab and down the length of the boom. He could cut a straight line without any markings, and if he hit a boulder he wouldn't scrape at it, just skimmed the top so Walsh could drill and set the charge. Once he came within inches of taking out cable TV for all of Union Hill, but instead of cutting through he lifted the line – stuck between two of the bucket's teeth like dental floss – moved it aside, and went back to clearing the trench.

He should have made foreman long before Robert had, but he said he preferred it up in the cab of the track hoe, behind the controls. He didn't want to be in charge, didn't want to deal with management and progress reports. He didn't want to park that ugly-ass one-ton in front of his house every night.

But Robert knew better. He understood how Boonton Ex worked. He'd heard the jokes the supers made and knew how the owners voted. Al's full name was Alfonso Colon Cordera, and he lived in Dover, just off Blackwell, with most of the Puerto Ricans in the county. He had five kids and his house needed a new roof, and he could have used the extra pay that came with being foreman. But he was short and dark and had an accent and a silver cap on a front tooth, and not once in ten years had he been offered a promotion.

And still he didn't gripe and whine the way Walsh did, pacing above the ditch, saying, "I'm not getting back in there. It's fucking treacherous."

What did he have to complain about? He was tall and sandy-haired and square-jawed, and he didn't have a name that would hold him back at Boonton Ex or anywhere else. He'd be a superintendent himself while Al's roof sagged over his five kids. Nineteen, and already he drove a pickup that cost twenty-grand and lived alone in a duplex his father had built and paid for, but still he couldn't put in a day's work without moaning about how hard the world treated him, how life was so unfair.

"I'm not getting back in this fucking hole," he said, already climbing down. "I'm no garbage man."

"What are you then?" Robert asked. "Because you sure as hell don't look like a pipe-layer."

"Dude, I lay my pipe all over town. Getting so I can hardly even walk."

The truth was, Walsh did know how to work, even when he was mouthing off. He kept up with Al, something Teo hadn't been able to do at all, something even Robert had struggled with when he was still down in the ditch. Walsh's father was a contractor, and the kid had grown up framing and laying foundation. And it was his father who'd gotten him the job, so he could learn new skills and maybe expand the business. He wouldn't be a foreman or super. He'd be a contractor himself, with a house six times the size of Al's. His back bobbed above the surface and then disappeared below, his spine cutting a ridge down the middle of his safety-orange vest, his face lost in clouds of dust, his voice setting Robert on edge.

"How many kids you planning to have anyway?" he shouted, loud enough for Al to hear over the rumble of the track hoe's engine and through foam rubber ear plugs. "Fifteen? Twenty? No wonder you're always broke. Kids are fucking expensive. My truck's cheaper than a kid. Why do Ricans have so many god-damn kids anyway? You got something against rubbers? Mortal sin or something? I'm a big fan of rubbers. I'll wear two with a girl I don't know. I don't care if I can't feel as much. I feel plenty. You're not against rubbers, are you, T.? Oh, wait a minute, you gotta get laid once in a while to worry about rubbers. What about you, boss? You cover the stick or go freewheeling? I mean, before your woman kicked you out the house?"

Teo ignored him, and Robert did his best. It was easier for Teo, since he was a dozen yards away, fetching gravel from the dump truck, then pouring and compacting it over freshly laid pipe. The man on backfill was always separated from the rest of the crew, and with Walsh yapping all day, maybe it was a blessing, though usually it led to trouble. It took a certain kind of personality to be off on your own all day, without much contact or oversight, and each of the previous backfill men – Teo was Robert's fourth since making foreman – would start to slip, taking extra smoke breaks, showing up an hour late, spacing out in the middle of a job.

Teo was the oldest on crew, almost forty-four, with a two handed gut and sore joints, but he was solid and steady and never questioned Robert's direction. He'd worked underground construction once before, he said, in his late twenties, up near Albany. What he'd done between then and now he never mentioned, and no one ever asked. But from his tattoos and haggard face, his smoke-roughened voice, a tic in one cheek Robert had seen before in alcoholics, you could guess the kind of life he'd been living. Now he was trying to turn it around, showing up on site before anyone else, occasionally bringing coffee and donuts for the whole crew, always deferring to Robert's authority. He was quiet and solitary, but he had a look he'd sometimes give Robert, a little nod and half-smile partly hidden by his shaggy mustache, reassuring and complimentary, and when he was around Robert felt supported. If anyone was promising backfill material, Teo was, and as soon as the last backfill melted down, Robert was only too happy to shift Teo out of the ditch.

But nothing was ever easy. He'd heard Teo talk about his father maybe a dozen times in two years, mostly offhand, passing mention. "Need to take an afternoon next week, if that's all right. Bring my pop to the doctor." Or, "Didn't sleep for shit last night. Pop was up coughing till two."

On Monday, their second to last day on a storm sewer in Montville – a cakewalk compared to the new job – it had been, "Pop passed last night."

It was early morning, and Robert was groggy, and the

word passed made him think of tests and college and, oddly, of the taste of day-old pizza – and then, no surprise, of Lisa climbing out of bed in that way she had, one foot reaching for the floor, the other resisting, waiting until the last moment to slip out from beneath the sheets. "Passed what?" he asked.

"Long time coming," Teo said. "But still." Only then did Robert hear the catch in his raspy voice, the tic in his cheek making one side of his mustache jump. "Funeral's Saturday. Don't need no time off. But, you know. Might be rattled some. Not my best. Thought you oughtta know."

"Want to take a few days?"

"Used up all my vacation already. Can't afford to lose the pay."

Just like that, and Robert had something to worry about. He would have liked to put Teo back in the ditch, where he could keep an eye on him, where he might feel taken care of. But Walsh hadn't trained on backfill, and Robert needed the kid's speed on the job if they'd have any chance of coming in close to budget. Instead he spent more time than he wanted glancing down the mainline to gauge Teo's mood, to catch him if he started to slide, as the others had. He found himself watching how Teo pulled his gears, how he wiped sweat from his brow, wondering if he did it differently today than he had before, if there were signs of an impending break. He must have been staring hard enough to tune out Walsh's banter, and long enough that he lost track of what he was doing.

"Boss! Hey, boss! You forget about me?" Down in the ditch, Walsh was waving both arms over his head. Robert lowered the next length of pipe, and Walsh pretended to hump the end of it. "Falling in love, boss? Need those rubbers after all? Get yourself a little backfill?"

Before he could say anything, or bonk the kid on the head with a wrench, there was a terrible cracking a few yards ahead. The bucket had hooked an old stump, its roots thicker than Robert's chest. They bent unnaturally and then gave way, small explosions of splinters where they split. Walsh bolted to the surface and paced on the far side of Al's machine. "I'm no fucking garbage man, man," he said. "No way I'm getting back in that hole. No fucking way."

THE SECOND DAY they struggled to make fifteen yards. They spent most of their time pulling shredded tires and reinforced concrete out of their way, and then re-grading the ditch with sand Robert called in and waited three hours for. Walsh bragged about the girl he'd been with the night before, some chick he'd met at a party, he said, no one special. He did her in the bathroom while someone was waiting to use it. "Not much of a face, you know, but dude! Smokin' body. She was wet before I even touched her. Put my pipe right in that mainline."

The day was bright and bleak, and after an hour the insides of Robert's nose had caked with dust. Through it filtered the smell of singed rubber and flinty smoke from sparks. Teo had shown up on site early, as always, and as always he was solid and steady, helping clear the trash when he didn't have gravel to compact. His eyes were glazed but focused, mustache drooping over his mouth, arms working the levers of his backhoe mechanically.

Too solid, Robert thought. Too steady for someone grieving. He'd rather have had him show some sign that this wasn't a normal week, that it was only seventy-two hours until his father's funeral. He tried to imagine the pain Teo was in, or the relief he felt, or the guilt that kept him awake at night. It was part of Robert's job to empathize, to anticipate problems, and at lunch he took Teo aside and asked again if he wouldn't be better off taking a day or two away. Teo squinted, pulled up his hard hat, ran a hand through the matted hair beneath. "Don't need me here?" His hoarse voice was choked and uneven. Creases went straight back from the corners of his eyes. His nose was crooked from at least one break. Robert found it disconcerting not to be able to see his lips through the dark bristles covering them. "Doing something wrong?"

"That's not it," Robert said. "It's just ... I'm sure it's a rough week."

Teo nodded and gave that half-smile, which Robert took again to mean that Teo approved of the job he was doing, that he was glad to work for him. Today it seemed to be telling him not to worry about how far behind they were, how much they'd have to do to catch up. "Rather work," Teo said. "Better than sitting around thinking. Pop and me –"

Before he could say more, Walsh was calling, "Shit. Look who's coming."

Gordon Millbrook walked the length of the mainline, shaking his head, wearing khakis and an ironed blue denim shirt, his fresh hard hat spotless and gleaming in the midday sun. "I'm surprised," he said. "I thought you guys could handle it."

"Hey, man," Walsh said, through a mouthful of sandwich. "Why don't you get down in that fucking hole –"

"We'll catch up," Robert said, shooting Walsh a look.

"I don't know," Gordon said. He'd grown tubby in his four years as super, cheeks red and bloated beside his slip of a nose. His frown had a hint of grin in it. "I thought you'd do at least forty a day. This," he said, scratching an ear, squinting up into the sky, "this is just disappointing."

Robert could have argued, could have said it was Gordon's own damn fault for taking the job and bidding too low. He could have made excuses about the crap in the ground and the sand that took forever to show up. But he guessed Gordon might have had other reasons for putting him on this job – to take him down a peg, to level the playing field. It didn't suit the front office to have one crew always show up the rest, especially one run by the only college graduate in the company not already a super. "I've got the sand here now," he said. "We'll make up ground this afternoon."

Gordon lifted his hard hat, ran a hand through hair not matted at all. "I won't hold my breath," he said.

When he was gone, Robert called a quick end to lunch.

Walsh groaned and lay back on the ground, pulling his own hat down over his face. "I gotta digest, man," he said, filthy poly muffling his voice.

"You can digest and lay pipe at the same time."

"It's bad for you to start moving right after you eat. Gives you cramps."

"You'll have worse cramps when I jam a pipe in your kidney."

Walsh pulled himself from the ground, mashed his hat on his head, kicked a clod of dirt. "This is an uncivilized profession. No wonder all you guys are total fuck-ups."

At the end of the day, after Robert had loaded the one-ton, after he'd called in his progress report and noted the receptionist's surprise at his low numbers, Al came up to him looking embarrassed, hands behind his back, face lowered. "Not feeling so hot, Rob."

"We'll have a better day tomorrow," Robert said.

"I mean I'm getting sick."

"Chills?"

"Throat," he said. "Head full of mud."

"Just a cold," Robert said.

"I know it's a bad time."

"We need you up there."

"Don't know how good I am like this."

"Better than some on-call guy with his head up his ass."

"You know I care about the crew. Our record."

"Your call," Robert said, with an insistence he was sure Al would understand, and wondered, not for the first time, how often Al imagined running the crew himself, how often he questioned the way Robert went about the job. "See how things look in the morning." Al swallowed, winced. Robert looked out over the clearing, trying to picture a thriving development on top of all this rubble, sprawling houses with hardly any lawn, garages as big as his new apartment. But he saw only graded dirt where streets would go and the beginning of a sewer trench. Anything beyond the present now seemed impossible. He reminded himself he'd made foreman for a reason, that a few setbacks weren't enough to throw him – the same way he reminded himself that nothing was final between him and Lisa, that the future was still open. Only his vision of the future always looked like the past: Lisa greeting him in her New Brunswick apartment, her clothes on the floor before they made it to the bedroom. "We'll catch up tomorrow," he said. "We've handled worse than this. Remember that job on Vreeland?"

"Trying to forget."

"Or South Beverwyck?" Al shrugged. "We'll catch up."

"If you say so."

"Get some sleep. And if it turns into the flu – "

"I'll see you tomorrow," Al said. He massaged his neck and tried to clear his throat, wincing again. "I leave it to you, you'll fuck up my trench."

ROBERT SHOWERED AND put on fresh clothes, but made sure to keep it casual. Clean T-shirt, jeans that had less than three months' wear, new motorcycle boots with only a scuff or two on the heel. He'd sold his bike three weeks ago, but Lisa didn't know that yet. She didn't know he'd quit drinking beer after work, either, or that he'd started reading before bed, first picking up the anthropology texts that had held his interest in college and now put him to sleep, and then moving on to thrillers that kept his eyes open a few minutes longer. He was waiting for the right moment to tell her these things, when it wouldn't sound like pleading, when he wouldn't seem pathetic. Best to let her find out for herself, after he'd moved back in. Best to have her take him as he was, without expectations.

Once a week they had dinner at Marco's on Route 46. He'd agreed to give her space, to meet in a neutral setting. He'd been back in the house only twice in the last two months, most recently on the pretext of searching for a toolbox. Already there were changes. In the living room was a movable rice-paper screen, and on both end tables, floral ceramic vases. At each place setting on the dining room table were a pair of painted chopsticks propped on wooden platforms. From the stereo came piano notes without any melody. Three nights a week Lisa drove to Montclair State to take classes in Japanese language and culture – for work, originally, though now the culture had followed her home. After graduation she had tried to find a job in labor organizing, but no union would hire her without experience or a master's degree. Instead she got a job in the personnel department of a fiber optics firm, most of whose employees were imported from Japan. After Robert finished digging around in the garage – plenty of tools, but no box – she invited him in for tea, and for a moment he was encouraged. Then she made him take off his boots. The tea was bitter. The music was by Takemitsu, she said. Did he like it? She was thinking about a trip to Tokyo in the fall. She knew he hated to fly.

Marco's was noisy with business dinners and high school kids on their way to the prom, the boys looking somber in tuxes, the girls hysterical in brightly colored satin gowns and carnations pinned to their wrists. He was stuck waiting fifteen minutes in the entryway. On the wall beside him were photos of Marco, the grizzled owner, posing with celebrities he'd served – Robert DeNiro, Ed Koch, Quincy Jones, all looking uncomfortable with Marco's hairy arm draped around their necks.

Lisa was late. She'd made the reservation for seven, but already it was pushing seven-twenty. Nobody eats dinner at six, she'd told him recently, one of the many things she'd decided in the past year. One night a month before he'd moved out she'd insisted they go to Il Capriccio, a price-fixed place with valet parking, where they'd paid an outrageous amount for two bottles of Tuscan wine, which, Lisa said after the third or fourth glass, was better than sex. They hadn't sat down until eight, and she was still sipping at eleven. He had to get up at five. Lately she'd been suggesting they meet for sushi in Morristown, an extra twenty-minute drive, but he stood his ground, claiming a special fondness for Marco's.

The prom kids passed a flask under the table, pouring shots into their cokes. One girl was tanked already, elbow on her bread plate, pink satin drooping off her shoulder. Her napkin fell to the floor. Robert picked it up and handed it to her as the host led him to his two-top, right in the middle of the noisy front room. The girl's dark hair was curled and pinned above her long neck. Her skin was tan even where the strap had fallen away. She had a tiny diamond stud in her nose and a bigger silver one in her tongue. She thanked him when he handed her the napkin, then balled the cloth in her fist and threw it back on the floor. She laughed, loud, and her pasty-faced date tried to shush her. When Robert sat, she waved to him. He raised a finger, and she laughed harder. Her date shushed her again, and she turned on him, face suddenly pinched and ugly. "I'm *not* being loud," Robert heard over all the other voices in the room. Then they argued, and he was forgotten.

Lisa showed up at seven thirty-five. He'd already finished half a Peroni and a basket of bread. He'd read the menu four times. "I just can't do seven anymore," she said, slinging her purse over the back of her chair. "The expansion, and classes. I'm lucky some nights if I get out of there by nine."

"You work too hard," Robert said. It was true that some nights she wasn't home at nine, or even nine-thirty. He drove by occasionally, twice a week at most, just to get a glimpse of the place and make sure no strange cars were in the driveway, no Japanese men knocking on the front door. Once he waited until after ten, behind some trees at the end of the block, and then drove home nauseated and shaking. Back in his apartment, surrounded by heaps of laundry, stacks of dirty dishes, a wall of empty Pepsi cans, he dialed their number, ready to leave a long, angry message, calling her out on her lies. He rehearsed as the phone rang. Don't want to hurt me more than necessary? Not going to see anyone until we resolved things? Going to be honest with me no matter what? But then she picked up. "Oh, hey," he said, instead of what he'd planned. "Sorry to call so late. I was just wondering ... Did you maybe see my weight belt around? Maybe in the basement? I'm thinking about taking up lifting again."

"I'm tired, Robbie. Why don't you make a list and bring it Wednesday."

Now she said, "So either we make it later, or make it every other week. Or once a month. Or just figure out something else."

"Later's fine," he said. "I'm flexible."

"I know you've got to get up early."

"I don't need as much sleep as I used to."

"Once a week might be too much for me," she said. "It's hard for me to plan around."

"That's what we agreed on."

"I know what we agreed. I'm saying we might need to make some new arrangement."

"I'm flexible," he said again, and picked up the menu, scrutinizing it as if he didn't know what language it was written in or what purpose it served. "So. The expansion. It's going okay?"

She told him about all the problems, the offices that weren't yet ready for the new engineers, departments wrangling over talent, executives trying to micromanage everything. She sounded like the businesspeople at surrounding tables, and looked like them, too, in a gray suit and blue blouse, collar open to expose a wedge of neck and chest. She was professionally harried, hair up in a loose knot, jacket sleeves wrinkled, lipstick perfect. She'd just turned twenty-seven, but she was put together, self-possessed, at once more beautiful and harder-looking than when he'd first glimpsed her at nineteen. That was when she'd gone everywhere barefoot and rarely wore a bra, when she twisted her hair into a hundred braids and painted her hands with henna. "I have to remind them they're just making telephone wires," she said. "It's not like they're changing the world or anything."

He'd been to her office a dozen times but still couldn't picture what she did there all day, surrounded by cubicles, oppressed by buzzing fluorescent lights. It made sense that she'd feel stifled, though why she took it out on him rather than her job he couldn't understand.

The waitress told them about specials, and Robert ordered what he'd known he'd order before he even showed up tonight – chicken in mushroom sauce, a side of fettuccini. Lisa asked about wine and made the waitress stand uncomfortably while she decided on food, finally settling on mussels, something Robert had never seen her eat before. When the wine came he asked if it was better than sex, and when she didn't answer, said, "Probably been too long to remember." She smiled, impatiently, and he knew how phony his own laugh sounded.

He asked about the house and the yard and if the bamboo she'd had him plant last spring was getting out of control. He talked about work, reporting all his own problems – Al's cold, Teo's dead father, the super's scolding, the awful ground – and how, starting tomorrow, he was going to attack the job with all his resources, not let anything stand in his way. She pried apart the mussel shells, seeming disappointed to find so little meat in each. He told her about Walsh's stories, most of which he doubted – screwing a girl in the bed of a pickup going ninety down the Turnpike; walking in on a threesome at a party, and without asking, joining in as a fourth; bedding a married bank teller in order to avoid an overdraft charge on his checking account – and soon he had Lisa laughing, shaking her head in disbelief. Her laughter was the one thing he could count on, the thing that had changed the least in the three years since they'd gotten married. It had a ringing quality to it, low notes rising to high, a surprised, delighted sound he'd always felt belonged to him alone, even when he heard it around other people. It left her a little breathless and flushed. He filled her wine glass. She took a sip and said, "It might all be true. Some women can't resist guys in work clothes."

"If I remember right," he said, leaning in, "you used to be one of those."

"Who says I'm not still?"

"You resist me pretty well these days."

"That doesn't mean it's been easy. And if you really want to know," she said, smiling a bashful, mischievous smile, holding up her glass, "no, this isn't better than sex. Not even close."

He waited until she'd drained most of it and then said, "I've been thinking."

"That's new," she said, and laughed again.

"I've been thinking it's time for me to move back in." This time her laughter was forced, and she covered it by lifting the glass to her lips. "I've been thinking we should talk about it."

"Did you come up with that yourself?" she said, in a teasing voice he knew well, slyly defiant, meant to undermine him. "Or did your whole crew have to help you?"

"It's been two months. I don't see how any more time's going to make a difference. To clarify things, I mean."

"Oh, Robbie. Do we have to be so serious? Can't we just enjoy ourselves? It's been a long day."

"Fine," he said. "Forget I said it."

"It's not like it's been easy on me, either," she said. "Two months in a big empty bed."

"Remember when we first got together? We could hardly go two hours."

"Don't remind me."

"And when you were still in New Brunswick, and I'd drive down after work. You wouldn't even let me wash my hands."

"That smell," she said. "It did something to me."

"I still smell the same."

"I'm sure you do."

"Maybe even worse."

The laughter burst from her again, rocking her forward. He would have done anything to hear that sound every day. But he didn't want to show it. He leaned back in his chair, dabbed at his mouth with his napkin. He had to stay focused, determined, unrelenting. She caught her breath and said, "If that's all there was to it –"

"Who says it doesn't have to be?"

He heard the ruckus before he saw its source. Lisa turned around in her chair. The prom kids were getting up from their table, staggering on their way to the limo waiting in front. The girl in pink satin broke away from her date and weaved across the dining room, a shaky line ending at Robert. Her shoes, strappy white sandals with four-inch heels, dangled from one hand. "He," she said, and poked a finger into Robert's shoulder. "He picked up my napkin. He's a gentleman." Then her hand was flat against him, the only thing, he guessed, keeping her from falling into his lap. Her date came to collect her, but she pushed him away. "I'm not gonna fuck him," she said. "No matter what he thinks." She dropped the shoes, clapped a hand over her mouth, and made a run for the bathroom. Her date hurried after her. Lisa watched them all the way to the door. When she turned back, her smile was gone. In its place was the harried, hardened look she'd had when she'd first come in, and she set her wine glass, still a quarter full, on the far side of her plate. "Jesus," she said. "I'm glad I'm not in high school anymore."

"So," Robert said. "What do you think?"

His chance had passed, and he should have let it go. There was no humor left in her voice when she answered. "About what?"

"About me maybe moving back in."

"Oh, Robbie."

"Or maybe I could just stop by some day after work. Before I shower."

"There's more to it than that. You know there is."

"If you met someone else," he said, and felt a rush of blood to his chest and neck, a constriction of some kind, a terrifying ache.

"We've been through this already. It's not about someone else. I've told you that all along."

"I've been taking better care of myself," he said. "I started doing push-ups again."

"Do you think this is easy for me? Do you think I wanted it to happen? It's awful," she said, and her face changed again, red blotches appearing now on her cheeks and chin and below her ears, tears springing to her eyes. She snapped a mussel shell in half and made an odd sound through her nose. For a second he thought she was going to start talking to him in Japanese. "Can you imagine how terrible it is, suddenly realizing you've – and you're going to go completely crazy if you don't – "

"I sold my bike," he said quickly, that ache in his chest solidifying, a longing for the old Black Shadow Lisa had tried to talk him out of buying, for the barefoot girl with braids who would have ridden happily on back, her breath warming his neck.

"It's not about the bike, either. You know it isn't."

"I started reading again," he said. "I might make super next year."

"Look, Robbie," she said, and the expression she turned on him now was so much worse than the cold, distant one he'd come to know over the last year. Her hands folded on the table, her smile sad and sincere, full of pity, her cheeks soaked. "You're right. More time isn't going to make any difference."

IN THE MORNING, back on the job site, the sun was too bright. The dust stung his eyes and made his nose itch. The noise of the machines rattled his skull. Lisa had kept him out too late, and he hadn't been able to fall asleep. All night he kept thinking of the way she'd snatched the bill as soon as the waitress dropped it, insisting on paying. Then the brief hug she'd given him in the parking lot before clicking off to her car, in those dress shoes that seemed so foreign to her feet, or else feet that were entirely foreign to him, part of a foreign body – the body of a harried professional he knew only casually, in passing. After her car pulled away, he stood on the blacktop, watching the rumbling limo packed with high school kids, and thought he was on the verge of putting his finger on it, the moment of rupture, the place he could return to and restart. But before it came to him, the girl in pink satin stormed out of the restaurant and pitched headlong into the limo's open door, her pasty-faced date still chasing her down. At home he abandoned his anthropology books and thrillers for the TV, watching until late night shows gave way to infomercials, drinking the beer he'd avoided for weeks. Finally he jerked off, first trying to picture Lisa as she'd been in college, a slim, cheerful, trust-fund hippie with dirty feet; and then, with a measure of shame, the tan high school girl from the restaurant, with the studs in her nose and tongue.

Teo was on site when Robert showed up, and so was Walsh. Al was five minutes late, looking puffy-eyed, with bits of tissue stuck to his upper lip. Robert gathered them together and laid out the plan for the day. If they didn't pick up the pace, he said, Gordon would make them work through the weekend. It was an empty threat, meant to prod them, but right away Walsh started griping. "Bullshit, man. Why don't they bring in a goddamn garbage crew? How the fuck they expect us to go any faster with all this shit in our way?"

"Go home if you don't want to do it," Robert said, the edge in his voice surprising him as much as it did Walsh, whose mouth opened and closed without a sound. "Cry to someone else."

"I'm just saying –"

"You heard me," Robert said. "Go home."

"I know it's not your fault –"

"Ask Daddy for a new job."

"Hey, man –"

"Or shut up and get in the hole."

He did shut up then, for the first time in as long as Robert could remember. Teo shuffled his feet. Al coughed into his hands and wiped them on his pants. Walsh didn't say another word until he was in the ditch. Then he muttered, loud enough for all of them to hear, "Fuckin' A, man. What's his problem? Just saying it's bullshit we gotta clean up all this garbage. I'm no fucking garbage man. What an asshole. No wonder his woman sent him packing."

Al climbed into the cab of his machine without glancing at Robert. No doubt he was thinking again of how things would be different if he were foreman – that they wouldn't be behind at all, that he'd know how to keep Walsh in line. But he wasn't foreman, and never would be, and Robert was tired of feeling sorry for him and his five kids. Walsh was right. Why have so many if you couldn't afford to put a roof over their heads? Al started to cough again but this time held back, head flinging forward, hand over his mouth, no sound. He straightened, gasped, said, "I'm fine," and started the engine. The track hoe's boom jerked up and then stretched out, the bucket easing down.

Teo hung back until the other two started working. His tic was going like crazy, his beaten face spastic on one side, the other weirdly still, as if it were made out of wood. His raspy voice was hardly more than a whisper. "This weekend," he said. "Pop's funeral."

"And?" Robert said.

"Saturday," Teo said. "I can't work."

"What am I? Fucking babysitter? Work if you want. Take a hike if you don't." Teo blinked and ran a hand over his mustache, down his chin. Sour spit filled Robert's mouth, and he turned aside to hock it in the dirt. "Look, T.," he said, but Teo had already turned away, heading for his machine. "We'll catch up," Robert called after him.

And they did start to catch up. By lunchtime they'd made twenty-two yards. In the early afternoon Al was tearing through the mess of dirt, filling a dump truck with concrete and rock and rusted metal, the clanking rhythmic now, the smell of damp earth stronger than that of dust or smoke or rubber. Walsh was laying pipe and talking nonstop, telling them about another girl, or maybe the same girl he'd told them about the day before. "I don't know, man, some dudes like a big ass. Better the cushion and whatever. Not me. I like a tiny little ass. I'd fuck a skeleton if

I could. I bet you're a big ass type, huh, boss? I know Al is, all them Ricans are. What about you, T.? You like a big can?"

But there was no way Teo could hear. He was working the plate compactor, pounding gravel down into the trench, covering up their work so no one in the half million dollar homes would ever know they'd been here. And now Robert could see it. The gaudy development, tasteless houses with white brick facades, imported luxury cars pulling into enormous garages, overpaid professionals – like Lisa, like her parents – walking beneath vaulted ceilings, all of it slowly sinking into the rubble. He found himself arguing silently with Lisa as he lowered pipe to Walsh, thinking how unfair it was for her to have wanted one thing all those years ago, and then to suddenly want something else. Why couldn't she have changed her mind after that first summer, when he'd still had the chance to do something different? Where would he be now if she hadn't liked the smell of his sweat so much?

An hour before quitting time, Gordon Millbrook stopped by to check on them. The smug satisfaction disappeared from his pudgy face when he saw how far they'd come. Robert walked him down the length of the mainline and back, more than forty yards. "We're getting there," Robert said. "Longer I talk to you, the less I get done."

He decided that from now on he was going to recognize his mistakes as soon as he'd made them, and when Gordon's truck pulled away, he left the ditch and went back to talk to Teo, to give him a supportive word or two. But Teo had his sunglasses on, earplugs in, head down, guiding the plate back and forth over the mainline. He didn't hear Robert call or see his waving arms. This wasn't a place for grief, Robert thought. Not a place for feelings of any kind. He'd send Teo home and do the backfill himself, punch his time card for him so he wouldn't lose the pay. He could feel the vibration of the plate from ten yards away, up through his feet, all the way into his jaw. Fifty years after all the gravel had been dug out of this hole, and now they were putting it back in. It struck him as stupid and sad, the endlessness of it, digging holes and filling them, digging and filling. His whole adult life so far, surrounded by foul-mouthed kids and hopeless drunks and illiterate drifters. He was one of them now, though why he'd ever wanted to be, he now had no idea.

Robert called out again, and this time Teo switched off the machine. He took out an earplug, pulled off his sunglasses, shaded his eyes with a hand. His face seemed different, something about the wrinkles around his mouth or the set of his jaw. The tic was still. The tattoos on his arms were so faded they looked like ground-in dirt. Before Robert could apologize, he said, "About Saturday. I been thinking."

"Yeah, man, about that. I didn't mean –"

"Thinking I'll work if we need to."

"No way we're working Saturday," Robert said. "Fuck Gordon, okay?"

"Don't need to see the asshole into the ground. Said good-bye enough already."

It was a strange thing for him to say, and stranger still was how uneasy it made Robert that he'd choose to say it to him, as if he'd mistaken him for someone else. The ground still trembled, even though the compactor was silent. The trees at the edge of the clearing seemed to wilt under the late afternoon sun. "Maybe you need a few days," Robert said. "I'll make sure you get paid. Gordon doesn't need to know anything about it."

"I tried," Teo said, and gave that half-smile, only now it didn't seem to have anything to do with Robert or the job he was doing, and he wasn't sure it ever had. "Thought I could make up for all that old shit. Come back here and take care of him, but he doesn't thank me once. Just lays there and dies."

There was something inappropriate about what Robert was hearing – not just the words but the raspy sound of Teo's voice, which seemed to scratch and burn its way out of his throat. He was still waiting for something that made sense, a simple break like he'd seen with those who'd come before. "Look man," he said. "I know I've been hard on you guys. It's not about your work. You know, Gordon ... And this shit with Lisa ... " He wanted to stop himself. It was all so inappropriate, so out of place with these big ugly machines, with the deep gouge in the yellow-brown dirt. "How are you supposed to come to work and do what you've got to do when something like that ... like your father ... A few days would do you good."

Teo put his sunglasses back on. He replaced the earplug and kept his hand there, cupped against his head. "Clocked me once so hard my ear rang three days," he said, and came out with a scratchy little laugh. It was the first time Robert had heard him laugh, and it was so unexpected it sent a shudder through him. "Nearly burst the drum. Motherfucker. Can't tell you how many times I wished he'd croak."

Here it was, Robert thought, the breakdown he'd been waiting for, that always came, no matter how solid someone seemed. But Teo only gave him that odd smile again, and now Robert had the feeling that it was a condescending smile, that meant Teo thought he had no idea what he was doing. The backhoe's engine started up, and the compactor pounded down. The vibration made his ears hum, but along with that sound was another, unfamiliar, like tires screeching, only higher pitched. At the end of the mainline, something was wrong. A tooth of the track hoe's bucket had hooked an old cable, three inches thick, rusted and caked with dirt. This time Walsh didn't jump at the sound. Al didn't seem to hear it either. Robert wondered if his own ears were tuned to a different frequency, like a dog's. And then the sound was lost to him, too, as the drumming of the compactor came closer.

Both ends of the cable disappeared into earth, and as the bucket rose it tented over the ditch and stretched like the band of a slingshot. Walsh's head was a few feet from it, bobbing above ground and then below, lips moving. His vest was bright and useless, the utility board's slogan on its back – *Dig Smart New Jersey!* – a stupid joke. Safety-orange, Robert thought, picturing all those dark suits Lisa had on both sides of her closet now, spreading across the space where his own clothes had been. What made a color safe?

He waited for Al to set the cable aside, gently, as he did everything. But Al's face was puffy and red, his eyes slits, and the boom and bucket kept rising, turning toward the dump truck, the cable straining against it, lifting from the dirt but not releasing. Robert couldn't help feeling sorry for him again, having to watch a white college kid get promoted into the job that should have been his, for the five children who would grow up poor and brown and without much chance in the world. Compassion had no more place here than grief, and neither did pity, but now he felt sorry for Walsh, too, this kid who had every-thing he wanted, sex and money and cars, who never worried about anybody but himself, talking on and on about women who lusted after him, who saw nothing in him but his tan neck, his muscled arms, his sweaty chest – and him thinking that was all he needed.

The boom stretched against the taut cable, the ground shook beneath Robert's feet, and his knees felt sore and fragile. He'd seen so much trouble in seven years. Guys falling into ditches, breaking arms and legs. Eyes taken out by zinging rocks. One pipe-layer who electrocuted himself on live power, singed off all his hair but lived. His own hard hat had a dozen dents and dings, any one of which could have meant his skull if it hadn't been covered. In his lower jaw were three crowns where those teeth had been knocked loose by the falling spool of wire. He'd never found out who dropped it, but he'd carry the mark of it for the rest of his life, while Lisa would walk away unscathed.

He could picture her, asleep in his college bed, naked under a damp, twisted sheet, one dirty foot dangling over the edge of the mattress. His memories were full of pictures like these, but he wouldn't find the moment that would give him answers – or else he'd find it in such abundance that the answers wouldn't matter. Part of him had known this all along. He'd tried to build something stable on the flimsiest of foundations, taking for granted that his hopes for it would be enough to keep it standing – though as Walsh's head rose once more, as Teo shut off the compactor and shouted, as Al checked the movement of the boom and eased it away from the dump truck, it seemed to him that all ground was shaky, that nothing in the world was solid. And this comforted him enough that by the time Al set the cable safely on the ground he already forgave himself for the way his feet were planted, his mouth shut, his mind clear and eager, waiting for the snap.

Saab

SIX MONTHS AFTER THE START-UP WENT UNDER, ARI Feldman's marriage followed. For tax purposes, the house was in Nan's name, and so was the remaining car. He wouldn't fight for any of it, he decided. There was more dignity in simply walking away, and now he wanted only to bury himself in a new, barren life, without anything to remind him of what he'd had. After spending most of a month sleeping in the guest room, he packed his clothes and toiletries, nothing else. He'd leave behind a dozen bottles of single malt, his collection of blues records, a signed photograph of John Lee Hooker. Decisions, he'd always believed, should be final the moment they were made, carried out to an end despite second thoughts, and he didn't let himself hesitate as he passed the Hooker photograph on his way out the door. Rather than call on old friends, most of whom he owed money, or his parents, whom he owed more, he spent three nights in a motel beside the freeway, not bothering to shave, showering only once, and then answered an ad for a studio in a South Chatwin neighborhood he'd never heard of, the lowest rent he could find. The property manager spoke to him shortly, named a time and address and hung up before he had a chance to thank her. He checked out of the motel – why pay for an extra night if he might not need it? – and carried all his belongings to the side of the road. He had to change buses three times, making his way from one corner of the county to another.

The property manager showed up forty-five minutes late.

While he waited he found himself imagining where she might live – up on the ridge that cut across the northern horizon, maybe, or out on Lenape Lake. Someplace that didn't smell of overripe fruit and cat litter. But then she drove up in a white Saab convertible, a decade old, with a shattered taillight and a gash in the roof patched with crumbling duct tape, and parked where the curb was painted yellow. So maybe not on Lenape Lake, he thought. One of the garden apartments on Route 46, more likely, or the stretch of tract housing in Rockaway.

The engine idled. From the steps where he sat with a suitcase and duffel, a pair of coats draped over his knees because he had nowhere else to put them, he could see the woman bending between the front seats, her mouth working furiously, her fist rising and coming down. Finally, the car went silent. She called to him before she was all the way out from behind the wheel. "I have to turn it on and off with a paperclip. Goddamn key broke off in the ignition. Day after I signed the papers. Never buy one of these, Euro piece a crap."

There was no apology in her tone, no sense that this was an excuse for leaving him waiting. She couldn't have been older than thirty-five – Ari's age – but her voice was husky, and a gray streak ran through her dark hair, beginning just above her right temple and disappearing in a loose ponytail that clung to the back of her blouse. Her nose was slender, her jaw narrow, thrusting. She wore a pinstripe skirt with tennis shoes and socks over black hose, the matching jacket bunched in one hand, a pair of pumps in the other. "I'm a mess," she said, glancing down at her feet. Then she shook her head, made a dismissive gesture with both hands, and asked accusingly, "What the hell do you care?" She dropped the shoes and jacket on the front stoop and flipped through a metal hoop crowded with keys. Even when she stood still her shoulders had movement to them, a swagger, and her legs were spread apart as far as the skirt would allow. "You've got money, don't you?" she asked, pausing, a key hovering over the deadbolt. "I didn't just drive all the way over and you can't afford the deposit."

"I can pay," he said, tossing the heavy duffel as casually as he could onto his shoulder. The weight of it knocked him off balance, and he nearly toppled into her.

"Careful," she said. "I won't put up with any bullshit."

"It was an accident," he said.

"You can forget about the apartment right now."

"An accident," he said. "Really."

Her eyes narrowed. She unlocked the door.

The house was three stories tall, made for a single family at the turn of the century, now carved into a dozen units. The front door still had its original leaded windows, but the oak floors, whose fine grain and deep color he could only imagine, were buried under matted fawn carpeting. The hallway smelled of fried fish. She led him up to the second floor, turned a quick corner, and opened a door cut awkwardly beneath the stairwell. Inside, the single hanging bulb sputtered and then glared. It took him only a moment to survey the room, walking the four paces in each direction. On one side, to fit under the stairwell, the ceiling slanted all the way to the floor. The window above the kitchen counter – the only one in the apartment – looked out on a rotting tool shed whose roof had collapsed. Beyond was the back entrance of a diner, where cooks and dishwashers smoked somberly beside a row of trash cans and stacked wooden pallets. His new neighbors. A cheerful bunch, he thought, just like him.

He glanced at the water stains above the toilet, at the dozen holes where pictures had once hung, at the shower curtain rod bent and sagging, the knob of the closet door dangling from a single screw. The stovetop was lacquered with grease and dust. Only two of three burners grew hot when he switched them on. The fourth was missing its element altogether, two wires sticking out of a metal stub. It was impossible to look at this and not think of the spacious Colonial in the old part of Mendham, with the hardwood floors he'd had refinished, the clawfoot tub, the six-burner gas stove he'd paid a fortune to have installed. He held tightly to his suitcase. He wouldn't react, wouldn't show a sign, he swore, of the despair that threatened to swallow him, of the disaster his life had become. The property manager stood in the doorway, arms crossed, one tennis shoe tapping. She didn't apologize for anything, didn't mention repairs. "Well?" she asked.

He shrugged. What other choice did he have? Sleeping on a friend's futon, or in his parents' guest room? Throwing himself on their mercy, living with the shame of it, with the pity he'd see in their eyes, with their silent judgment of his failures? "Yeah. Okay. I guess I'll take it."

Her face momentarily lost its sharp edge. Her eyes lowered, and she pushed loose strands of hair behind her ears. Was this embarrassment? Insult? "I'm not twisting your arm here," she said.

"I said I'll take it." Anger came to him swiftly, pleasantly, an old friend. "You want me to do cartwheels?"

Her neck tensed, her body went rigid, face again all pinched nose and chin. "Rent's due on the first," she said. "One day grace period. Twenty-dollar late fee per week. First and last up front."

Finally he set the suitcase on the floor and let the duffel fall from his shoulder, which immediately began to throb. The woman crossed her arms when he took his checkbook from a back pocket.

"Fifty bucks if that bounces."

"It won't," he said hotly, hoping it was true – or hoping, at least, that his overdraft protection would cover it if it wasn't. "You can cash it today."

"Make it out to R.T. Rentals."

Great name, he thought. Very personal. The human face of real estate. "Is there a maintenance person? A handy-man?"

"Are you kidding?"

"Who do I call with problems?"

"Call a lawyer," she said, and let out a husky chuckle, pleased with herself. She plucked the check from his fingers and handed him a pair of keys. "Or a shrink. Or a priest, if that's the kind of thing you go for."

THE MANAGER'S FOOTSTEPS echoed all the way down the stairs. He opened his suitcase in the middle of the floor and flipped absently through his clothes, dress shirts and slacks, a dozen ties, things he had no use for now. Nor did he have anything to hang them on. Hard times build character, his grandmother would have told him if she were still alive. They bring people together. Then she would have started a story about her family's struggles during the Depression, how his grandfather had had to sell the drugstore, how the children – his father and aunts – had worn holes in their shoes, how they'd all learned to eat half their regular portions and were still thankful for what they had. He never reminded her of the other drugstores his grandfather had lost, those during the boom years following the war, when most people were making their fortunes. What kind of character had *those* times built? Whom had *they* brought together?

He dragged the duffel to the closet. The knob came off in his hand, and he threw it to the floor with some satisfaction. He thought of other things he could break – the shower rod for sure, the stove, maybe, the dripping faucet. He pictured it all twisted and smoking at his feet, the whole apartment, the house, the unfamiliar neighborhood, the entire town. It was easier, he supposed, once a life had begun falling apart, to hasten it on its way.

Go easy on yourself, Nan had said at the beginning, soon after the company folded, taking with it his options, his savings, all his hopes. You're resourceful. You're resilient. You'll bounce right back. And he'd agreed with her – he hadn't known the first thing about computers or about children, but he'd had no trouble selling a fanciful idea to eager investors. People who'd cashed in early had made millions. One couple had sent him a bottle of champagne and a picture of their boat anchored off Baja. For a while he listened to her, trying to take each new disappointment lightly. But she didn't understand the humiliation he felt – or if she did understand, then she was simply a part of what humiliated him, one more reminder that he was well-educated, skilled, experienced, unwanted. He did try to go easy on himself, but what turned out to be easiest was to let Nan go with the rest of it, to give up everything with one devastating shrug, a snake shedding the last of its skin.

Get over yourself, she'd said toward the end, hardened by then to his brooding, to the long silences with which he was trying to punish her, to the suffering he would never admit to no matter how many times she named it and told him she wanted to help. He was glad to be done with her optimism and encouragement, cheered even by signs of anger and resentment. She stood with hands on hips as he packed his bags, eyes clear and barely blinking, all compassion replaced by bitterness and frustration. He felt lighter, it was true, having portioned off a measure of pain onto her. But a shiver of shame ran through him as he snapped the latch on his suitcase, and a pang for the beauty he still wanted to see in her face but couldn't. Her lips and cheeks were pale, the skin beneath her eyes discolored. He'd done more damage than he'd thought himself capable of, wrecking what he'd once imagined indestructible. Suddenly he hoped to hear a catch in her voice as she said goodbye, the slightest waver, some small signal that her core – that sappy, bountiful, forgiving heart he'd first encountered skeptically at twenty-five, only tentatively believing his luck – was still intact, however deeply buried beneath the scars he'd left.

But her words were steady, bladelike, as he headed for the door. "The world doesn't stop with you, Ari. You know that, right? After you're gone, people still get up and make their coffee and go to work."

WHEN HE CAME out of the building – heading where? to buy groceries, maybe, to get to know the neighborhood, anything to get away from the awful apartment–the Saab was still parked at the curb, the property manager bent over the seat. It had been ten, fifteen minutes since she'd left his apartment. From around the corner came loud laughter, the cooks and dishwashers, one of them shouting gleefully, "Unh-uh. No way. No fucking way." They didn't sound so different from the kids in his old neighborhood, who played basketball in newly blacktopped driveways, whose parents bought them baggy designer clothes meant to make them look like inner-city thugs. On the street the air was fresher than he'd remembered, the smell of nearby trashcans seeming faint now, a relief after fifteen minutes in that stifling, mildewed room. The sidewalk was lined with maples, young ones, but big enough to give shade all summer and to clog the gutters with leaves in the fall.

He was going to enjoy this–walking by as the woman struggled with her car, eyes forward, chin high. He thought of his grandmother again, in an assisted living facility for the last eight years of her life, the way she managed to lift her nose at the women who used walkers or wheelchairs, even as her own legs grew weak, twice causing a fall. It was a meaningless pride, he knew, both his grandmother's and his own. But what else did they have? He savored the thought of the manager watching him pass without seeing her, as he casually turned a corner. But he also wanted more than what he could only imagine and glanced quickly to the side as he came even with the car.

It was a mistake. He caught her eyes, crinkled and teary, her face blotched and red. Her ponytail was falling out of its band. She clenched a clump of hair in one hand, the gray streak that should have made her look older but didn't. He couldn't walk by now. He wasn't cruel enough for that, or maybe brave enough. Why had it been so much easier with Nan? He opened the passenger door. The woman's husky voice barraged him, blubbering now, but no less aggressive than before. "This fucking thing," she said. "It's not even half paid for."

He leaned across the seat, careful to keep his feet outside

the car, on the pavement. Such a strange place to put the ignition, between the two seats, just in front of the emergency brake handle, the jagged hole now stoppered with metal. "Why would they put it here?" he asked. "Makes no sense."

"Goddamn Euros," the woman said.

"Let me give it a try."

When it was new the car had certainly had style, but now its leather seats were worn to threads, its floormats frayed, its dashboard scratched and dusty, the glove compartment ripped out along with the stereo, and he couldn't see in it much more than rusting metal, ready for the scrapyard. She handed him a mangled paperclip, which he twisted into a large loop and worked down alongside the broken key. "I'll never be able to sell it," she said. "It'll bury me." He was close enough to smell the lavender scent of her hair, her salty cheeks, her smoky, stuttering breath. He was all the way in the car now, knees on the seat. She sniffled beside his ear, a watery, whistling sound. He jiggled the clip and then turned it, hard. The engine revved, the car came to life. He was still capable of something. He wasn't entirely useless yet.

"Christ," the woman said, and let out a raspy sigh. She held the steering wheel in both hands and took several deep breaths, in through the nose, out through the mouth. "Thanks," she said, without looking at him.

He waited for her to say something about the apartment, to apologize for all the things wrong with it. She'd blame the owners of course, the faceless slum lord, but that was better than nothing. Several seconds went by, and she didn't speak. The silence bothered him. Down the street someone had dragged a mattress to the curb, and later, he thought, he'd haul it up to his room, would sleep on it despite any stains or rips or springs poking through the fabric.

He wanted to explain. He wanted her to understand that he didn't belong here, that circumstances had gotten out of his control. He could show her where his wedding ring had been.

He could show her how quickly, how naturally, he could make a perfect knot in a necktie. "This is all new to me," he said.

The manager had recovered her composure. Her eyes were dry now, kinder than before, and he thought maybe he'd judged her too quickly, that she wasn't the hard, heartless person he'd imagined. Her hands were loose on the steering wheel, one finger tapping lightly. "What's this?" she asked.

"I just want you to know – "

"I thought I said no bullshit," she said, but not angrily.

"I used to – "

"Nothing against you," she said. "But I've got enough problems already."

He had a hard time finding the right words, but couldn't stop himself from searching. The truth was, he didn't want to be resourceful. He didn't want to be resilient. He'd made his one big try in life, and it had bombed – now all he wanted was sympathy. "I made people rich," he blurted. His voice broke as the words came out. He nearly choked on the terrible irony his wife had failed or refused to recognize. "People are millionaires because of me."

The woman didn't seem to hear him. She began fixing her ponytail, checking herself in the rearview mirror, glancing at him sideways. "Not that you're awful looking or anything," she said. "God knows I've been with worse." He should have kept his mouth shut. He should have stayed in the apartment where he belonged, surrounded by broken appliances and grimy windows. One of the cooks or dishwashers was shouting again, "Give it back! Give it back, motherfucker, or I'm a kill you!" This time there was nothing playful in the voice, nothing innocent. These weren't the pretend thugs of his old neighborhood but the real thing. The woman pressed down on the clutch and shifted gears. The car rolled forward slowly, and he was only too happy to let her take him away from here, back to the world he knew. He had to close the passenger door to keep it from bumping the trunk of a nearby maple. "But you know," she went on, jerking a thumb behind her, in the direction of the dilapidated house. "Two people with troubles. Bad idea all around."

They passed the mattress and began to pick up speed. The image that came to him was of Nan in their bedroom, waking up late as usual, after hitting the alarm clock's snooze button five or six times. He saw her jumping into the shower without first testing the water, nearly scalding herself and crying out in surprise – though how she could be surprised when she did it so often he'd never understand. Then, in the kitchen, making her morning coffee, grinding it too fine as she always did, putting too much in the basket, wincing at the bitterness, then adding more water directly from the tap. Nothing she did was easy – she created new challenges for herself every moment of her life. It exhausted him to picture her rushing out of the house with her mug, coffee sloshing onto her coat, the car screeching frantically into traffic. He was tired, and had been for as long as he could remember.

They were nearing an intersection, the tree-lined street giving way to the busy avenue where the bus had dropped him off an hour earlier. He could hear the clicking of the turn signal, but from where he hunched he couldn't see which direction she was taking him. He didn't know if he cared. But maybe it was a mistake to let her take him anywhere, to further subject her to his bad fortune. "Stop," he said feebly. "Let me out."

Her face was turned away from him, watching for an opening in the line of speeding cars. "Sometimes it's easier when you've got someone to talk to," she said.

He could have opened the door and walked away but didn't. How could he go back to that stuffy room, that suitcase full of ties? Wherever they were going had to be better. She gunned the engine, and the roar of it sent a ripple of terror through him. "Let me out," he said again, sinking down into the seat.

"Least I can do is buy you a coffee," she said. "It's not every day someone bothers to give a shit, you know?"

LILY. THE NAME didn't fit the brash manner, the strong shoulders visible beneath her thin blouse, muscles cut by the lacy straps of a dark blue bra. Nor did the delicate way she ate her scrambled eggs, scooping a few flakes onto a corner of toast, biting down gingerly with her front teeth. She hadn't taken him far, only circling the block and pulling into the parking lot behind his new house. Not far enough. The diner was small and nearly empty, smelling of burnt coffee and citrus air freshener, their booth sticky. Out the window he could see the row of trash cans, the cardboard crates, and beyond them the tool shed, its back wall covered in graffiti, dozens of overlapping tags in black and white and red spray paint, a tapestry of sorts, oddly beautiful. High above was the streaked glass of his own tiny kitchen window, sparkling in the late morning sunlight.

Lily had gone to the bathroom to wash up, and when she'd come back her ponytail was gone, her hair brushed and framing her face, the gray streak falling over one eye. "I'm a disaster," she said. "I need to pack my eyes in ice."

It may have been true, but she was far more attractive now than she'd been before, a softness about her features brought out by the tears and the sleepy look that had followed them. She let herself slump against the vinyl seat, and a melancholy, ironic smile made her look more vulnerable than he could have imagined possible half an hour before. He drained most of his coffee while she picked at her eggs, telling him about her ex-boyfriend, the owner of a small landscaping company, who'd left her for the roommate of his twenty-six-year-old sister.

"We were together eight years," she said. "We were pretty much married. Better if we had been. I wouldn't have gotten fucked so royally."

He threw her out of the house, she told Ari. He wouldn't let her come get her stereo or her dog. She had kids from a previous marriage, and though she didn't have custody, they came to visit at least once a month – and now they had to sleep on air mattresses in her cramped living room.

"And on top of everything else, that damn car."

She still hadn't apologized for the apartment, hadn't asked how he'd ended up here. "Things'll turn around," he said, recognizing right away how much he sounded like Nan. But unlike Nan, he didn't believe what he said, not for Lily. She wouldn't hit bottom and bounce back. She'd sink down in the muck and stay there. From the sound of things, he suspected she was used to being stuck in it, knee deep. But she didn't need to hear it from him, not when she looked so fragile, so exposed. He could let the truth slide for now. What was the harm in a little encouragement? He gulped the last of the watery coffee and said, "You'll come out okay."

"I had that dog ten years," she said. "Since before I met the fucker." Her voice went phlegmy. Her lips flattened out when she spoke, nearly disappeared altogether. Her eyelids blinked away more tears. She'd raised him from a puppy. A boxer mix, with a little lab, a little chow. His name was Oliver. A big, beautiful dog. Her baby.

"You should get a lawyer," he said. Or a priest, he was tempted to add, but caught himself. He had more pity to spare than he realized, especially now that her hair was down, her lips parted, blouse falling forward to show more of her bra than just the strap. "I know a guy. Or used to. I could give you his card. Just don't mention my name."

The boyfriend had never liked Oliver, she said. The sister's roommate was allergic. For ten years the dog had slept on the bed with Lily, and now he wasn't allowed in the house. They didn't take him for walks, just left him sitting in the backyard. She didn't even know if they were feeding him. For the past two weeks she'd snuck over every day with biscuits to slip him through the fence, and each time Oliver whimpered at her and licked her hand. Her eyes reddened again as she told him how depressed the dog sounded, how lonely, and he was surprised to find pity giving way to the first idle stirrings of desire, picturing her on the king size in his old bedroom, or across the desk of his former office, now leased to an insurance agent. "You can't explain anything to an animal," she said. "That's the worst part. If I could just make him understand, I wouldn't feel so awful."

"At least you get to see him."

"It's killing me. I don't know if I can do it anymore."

"If they don't want him, why not just let you have him?"

"The asshole wants to torture me."

"Then you should just take him," he said, shrugging. At one time outrage had propelled him to action, spurring him to sue a former business partner for copyright infringement, and a contractor for trying to pad a bill with phony expenses. He felt it still, but distantly, thinking here was one more example of how unfair the world was, how unforgiving.

"I'd get arrested," she said.

"But he's yours."

"There's a restraining order." She dropped a crust of toast into the greasy remains of her eggs. "It's a long story."

He leaned away and thought, Hell no. He didn't want her. He should know better. Wanting was what landed him here in the first place. He shrugged again and shook his head. "You could get a new dog."

The waitress tried to refill his cup, but he waved her off and told her to bring the check. He wouldn't let Lily pay, he decided. He didn't want to owe her anything. She was staring at him now, her expression altered, a sheepish little smile on her lips, a startled look of recognition, as if she were seeing him for the first time. Now, finally, she'd ask how someone like him had found his way here, and how he planned to work his way out. But it was too late for that, she'd taken too long. He determined not to tell her a thing.

"It'd be different," she said, tucking her hair behind her ears, once more giving her face that pointed, forceful look, "if I had someone to help me. Then it'd be easy."

For a second he didn't say anything. Then he laughed, a weak, ineffectual sound. "Not a chance."

"Ten years," she said. "Can you imagine how he feels?"

"What about the restraining order?"

"I've got to stay fifty yards away from the house. And from the fucker," she added, her voice going low, bottom lip pulling away from her teeth, two of which overlapped. "And his tart. But that doesn't mean someone else couldn't go get Oliver. I'd keep the car running. You could grab him and we'd be gone before anyone knew the difference."

He turned away. Beyond the window, the tool shed caught his eye again, the scrawl of graffiti muted now that a cloud was passing overhead. The words were indistinguishable, but he could make out individual letters, a bubble "S" in the lower left corner, a "T" with devil horns just below the collapsed roof. And there, where splintered boards leaned against each other, making a little cave, he saw movement, a flash of fur. A rat. The coffee churned inside him. "They'd still come after you," he said. "You'd probably still get arrested."

"I'd hide him a week or two. They couldn't prove anything."

"Hard to hide something so big."

He caught movement again, glowing eyes in that cave on the shed's roof. Too large for a rat's eyes. He watched until he could make out a raccoon's bandit face and breathed easier. A raccoon he could live with. When he turned back her eyes were still locked on him, dry and searching. Her face was less appealing now, no longer pretty in that ragged, defenseless way. Why did some women look so much better when they were crying?

"No one would ever look for him at your place," she said.

"You've got to be kidding," he said, but then she reached out and snatched his wrist. Her grip was firm, but her fingers played lightly over the skin of his inner arm. He didn't try to pull away.

"No one's home right now," she said. "The neighbors never pay attention."

"I've got to unpack," he said. "I've got to get a new shower rod."

"It won't take more than fifteen minutes," she said. The waitress dropped off the check, and Ari avoided her eyes. What did she think of the two of them here together, at eleven in the morning on a weekday, a man badly in need of a shave, a woman who'd obviously been crying? Did she think he'd been beating her? Did she think they belonged together, that they were part of the same world? Lily had a bill out of her purse before he could reach for his wallet. "I've got a crowbar in the trunk," she said, and took his hand again, her fingers rough and chapped, blunter than Nan's, but working the blood under his palm. Her face was close to his, that smoky breath in his nose, those bra straps only inches from him. "Please," she said. "I won't be able to thank you enough."

THIS TIME THE car started right away, with the first turn of the paper clip. She thanked him again as she put it in gear. It was surprising, she said, to find someone who gave a shit about anyone other than himself. Her tennis shoes pumped the clutch and gas, her black hose making a swishing sound as her legs rubbed together. Her skirt had ridden up well above her knees, and she left it there. For his benefit, he supposed. Why did it infuriate him? Because she'd hooked him with so little? Or because he couldn't keep his eyes from drifting to that dark seam between her thighs? Her chapped fingers left the gearshift, tapped his knee, and took their time returning to the steering wheel. "Things'll turn around for you, too," she said. "I can tell."

"Psychic," he said.

"Someone as nice as you, who'd go out of his way–"

"How far is it?"

"Fifteen minutes."

She didn't know the first thing about him. Not where he'd been or where he was going or why. Another word and he was through. He'd tell her to turn around, he'd leave her to her stolen dog, her broken car, her pathetic life.

But Lily kept her mouth shut, and he let her drive.

Battered as it was, the Saab rode smoothly, a pleasant rumble to its engine, a forceful thrust on straightaways. In the worn leather and scratched chrome he could glimpse now a hint of its original class. He understood why Lily would have wanted it – with a little imagination, sitting behind its wheel, you could believe you were on your way up in the world instead of nose-diving down. In her place, he might have bought it, too.

They were heading south, past new strip malls and office parks, over the ridge of Union Knoll, and then east, away from Lenape Lake. Brick-fronted Tudors gave way to modest bungalows and then to sagging ranches. Against his will, Ari pictured his Mendham Colonial again, the hardwood floors, the clawfoot tub, the six-burner stove. For three days now Nan had been living there alone, driving the sporty Acura he'd bought outright. She'd been drinking his single malt, listening to his blues records, looking at his photo of John Lee Hooker.

And this was what bothered him most: knowing that as much as he might want to, he wouldn't be able to just let it all go. It might be noble to slink away with nothing, to make a clean break. But that Scotch stuck in his mind, and those records, and that photograph he'd bought on a business trip to Chicago. Hooker had died almost a year ago, and now Ari was living in an apartment that might have shown up in one of his songs. Nan didn't understand the music, even if she claimed to like it as much as he did. She wouldn't change the needle on the turntable, wouldn't take the pains he did not to scratch the vinyl. She'd go about things in her usual careless way, spilling red wine on the oak floors, leaving sticky splatters on the stove, offering his good whisky to some asshole who didn't know the first thing about Scotch, who couldn't tell the difference between Speyside and Islay. And then one day the cheerfulness would return to her face, a day when he could no longer drive her to anger or tears, when he'd punished her as much as he could. What would he do with himself then?

Lily pulled to the curb and yanked the emergency brake.

The house she pointed to had a low-pitched roof with shingles missing, paint flaking from the siding. Horizontal blinds blocked a picture window, a few slats twisted, a few others broken. "We'd better hurry," she said. "In case anyone's around." "I thought the neighbors didn't care." She didn't answer. She was pulling her hair back into a ponytail, stretching the skin tight over her temples. The lawn was scraggly, spotted with dandelions, sparsely planted with shrubs, in need of watering. "Wait a minute," he said. "This guy owns a landscaping company?" "Ready?" she asked, and this time he was the one not to answer. He didn't move, either. She put a hand on his knee again, and left it there. This was her idea of no bullshit? "I'm not twisting your arm," she said.

"You want backflips?" He tried to laugh, but all he could manage was something high-pitched and nervous, and cut it short.

"Around the left side," she said, moving the hand higher on his leg. "The gate's just past the patio."

The Saab's roof rippled as he closed the door behind him, a bit of duct tape coming loose and falling to the ground. A dog barked once, deep and threatening, not a sound made by something sad and mistreated, he thought, by something named Oliver.

His grandmother's hard times hadn't included chain-link fences and tipped-over lawn sculpture, a stone angel or imp, face down, its back covered in moss and lichen. Her stories were romantic and hopeful and had never failed to move him, had never failed to make him feel the stony pavement under her feet as she scavenged food for her family, or the cold of the wind blowing through her threadbare clothes. She'd spun them whenever Ari complained about running an errand for her, or during her last years, whenever she needed a loan he knew she'd never repay.

Lily handed him a crowbar, along with a leash and a handful of biscuits shaped like bones. He surprised himself by laughing. The shape tickled him. What did a dog care whether a biscuit looked like a bone or a steak or a lampshade?

"If he tries to bite you," Lily said, "just give him a poke with the end of that."

The anguish he'd seen in her face was long gone, along with all his pity. But there was something else that made her desirable now, something he couldn't put his finger on, and again he pictured them together, this time on the torn mattress in his new apartment, the bare bulb swinging overhead. The iron bar was pleasantly heavy in his hand, rust flaking off under his fingers. It wouldn't take much to break the lock, he guessed. He knew how to break things.

The swaggering movement had come back to Lily's shoulders as she scanned the street. "Fuck it," she said, and made a sudden break for the front door. "Hurry," she called behind her. "Before anyone sees us."

"Aren't you supposed to stay in the car?" The dog barked again. Ari stood at the edge of the scorched lawn and peered around the side of the mean little house. The glare of sunlight on the picture window blinded him, a strange intoxication making him giddy.

"Come on," she said.

"Isn't he around back?"

"You've got to let me in here first," she said. "I need the stereo."

"Jesus. What about the restraining order?"

"The fucker," she said. "I'll show him restraint."

He followed her up the concrete path, where tufts of grass stuck up through the cracks, some of them ankle high. Nothing felt better than momentum. It was what he enjoyed most about making a decision, the sudden freedom, the blissful release into whatever current would carry him. The dog let loose now, a steady chorus of angry barking, the metal fence rattling. Ari pictured it hurling itself against the chain links, teeth bared and snarling.

"Friendly puppy," he said.

Lily took back the crowbar and worked the hooked end between the frame and door. The street was empty except for the Saab, a squat, snub-nosed thing, furtive-looking and strangely alive. It was warm enough now to ride with the top down, though he supposed the roof's hydraulics no longer worked, or else Lily would have had it down already. In twenty minutes they could be in Mendham. There they wouldn't need a crowbar. In his suitcase, along with ties and dress shirts, cufflinks and shoe polish, he'd tucked his extra set of keys. He wouldn't have packed them, he decided now, if he'd never intended to go back.

"I want the stove fixed," he said. "And a knob for the closet door."

"I need your help here," Lily said through clenched teeth, pushing at the crowbar, arms straining, eyes squinted, her face looking obstinate, half-crazed, hideous, enticing. "I can't do it on my own."

He grabbed hold of the handle, leaned his weight against it, and listened for the crack of wood, the sound of a new beginning.

West End

I.

THE WOMAN HAD BEEN A FIXTURE OF MY CHILDHOOD. Almost every week I'd seen her limping around Victory Park in Chatwin's West End, with that strangely erect, stately posture that didn't match the way she swung her bad leg out from the hip. Back then she looked impossibly old, her cheeks grooved, hands clawed, veins showing on her pale neck. She kept her hair long and pulled back in a bun, the skin over her temples stretched taut, her broad nose made prominent by the narrow outline of her face.

"Polio," my father said without prompting one Wednesday evening, on our way to Temple Emek Shalom in North Chatwin, where I went to Hebrew school reluctantly, preparing for my bat mitzvah. As usual, we were stuck in traffic around the old town square, a nightmare of crosswalks and one-way streets and turn-only lanes, and the woman passed close enough for me to see how her leg brace buckled to her shoe, how it clamped around her stockinged ankle and rose up beneath the hem of her skirt. A dozen times before I'd been on the verge of asking what was wrong with her, but now that my father had told me, I decided I didn't want to know. The woman turned to me, and before I could look away, smiled with her mouth closed and raised a hand, a cigarette burning between two fingers. "When I was a boy," my father went on, "that was the scariest word in the English language."

Everything about the park scared me then. The creaking

branches of the last surviving elms in the county. The imposing bronze statues of Revolutionary War heroes on horseback. Winos in army surplus jackets gathered around picnic benches, swapping bottles and shouting at passing cars. And on all sides, the dark, sooty buildings that looked as if they might crumble in the mildest breeze.

How can a person change so much in just ten years? In 1995, when I was twenty-two, I saw more mystery and romance than menace in the neighborhood's dilapidation, in the sooty bricks and the huge trees and the statues grizzled with pigeon shit. I'd just graduated from college and was fresh off a month-long trip through southern Europe with a boyfriend I'd once been sure I loved. In Greece and Italy and Spain I'd been intrigued less by ruins than by ancient buildings still in use, houses and apartments inhabited for hundreds of years, stone steps worn down by generations of passing feet. Coming back to the States to see slapdash new construction everywhere was unexpectedly disheartening.

Soon after the trip ended, I packed my few belongings and came home to New Jersey. This wasn't something I'd planned. I'd expected to stay in Boston, where my boyfriend, David Zeitlin, was starting law school, or else move in with friends in Brooklyn. But then my father was diagnosed with colon cancer, and my Brooklyn friends found a place too small for three people, and it turned out I no longer loved David after all. A few days after arriving at my parents' house I found a job as a communications assistant with a marketing agency in downtown Chatwin and rented a studio apartment nearby. I bought myself new clothes at a discount store, slacks and blouses and pencil skirts, things I hadn't worn once in the last four years. I got a new haircut, a short curly bob meant to show off my jawline. I polished my shoes and painted my nails.

The studio was in an old residence hotel of the '30s and '40s, a beautiful neglected building with a brick façade and wide leaded windows looking out on Victory Park. The West End had been Chatwin's cultural center at one time, with a pair of movie theaters, a dozen restaurants and nightclubs, and a small concert hall across from the library. But whatever culture the town had now was a mile south in the Heritage Mall on Route 206. The theater on the southwest corner of the park was boarded up, and the other housed a vacuum cleaner outlet, the marquee advertising sales on Hoover and Eureka. The concert hall was surrounded by a cyclone fence hung with signs announcing its demolition in the fall. The library had been replaced by offices for county transportation and waste management departments.

Still, layers of soot couldn't hide the elegance of the old buildings, some of which dated back to the early nineteenth century. The trees were even older, their trunks straight and sturdy, free of blight, their canopies shading all but the edges of the park. A few specialty boutiques had opened in long-empty storefronts – a wine importer, a dress shop I couldn't afford even to browse in, the salon where I'd gotten my haircut – and three of the nightclubs had been revived as gay bars, their windows decorated with rainbow flags and neon beer signs. At night, slim, gorgeous boys walked hand-in-hand around the square, and even during the week spacey house music drifted up to my apartment until two in the morning.

Most of the other residence hotels had been converted into assisted living facilities, residential drug treatment centers, halfway housing for the mentally ill. A few were used as offices or storage. But even neglected they were gems, with brass front doors, tiled and mirrored entryways, pillared porticos, elevators with heavy wrought iron grates. Their elegant names were printed in script on their fluttering awnings: The Gentry, The Knight's Arms, The Lincoln.

My apartment was in The Victory Manor. The expansiveness of the name partly made up for the narrow studio with its tiny kitchen, for the closet that accommodated only half my clothes, leaving the rest to sit in milk crates beneath the window. The bed took up most of the space in the room. It was on tracks, and at one time had rolled away into the wall, but the wheels had long since rusted in place. The evening I moved in I ate my dinner on it, propped up by pillows, looking down on the park and the traffic around the square, sparser now that the state had built a bypass connecting Route 206 with the interstate. The winos had spread themselves to all four corners, begging change from cars stopped at traffic lights. A pair of slim boys in tight jeans strolled to one of the clubs. A Vietnamese man lined his arms with birdseed and stood Christ-like beneath one of the statues, giggling as pigeons swarmed him.

And there was the old woman crippled by polio, lurching along with a knitted grocery bag dangling from one arm, somehow managing to keep her back straight, her head lifted high. She hadn't aged, or else my own transformation over these ten years had made her aging insignificant. I wondered how I could have been afraid of her, how I could have failed first to pity her. But now I thought she didn't deserve pity, either. She carried herself so easily, with such pride, despite her brace and the awkward way she had to throw her damaged leg forward with every step.

I watched her skirt the park and cross the street. Then she slipped out of view. To follow her I left the bed and my dinner and went to the window, guessing that she was heading to one of the assisted living facilities, or maybe one of the halfway houses. But by the time I got there she was gone. It made me uneasy to think that she'd just disappeared, or that I'd dreamed her there, an image conjured from childhood.

But then I spotted her again, just below, sprawled face down on the sidewalk. I hesitated just a second before running out of the apartment and down the stairs, disturbed to think that something so drastic could have happened while I was looking in the wrong direction. The woman hadn't moved by the time I made it to the street. Her head was turned in a way that seemed unnatural, one of her arms caught beneath her body. I thought she was unconscious and was ready to run for a payphone, but then her good leg stretched out, foot scraping at the gutter. "Are you hurt?" I asked, crouching beside her, feeling foolish as soon as the words left my mouth. I tried to make up for them by putting a hand on her back. "Should I call an ambulance?"

"Lift my shoulder," she said, not sounding hurt at all. Her voice was whispery and musical, with a trace of European accent overlaid with a thick New Jersey one. I did what she asked, and she freed her arm and then, with surprising strength, pushed herself up to her knees. I tried to help her to her feet, but she slapped my hand away. "I didn't fall," she said, giving me a startling, accusatory look, and then brushed off the front of her blouse and skirt. "I dropped something and bent down to pick it up."

What could I say to this? I only nodded, and to cover my confusion, retrieved her bag, which had slid a few feet away. Through the loose knit I could see that all she carried were three packs of Newport Slims. Across the street, one of the drunks, a sunburned vet with pencil-line mustache and long white braid, called out, "Hey, beautiful ladies, how 'bout one of you spare me a dollar for a cup a coffee?" Behind him the Vietnamese man was a live, squirming statue, only his laughing face visible through a screen of feathers and beaks.

"Let me at least walk you home," I said, handing over the bag, which the woman scrutinized, making sure nothing was missing.

"I've never had any trouble walking," she said, and without another word hurried past me, moving quickly despite that difficult gait, strangely mechanical, like some battered robot in a science fiction movie. The wino had crossed the street and now circled me, explaining why he needed a dollar, not for coffee anymore, but to catch a bus to see his ailing mother. She had kidney problems and then heart problems. And then it wasn't his mother but his sister and finally his aunt. The only way I could get him to let me go was to promise to toss down a dollar from my window. And when he moved out of my way, I saw the old woman duck under the awning of The Victory Manor.

Why should I have been so surprised? Why did it trouble me so much to discover that she and I had ended up in the same place? I can understand now, at least in part: She'd interrupted the fantasy I'd been indulging, sitting on my bed, recalling photographs I'd seen of my paternal grandmother before her marriage, when she lived in a studio of her own in Manhattan and worked in a secretary pool, when she spent her evenings in dance halls and wore sleek dresses and had perfect hair, her arm around different young men in each picture, her eyes sly and expectant. I'd been working up a pleasant image of myself taking her place in those photos, but now another image, unasked for, complicated that one. I didn't want to think about a crippled old woman living alone in a tiny room. By the time I made it upstairs I was filled with pity, mostly for myself, the apartment even smaller than I remembered, the immovable roll-out bed with my plate of vegetables and rice in its center more drab, the window grimier. Without looking to see if anyone was waiting below, I held a dollar over the sill and let the breeze carry it down.

2.

MY PARENTS' HOUSE was in one of the quiet residential neighborhoods just south of Heritage Mall, a mile from the West End, and I'd grown up listening to my father complain about traffic around the park and about how the boarded-up theater was an eyesore and should have been razed. If I wanted to come back to New Jersey, my parents asked, why not live at home, where I could save money and eat decent meals? I was a grown-up, I could come and go as I pleased, so long as I kept my room clean and helped with the dishes, and maybe, once in a while, did the grocery shopping. Or if I didn't want to hang around with old folks all the time, why not find a roommate to share a bigger place? Weren't any of my high school friends still around?

Weren't there lovely garden apartments just around the corner from the mall?

I didn't tell them that I hadn't been in touch with a single high school friend since I'd left for college. I didn't tell them I'd never liked my high school friends much anyway, that friendships then were based on convenience. I didn't tell them coming back to Chatwin had nothing to do with wanting, that these were the cards I'd been dealt and that I was trying to accept them with dignity. What I did say was that I liked the apartment because I could walk to work and to the train station. I planned to spend my weekends with friends in the city, I told them, and this was more convenient than having to drive downtown and pay for parking.

"And your car?" my mother asked the evening after I signed a six-month lease, a week before my father's surgery. She stood at the living room window, staring out at the twenty-year-old Nova I'd bought my junior year of high school, filthy now, with a jagged crack across the windshield. I was stretched out on the couch behind her, with my feet up on one arm, partly to be comfortable and partly because I knew it was harder for her to fight with me when I was lying down. "You're just going to leave it in our driveway?"

"I can put it on the street if you want."

"So all the neighbors have to look at it, too."

"Fine," I said. "I'll keep it by the park."

"And have it broken into in five minutes flat," my mother said. "It can stay in the driveway. It's just a car. It's not a big deal." She shrugged and gave a dismissive wave, as if I were the one who'd brought up the issue of the car in the first place. "What I really don't understand is why you'd want to live in some slum."

"It's not a slum," I said. "It's working class."

"Sure," my mother said. "Those bums in the park, they work pretty hard."

"So don't visit," I said. "Forget I'm even there."

As was her way, my mother suddenly looked wounded,

her eyes watering and nose going red. She turned away and said, "You can at least come over and have dinner once in a while. You don't have to be a complete stranger."

And as was my way, I was suddenly contrite, my defensiveness gone, my tone forgiving. "Of course," I said, sitting up. "That's why I'm here. I want to help. If Dad needs anything—"

"Who says I need anything?" my father said. Until now he'd kept quiet, sitting on his favorite armchair, reading the paper. His feet were propped on an ottoman piled with old phone books, his body twisted to take pressure off his right side. He'd lost fifteen pounds in the last three months, and his torso, once robust, looked deflated. "You don't have to come back here for my sake. No need to turn your whole life upside down for a little—" He gestured at his belly and clucked his tongue. "A little trouble in the pipes."

"He calls three tumors little," my mother said.

"Only one's a tumor," my father said. "The other two are polyps."

"Splitting hairs," my mother said.

"I'm just saying, she doesn't need to give up her whole life, her nice boyfriend and everything—"

"I was sure you and David would end up getting married," my mother said. "He'll make such a good lawyer."

"You should go back up there to Boston," my father said. "This little—" He waved at his guts again. "This'll be finished in no time. And then you and David can come down to visit—"

"All this coming and going," my mother said. "Did you hear about Iris's Todd? You know, my cousin Iris? Her son and his wife, they're breaking up. You and David. Todd and Jody. Why can't everyone get along, like your father and me?"

"Not everyone's got infinite patience like I do," my father said.

"I just don't understand it. You and David looked so good together. And Todd and Jody, they've got two kids. How can they split up? Almost ten years they've been married. Divorce, tumors. What's happening to us?" She came to the couch, threw her arms around my neck, and sobbed. "Oh, Amy. I'm so glad you're home. I don't know how I'd do this by myself."

"She cries all day," my father said, grinning to keep himself from falling apart. "I'm the one who's got to go under the knife and get poison injected into my veins. You think I'm happy about it?"

"Live in whatever slum you want," my mother said. "As long as you're nearby, I don't care. I'm just so glad you're here."

3.

FALLING OUT OF love with David Zeitlin must have happened gradually, over the course of the spring, or maybe over the course of the past year. Realizing it, though, came as such a shock that it took me two weeks between deciding I couldn't possibly spend another night in his arms and gathering up the courage to do something about it.

We'd been together since halfway through sophomore year, and in hindsight I can see that I'd already begun drifting away from him by the time we left for Europe. As we made our way through Greece and Italy and Spain, he wanted to play tour guide, taking me to sights he'd read about in a budget travel book. But I'd been a classics major and had made my own itinerary, culled from a Mediterranean archaeology class I'd taken the previous semester. He was hopeless at reading maps, had no sense of direction, and embarrassed me by asking questions of locals in slowed-down, too-loud English. He was squeamish about exotic foods, eating only the dishes he'd eaten in the States: gyros, pizza, paella.

I was too distracted to enjoy the ruins I'd studied, too impatient to test out my Greek and Italian and limited Spanish. We stayed in hostels and bunkhouses, and any sex we had was discreet and unsatisfying, or, on occasion, drunken and mortifying. At first I located this as the source of my frustration, compounded by David's not seeming to mind. When I suggested we get a hotel room, to give ourselves a night alone together, he shrugged and said it was too expensive. He liked those scruffy Australians we met everywhere we went, who often provoked him into drinking contests from which he'd emerge miserably hungover, unable to eat for a day and a half. On our first visit to the Acropolis, he puked into an overflowing trash can and had to lie down on the steps of the Parthenon, arms covering his eyes. In Barcelona he insisted on calling Gaudí "Gaudy" and Park Güell "Park Gruel," even after I corrected him a dozen times. After the first week of traveling I was exhausted, craving quiet and solitude. I told myself I was growing up.

Whatever had once made me love David – his melodic laughter, his confident tenderness, his unwavering loyalty – had begun to submerge beneath the rising waters of my impatience. The problem, though, was that I'd never stopped being attracted to his curly hair, gone bushy during our month away, to his dark eyes and wide chin and firm lips. I'd never stopped liking his lanky body, his gentle touch, his sweet, loamy smell. I couldn't imagine not feeling his skin against mine at night or tasting his salty breath in the morning. Like my mother, I'd sometimes allowed myself to play over the idea of marriage, most likely after David finished law school and got a job and started paying off his loans, though while planning our trip I'd secretly imagined him proposing in a quaint Italian village or on a misty trail in the Pyrenees. The prospect was simple and comforting, a solid plan I could hang my life on, and considering I had no other plan to replace it – I had vague expectations of going back to school one day and becoming a scholar of Latin poetry – the fantasy was one I let myself indulge more frequently the closer we came to graduation.

And even after I knew it would never come to life, the fantasy stuck with me. To let go of it was frightening – not because I didn't think I'd be okay on my own, that I wasn't capable of taking care of myself, but because I knew I *would* be okay, that I was more capable than I sometimes wanted to be. I'd been working since I was twelve, when I started babysitting for two families down the street, and by the time I got my license I'd saved up enough money to buy the Nova. Though my parents said I shouldn't have to have a job while I was in college, I got one anyway, shelving books at the university's library, paying my own rent after I moved out of the dorm. Independence came easily to me. Too easily, I sometimes thought, worried that I'd never be able to let go of myself enough to be content with another person, to have the sort of crucial, if neurotic, relationship my parents had, the kind I figured was necessary for long-term happiness, or at least long-term stability.

Now it seems ridiculous to think of myself at twenty-two, fearing I might end up alone, believing that David – whose idea of romance included sex on a bunkbed with a drunken Australian snoring beneath us – might be my one chance at a normal life. But I did believe it, and even though by the time we made it home from Europe I knew we were finished, I could hardly admit it to myself, much less to him. For two weeks I lay in his arms every night, breathing in his smell, playing my fingers over his hairy knuckles, feeling his sweaty middle against my back. I went through the motions of intimacy, giving kisses I hoped were passionate enough, speaking words I didn't mean. I had just over two weeks left on the lease of my old apartment, and then I was supposed to move into David's. My roommates had already moved out. David kept pressing me to start packing, but I put it off as long as possible, feigning laziness he should have seen through. When had I ever been lazy before? But being lazy himself, he didn't question it, trying instead to motivate me the way I'd often tried to motivate him, pushing gently against my reluctance with affectionate words and gestures, trying to seduce me into doing what he wanted, and finally offering to do it himself.

If anything, I should have been worried about David, who couldn't take care of himself at all. In four years he hadn't scored lower than an A- in a single class, but there was little he knew how to do besides writing papers and studying for tests. He didn't know how to cook anything that couldn't be micro-waved and would have lived in squalor if I didn't occasionally clean his bathroom and kitchen. After he'd overdrawn his bank account four months in a row, I started balancing his check-book. I mailed in his law school applications and registered him for the LSAT. In general, he was a cheerful mess, and without me I was sure he'd quickly fall to pieces.

But while I did suffer plenty of guilt during those two weeks, imagining the disaster of David's life after I'd left him, there were moments when the knowledge I carried gave me a certain pleasure, a sense of power and volition that excited me. As David kissed me, as he moved on top of me, as he spoke to me in his breathy, post-coital voice about his summer internship, or about the classes he was registering for in the fall, or about the trip we were supposed to take to his parents' timeshare in the Berkshires, I played over the words I would tell him when I was ready, and then the words of comfort I'd offer afterward, the consoling touch, the final acts of caring and passion and intimacy, all of it terribly hard and sad and gratifying. The secret made me giddy and lighthearted, and during those two weeks I enjoyed David's company more than I had since our first days together. I didn't mind watching the silly comedies we'd watched twenty times before – David reciting lines along with Gene Wilder and Leslie Nielsen – didn't mind eating the steak he microwaved to leather, didn't mind the mess he left in the sink. We looked through our photos from Europe, and when he said, "Don't you miss that crazy Gaudy?" I laughed. When he ran a finger down my neck and along my collarbone, I even wondered, briefly, if I were making a mistake, if in breaking up with David I would be closing off an important part of myself, the part that liked to joke around and drink wine and be taken to bed and not have to think beyond the moment I was in.

But then the two weeks were up, along with my lease. I packed what I wanted to keep and hauled the rest out to the curb to let the neighbors pick through. David borrowed a friend's pickup and carried the heavier items – my records, the vintage stereo I'd inherited from a great-uncle, the files stuffed with four years of hand-outs and exams and essays scrawled on by my favorite professors – up the three flights to his place. I watched him with a strange curiosity, thinking I could make him do anything, that my power over him was boundless. I knew how awful I was, letting him struggle up the stairs, sweating and breathing hard, but for the moment I reveled in my awfulness, and only after we'd finished and he'd returned the truck did I finally feel ready – that is, brave enough – to say the words I'd been rehearsing for two weeks.

In a certain way, the timing was perfect. Here we were in his already messy living room, now jammed up with my boxes and crates and bags of clothes. It was late afternoon, and we were sweaty and hadn't eaten since breakfast. On the spot, I decided this would be a test, and within seconds David failed. Rather than help me tidy or order take-out, he grabbed a stale box of chocolate chip cookies from the kitchen, popped a tape in the VCR, and flopped on the couch. I pretended to rummage through my boxes, looking for things to put away, and kept an eye on him. Here was everything that drove me crazy – his idleness, his childish habits, his complete obliviousness to my needs. If my leaving him came as a surprise, that was his problem, I thought, not mine. He bounced a heel on the edge of the couch and said, "Leave it, babe. We've done enough for one day."

Now or never, I thought, and believed it. That was how crucial every decision seemed to me at the time, how momentous. I took a good look at David's innocent, oblivious face, at his long eyelashes, his broad shoulders, those strong, gentle hands, and reassured myself they were things I could do without. I opened my mouth to speak. But what came out wasn't what I'd planned. Instead I told him I needed to make some phone calls, that I'd join him in a minute. I closed myself in the bedroom and dialed my old roommates, Debbie and Hope, who were staying with friends while they looked for a new apartment. I thought I'd just check in with them, to find out how the search was going, and ask, casually, if they'd seen any places with space for a third. But when Debbie answered she said they'd already found a place, an adorable two-bedroom in Boerum Hill, a block from the Pacific Street station. "We miss you already," she said, and Hope, who'd slept with a dozen men during the year we'd lived together but had never in her life, as far as I knew, had a relationship that lasted more than a few weeks, asked, "So? How's the shacking up? You and the hubby getting along?" I congratulated them on the new apartment and told them I couldn't wait to visit. Then I called home, thinking, desperately, that my mother might offer some unexpected bit of wisdom. But when she heard my voice, she cried, "Oh, Amy, where have you been? I've been trying you all morning. I've got terrible news."

Punishment. That was my first thought. I was being punished for the last two weeks, for my heartless insincerity, for my selfishness. I ran into the living room, threw myself on David, told him what had happened, and told him I'd have to leave. "Of course," he said. "I'll come with you." In a voice partly hysterical, partly calculated, I explained that I wasn't talking about a visit. What I meant was that I was moving out the same day I'd moved in, that I'd stay in New Jersey until my father was well. David was cautiously sympathetic, tentatively comforting, competing impulses bringing a lovely, vulnerable confusion to his sensitive features. "You're coming back, right?" he asked.

"I can't think about details right now," I said. "I just know I've got to be with them, and whatever happens –" Only now did the full impact of my mother's news hit me, along with a sudden flash of images – funeral service, headstone, my mother alone in the house – and I started crying. Or maybe I'd wanted to cry first and forced the images, which still seemed unreal, far from actual possibility. I couldn't stop believing that I'd brought this on myself, even as I grew ashamed for thinking that my father's cancer could have anything to do with me, for imagining myself to be so important, the center of the universe. To David I said, "Everything else'll just have to wait."

"Yeah, sure," he said, doubtfully, reaching for the remote and switching off the VCR. "The details." He glanced down at his lap. "They can wait. I'll help you load your car."

Once again I wondered if I was making a mistake, if the irritation I'd felt these past months weren't about David at all, but rather a symptom of other anxieties, a premonition of trouble brewing in my life making me lash out in anticipation. On the sidewalk beside the overstuffed Nova that fit only my clothes and kitchen supplies, he said he'd send me anything else I needed, that I shouldn't hesitate to ask. His dark eyes were even sexier with tears in them, his lips even more tender than usual when I kissed them. I was on the verge of changing my mind, of promising that I'd be back as soon as possible. But then his face hardened, arms crossing over his belly, as if he expected me to slug him. His look was one of pain and regret and determined self-protection, not so different than the one he wore after a long night of drinking with Australians twice his size. "Don't worry about me," he said. "I'll be fine."

4.

MY FIRST NIGHTS in The Victory Manor I hardly slept. It was too warm for blankets or even sheets, too warm to close the window. Noise rose up from the street, loud cars passing, people laughing and shouting, bass thumping in the nearest of the clubs. I'd been used to sleeping nude, but here even with the curtains closed I felt exposed to the world. I wore a T-shirt that got wound around me in my restless flopping and then took it off, growing immediately self-conscious in a way I never had in front of David, even though he'd made sure to tell me whenever he thought my thighs were getting the slightest bit thick or my belly anything more than flat. It struck me that I no longer knew how to sleep alone anymore, and I worried there were other things I could no longer do, either, that my independence had begun to falter. The previous year my father had filed my taxes for me, and for Hanukkah my mother had bought me underwear I badly needed. A month before I'd graduated I'd nearly lost my job in the library when my supervisor caught me standing in the stacks, reading, my full cart idle beside me. Two and a half years with David, and now I was on the verge of being helpless, and the longer I lay awake the more I berated myself for letting down my guard.

It didn't help that my upstairs neighbor stayed up late most nights, running an electric sewing machine. The thrumming came down through the ceiling as electronic beats rose up from the street, and even if I exhausted myself with criticism and abuse, pacing naked around the bed and back, I was still kept up for hours. I pictured a seamstress from turn-of-the-century photographs, a sad-faced woman in a Lower East Side tenement, taking in mending jobs for extra money after working long hours at a tailor's shop. I didn't know if there were seamstresses anymore, but if there was anyplace one would live, this was it. I was too shy to go up and ask her to stop working, me who could no longer do anything for myself. Who was I to tell someone she shouldn't make a living?

Most nights I finally curled up on one side of the mattress, hugging a pillow to myself lengthwise to simulate another body, and either waited until I drifted off or until sunlight began to filter through the shades and my alarm threatened to sound. A few times, though, I put on clothes and went back out into the world at midnight, one, two, walking around the square and peeking into the boy bars, at bodies gathered around tables or on the dance floor, at sweaty arms and gleaming smiles and hungry eyes, and felt a longing so powerful and pure I almost went inside and threw myself at men who had no interest in me, hoping they'd take pity and give me a few minutes of attention. After a while I'd cut back through the park, which the drunks policed at night, keeping it safe enough for young women and slim gay boys to walk through at any hour. I handed off change to some and once impulsively took a sip from a proffered bottle. The liquid that was supposed to be wine was tangy and sour and burning, and I was sure I'd been tricked into drinking poison. I rushed home to gag myself. By the time I made it to the apartment and knew the wine wasn't killing me, I thought instead about disease, how stupid I was to let my lips touch something that had touched the lips of men who hadn't bathed for weeks. I spent the next twenty minutes scrubbing my face.

Another night, when I came back inside, there in the lobby, sitting on one of two threadbare wingbacks flanking the elevator, was the old woman, the polio victim. Her grocery bag was folded in her lap. The leg with the brace was tucked under the chair, and sitting, she looked perfectly normal, or better than normal for someone her age – there was that stateliness in her posture, the elegance in her tightly bunned hair, her alert eyes, her long pale neck. What she was doing up so late I couldn't imagine. As I pressed the elevator's call button, she smiled at me with her mouth closed and pulled herself up from the chair. If she remembered me from the street, she didn't acknowledge it, though there was something furtive about her expression, as if we shared a secret. "A lovely evening," she said, and then I understood why she didn't show her teeth when she smiled – there was a gap between the front two, and their exposed edges were stained a dark brown. She introduced herself: Elizabeth Elkin. I gave my name in turn, and she said, "Miss Markowitz. A pleasure." Her whispery voice was playful, the accent more European tonight than New Jersey. She asked how long I'd lived in the building, and when I told her she laughed. "So many come and go," she said. "I've met hundreds of Miss Markowitzes in my time."

She'd been here forty-three years, she said as the elevator arrived. I opened the heavy door and pulled aside the grate to let her in. Miss Elkin – I couldn't think of her as Elizabeth – pressed the button for the fifth floor, one above mine. The seamstress, I thought, and again felt ashamed for having let the noise bother me. What else would an old crippled woman do to make ends meet? "I do remember another Miss Markowitz," she said. "Or perhaps it was Horowitz. Oh, it was years ago now. She was a bit shorter than you, very petite, but with a sweet smile like yours. She lived in the apartment next to mine, and I'd have her in for tea some evenings. Not for long, of course. They never last long. But she was a lovely girl, very personable." The mustiness of the elevator was cut by the smell of menthol and face powder.

We reached my floor, and I said goodnight. Miss Elkin cleared her throat, shifted weight off her bad leg, smiled. She wanted something from me, but I couldn't imagine what. The thought made me defensive, afraid of being taken advantage of. "Miss Markowitz," the old woman said. "Would you mind?" She raised her eyes to the ceiling. I only stared back. "I have trouble," she said. "With the door."

My shame deepened, a flash of heat. "Of course," I said. "I'd be glad to."

"I managed to get myself stuck once, a number of years ago," she said as we rose another floor. "Since then I've decided it's best not to go up alone." She thanked me with a graceful handshake when the car stopped, her palm moist and surprisingly soft, her grip solid. I held the door open for her, and she limped only a few steps before stopping to reach into her bag and pull out a cigarette. "A terrible habit, I know," she said. "But it's hard when you've got no one but yourself to scold you. Good night, Miss Markowitz."

This time the pity I felt really was for her. There was no comparison with my grandmother, who, after her brief independent stint in the city, had four children and died within a year of her husband of five decades. I stood in the door of the elevator, watching her limp away, close to tears. I was so tired. Miss Elkin went past the door I'd expected her to enter, the one to the apartment above mine. She kept going to the end of the hall, the last door before the fire escape.

A seamstress? Where had I gotten that idea? I wondered about it for only a second before moving on to the more important question: If it hadn't been her, who'd kept me awake all these nights? I was suddenly furious, glad I hadn't shed any tears, which would have been shameful, too, a way to make myself feel better. After Miss Elkin closed her door I stormed out of the elevator and pounded on the one behind which the sewing machine was drumming. Instead of some sad-eyed woman in a shawl, a skinny boy opened the door, short and groomed and gay. For a second I was confused, and I stammered, less angry than I wanted to sound, "You're ... you're the one who's always sewing?"

The boy, maybe twenty-three or twenty-four, smiled and glanced over his shoulder. "I'm opening a boutique," he said. "Where the liquor store used to be."

He hadn't realized someone had moved in downstairs. The apartment had been empty for almost a year, and before that had been occupied by an old man too deaf to be bothered by the noise. He promised not to run the machine past ten anymore. "It's nice to meet a new neighbor," he said, and shook my hand. "The store opens next month. You should stop by and check out our stuff. Just men's clothes," he said, tugging at the collar of his tight satin shirt, then gesturing at his trousers, which hugged his hips and flared at the cuffs, "but maybe you can find some-thing for your boyfriend."

David in satin and bell bottoms. I couldn't keep from crack-ing a smile, and the boy, who introduced himself as James, invited me in for a drink. Inside his apartment, I couldn't believe I was still in the same building. One floor above mine, and here there were no signs of age and decay. The walls were freshly painted, the wood of the windowpanes and built-in shelves polished, the window itself spotless. The bed was tucked away in the wall, making the room seem spacious and open, even a little grand, despite the sewing table, bolts fabric, and racks of clothes blocking the way to the kitchen. On a rolled-arm sofa beneath the window lay another boy, shirtless, reading a magazine. He wasn't pudgy, exactly, but soft, with the whitest skin I'd ever seen, and a strikingly handsome face, the kind advertisers love – broad forehead, ridged brow, big eyes, pouty lips, cleft chin. In the middle of his chest a dark patch of wiry hair looked strangely lewd. He didn't glance up from the magazine when I came in, but said, turning a page, "Listen to this: stretches of unbroken beaches, open-air restaurants, a vibrant outdoor market. Hire a fishing boat and have your catch grilled for you. Lobster, squid, snapper, crab. Anything you want. I think we should go."

"This is our neighbor," James said, skirting the sewing table and then clinking glasses in the kitchen. "Say hello. Learn some social skills already."

The boy on the sofa brought the magazine closer to his face. "He always brings someone in just when I'm ready to go to sleep."

"No one ever taught Stephen to be polite," James called. "I think he was raised by gorillas."

"It's late," I said. "I should go."

"No, no," Stephen said, flinging the magazine to the floor. "If you go now he'll blame me for running you off. I'll never hear the end of it. Stay and have your drink."

James handed me a glass and went to the nearest clothes rack, shuffling through the hangers. He was about my size, with delicate hands and wrists, and if not for my hips we might have been able to share a wardrobe. He had a slightly beaky face and hooded eyes, and his smile was crooked as he held up a shirt, a collarless oxford with French cuffs and a silver sheen. "What do you think?"

"It's beautiful," I said, and took a sip of the drink, which set me coughing. It was mostly vodka, with a dash of cranberry.

"What he wants to know is would you buy it," Stephen said. "Would you pay an outrageous price for something you could get for five bucks at the nearest thrift store."

"Don't you think your boyfriend would love it?" James said.

I answered with a mournfulness that was only partly feigned, "I don't think I have a boyfriend."

"What's there to think about?" Stephen asked, sourly, but then sat up and leaned forward, clearly eager to hear more. There was a little smile on one side of his sleepy face, sarcastic, maybe, or possibly even sympathetic. "You either do or you don't."

"Haven't you heard of something called ambiguity?" James said.

"Not when it comes to whether or not you have a boyfriend."

"He wants everything to be black and white. Gay, straight. Happy, sad. Love, hate. No middle ground. He can't stand messiness."

"I don't blame him," I said, and without thinking took a seat on the floor and started talking. No one had heard the whole story yet. I'd told my parents that David and I had broken up for good, that it had been a mutual decision. I'd told Debbie and Hope that we were taking a break for the summer, hinting that it had been David's idea. But now I spilled it all, how I'd chickened out when I'd had the chance to end things, how I'd used my father's illness as an excuse to get away. I even admitted that I didn't answer my phone when I thought David might be calling, instead calling back when I knew he wouldn't be home, leaving sweet messages on his answering machine, stringing him along. Stephen listened attentively, nodding or shaking his head, and I found myself having to turn away from his beautiful face and naked chest, that inappropriate patch of hair in its center. James went back to his sewing table, threading seams and occasionally stopping to make comments like, "You shouldn't be so hard on yourself," or "I would have done the same thing."

When I finished, I said, "I'm horrible."

"You are," Stephen said, delighted.

"Don't listen to him," James said.

"I know I am. I have to stop calling him."

"You've got to be in truth," Stephen said.

"What does that even mean?" James said. "Be in truth."

"Just what it sounds like. Quit lying."

"Why don't you just say 'tell the truth' then."

"It's bigger than that. It's a state of being. A state of being in truth."

"You're so full of shit," James said.

"Fine," Stephen said. "Wait till I tell you I've got to go take care of my dying grandmother and never come back. Then we'll see how full of shit I am."

"God," I said. "I'm awful."

"You are," Stephen said.

"Ignore him," James said.

"Don't get me wrong," Stephen said, lying back on the sofa again, hands under his head. "I'm not judging you or anything. Or maybe I am. But you seem pretty cool anyway. We should all hang out more when I'm not so tired I want to puke."

When I finally went back to my room it was nearly dawn. The air was stuffy and still. I tore off my clothes. From outside came the first sounds of morning traffic, and from above the thrum of the sewing machine, a cruel, irregular beat.

5.

COMMUNICATIONS ASSISTANT WAS a glorified title for my job, which consisted mostly of stuffing envelopes with brochures and letters, running them through the postage meter, and walking them the two blocks to the nearest mailbox. I was probably lucky to find any job at all, given my limited experience and impractical degree, but at the time I quickly felt belittled and underappreciated, my talents wasted. The truth is, I was hardly qualified even for this – I wasn't used to being on my feet all day, or concentrating energy for so long on a single task, and without a full night's sleep since starting the job, I often found myself drifting off as I had while shelving books in the library, mind wandering, only to snap back ten, twenty minutes later, a brochure in one hand, an envelope in the other. But in the library I'd never worked more than four hours at a time, and there I had books to distract me. Here I had only a glass wall to stare at, separating a hallway from the agency's conference room, where I had my stacks of papers spread across the long seminar table. The glass was soundproof, installed so the design team could listen to audio tracks without disturbing the rest of the agency. All day I watched designers, writers, account managers pass in front of the window, carrying on conversations I couldn't hear. Occasionally one of them peered in at me, as if I were some exotic animal that had taken up residence where it didn't belong. I had an impulse to dance like a chimp, clawing at my armpits, but mostly I kept my head down, pretending the glass was a two-way mirror.

The agency, Immediate Marketing, Inc., was run by two sisters who broke into shouting matches at least once a week. Anna Pannepinto was the younger by five years, but she was also the company's founder, President, and C E O. She was in her mid-thirties, a fitness nut who spent two hours in the gym every morning before coming to work. Her hair was bleached, and she wore contact lenses tinted a deep, sparkling blue that didn't match the color of any eyes I'd ever seen. Her suits were flashy and revealing, jackets tight around her slim waist, blouses cut low, skirts short enough to show off most of her muscled legs. She came rushing in and out of her office all day, calling for meetings when there was nothing to meet about, bringing decorators in to arrange her artwork and dozens of houseplants. Every day she had a new idea for expanding the business, and whenever she talked profits those blue lenses grew brighter, more alien, her fingers fiddling with a cross around her neck every time she named a figure.

Maxine Valva's title was Managing Director and Chief Financial Officer, but her primary function seemed to be keeping her younger sister's manic energy from sinking the company. At least once a week she stormed into Anna's office with an expense sheet, slammed the door closed behind her, and lectured about responsible management and sustainable growth, her voice husky, masculine, always louder than it needed to be. In response Anna called Maxine names and accused her of jealousy. She'd always hogged their mother's attention, she'd never wanted Anna to have anything of her own. Maxine said that Anna was spoiled, that the only reason she'd had any success was because she flashed her tits to the whole world. If I were on my way down the hall, taking a load of mailers to the postage meter, I'd catch every word as clearly as if they were standing toe to toe in front of me. Everyone else went on working, utterly deaf to the crescendo of hysterical voices.

Eventually Anna would threaten to fire Maxine, and Maxine would quit on the spot. Then she'd storm back to her office, grab her purse and pictures of her family – unlike Anna, who talked about dates with AT&T executives and ex-boyfriends in Brazil and Germany, Maxine was married and had two kids – and head for the door, where Anna always stopped her, blubbering apologies, begging her to stay. Anna would promise to drop her newest pet project, to stay focused on the agency's core services. After crying for hours she'd take out her contacts, and then her face was as drab as Maxine's, though gaunter, gray irises swimming in red. A few days later the project would be on the books again, and the fight started over, with the same recriminations and insults, neither seeming to remember that they'd been through the whole act a dozen times before.

Hiring me was the result of one of Anna's whims, a project Maxine had lobbied against and quit over more than once. Without consulting her, Anna had begun to offer conference promotion services to bring in high-paying clients. A tech firm in the city hired her to drum up registration for a meeting on the future of outsourcing, and a Montreal fiber optics company turned over promotion materials for its annual convention to her. To keep Maxine from leaving, Anna was doing the project management and production herself. She brought me on to do the grunt work, paying me so little my wages would hardly affect the bottom line.

Still, Maxine wasn't happy about it, and she didn't hide her hostility. She hardly ever spoke to me, but whenever she passed in front of the conference room window, she stopped and peered in, always managing to catch me when I was daydreaming, staring off into space. She was short and stout and dark-haired, her clothes drab, bordering on frumpy, the skin around her mouth and eyes prematurely creased, though not from smiling. The only feature she shared with Anna was her perfectly shaped nose, slimmer than mine and evenly proportioned.

Because everyone else in the office was afraid of Maxine – and afraid, too, of the agency folding if one of Anna's whims went sour – they kept their distance from me. I'd exchange a few words with the designers at the coffeemaker every morning, and with the account managers at the water cooler during the day, but at lunchtime they all headed off without me. Not once did I get an invitation to join them for happy hour, though I'd hear them talking about stopping at The Killarney on the way home, the yuppie gathering place on the roof of Heritage Mall. There were good-looking young men among them, single as far as I could tell, but none bothered to flirt with me. I was used to getting attention from men, even when I'd been with David, but now I was invisible, despite my new clothes and haircut. It was part of my punishment, I decided, another form of penance – a thought far more consoling than believing no one was attracted to me.

For lunch I picked up a plastic tub of salad from a deli a few doors down from The Victory Manor, and then sat on a bench in the park, trying to read Catullus. I'd always felt I was getting away with something when assigned to read his erotic poems for class, living a dirty secret out in the open. But now, only a month past graduation, my proficiency with Latin was fading, and struggling through unfamiliar words was too much work to be titillating. The passion I'd developed for the great poets seemed a part of someone else's experience, something I'd read about or heard on a tour of Rome, while David shuffled along, queasy, beside me. After a few minutes I'd set the book down on my lap. The park was busiest at lunchtime, the drunks gathered around their picnic benches, young mothers wheeling strollers around the big elms, old couples from one of the assisted living facilities taking laps around the statues, leaning on canes or pushing walkers. Some brought bread to feed the pigeons, but none could compete with the Vietnamese man, brown and withered, howling with delight as the birds picked him clean.

A few other office workers ate lunch and read newspapers and magazines, each on her own bench, none making eye contact. I didn't feel as if I belonged among them, even though I wore the same slacks and blouses and skirts with bloodless gray tights, the same pointed shoes with square heels that distinguished me as a functional member of society. I tried to see myself as others must have, just beginning to make my way in the world, but after three days at Immediate Marketing and a week without sleep, I began to associate myself instead with the bums drinking from bottles in paper bags. For the first time I felt I had nothing to contribute to the world, not even as a curiosity like the man covered in pigeons.

Most days on my way back to the office I popped into the former liquor store, where James was tearing out everything but the walls. He had usually just arrived by then, still sleepy, in coveralls and workboots, his hair sticking up in back. He looked small in the baggy clothes, his delicate shoulders swimming in loose fabric. Stephen was rarely with him, though he didn't have a job to go to – he worked only on the weekends, a few hours at a pet food store near the mall. "He's part vampire," James told me. "Sleeps till four every day."

It was hard to picture a boutique in the space. It looked more like a bomb crater. James wanted it as spare as possible, nothing but clothes racks, a dressing booth, and a cash register on a pedestal, everything, including the floor, painted white. "I'm into the sterile look," he said. "When you're trying on clothes you should feel totally clean. You put on a pair of pants and you should believe they were made just for you, that no one else would even consider wearing them. Don't you think?" I agreed with everything he said, not because I had an opinion one way or another, but because there was so much doubt in his voice, and on his face an honest, overwhelmed expression that pleaded for affirmation. He admitted that he'd borrowed money from friends and family and a sketchy title loan company with criminal interest rates.

"You've got a car?" I asked.

"No," he said. "Just a title."

"Whose is it?" He shrugged. "Someone you know?" He shook his head. "Where'd you get it?" Another shrug. "You *stole* it?"

"Is it my fault some idiot parks his Jeep in this neighbor-hood and doesn't lock it?" He covered his face with his hands. "Oh, God. I'm so screwed if this place doesn't take off."

The few times Stephen was there, wearing sunglasses and a wide-brimmed hat, slouching on a sawhorse, yawning incessantly, James was confident and optimistic. He talked about how much stock he'd keep on hand, and how much he thought he'd sell in the first year, all while knocking the old liquor store shelves off the walls with a sledgehammer and chiseling up floor tiles. Stephen didn't lift a hand to help him, nor did he offer. He was free with his opinions, though, calling out from the front, where we both stayed close to the door to keep dust off our clothes. "Don't you want *any* furniture? You're just going to *stand* all day and wait for people to come in?"

"I'll get a stool," James said.

"What's wrong with a sofa?"

"It'll ruin my clean lines."

"You can get a white one. It'll blend into the wall."

"You don't understand aesthetics at all," James said, taking a whack at a metal shelf, which crumpled around the head of the hammer. He had to pry it off.

"I'm not the one who's going to be on my feet for hours,"
Stephen said.

"As soon as I'm in the black I'll hire someone else to do it,"
James said. "You want a new job, Amy? The hours are long and
the pay's terrible."

"I'll think about it," I said.

Stephen pulled up his sunglasses to show me the pale,
somber eyes that never seemed to match his mocking tone and
whispered, "He's not the brightest light in the sky."

He'd begun taking on this confidential tone with me whenever I saw him in The Victory Manor in the evenings, and it
always surprised me to have his lovely face lean toward me, with
a look of hushed intimacy that made me feel special, singled
out. He and James had taken me to one of the clubs on the square
the night before, and while James was at the bar Stephen told
me how they'd met, a year ago, at a birthday party for Stephen's
cousin. That was back when Stephen was still making an effort
to be straight, dating a girl who had few expectations for happiness in her life. "I was standing there with her, and he came
right up to us," Stephen said, keeping an eye on the bar. "It was
totally heartless. He didn't look at me at all, just handed my
girlfriend his phone number and told her she should call him if
she ever needed any stitching done, hems or anything. She
thanked him, and when he walked away, she gave me the number.
Smart girl. Total train wreck, but she knew when to give up."

Now he went on, still whispering, "He didn't graduate
high school. Had something like a one point two GPA. I never
imagined myself with a dropout. If he wasn't so damn sexy."
Then he leaned back and called out, "Are wearing anything under
that monkey suit?"

James swung the sledgehammer onto his shoulder, knocking himself off balance. He staggered a step or two, recovered,
and gave his crooked smile. "Am I ever?"

"I get sweaty just watching you," Stephen said. "It's the only
reason I get up in the morning."

"You never get up in the morning."

"Well, I'm up right now," Stephen said, standing.

"All the way up?" James asked, coming toward us.

The heat between them made me start sweating, too. My legs itched under my gray tights. It felt all wrong for me to be standing here with them in the dusty rubble of the shop, and anyway it was time to get back to work. They were face to face, separated only by the sawhorse, and didn't acknowledge me when I said goodbye. Only when I opened the front door did Stephen call after me, "Just so you know, Amy, if I were still the slightest bit straight, you'd be the first person I'd invite to join us." I was still flushed by the time I made it back to the conference room, and for the next hour worked with my back to the glass.

6.

THE NIGHT BEFORE my father's surgery, my mother charged through the house vacuuming and dusting and scrubbing surfaces, as she did before a long vacation away. They'd be gone for only a day and a half, but still she wiped each of the dining room chandelier's three dozen crystals with a cloth diaper until they gleamed. My father didn't joke with her as usual about polishing the silver so burglars would know it was worth stealing. He sat in his armchair, reading the paper, the pile of phone books on the ottoman grown higher, his body even more twisted. "Bernice," he said, as my mother fluttered past him with a feather duster. "You're making me dizzy. Can't you clean upstairs?"

I was in the kitchen, making a light dinner for my mother and myself, beating eggs for an omelet, slicing radishes and cucumber for a salad. My father wasn't supposed to eat for twenty-four hours before the anesthesia, but he'd hardly eaten anything in the last two months anyway. He was down to a hundred and seventy-one pounds, what he'd weighed when he and my mother had married. "This little – " he'd said earlier, waving at his belly. "It's probably saved me from a heart attack. Did you know I broke two hundred the year before last? Another one of your mother's lasagnas and I might have keeled over. This thing, it's better than Atkins." My mother glanced at the ceiling and muttered something I couldn't hear. A prayer, most likely – she'd started going to services again, for the first time since I was in high school. "Heart attack," my father said. "The two scariest words in the English language. Much worse than colon cancer."

Now he called me into the living room and pointed to the sofa. "Sit for a second," he said, and gave me a smile that made me grip the cushion. His face had aged even in the two weeks I'd been home, growing pale, cheekbones appearing where before there'd been only flesh, hollows forming at both temples. His hair had gone white years ago, but it was still thick and full and wavy. It was hard to believe it might soon begin to fall out, along with his eyebrows and mustache and the soft dark fuzz on his arms. "While your mother's out of the way," he said, and craned his neck to see into the hallway and up the stairs. His voice was hushed in a way that set my heart chugging. "I thought we could take a minute. Just in case – "

"Dad," I said. "Nothing's – "

"I know, I know," he said. "It'll all go fine. I'll come out lean and mean and bald as Kojak." He smiled again, half-heartedly this time, and I felt compelled to smile back though I didn't want to. "In any case. My will. It's with Bronstein, the lawyer. You remember him. He was at your bat mitzvah. Heavyset guy, big ears."

"Sure," I said, though the description fit any of a dozen men who'd drifted into and out of my childhood, when I'd been distracted by other things, friends and grades and boys. Why hadn't I paid more attention?

"Anyway, his office is on Beverwyck. Phone number's in my rolodex."

"Got it," I said, impatient, ready to stand.

"There's also the account numbers. The Paine Webber, the Chemical. It's all in my files. Shouldn't be hard to find. The mortgage, too, and the car titles. Your mother, you know, she'd be running around like a crazy person, and she wouldn't think about any of the important things."

"Okay, Dad," I said, and this time I did stand. I glanced at the ceiling, at the sound of the vacuum passing overhead, and was tempted to offer a prayer of my own. "You shouldn't be worrying about any of this. The doctor said the surgery's routine, and – "

"Wait a minute," he said, and his expression changed now, to one more serious than I'd known him capable of, his brows constricting, his tongue probing a spot behind his lower lip. He checked the stairs again, adjusted himself on the chair, and lowered his voice even further. "There's something else. Something Bernice doesn't know."

I sat. My hands went instinctively between my knees. I waited for the confession, for something unexpected, something shocking – a long affair, a second family, a secret identity. It surprised me to realize how much I wanted to hear it, to be shaken and at the same time comforted by someone else's transgression. I was ready, too, to admit what I'd been doing to David, to reveal how dishonest I was, and how much, at first, I'd enjoyed it.

"You know your mother," my father said. "How she is with money. You grow up poor, you think it's never going to last." He shook his head and shrugged. "I don't know what I was thinking. Twenty years ago. You were just a toddler. We weren't rolling in it or anything, but I'd just gotten the job at Lambert, and I must have been feeling flush... This salesman ... Anyway, it doesn't matter how he suckered me. I bought a piece of property. A big piece. In Florida. I guess I thought we'd build a cabin on it, use it for vacations. That was when I was still fishing – remember? – and there was a lake ... But as soon as I put the money down ... Your mother, she'd kill me if she knew."

"Big?" I asked. "How big?"

"Big," he said.

"Like an acre? Two acres?"

He coughed, winced, pressed a hand to his side. "Thirty."

I made some kind of noise of astonishment and for a moment forgot all about his surgery and his cancer, about David and my job and my squalid apartment.

"It's just swampland," he said. "The edge of the Everglades. At least it was then. Now it's about half a mile outside West Palm."

"And you've had it all this time? And it's just been sitting there?"

"It's gone up in value," he said, sheepishly, but also with a touch of pride. "It's gone up a lot."

"Why don't you just tell her?"

"Tell me what?" my mother asked. There she was in the doorway, the duster resting on her shoulder, the red frizz of her hair made fiery at the edges by the hallway light.

"That you're making me nervous with all this bustle," my father said, not missing a beat. He'd been lying to her for twenty years and must have been used to it by now. I admired how naturally he managed it. "I wish you'd just relax already."

"What's that burning?" my mother said.

I sprang up and ran to the kitchen, but it was too late. The omelet was scorched.

"Let me do it," my mother said. "If I can't clean at least I can feed us." She took the smoking pan, scraped the mess into the trash, and in five minutes had everything under control, onions browning, cheese grated, eggs beaten. I stood by and watched. I'd been cooking since I was nine years old and hardly ever burned anything. But now I was as useless in the kitchen as at the agency. I didn't know what I was doing here at all.

"I wish you'd at least eat a few bites," my mother called into the living room. "You need strength for the recovery, don't you?"

"Doctor's orders," my father said.

"A nibble wouldn't hurt you."

"Choking on my own vomit," he said. "That's how I've always wanted to go."

7.

AFTER THE SURGERY my mother asked me to come to services with her on Friday night or Saturday morning, but I went into the city instead. My weekends there were disorienting. I'd grown sensitive to the crush of urban life, to noise and smells and the blur of cars and bodies, and by the time I'd navigated the trains and subways from Chatwin out to Brooklyn my head was ringing. Seeing my old roommates in their new apartment was confusing, too, how easily they moved around each other in the small space, how comfortable they were sitting side by side on the love-seat in their living room, no more than an inch separating them. When I'd lived with them they'd fought constantly, and on more than one occasion I'd kept them from ending the friendship, negotiating truces and serving as go-between. Now they laughed together as they told stories of their first days in the new place, the landlady who'd tried to cancel their lease because she thought Hope was Puerto Rican, the terrible time they'd had with the moving van, one of them having to stand beside it the whole time to keep neighborhood kids from tagging it. They'd also both gotten haircuts – shorter than mine, stylishly highlighted – and new clothes. Debbie, who'd once had a closet full of long Indian skirts and baggy pants with stripes down their sides, now wore black jeans and a tight black tank top. Hope had started jogging and dieting while I was in Europe and lost five pounds. She'd also been spending time at the beach or the tanning salon – hence the landlady's mistake – and now had on a short shaggy dress she might have run through the dryer too long, and chunky open-toed heels that were unapologetically trashy. She'd slept with a near-stranger in the last week and was waiting for a phone call we all knew would never come.

"Amy, you *have* to move out here," Debbie said. "It's *so* much fun. I mean, after your dad's better and everything."

"How *is* your father?" Hope asked. Even with all the running and dieting she was still a bit chubby, and when she crossed her legs her dress rode up over her heavy thighs. "You poor thing. I can't imagine what you've been going through."

"He's doing okay," I said. "At least the surgery went well. The chemo, though, my God –"

"Awful," Debbie said quickly, ready to change the subject as she did whenever a difficult topic came up. She didn't run but she didn't eat, either, and her waist was small enough to get two hands around, her arms long and stringy and effortlessly graceful. She was prettier than Hope would ever be, though not as sexy. Her boyfriend was on a Fulbright to Italy for the year, and next summer she'd join him. Once there I had no doubt she'd get the sort of romantic proposal I'd once idly fantasized about. Her smile was fixed and saccharine, and I decided now that I'd never entirely trusted her. "Really, as soon as he's okay, you should find a place nearby."

"It's not fair at all," Hope said. "This thing with your dad, and then Zeitlin being a shit. He doesn't know what he's giving up. You hear anything from him lately?"

"We've been exchanging messages. He wants to come down and see me in a few weeks."

"I bet he started getting with Nissa. You remember, that tart from Milwaukee? He always had his eye on her."

"We're late," Debbie said, checking her watch and jumping up. "I told Maddie we'd meet her at seven."

"Maybe Russ'll be there," Hope said.

"That asshole," Debbie said. "He never called you."

"They're all liars," Hope said and shrugged. "But some are sweeter than others."

They took me to hip dive bars and dark music clubs and sometime after midnight a hole-in-the-wall falafel joint, and I lost track of what neighborhood we were in, what subway line I'd take if I got separated from them. I was the one who should have felt at home here, having grown up in the city's shadow. I'd come in with my parents all the time as a girl, to visit my grandparents when they were still alive, to see musicals and concerts and art shows, and then as a teenager took the train in with my friends, hitting all-ages clubs, bumming cigarettes from strangers, buying terrible fake IDs at the jumbled photo and electronics stores on 42nd Street, most of which were gone now, along with the porn theaters and peep shows. It was Hope's and Debbie's city now, and I was entirely in their hands as we bounced from one haunt to another, their circle of friends growing larger and more raucous with each new stop.

It was disorienting, too, to have men hitting on me again, scruffy boys with pierced ears and fresh tattoos, their faces getting closer to mine the more they drank, their smiles sloppy and ravenous. One had designs on taking me home, and I might have considered it if Hope didn't pull me aside and whisper, "He's a shit. He'll screw you and next time he sees you pretend he doesn't know your name." I stayed away from him then, and an hour later Hope was sitting beside him, his hand in her lap. They disappeared together, and I was livid, but before I could say anything, Debbie shook her head and sighed. "Don't worry about her," she said. "She's not as fragile as she seems." I took Hope's bed for the night, but even drunk and spinning I slept only a few hours and hopped an early Sunday morning train back to Chatwin.

Soon after I left the station, I spotted Miss Elkin across the park. Or rather, what I spotted was a tiny lurching form against the dark trunks of the elms, moving so quickly that at first she seemed transparent, a projected image less substantial than what was behind it. She was far enough away that I couldn't catch up even if I hurried, and I doubted she'd hear if I called to her. But I did my best to keep her in view.

I was fascinated by Miss Elkin, I'll admit, in a clinical sort of way. I'd begun to invent a history for her, or several histories, and this, I think now, is what appealed to me most–that she served as a blank slate upon which I could test out different versions of how a person might end up as she did, old, destitute, alone. Most of the possibilities I came up with were naïve, I knew even then. I envisioned a terrifying childhood for her in Europe, one in which she narrowly escaped the horrors of war and death camps, only to end up an orphaned refugee in a strange country. I gave her a lover who died in a tragic accident – sometimes in a car, sometimes a plane – and another who abandoned her weeks before a planned wedding. I had her in a hospital, receiving experimental surgery on her leg, discovering only months afterward that her limp would remain as severe as ever. I heaped sorrow on her, killing off her parents and siblings, her friends and romantic interests, her beloved pets. I was trying to decide how much grief a person could bear, believing I couldn't bear any.

Halfway across the park I lost sight of her. She slipped behind the last column of trees before the street, and even after I maneuvered around them, it took a moment to spot her again. She wasn't where I expected her, lurching toward The Victory Manor, and even with her speed I didn't think she could have made it inside already. And then I saw: a bundle of clothes on the sidewalk, one foot moving, the other still. I froze. What kept me from running to her wasn't how hostile she'd been the last time I'd helped her up, how she'd slapped my hand away; it was embarrassment, a sense that I'd seen something I shouldn't have. And even if I had run, I wouldn't have made it to her in time. In a moment she was up on her knees, and after another on her feet. She didn't need anyone's help, I thought, excusing myself for standing by and watching. She brushed herself off, arranged her bag on her arm, and moved off as if nothing had happened.

By the time I made it into the lobby, she'd already taken up her spot beside the elevator, braced leg tucked under the wingback badly in need of re-upholstering. She was smiling, unruffled, and to anyone who hadn't just seen her outside, she looked as if she'd been sitting here for hours. "Miss Markowitz," she said. "How nice to see you. I thought you'd gone."

"I just moved in," I said.

"You'd be surprised how quickly some of them leave," she said. "They meet a man and get married, or move back home with their families."

"I'm not going anywhere," I said, firmly. "Just up to my room." All morning I'd drifted in and out of nausea, and now my head hurt. I'd spent most of the night angry, at Hope for taking away the scruffy boy with his tattooed arms, at myself for needing those arms so badly, and for finding myself longing for David Zeitlin, who now, according to Hope, might have had his arms wrapped around a tart from Milwaukee. I resented Miss Elkin imagining possibilities for my life as I'd been doing for hers.

She waited with me as the elevator took its time descending, and only then did I notice the fresh scrape on her elbow, raspberry colored, with bits of dirt stuck in the center. I looked away. "That other Miss Markowitz," she said. "Or did I say Hurwitz? It's funny, I can see faces as clear as day, but names sometimes escape me. She was a shy girl, not as pretty as you, but when we sat together she would tell me about the men in her life. I have to admit," she said, her voice going low, "I enjoy hearing about such things." She paused, maybe expecting me to offer some tidbit about my own love life. The elevator car arrived. I opened the door for her and this time pressed the button for the fifth floor.

"The other Miss Markowitz," Miss Elkin went on as we started to rise. "She had such trouble with men. This one loved her but he drank too much and never had any money. This other one she loved, but he was involved with someone else. I would hear them coming and going from her apartment. Not that I listened. I always mind my own business. But she'd come in and cry over them and tell me she was giving them both up. And then she met another man, right here in this building, on the stairs, maybe, or in the lobby. Maybe even in this elevator, I can't remember." We reached her floor, but Miss Elkin wasn't in a hurry to get out. The smell of tobacco and menthol on her breath made me dizzy. I yanked the grate open, feeling sick again, my head throbbing. "You never know where it happens," she said. "You've just got to keep your eyes open."

I wondered if she realized that most of the men in the building these days were interested in other men. I didn't bother to tell her. She invited me in for tea, as she'd done with the other Miss Markowitz or Hurwitz, a mousy girl, I imagined, who'd met an equally mousy man on the elevator. For some reason I didn't want to see the inside of Miss Elkin's apartment, preferring instead to stick with my imagined version of it, which was cluttered with photographs of all the people she'd lost, her only company. I apologized and muttered an excuse, the first thing that came into my head. "I've got to go visit my father," I said. "He just got out of the hospital. But another time, I'd love to."

"Of course," Miss Elkin said, offering her polite smile and handshake, giving her best wishes for my father's recovery, hiding any insult. She thanked me for holding the door, and her limp seemed more pronounced than ever as she hobbled away, her brace clattering on the hallway's matted carpet.

Back in my own room, I threw myself on the bed and was asleep twenty minutes before the phone woke me. I let the answering machine pick up and listened to David's crackling voice, speaking with an indifference that was obviously forced. "Hey. Just calling to see what's up. Guess we missed each other again. No big deal, I'll just keep trying. I was thinking maybe next weekend I'd come down. Or the one after. Or whatever. Hope you're dad's doing better." I hugged the pillow, resisting the urge to pick up, and before I could fall asleep again the sewing machine was pounding a rhythm out of sync with the terrible pounding in my head.

8.

ONE MORNING THE next week, after I'd been stamping envelopes at the postage meter for more than an hour, Maxine Valva appeared in front of me, arms crossed, with an oddly perplexed, exasperated expression, as if she couldn't understand, for the life of her, what I was doing here. She and Anna hadn't fought for a week. Anna's newest projections of income from the conferences were higher than expected, and she'd been flitting around the office, fingering her cross and taking measurements for new furniture. She'd begun to muse out loud about being named Entrepreneur of the Year by the county's Association of Young Business Leaders.

Something about Maxine rattled me. More than just her unfriendliness, it was that she'd made up her mind about me before I'd even started the job. It was unfair, I thought, for her to judge me without cause, to fail to see me as I really was. What a mistake on her part not to realize I was an asset to the company, though in her presence I couldn't prove it. The longer she watched me, the clumsier I got. I dropped an envelope and then punched it crookedly, a corner of the stamp missing the edge of the paper. She uncrossed her arms and asked if I weighed each envelope separately.

"They all have the same stuff in them," I said.

She took two off the top of the stack and brought them to the scale. I knew why she hated me – I was part of everything she envied in her sister, a mark of all their differences. I decided on the spot to hate her back, as Anna must have hated her so often, her spreading backside, her frumpy clothes, the dark hair at the edges of her lips. She's jealous, I thought, and felt a comforting superiority, grateful for my firm thighs and full lips, for a voice that David had once told me was sultry.

Both envelopes weighed nine ounces. *See?* Maxine disappeared into her office and returned with a pair of scissors. To my astonishment, she opened them and held the blades to the center of an envelope. She'd lost her mind, I thought. Jealousy had driven her crazy. But then she adjusted the envelope and snipped off a corner of manila paper, about the size of a thumbnail. It fluttered to the floor at her feet – fat feet, in ugly brown mules. She put the envelope back on the scale. Eight point eight ounces. Twelve cents less per envelope. "It isn't your money to throw away," she said, and handed me the scissors.

When Anna came into the office an hour later, gym bag slung over a shoulder, legs bare to mid-thigh, heels clicking across the tiled floor she must have paid a fortune to install – checkered black and white like an Italian villa's – I had a collection of paper corners at my feet, dozens of yellowed thumbnails.

"What in the world are you doing?" she cried.

"Saving you money," I said.

Her eyebrows lifted, those false irises flashing electric blue. "I knew it."

"Knew what?"

"Maxine. She's always wrong about people."

"What did she say about me?"

If I kept it up, Anna told me, I wouldn't be stuffing envelopes for long. "I have an instinct when it comes to potential," she said, picking up one of the packets and examining its clipped corner. "That's how I got to be where I am." As soon as she said it, her look of pleasure disappeared, and a bitter one replaced it. "You know where I'd be now if I'd listened to her? Married to some idiot, like she is, with more idiot kids than I knew what to do with. That's the first thing you've got to learn," she said, handing back the envelope. "Never listen to anyone. Just do what feels right, and do it only for yourself."

Then she sent me out to pick up her lunch, cottage cheese with a side of fruit salad.

9.

WITHOUT HAIR, MY father looked surprisingly distinguished. His head had a nice shape to it, hidden all these years by those dense waves, a good fit on his now slender neck. Two weeks of chemo had taken his weight down to what it had been when he was twenty-four, a post-doc making less than ten-thousand dollars a year who didn't know how to feed himself before my mother came into his life. "This is what I get," he told me, after throwing up for the third time in an hour. He was back on his armchair, straightened now, without phone books to prop him. My mother had been fluttering around with the duster, and he'd sent her upstairs, telling her he didn't need any help getting nauseated. Now the vacuum roared overhead. It was an effort for him to talk over the noise. "When I married her I told myself I'd always be honest. That was the only rule I made, and I couldn't stick to it."

"No one's perfect," I said.

"I'm not even close."

"Why don't you just tell her now?"

"She'd never forgive me."

"It's not like you lost money or anything. You did well. You could call it a surprise."

"She hates surprises. Remember that party I threw on her fiftieth birthday? She still holds it against me."

"In any case," I said, "it doesn't have anything to do with you being sick. I don't believe that for a second."

"You don't know what kind of tunes the Old Fiddler plays," he said, jerking a thumb at the ceiling. "All that praying she's been doing. It's got to have some kind of effect."

"You're an atheist," I said.

"I believe in curses," he said. "And cosmic jokes."

As if to prove it, his face went pale, and he clapped a hand over his mouth. I helped him into the bathroom, stroking the back of his silky head. He was still bent over the toilet when my mother came downstairs, and she started heating soup on the stove.

"Give me a break, Bernice," my father said, wiping his mouth with a dishtowel he'd usurped as a handkerchief. "Can't I have five minutes without heaving?"

"Every bit that comes out you've got to put back in," my mother said. "Tell him, Amy." I knew better than to say anything. She'd quit crying in the last two weeks, going around instead with a desperate, unnerving cheer, trying to convince everyone, especially herself, that the worst was behind us. As she poured soup into bowls, she said, "Did I tell you? I talked to Iris yesterday. Todd and Jody decided to give it another try. Not just for the sake of the kids, either. They missed each other. Isn't that wonderful?" I didn't answer. "You should give your David a call," she went on. "Now that things are under control here–"

Coming out of the bathroom, my father groaned, hugged his belly, and said, "She calls this under control."

"You ought to go up there and visit him," my mother said. "You can see if maybe, you know, you two still have feelings for each other."

"We don't," I said.

"I don't understand it," my mother said, pulling a chair out for my father, who eased himself down, grimacing. "You were so happy together. I can tell these sorts of things. Something must have happened."

"What do you want to hear?" I said. "That he caught me in bed with the milkman?"

She was determined not to be hurt. The desperate grin was frozen on her face, as on a cadaver's. "I know what it was."

"Something did happen," I said. "He kept calling Gaudí 'Gaudy.'"

"You got scared, that's all. You were afraid of getting too serious. It doesn't mean you can't go back–"

"I like it here," I said, the plainest lie I'd told in my life. Across the table, my father gave me a warning look, or maybe a look of support. He brought a spoonful of soup to his mouth, sniffed it, then turned away and closed his eyes.

My mother was delighted. "Of course you do," she said. "That doesn't mean you can't be together. If he loves you he'll make sacrifices. He can finish law school, and then you'll move back. Somewhere nice, not some slum apartment on Victory Park. Really, you should call him. After dinner, go ahead. You can use the phone in our bedroom. Close the door, take all the time you want. We've got new long distance. Good rates at night. You don't even have to reverse the charges."

10.

BY NOW JAMES and Stephen had adopted me. Most weekday evenings, after I left my parents' house, I spent a few hours in the room above mine, mixing experimental cocktails while James stitched and Stephen read travel magazines and complained that they never went out anymore, never did anything fun. The boutique was set to open at the end of the month, and James was in a silent, stoic panic – silent and stoic in front of Stephen, at least – making far more clothes than he needed. He'd finished tearing out the shelves in the old liquor store, patched up most of the walls, and started painting the floor. But now he was having second thoughts about white. Was it too sterile? he asked, casually, as if he didn't care much one way or another, as if his entire life wasn't on the line. Would it intimidate people?

"You need a place for people to lounge," Stephen said, lounging on the sofa. "The color doesn't matter." He was in boxer shorts, nothing else, the spray of wiry hair spread unevenly between his nipples, thicker on the right side. "I keep telling you that, but you never listen."

"White doesn't intimidate me," I said, handing James a pink cocktail. All my drinks had grenadine in them – without it they looked like water from rusty pipes – and most tasted like cough syrup. "If I did, I'd never be able to look at Stephen's chest."

"If you want people to buy your clothes you've got to make them comfortable," Stephen said. "You've got to give them a place to hang out."

"You should see his ass," James said. "You wouldn't think it could get any whiter, but you'd be surprised."

I was used to seeing Stephen's chest by now, and he was used to me stretching out on the sofa opposite him, tucking my bare feet under his arm. I told him he was my surrogate boyfriend, and he said that was fine as long as I didn't want any surrogate sex. I liked his smell, and the feel of his legs pressed against mine, and the indifferent way he let his hand drape over my knee. He'd pass me his magazine, turned to a picture of some tropical beach or exotic marketplace and say, "Let's run away together. I'm so bored here." I'd tell him about sights in Greece and Italy and Spain, and he'd ask if David and I had done it in the Vatican. Had he ever been to Europe? I asked. He shook his head. Had he ever been out of the country? Another shake. Had he ever been on an airplane? Silence. He'd lived in New Jersey all his life, James said, and had never once even gone into Manhattan.

"You've got to be kidding me," I said.

"He doesn't even like riding the bus."

"I went to Philly once," Stephen said. "Eighth grade. The Liberty Bell, cheesesteaks, big deal."

"Come with me this weekend," I said. "I'll show you around."

"I've got to work," Stephen said.

"For a whole three hours," James said.

"We'll go during the week then. I'll take a day off."

"If I'm going anywhere I want it to be Hawaii or the Bahamas. What's the big deal with New York, anyway? Tall buildings and concrete, who cares."

"He's afraid of AIDS," James said. "He thinks you can get it just breathing the city air. High school sex ed classes fucked him up forever."

"All I know is I want to get out of *here*," Stephen said. "We've been cooped up in this room for *days*. I want to get a real *drink* already. No offense, Amy, but yours taste like rubber bands."

"We'll go out tomorrow," James said. "Tonight I've got to finish these shirts."

"Me and Amy'll go without you. Maybe we won't come back. We'll run off to Fiji." James didn't answer, but his face was more serious than I'd seen it before, eyes locked on a seam, hands tense as he guided fabric under the needle. "He hates the idea of us being alone together," Stephen said. "He thinks you'll turn me back to women. He doesn't believe I'm all the way gay.

Just because I used to do it with girls. Look," he said, and without warning grabbed my foot, pressed it into his crotch, rubbed it up and down. "Nothing, okay? Can we go out now without a chaperone?"

The sewing machine stopped abruptly, and James stood up. "Let's go already," he said. "I can't work with you griping all the time."

I gave them a little distance, keeping a few feet ahead as we walked across the park – in part to assure James that I had no intention of turning his boyfriend back to women, and in part because Stephen had lied. It hadn't been nothing. In fact, it had been the opposite of nothing. As soon as my foot had touched him, he'd gone hard against it, and then hid it from James by standing, turning his back, and pulling on a pair of jeans. On our way out of the building he'd given me a look I couldn't quite read, maybe amused, maybe ashamed, and to let him know it was no big deal, I squeezed his arm. He shrugged me off. Now I glanced behind and saw that the two of them were holding hands, Stephen snuggled up to James more affectionately than usual, James smiling and whispering in his ear. "Slow down, will you?" Stephen called. "Why are you running?" I let them come even with me and took up their pace but stayed on James's side, not Stephen's. James put his free arm around my waist, and the three of us marched under the elms, past a group of drunks too far gone to bother asking for change. My foot held a memory of Stephen's shape beneath his boxers. With every step I felt it against the leather of my sandal, the suddenness of it, the shock of recognition, the way it made my breath catch in my throat.

"We need to find Amy a new man," James said. "Even if she can't dump the old one."

"What about being in truth?" Stephen said.

"I'm more into being in fun," James said.

"It's better for us if she's single," Stephen said. "We need someone to save our table when we dance. Didn't you know that's the only reason we bring you along?" Though he said it in the same offhandedly nasty way he said everything, this I couldn't shrug off. He couldn't have seen my face, but from my silence he must have guessed how much his words had stung me. "God," he said. "Everyone's mad at me today. I should have just stayed in bed."

"You did stay in bed," James said. "Till after four."

"I'm sorry, world," Stephen shouted, tilting his head back, as we reached the far end of the park. "I atone for all my transgressions." I was ready to turn around and go home when we came to their favorite bar, The Scandal, but as James paid the bouncer, Stephen put his arms around me, and with an exaggerated, abashed look, eyebrows raised, asked, "Forgive me?"

"You're supposed to apologize before asking forgiveness."

"Didn't I do that already?"

"Not to me."

"You're so particular," he said. "Well, consider it done, then."

"Okay," I said, reluctantly. "Then consider yourself forgiven."

It wasn't even true that they needed me to save the table while they danced, because only James ever danced, while Stephen and I sat in a booth and drank. Stephen said dancing tired him out too much, but he liked watching James grinding with other men. "Don't you get jealous?" I'd asked the first time we'd gone out. "Of course I do," he'd said. "Jealousy gets my blood pumping. It's totally erotic." I was more comfortable in The Scandal than in any of the bars I went to with Hope and Debbie in the city. The space was open and dim, the wooden tables polished, the music pulsing and languid. Even if I was the only woman in the place, I felt as if I belonged here. Now when James hit the dance floor Stephen leaned across the table and said, "Okay. We need to talk."

"Sure," I said, nervously, thinking about my foot and his crotch, ready to say that it didn't mean anything, that it could have happened to anybody, that James didn't have to know.

But what had happened on the sofa wasn't on Stephen's

mind at all, or if it was, he had no intention of addressing it. "It's time to deal with this David thing," he said.

I relaxed, turning sideways, feet up on the seat beside me. "I know," I said.

"Don't laugh. I'm serious."

"I'm not an honorable person."

"Not remotely," he said. "It's been, what, a month?" Stephen had his back to the dance floor and couldn't see what I saw: James with his arms over his head, hips thrusting, shirt sticking to his chest, sweaty men on all sides. "Finish the guy off already."

"I will," I said. "As soon as my dad's better, I'll go up there—"

"What's your dad have to do with it?"

I shrugged and sipped my cocktail, which was indeed better than any I'd ever made. What could I have told him? Not what had come into my mind, surreptitiously, over the past couple of weeks, less a fully formed thought than an intimation— that I shouldn't make any changes until my father was well, that if I just held steady, he would, too, and when he was stable I could go on with my life. For now I was intentionally keeping myself in a limbo that included David and the cramped apartment and the job I hated. It included spending my evenings with Stephen and James, too, and realizing this, I suppose, more than anything, is what kept me from speaking now.

"Look," Stephen said. "I'm not saying it for David's sake. Do you think I care about some random straight guy I've never met? I'm sure he deserves it. Worse, probably. It's you I'm worried about."

"Worried," I said. Why should he worry about me when he was the one getting erections and lying about it to his boyfriend?

"I know how this kind of thing goes. It gets under your skin. It's oppressive. You've got to free yourself from it. You've got to, I don't know—"

"Be in truth," I said.

"Exactly."

"Who says I don't want him up there waiting for me," I said. "Maybe I really will go back to him."

"Jesus, that's what I mean," Stephen said, flinging himself back into the corner of the booth. "You *might* go back to him. Fuck might. You either do it or you don't. You can't just ... mess around with people's lives while you make up your mind. God."

"Whose lives am I messing with?"

"Everyone's."

"I mean specifically."

He turned away. "Do what you want," he said.

"Yours?"

He didn't answer. I finished my drink, left him in the booth, and joined James on the dance floor, throwing myself into the middle of all those churning bodies. It took me a minute to find the rhythm, and by the time I did there was a circle of dead space around me, as if my awkward moves had soured all the air they'd touched.

II.

FOR THE TIME being I'd given up reading Catullus. He was too sensual, too arousing when my days were so mindless and dull, my sleepless nights spent alone in a big empty bed. I no longer brought a book to the park at lunch, instead watching the old people looping the statues, the pigeon man swarmed by birds, the drunks passing their bottles. I stared at my own crossed legs, at my ankles in gray nylon, at the concrete sidewalk scattered with flattened gum.

And then, one day almost three weeks after my father's surgery, another pair of shoes appeared beside mine, black wingtips in need of a polish. I took my time glancing up, and there on the bench was a young man in suit and tie, with dark hair cut short and gelled. I was too startled to decide whether he was attractive or not, too surprised to tell whether he'd sat too close. He hunched forward, elbows on knees, staring straight ahead. I said hello, and he nodded. I tried to follow his gaze, but he was staring at the space between an elm and the pigeon man: nothing but street, a few passing cars, and the vacuum cleaner outlet as backdrop. I took a bite of salad. Without stirring, the man said, "Smells good."

"It's okay," I said.

"Real good." His voice was hushed. He *was* attractive, I decided, his chin and mouth well-shaped, his brow nicely ridged, though his nose was bulbous and crooked at the bridge. He had two round little scars beneath his ear, and another on his neck, and noticing them I decided he was in fact sitting too close, with a good two feet of empty bench on his other side.

"It's mostly lettuce," I said. "I wish they'd put more carrots in it. The vinaigrette's good. That must be what you smell."

"Fresh," he said.

"I guess. The lettuce is a little wilted."

"Fresh and young," he said, his hushed voice lowering to a whisper. He closed his eyes and lifted his nose. "Fresh, young…"

I waited for him to finish. What word would he use? My fork kept moving, into the plastic tub of lettuce, back up to my mouth, teeth mashing soggy leaves. Say it, I thought. *Fresh, young pussy.* David had always wanted to talk dirty in bed, and that was his favorite word to whisper in my ear, though he said it self-consciously, hesitant, as if he expected me to slap him. For a moment I was angry enough to stab the man in the neck with my fork, to add another scar. But the fork was plastic, too, and would have shattered before it did any damage. He went on sniffing air. I wasn't afraid of him, not then. He seemed harmless, his smooth cheeks boyish and soft, hands almost as small as mine resting gently on his knees. I was wrong about his being attractive. His belly sagged onto his lap. His lips were loose at the corners, like a dog's. A foot of space separated us on the bench, and I told myself if he came an inch closer I'd stand up and scream or smack him with the lettuce tub or take off running. But he didn't move, and neither did I, except to uncross my legs and cross them away from him, pulling my skirt down as far as it would go. His head bobbed forward and back. His breath filled his lungs slowly, a slight wheeze to his inhale, and then came rushing out. I didn't know what he was smelling – my shampoo, maybe, or my hand lotion – but it wasn't coming from between my legs.

Across the park, birds whirled in a tight vortex around the pigeon man who threw back his head and laughed. An old couple hobbled by on canes. One of the drunks started shouting, and another shouted to quiet him down. I finished my salad and set the tub on the bench between me and the stranger, who was still now, his breath even, eyes closed. I wondered if he'd fallen asleep. It was time for me to head back to work, but I wouldn't budge before he did. I didn't want to look like I was running away. I settled in, hugging myself, daring him to finish what he'd started to say, or to say something worse. And then I was wishing he'd say anything, that he'd look at me, just once, to see who it was he'd insulted, to see the face that went with the fresh young pussy.

But then he was up off the bench without any warning, without rocking himself forward or stretching his arms or pushing off with his hands. And without glancing at me he walked off, wobbling slightly, feet coming down flat on the pavement, arms stiff at his sides – the gait, I guessed, of the mildly deranged, a resident of one of the halfway houses across the park. By the time he disappeared behind the nearest statue, all my anger had left me. Something replaced it, but I couldn't name the feeling, and can't now. All I know is that it set me crying on the bench with nothing but my damp napkin to wipe my face. I tried to gather myself but couldn't and started walking instead. The old liquor store was empty, stark white, James's paint cans lined up along the plate glass, the brushes cleaned and set neatly on top. I was still crying by the time I made it back to the agency, hurrying past Maxine's open door, and the designers who ignored me now as always. I went straight for the women's bathroom, which Anna had decorated to look like a turn-of-the-century boudoir, with brass fixtures, marble countertop, and a plush velvet chaise longue. I stayed in there ten minutes, fifteen minutes, and thought I'd never be able to leave. But then there was a knock, and Anna's voice asking if I'd let her in. I threw the latch and hunched back on the velvet cushions. Anna was wearing an outrageously lacy blouse, see-through to the edge of her bra, and a skirt split on one side to the top of her thigh. Her heels were high enough to flex her calves, a distinct line where muscle met bone. Maxine was right: She looked more like a stripper than an executive. Her expression was concerned and condescending, lips pursed, hand patting my knee as she squatted in front of me.

"What is it, honey?" she asked. "Is it a guy?" I shook my head, but either Anna didn't see or didn't believe me. "Listen, they're not worth it. There's always another one waiting." I kept crying, and Anna quickly lost patience with me. "Look, Amy, you might be a smart kid – you figured out those envelopes – but you'll never get anywhere if you let some prick throw you off your game."

"It's not a guy," I said.

"Then what is it?"

"My father," I said without thinking. "He's ... He's got cancer."

As soon as I said it, I wanted to believe I really was crying over my father. No jerk in the park should have set me off this way. I'd always thought of myself as the kind of person who could handle insults, who had a thick enough skin to withstand whatever the world threw at me. But now it felt as if I had no skin at all, only raw nerves exposed to abrasive air.

Anna's impatient look faltered, uncertainty taking its place. Her hand left my knee. She leaned back on her heels, away from me, as if my sorrow might be contagious. I'd never seen her at a loss for words before, but now she was silent. When she finally did speak, it was only to tell me to stay in the bathroom as long as I wanted; the other women could go to the insurance office next door. I was done crying by then – done, actually, the moment I'd mentioned my father – but I waited another ten minutes before returning to my stacks of letters and brochures in the conference room.

For the rest of the day Anna avoided me. On my way out I saw her in Maxine's office, standing behind her sister's chair, leaning in close to look at a spreadsheet on the computer screen. Her hands were on Maxine's shoulders. Her expression was tender, intimate, and Maxine spoke quietly enough that I couldn't hear her even with the door open. They looked like the closest of friends.

12.

THAT WEEKEND, I went into the city and slept with a boy named Ryan on a lumpy futon without sheets or blankets. The rough texture of the cover fabric left my back tingling the next morning as I padded around his apartment, barefoot, wearing only an oversized T-shirt he'd lent me, the front printed with the logo of a music festival in Minnesota. In the kitchen, pouring myself a glass of water, I ran into Ryan's roommate, taller than Ryan and better-looking, with shaggy mod hair and an appealing mole on his chin. I chatted with him about the band I'd seen the night before and flirted with him a little, saying I hoped to see him again.

Back in the bedroom, Ryan was up and dressed, a guitar in his lap. He'd raised the futon. His hair was long and lank, and without his glasses his face had a squinty, lost expression, a surliness I didn't remember from the night before. Hope and Debbie had left me at a bar with him, Debbie saying she had to get up early, Hope disappearing with a boy she'd earlier claimed she'd never talk to again. The girls weren't getting along so well anymore, both taking me aside during the evening to tell me how the other was driving her crazy, how they might have to look for separate apartments. If I were thinking about moving in, each said in turn, I should let her know as soon as possible.

I went home with Ryan because it was easy, and because I decided it was something I needed. I wasn't thinking much about my own gratification, and in any case Ryan was too drunk and clumsy for me to enjoy myself. What I wanted was clarity, a crossed line, a step I couldn't reverse. I wanted solid evidence to offer David for why he should hate me, why he shouldn't take me back. And maybe what I also wanted, though I didn't know it at the time, was for some boy to hurt me, to break my heart as I'd break David's, to replace my guilt with simple, straightforward grief.

But Ryan wasn't the one to do it. I wasn't bothered by his indifference, real or pretended, as he strummed his guitar and watched me gather my things. When I pulled off his music festival T-shirt he set the guitar aside and came to me. I let him kiss me for a minute, his hands dry against my bare back – the fingers of one callused from chords, the nails of the other long for picking – and then eased him aside and put on my clothes. He asked for my number, and I told him to call Hope and Debbie. I was sure we'd all get together again soon. On the train ride home it wasn't David I thought about telling, but Stephen, imagining how he'd scold me, how I'd tell him things were black and white now, that I could finally be in truth. I was pleased by how casual it could be, this sex and intimacy and leave-taking, by how strong I felt in my own indifference. If only I could keep it this way, I thought, and never care about anything.

But when I got home there were six messages on my machine, two from David, which I fast-forwarded, the rest from my mother. She was crying again. "Where are you? Why don't you answer?" My father was in the hospital. He hadn't been able to keep food down for three days and had to be put on an IV. He was retaining water. His electrolytes were dangerously low. When I got to his room, he lifted a swollen arm, tubes dangling, and said weakly, "I should have been eating this way my whole life. All this chewing and swallowing, what a waste of time."

He slept for a day and a half, and my mother and I took

turns watching him. I studied the movement of his chest, the steady rise and fall, and any variation – a snore, a sputter – made my own breath halt. I closed my eyes and chanted silently. In. Out. In. Out. In. Out. Eventually I fell asleep, and an hour later woke with a jolt, stiff on the hard chair, convinced that my father was gone, that my inattention had let him slip away. But his chest rose and fell, and I went back to chanting, pretending that I had some say over the action of his lungs, the beat of his heart. It was better than sitting there and doing nothing.

James joined me for one of my shifts, taking a break from painting and sewing, a break I knew he couldn't afford, with his shop set to open in just another week. When it came to friendship he was far more black and white than Stephen; if he counted you among his friends he'd wouldn't hesitate to spend four hours in a hospital room watching your father sleep, if that's what you needed. His caring for me was pure and unsullied, and I was grateful for it, but he couldn't offer much more than his presence, occasionally stroking my back, trying to distract me by talking about his grand opening and the DJ he'd hired for the night, not as good as the one at The Scandal, but not bad. He said Stephen would have been here, only he was afraid of hospitals, they were too messy for him, no clear lines between life and death, everything in flux. I thought I knew better – Stephen had been chilly toward me since our last night out, the night of my foot and his crotch – but didn't say anything. It wasn't fair to James that it was Stephen's presence I would have preferred, his sweet, musky smell, the bored way he flipped through his magazines, the sudden conspiratorial look he'd get when he decided he had something important to tell me.

James said, "I think love's too messy for him, too. He wants to feel the exact same way from one second to the next. He can't handle fluctuation. It drives him crazy." He leaned forward, hands clasped, his bright, eager eyes set on my father's bald head and sunken cheeks. "I don't think we'll last another three months."

Ten minutes before my mother came to spell me, Stephen

did show up, wearing his hat and sunglasses, looking hungover or anemic. James glanced up at him with tears in his eyes. Did he read Stephen's arrival as a sign? And if so, of what? Stephen complained of the hospital's terrible lighting, and the air that smelled like one of my cocktails. "I don't see how anyone could get better in here," he said. "You get rid of cancer, but then you're totally depressed." He lifted his glasses and gave me a squinty look that might have been guilty or apologetic or might simply have been a tic of nervous energy. For ten minutes he stood between my chair and James's, a hand on each of our shoulders. The three of us stared hard at my father's chest.

I didn't go into city the next weekend. Debbie and Hope both left messages, saying that Ryan had asked about me, but I didn't call them back. It occurred to me now that I'd likely lose touch with them as I had my high school friends, that they, too, had been nothing more than friends of convenience, our connection broken as soon as we moved apart. The thought saddened me, but I accepted it as inevitable, something out of my control.

On Saturday morning I went with my mother to Temple Emek Shalom, where I'd squirmed through High Holidays services as a girl, where I'd first kissed a boy in a game of truth or dare down in the old gym in the basement, which had since been remodeled and turned into a ballroom, rented out for bar mitzvah and wedding receptions. I hadn't been back since I'd graduated high school, and the sanctuary looked smaller to me, less grand, the wooden pews replaced by plastic folding chairs. Where one of the antique windows had been broken by vandals, clear plate glass gave view onto the sooty bricks of the apartment building next door.

Right away I recalled the past agitation I'd felt here, when I was pained by my own boredom, by the cantor's meandering melodies, by the rabbi's feeble attempts to engage the young people in the room, slipping references to Michael Jackson and Police songs into his sermons. "If you'd just sit still for five minutes and listen, you might actually learn something," my mother would say on the drive home. "Didn't you hear what the rabbi said? How God always sees what you're doing and knows what you're thinking? 'Every breath you make,' right?" My father, who accompanied us only because my mother insisted he set a good example, slapped the steering wheel and snorted, which sent me into a fit of giggling. My mother looked out the window and said, "You're not helping, Alan."

The words of the prayers meant no more to me now than they had then. I wanted to be moved by the cantor's voice, wanted to have some profound insight into life and death and love, but I was so conscious of wanting it that I couldn't let go of the skeptical voice that undermined the melodies, the sermon, the solemnity, that said any spiritual feeling I might have was of my own invention. During the silent Amidah, my mother was rapturous, lips moving, eyes closed, body rocking, and after a moment I closed my eyes, too. Those images of funeral and grave-side I'd first pictured in David's apartment now finally seemed real, even as I tried hard not to believe them. I couldn't stop myself from adding my own prayer. Please, I thought. Let him pull through. Let him get better so I won't have to stay in Chatwin taking care of my mother, explaining to her about the property in Florida. Let him live, so I can get back to my own life. As if I knew what that was supposed to be.

My mother sat. The rabbi said a page number, and in the midst of rustling paper came a sudden thump and rattle, followed by a gasp from the entire congregation. On the other side of the clear glass, a cloud of feathers drifted downward. I'd snapped the prayer book onto my finger. My heart was racing. "Pigeon," my mother said. "Happens all the time. Ever since those Nazis smashed our window."

Afterward we ate lunch at a Chinese restaurant two doors down the street. "It was nice of your friends to come to the hospital," my mother said as I took a bite of wonton soup. "They're very … interesting." She'd told James and Stephen how sorry she was that I'd had to come home this way, that I'd disrupted all my plans. She was sure I'd be able to go back up to Boston as soon as my father was on his feet again. Did they know I had a boyfriend up there, a great guy, soon to be a lawyer? "I think ... I think, maybe, you should go back up there now," she said, staring at her placemat, ringed by cartoon symbols of the Chinese Zodiac. "I don't think you should wait."

"I'm not going anywhere until Dad's well," I said.

"It doesn't seem to be doing any good, you being here. He's only getting worse. Maybe ... maybe he'll do better if you leave."

I put my spoon down. I was surprised more than insulted, saddened to discover that my mother was as superstitious as I was. How deluded were we, thinking our actions had any influence over the world. What did cancer care about us? What did God, for that matter? I covered my face and cried. My mother apologized and took it all back. "The whole thing's making me crazy," she said. "For Godsakes, Amy, when's it going to stop?"

13.

THAT NIGHT, WHEN I thought he'd actually be home, I called David. Part of me hoped he wouldn't answer anyway, that he'd be off somewhere with Nissa, the tart from Milwaukee, or out drinking with college buddies who would soon become law school buddies. But another part of me was so relieved to hear his voice when he answered that the first thing I said was how much I missed him, how frustrating it was that I never caught him in. "Where are you all the time?"

It was a manipulative thing to say, I know – I knew it even then – but without hesitating, David rose to the bait. "I've got a life," he said. "I can't sit around waiting for you to call all day long."

Just like that, and I was exonerated – all the messages I hadn't returned, all the calls I'd made when I knew he'd be out, and he'd just accepted the blame. My mother was wrong, I thought. He'd make a lousy lawyer. I told him I'd been in the hospital for the past three days, and his tone shifted to that confused, hesitantly sympathetic one he'd had the day I'd left, offering awkward words of comfort, and I couldn't decide whether or not to feel sorry for him. "Do you still want to come down and visit?" I asked.

"Sure," he said. "I mean, of course. If you want me to."

"Come tomorrow," I said.

"Well, I mean ... I've got to work. I can't just bail without telling them. I'll come on Saturday."

"I need you here tomorrow."

Why did I feel compelled to keep testing him, when he had no chance of passing, when he'd already failed the one test that mattered?

He hesitated a moment, and then said, with his old lazy self-assurance, "Okay, sure. I'll be there by early afternoon."

He didn't make it until after nine. He left a message from a payphone at South Station, saying he'd missed his first train out of Boston. Then another two messages from Trenton. He'd forgotten to change trains in Newark. Did I maybe know which train to get on from there? Never mind, he said in the last message, he'd figure it out. Finally he called from the Chatwin station. I told him how to find his way to The Victory Manor and then let him stand in the hallway for a minute after knocking. When I opened the door his face went through a cycle of expressions, from tender and condolent to delighted and hungry. "Sorry it took so long," he said. "I got lost. Went around the wrong side of the park. Nice haircut."

After visiting the hospital on my way home from work – my father was awake and drinking fluids on his own, his electrolytes were up, but he couldn't yet get out of bed – I'd stopped to get a trim. I'd repainted my nails and taken a shower and lay on the bed naked, letting a rare breeze through the open window cool me. For a while I debated whether or not to stay this way until David showed up, but the longer I waited the less refreshing the air felt, and eventually I got dressed. "You always thought I looked better with long hair," I said.

"I was wrong. You look great." David didn't look so great himself. His hair was matted on one side, his face shaded with at least two days of stubble. I'd never known him to get acne before, but now he had a rash of it across his forehead and over his left temple. He put down his bag and kissed me, and his breath tasted like stale coffee. His hands felt unfamiliar against my back, clunky and insensitive, one sliding down onto my rear. I pulled away, expecting him to give me his wounded look, but he didn't seem bothered. He flopped onto the bed as if he belonged in it, shoes on the sheet, hands behind his head. "Cool apartment." He patted the mattress. "You gonna join me or what?"

"Later," I said. "We're going out."

On our way upstairs he told me what a crazy day he'd had, as if it was something imposed on him rather than something he'd caused himself—he'd missed his first train because he'd forgotten his credit card and had to go back to the apartment, and then no one in Trenton would help him. "It was like everyone spoke another language," he said as we stepped into the elevator. "Just like being back in Spain. Jesus, remember that guy in the Madrid station who kept yelling at me? What an asshole. Anyway, I made it, didn't I?" He said it with real pride, as if it were a major accomplishment, and I wondered for the first time since I'd left what state his apartment was in, whether he'd done dishes once in the last month and a half, whether he'd moved any of my boxes from where he'd first dropped them. Only now did he remember to ask about my father, and when I told him things were day to day, he put on a look of concern and slipped an arm around my waist. It was still there when we reached the fifth floor, and his fingers kept their grip as I heaved open the grate. And there on the other side was Miss Elkin, with her bag and lit cigarette, giving a big, closed-lipped grin when she saw us.

"Miss Markowitz," she said, letting smoke out of her nose. She dropped her butt on the floor and ground it out with her braced heel. "What perfect timing. Would you and your friend mind riding me down?"

She explained to David about her difficulty with the door, and told him she'd lived in the building twice as long as he'd been alive. I kept silent, and David had to introduce himself, continuing to cling to me even as he shook Miss Elkin's hand. She asked if we'd just met – at work, perhaps? or did Mr. Zeitlin live here in the building? – and David briefly related our history together, the political philosophy class in which we'd sat beside each other, flirting, the second semester of sophomore year, the trip we'd taken to Europe, the unfortunate way I'd had to leave when my father got sick. I'd never actually told Miss Elkin I was single – not explicitly – but all the same I felt caught out in a lie. If she thought so too, she didn't let on. She smiled at us both and said we were a lovely couple. When we reached the lobby, David held the door for her, and she said, "Mr. Zeitlin, a pleasure to meet you. And Miss Markowitz, as always. I'm sorry to hear your father's still not well. My best wishes to him and your family for a speedy recovery." She paused a second in the door of the elevator, and then added, "If all goes well I suppose you'll be leaving us shortly." She and David both stared at me. I said nothing.

On our way back up, David asked what was wrong with her leg. "Auschwitz," I said, without hesitation.

"Oh yeah? No tattoo."

I'd never seen a tattoo, either, but it had never occurred to me to look. "She didn't get a number," I said. "She was supposed to go straight to the gas chamber." I told him a story about her daring escape from the camp, a year of hiding in the woods, a Nazi dog that sniffed her out and clamped its jaws on her ankle until she'd brained it with a rock. I made it sound as if we were intimate, as if I'd taken the time and made the effort to get to know her. "Her whole family died," I said. "She didn't know a single person when she came here."

"Brutal," David said, and pulled me closer. "You never told her about me." I shrugged. He bent down and kissed me again, and this time I let his hands go where they wanted. They were gentler now, and his breath tasted better. I hated myself for not knowing what I wanted, or for wanting different things from one moment to the next. When the elevator stopped, I pushed him away.

James made a big to-do over David, giving his crooked smile and opening his wide, eager eyes, telling him he'd heard so much about him, that he was so glad David could finally make it down. "Amy's been horribly lonely without you," he said. "We've been trying to keep her entertained while she's here." I didn't know if he was putting on a show for my sake or for David's, but in either case I appreciated it. Stephen didn't. He stayed on the sofa, flipping angrily through his magazine. As usual, he was wearing nothing but boxers, but now he seemed embarrassed to have his white skin and wiry black hair exposed, covering his chest with an arm, crossing one leg over the other. When I introduced him to David he only nodded without lifting his eyes and turned a page. James explained the sewing machine and bolts of fabric, telling David he'd have to come shop at his store after it opened. And then he said, "Wait! You can try some things on now. I really need a model. Stephen never wants to wear anything I make."

He started shuffling through his clothes rack, asking David's size, handing him a dozen shirts and pants. David looked them over with a stricken expression, similar to the one he wore in Europe when scrutinizing unreadable menus. I went to the kitchen and made cocktails, with less grenadine tonight and more Rose's Lime. James took a sip and said, "Oh, you nailed it this time, Amy. Your best one yet."

David made a face when he tried his, but then gulped half of it down. Stephen waved his away. "I don't want to drink something that tastes like Band-Aids," he said. I handed it to him anyway and squeezed in beside him on the sofa. He kept his legs crossed tightly and held them away from me. But I tucked my feet under his arm, and unless he rolled off the sofa, he couldn't keep me from touching him. When David went into the bathroom to change, Stephen said under his breath, "You're really working on that honesty thing."

"I'm trying," I said. "That's why I told him to come down."

"To finish him off? Or to get back together?"

"One or the other," I said. He stiffened and leaned away. I wedged my foot under his back.

"He's pretty for a straight boy," James said.

"Maybe you can turn him," Stephen said. "Since you seem to think it's so easy."

James ignored him and said to me, "You've got good taste. For looks, anyway. I don't know about personality."

"You too," I said. "Especially on the second count."

When David returned, his loose jeans and T-shirt were gone, and in their place were tight red trousers and a fitted butterfly-collar shirt patterned with stars and crescent moons, far more flamboyant than anything I'd seen James wear. I burst out laughing, and so did Stephen. David looked like a gay Jewish pimp, and he hammed it up, strutting in front of us. Of course I wouldn't go back to him. I felt light and cruel and laughed harder, digging my foot into Stephen's armpit, trying to tickle him with my toe. He grabbed my ankle to stop me and kept his hand there. "You look amazing," James said, peering through a frame he made with his fingers, as if he were a movie director. "Now we just have to find you shoes."

"And then let's go already," Stephen said, putting aside his glass. "I can't drink any more of this swill."

David stopped strutting. "I can't go out like this," he said.

"You'll be such a star," James said.

"I don't think so."

"For me," I said.

He studied himself in the mirror, pulling anxiously at the shirt's hem, and drained the rest of his drink. "Not a chance."

I waited until he caught my eye. It took all my effort to keep a straight face. "Please?" I asked.

It was the clearest night of summer so far, moonless and

cool, and the lights of the park cut a straight, lavender-tinted path through its dark center. A pair of drunks hit us up for money, and David struggled to get his wallet out of the tight pants. When he did, all he found was a twenty, and handed it over. "God bless you, man," one of the drunks said, grabbing his shoulder with grimy fingers, smudging the satin. "You're a saint."

"Saint Huggy Bear," Stephen said.

In The Scandal, David downed three drinks in twenty minutes and did his best to ignore the looks he was getting, the smirks and laughter. By the fourth drink he was starting to enjoy himself, and after dancing with him for a couple of songs, I left him on the floor with James and a dozen other men who didn't seem to mind what an awful dancer he was, far clumsier than I. Stephen was enjoying himself, too. He was cheerful when I joined him in our booth, laughing when I said that James was right, it was a snap to turn a straight boy gay. He seemed to understand something of what was in my mind, even if I didn't say it. We put away several drinks of our own and talked about exotic locales we'd run away to, where no one would find us. He suggested places with names he liked the sound of, Casablanca, Kashmir, Tasmania. I talked about places I'd been in the spring – in this fantasy my imagination was somehow limited – describing Crete, Sorrento, Cadiz, thinking how nice it would be to visit them with someone who wouldn't gawk at women in bikinis, who wouldn't be afraid to try unfamiliar food. "Cadiz," Stephen said. "I like the ring of it."

"We'll go," I said. "As soon as my father's better." But then I thought we'd go whether my father got better or not, and felt a swelling destructive urge to brush aside everything I cared about, to shrug off all concerns but the most selfish ones, or the ones with the least potential to cause me grief.

"You don't mind leaving Superfly behind?" he said, pointing to David with his chin.

I shrugged. "What about James?"

"As soon as his shop opens, he'll forget all about me."

We'd find a room with a view of the sea, I said. I'd get a job teaching English to the children of rich Spaniards. We'd both meet dark-haired boys along the harbor, and the four of us would go adventuring together, to Gibraltar, to Casablanca. The light, cruel feeling was giving way to something more melancholy as I pictured Stephen holding hands with a fit, swarthy Latin boy, and I fought it off by telling him we'd buy motorcycles and ride up to the Pyrenees, we'd summer in the Swiss Alps, we'd grow old together under a warm Spanish sun.

"I can't wait," he said. "When do we leave?"

When David eventually came back to our table, he could hardly stand up. James was holding onto him, but still he swayed as if he might topple backward. "I think he's broken enough hearts for tonight," James said. "Time to get him home."

"He gets like this sometimes," I said on our way through the bar. "Usually when he's around Australians."

David sang, "*I come from the land down under, where the women jerk and the men come on her.*"

"I love that song," Stephen said.

"I don't think that's how it goes," James said.

"Those are the original lyrics," Stephen said. "They censored it for radio."

The lights in the park seemed even brighter now, the trunks of the elms made weirdly flat against the dark space behind them, the statues alive with rustling pigeons. David was still leaning against James. "Park Gruel," he said. "Gotta love that gaudy Gaudí. Strange muh-fucker, huh?" He reached for me, and I dodged his hand, and then without a single thought I was running, off the path, out of view of the lights, around picnic tables, over sleeping winos. I felt reckless and drunk and giddily free, and for a moment I didn't even realize Stephen was right there beside me, breathless, giggling.

"Where we going?" he asked. "Cadiz?"

"Let's hide," I said.

I took his hand and pulled him behind a shrub, where we

watched James and David staggering down the path, disappearing behind a massive trunk and then reappearing and then disappearing again, as if they were on a movie screen that flickered on and off, their faces lit up melodramatically like those of stars in old black and white reels, their shadows stretched out behind them. When they came close we made a break for The Victory Manor, hand in hand, both of us giggling now, bumping hips. Miss Elkin was in the lobby, but I only waved to her and pulled Stephen to the stairs. By the second floor he started to flag, heaving for breath, and I had to drag him the rest of the way. I started leading us to my door, but Stephen shook his head and pointed up. I didn't know why but didn't argue. In his and James's apartment, he gasped, "Here, in here," and without turning on the lights, pulled the bed a few feet out of the wall. We climbed in. "Watch your head," he said, and grabbing the inside of the trim, rolled us back.

What a strange thing to be hidden away inside a wall. We were in the building's belly and could hear the rumbling of its innards, water moving through pipes, gears pulling the elevator's cables, unidentifiable creaks and groans. It was completely dark and quickly stuffy. There was wood six inches above our heads, and underneath us the sheets were bunched and uncomfortable. I was surprised James would have left them this way, even if no one could see them. They smelled of sweat and sex and soap, but now I could smell Stephen's scent, too, a sweet muskiness and slightly milky odor, along with the spicy smell of rum on his struggling breath. "It's not Cadiz," I whispered. "But it'll do."

"Shh. I hear them."

The door opened and closed, and a razor-thin rectangle of light appeared around the edge of the bedframe. Footsteps sounded in the room, one set steady, one stumbling. As my eyes adjusted to the darkness, the soft outline of Stephen's face came visible, the small triangle of nose, the round contours of cheeks and chin. We lay on our sides, facing each other. He started giggling again, and I poked him in the ribs. And then I started giggling, too, and had to bite my lip, and then we both had to cover our mouths with pillows. Shadows crossed the light at our feet. Then the footsteps retreated, the door opened and closed again, and except for the rumbling of the building and the sound of a few cars passing on the street below, there was silence.

"What do we do now?"

"Let's stay for a while."

"Okay," I said. "We'll pretend we're in Cadiz."

"I don't know what it looks like," he said.

"Close your eyes." I described the harbor and the cathedral and the beautiful narrow streets ending at the sea. "There are parks everywhere, and open courtyards with people drinking coffee and wine. When the sun sets, the whole city gets this soft golden glow, and as soon as it goes dark, the water turns this incredible plum color, and the air smells like salt and olives and oranges." David and I had visited the city for less than a day and a half, and my memory of it was hazy at best. But now, my imagination kicked into gear. I made up what I hadn't seen or couldn't recall, including the sunset and the color of the sea at dusk. Stephen didn't question any of it. Our bodies were touching from hips down to ankles, and again from elbows to wrists. As I talked, our fingers intertwined. Stephen squeezed his eyes shut tight enough to wrinkle his nose, but I kept mine open, studying his face, which came clearer and clearer in the gloom. "One last thing," I said. "You see that long spit of land that curls out between the harbor and the sea? There's a small house there, two or three hundred years old, with beautiful carved stonework and a little turret at the top. That's where we'll live."

"Okay," he said. "I'm there."

He didn't seem surprised when my lips touched his. He let them part, breathed in, slipped a hand around my neck, under my hair. He went through the motions of kissing me, but it took only a moment to know they were only motions. I kept my mouth against his several beats longer than necessary, hoping it wasn't true. But I didn't need my foot against his crotch to know there was nothing happening. We separated and lay facing each other, hands still locked. I don't know that I've ever been sadder, but I didn't cry. I just took a last long look at his face in the near dark and decided that everything would be different for me from this point forward, that this was the final moment of all that my life had been up till now. Stephen's smile was part sympathetic, part resigned. "Forget being in truth," he said. "Truth sucks."

He pushed us out of the wall, and the light was so unexpectedly bright that for a moment I tricked myself into believing we'd been transported to Cadiz after all. I sat all the way up before realizing we were still in Chatwin, still in the West End, and that James was in the room, sitting on the sofa, staring at us. He didn't say anything, and neither did Stephen, and neither did I. All three of us averted our eyes. I let go of Stephen's hand and got off the bed. I had an impulse to straighten the sheets before I left but restrained myself. When I reached the door they were both still sitting as they'd been, Stephen cross-legged on the bed, James on the sofa with his elbows on his knees, head in his hands.

David was passed-out in my bed, snoring, the ridiculous shirt unbuttoned but still on, the red trousers pulled down to his knees. I stripped and lay beside him, straining to hear what was happening upstairs, imagining a fight brewing, some terrible scene. Occasionally I heard quiet voices, but those may have been coming from outside. Otherwise, nothing. It was the first night since I'd moved in that I didn't hear the sewing machine, and the first that I fell asleep with little trouble.

In the morning I woke to David's hand moving down my side, over my belly. His clothes were gone. He moved onto me, and we cycled through all our old positions, made all our old noises, and finished with all our old caresses. I was surprised to find I'd been wrong the night before, that nothing at all had changed, and even more surprised to find that I could enjoy being with David even as it embarrassed me, even as I chastised myself for enjoying it. Afterward we lay together without speaking. I felt humiliated without knowing why, and had the sense that David did, too. And then it occurred to me to say, "You've been fucking Nissa."

The sound of his breathing altered just slightly, for a second, and then continued. "I heard you got with one of Hope's friends in Brooklyn."

He took his time getting dressed in the change of clothes he'd brought, nursing a headache and uneasy stomach, and stuffed the clothes James had lent him into his bag. "Souvenir," he said. At the door I hugged him, and suddenly there was an easy companionability between us, maybe even genuine affection, a sense of a shared, if troubled, past, like that of soldiers returned from a foreign war. "You should probably come up to Boston and get your stuff," he said. "If you leave it to me, you know … you'll end up waiting forever."

I reminded him how to get to the station, what trains to take, where to switch, and to each piece of information he gave an uncertain nod. But even then I thought I'd been mistaken about him, that he could look out for himself just fine. After shutting the door behind him, I went to the window to watch him leave, but what I saw instead, a block and a half away, was a bundle of clothes on the sidewalk, two dark spots I knew to be shoes, a white puff I knew to be bunned hair. When David did appear below, I wanted to call to him, to warn him, but there wasn't time, and he probably wouldn't have listened anyway. He was running, bag over his back, and then crouching at Miss Elkin's side. I waited for her to swat his hand away, for him to jerk back and then stand by confused as she struggled to her feet. But instead, he helped her up, without any apparent resistance, and she leaned against him as he walked her back to the building. He delivered her to the front door and then made his way south, the opposite direction from the train station.

14.

FOR THREE WEEKS my father was in and out of the hospital,
with dehydration, and anemia, and infection. And then, almost
overnight, his condition improved. The infection cleared, his
iron count was strong, he was able to eat on his own again. He
came home from the hospital and took up his old spot on
the armchair, newspaper spread in front of him, a knit cap on
his head to keep his scalp warm as the days grew shorter. He
had two more chemo treatments left, but the drugs had finally
stopped making him nauseous. "You can get used to anything, I
guess," he said. "Even drinking poison."

On their twenty-seventh wedding anniversary, he told my
mother about the property in Florida. Only he didn't tell her it
was an investment he'd made two decades earlier but a gift from
his Uncle Albert, who'd died in the late seventies. He would
have told her about it back then, he said, but he knew she would
have wanted to sell it, and Albert had dictated in his will that he
keep it until its value doubled. And then for years he'd forgotten
about it. Now it was worth ten times what it had been when
he'd first inherited it. He kept a straight face as he said all this,
even when he caught my astonished stare. It was the most con-
voluted lie I'd ever heard, but I nodded along as if it made perfect
sense. He was going to sell the property now, he said, to a developer who'd build a gated golf community, with a big clubhouse,
tennis courts and an Olympic-size pool. "We'll get a house
there for our retirement," he said. "Haven't you always wanted
to live in the tropics?"

If my mother was skeptical, she didn't show it. The last few
months had taken the fire out of her. Now she looked almost
as drained as my father did. "I don't care where we go," she said.
"As long as it's not back to the hospital."

In early September cranes were erected on either side of
the old concert hall, and demolition balls began to swing.
In two days the building was leveled. Dump trucks carried away
the remains, big chunks of concrete and skeletons of twisted

steel, nothing that looked like it could have ever housed an orchestra and audience. Soon after, the vacuum cleaner outlet closed, and in its place came a designer shoe store, which gradually lured yuppies away from the mall. Shiny luxury cars appeared where before there'd been only dusty beaters. The police cracked down on the drunks in the park, clearing them out to shelters at night, and I no longer felt safe walking through after the sun went down. I kept my eye out for the man who'd sat on the bench beside me, sniffing air, but never saw him again. Still, I took to eating lunch in the agency's conference room, pushing brochures and envelopes aside, careful not to get salad dressing on anything important. Maxine wasn't happy about it, but Anna told her to mind her own business.

James's boutique had quickly taken off. He'd begun to pay off the loan on the stolen car title, and now with new commerce in the West End, the store was booming. He'd even brought in a line of women's clothes, sold on consignment by another designer. After a few weeks of avoidance and agonizing, I went in to browse and to apologize. James's smile was as eager as ever. He broke away from a customer to give me a hug and told me how much he'd missed me. Once again, the purity of his friendship shamed me. "I would have stopped by," he said, "but I've been in here every night." He'd set up his sewing station in the stock room and crashed on the white sofa he'd tucked in the back corner. He didn't have much reason to sleep at home these days. Hadn't I heard? Stephen was gone. He'd moved to Philly to live with old friends. He had a lot to sort out. It wasn't my fault, James said, and wouldn't even let me say I was sorry. "He did a job on both of us, didn't he?" I nodded but didn't know if I believed it or not. Who'd done the job on whom? But what I really couldn't understand was why he hadn't said goodbye. "He wanted to," James said. "But you know. He was never very good at doing what he thought other people should do. He said he hoped you'd forgive him for being such a coward."

Before leaving the store I bought a skirt and top I didn't

need. They cost most of a week's pay, and I didn't have any place to wear them. They were too sexy for the office – unless I wanted to compete with Anna – or Temple Emek Shalom, where I'd accompanied my mother to services most Friday nights since David's visit. The prayers didn't mean any more to me now than they had the first time I'd been back, but nothing made my mother happier, and for some reason I felt more relaxed in the old sanctuary than anywhere else; it was the one place I could let my mind go free and empty and not think about the past or future or even the present moment, which drifted along peacefully with the cantor's melody. I hadn't been back to the city for nearly a month, and now Debbie called to let me know that she and Hope were through as friends, and soon afterward Hope called to tell me that everything Debbie said was a lie, that she was a petty, backstabbing bitch. She wanted to know if I was ready to move out of New Jersey. She was looking for apartments, and there were better deals on two-bedrooms than studios. We'd have so much fun together, she said. We'd slay all the men in Brooklyn.

I told her I wasn't sure. My father was better but not out of the woods yet. And I couldn't just quit my job without notice. And I still had more than three months left on my lease.

The truth is, I was afraid to leave. There was something essential about my staying in Chatwin, I thought, something connected to what I'd done to David, what I'd done to Stephen and James, what I'd done to myself. Purgatory was a strange concept, foreign to my upbringing, an invention of people, I thought, meant to keep other people in line. But still, that's where I felt I belonged.

And then, on a Monday morning in mid-September, Maxine was waiting for me when I came into the office. She had a stack of envelopes in her arms. I didn't know what to make of it. She was smiling, and that confused me more. Without her puzzled scowl she looked almost pleasant, matronly and gentle, and it made sense that she had a husband and children who loved her. She handed me one of the envelopes and asked, mildly, where it was going. "Toronto," I said.

"And how much postage does it have?"

Not enough, apparently. I'd stamped them all the same, whether they were staying in the country or going out. All this time I'd thought the job beneath me, my intelligence ill-used, and it had never occurred to me that it cost more to send things to Canada. I'd never thought to ask. I put on a show of being horrified but my instinct was to laugh. I was tired of being capable, and now I could simply be the bonehead Maxine had always believed me to be. Returning her strained grin, I had to work hard to keep from busting up. The post office had sent back nearly a hundred of the mailers this morning, Maxine said, and the fiber optics convention started in less than two weeks.

"Is this all of them?"

"I think so," I said, though I knew it wasn't. The next morning another hundred envelopes came back, and then more than two hundred the following. Maxine's grin was long gone. On the fourth morning, nearly three hundred mailers returned. While I was getting my coffee, I heard Maxine shouting in Anna's office. "I don't care if her father's dying! She's finished! She's got to go!" Then, to my surprise, her voice went quiet. When I came back, Anna's office door was open. The sisters were in the conference room, silenced by the soundproof glass. Some of my co-workers had gathered outside, and we all watched, as if the glass were in fact a two-way mirror and not transparent from both sides. Anna and Maxine didn't notice us in any case. They had eyes only for each other. Maxine's hands went up over her head and crashed down at her sides. Anna yanked her own hair. Her eyes were red around their mesmerizing blue centers, her face nearly purple. I somehow expected their movements to be slowed down by the glass, as if they were fighting under water, but Maxine made a quick jabbing motion with her finger, and I flinched. Watching them was dizzying, but I couldn't pull myself away, and neither could anyone else.

One of the young designers, who'd said maybe a dozen words to me in the last three months, asked what had happened. I shrugged and said, "I think the little one broke the big one's Barbie." He laughed. So did several others around us. Then we all started joking, talking about our bosses as if they were little girls, cute and spoiled and harmless. When we broke for lunch, the others invited me to join them.

15.

"I'M SORRY," ANNA said that afternoon. "I know you're going through a tough time. But Maxine's right. The conferences aren't making enough money" – she looked down, sadly, at the cross dangling from her neck – "and we can't go on pouring resources into a losing proposition. It's not about the mailings. Anyone can make a mistake. Well, I don't know about making the same mistake seven hundred times ... " She stopped and glanced at me, the natural gray of her irises even more striking, I thought now, than the tint of her contacts. The exasperated expression Maxine liked to turn on me momentarily crossed Anna's features, and for once they did look like sisters. "Anyway," she went on, "it's not about that. I know you're a smart kid, and if your father weren't sick ... "

She wanted to help, she said. She'd take over my lease at The Victory Manor if I couldn't afford to keep the place. She'd use it as a second office, where she could get certain projects started without Maxine knowing about them. She had all kinds of great new ideas – "they'll make us a fortune," she said – but for now they were best kept to herself.

Miss Elkin was in the lobby when I came home. Her knitted bag looked heavier than usual – along with cigarettes it held two cans of tuna fish and a box of tea bags – and she had a bandage over her left eye. "Miss Markowitz," she said. "You're back early."

"Yes," I said. "A slow day at work."

She caught me eyeing the bandage, and touched it with

the tips of her fingers. "Just a little bump," she said. "Nothing to worry about."

"Of course," I said.

In the elevator she talked again about the other Miss Markowitz – or Horowitz, or Hurwitz – and how much she'd enjoyed having her in for tea. It was the thing she looked forward to most in those days, and she was so terribly disappointed when the visits stopped after Miss Markowitz met her new young man in the building. Everything changed about the girl then. She was always in a hurry, always rushing off with a strange look on her face, not distressed exactly, not quite anxious, but confused and a little stunned. "I didn't know what to make of it," Miss Elkin said as we reached her floor, and this time when she invited me in for tea – a wounded look like my mother's on her face as she remembered the other Miss Markowitz who'd abandoned her – I accepted. "Wonderful," she said. "I'm so pleased."

We passed James's door, and I experienced a pang for the sound of the sewing machine, and then a sharper one for the old sofa where I'd tucked my feet under Stephen's arm. Miss Elkin clattered down the hall, her brace jangling, and it took effort to keep up with her. "That look," she said, as she worked her key into the lock. "It wasn't a happy one, not the look of someone in love. There was something like torment in it. Oh, I know how love can be. Torment is often part of it. But this was different. I tried to imagine what was happening for her. Maybe her young man was already married. Or maybe he was a criminal of some kind. Or maybe it had nothing to do with the young man, maybe it was something in her family. Like your own sad look," she said, opening the door. "How *is* your father these days?"

Her apartment was tidy and cramped, just like mine. The windows were equally grimy, cobwebs decorating the high corners, and her bed, too, was frozen in its tracks, taking up most of the space. How could she have lived like this for more than forty years? While she made tea, I looked for photographs, any evidence I could find of the life she'd had before coming here.

By now I really expected to see creased sepia prints of a lost family in Europe, tucked away during years of hiding through the war and years of wandering in its aftermath. I hoped to see portraits of a lovely girl in a leg brace, her smile made mischievous by the gap between her front teeth, her arm linked with that of a nicely tailored man with slick, gleaming hair. I hoped to see pictures of a husband who'd died young, of children, now grown and living in California. I hoped to be wrong about the lonely life I'd envisioned, as I'd been wrong about Miss Elkin being a seamstress. But there was nothing here to tell me one way or another, not a single snapshot.

"The thing is," Miss Elkin said, hobbling into the room with two steaming cups on saucers, the liquid sloshing with each awkward step, but never spilling. "The thing is, I heard noises next door. You know how the walls are here. Not intimate noises," she added, and gave me a shy smile. "I don't make a habit of listening for such things." She placed the tea on a little table by the window, and I joined her there, looking out on the park, cleared of winos now, a Mercedes parked at the curb below, and a Lexus half a block farther up. Before she went on, she lit a cigarette and blew a stream of mentholated smoke at the ceiling. "I shouldn't even call them noises," she said. "I shouldn't soften it. It was shouting, awful angry shouting, and it would go on for an hour, and then doors would slam. It happened three or four times, late at night, and every time I told myself I should call the police, and then every time I told myself it wasn't my place to interfere."

The tea was strong and bitter, and the first sip burned my tongue. I didn't want to hear about this other Miss Markowitz. I'd just lost my job. I'd been released into some uncertain future, and I wanted to enter it alone, without the muddle of other versions of myself, even if they weren't named Markowitz at all. But Miss Elkin touched the bandage on her head and gave me a look I recognized, a pleading kind of look that made me think of David Zeitlin, though he'd never done this sort of pleading with me. It was the look I imagined on my own face if I could have actually gathered up the courage to tell him the truth, when I still cared whether or not he'd forgive me.

"It's terrible what happened to her," Miss Elkin said. "I'd almost forgotten it, until the first time I saw you in the lobby. You do so remind me of her, even though you're far prettier." She wasn't looking at me as she said it, and I wasn't sure that she wouldn't say the same thing to the next Miss Markowitz who arrived after I left. "One night the police did come. Someone else called them. I heard the commotion and decided it was none of my business, I would just stay where I was. But curiosity got the best of me. I peeked into the hallway just as they were wheeling her off. Her face was swollen and bruised. I'd never seen anything like it before. I could hardly recognize her. And after that she never came back. Her parents cleared out the apartment, and I walked by them as if I didn't know who they were or what had happened."

I didn't say anything. Miss Elkin puffed on her cigarette, sipped her tea, looked out the window. I waited for her to finish, to admit guilt, maybe, and ask for absolution. "I do wish you hadn't called her back to mind," she said, her voice sharp and accusatory. "Some things are better left forgotten." I was startled enough that I began to apologize, but without glancing at me she waved off my words, her cigarette trailing smoke between us. "There's no point in being sorry for living one's life."

When she did turn back from the window, her expression had changed again, this time sly, confidential, her raspy voice going girlish and gossipy. How were the young men in my life? she asked. There were two, if she remembered correctly, the one in the elevator and the one with whom I'd run up the stairs.

I hesitated a moment and then told her everything. About David and Stephen, about Ryan in Brooklyn, about the creep in the park, about the young designer at the agency who'd flirted with me at lunch and who I'd likely never see again. My stories delighted her, and she hung onto every word. The only thing I didn't mention was that I'd been fired and that I'd soon be leaving. "Well," she said when I finished, leaning back in her chair, satisfied. "I wish the best for you and this new young man at work. But I do hope you'll stay a while longer. I enjoy your company."

I could have told the truth then. Why try to spare her feelings when she'd find out soon enough that I'd gone? Lying, though, was far easier. I'd done it so often lately that it was becoming second nature. "I'm not going anywhere," I said. "Not anytime soon."

But Miss Elkin didn't believe me anyway. She finished her tea and lit a new cigarette. "I've seen more Miss Markowitzes come and go than I can count."

16.

AFTER LEAVING CHATWIN, I spent two years in the city, sharing an apartment first with Hope, then with a boyfriend, then renting one on my own. From there I went to Berkeley, where I'm still living now, a year or so shy of finishing my doctorate. Until recently I hadn't thought much about the three months I'd spent in the West End, which took on a dim, dreamy quality in my mind almost as soon as I moved away. I wasn't aware of pushing it out of my consciousness, but its absence surprises me now.

One mark of that summer did linger and should have been a steady reminder: My father's hair never grew back. At least not on his head. On his arms white fuzz sprouted, and his eyebrows came back thicker and darker than ever. His cancer never came back, either. After seven healthy years he retired, and by then the development of his former property outside West Palm was mostly finished, with a house for him and my mother on the fairway of the pro course's fifteenth hole. My old Nova had sat in their driveway all this time, and now they were giving it away, along with most of the furniture they'd had since I was a girl. My mother was replacing all of it. "This stuff is too dark for Florida," she said. "We're going to be sunny people from now on." Only my father's armchair was coming with them, though my mother insisted on re-upholstering it in off-white linen.

A month ago, when they were getting ready to leave New Jersey for good, I flew back east to help them pack. My mother tried to load me up with end tables and bookcases, with silverware and china, a beautiful set of my grandmother's. I refused it all. My apartment in Berkeley was bigger than my place in The Victory Manor, but I'd already filled it with things I enjoyed and didn't have room for much else. "I hope you won't stay out there forever," my mother said. "It's so far away you might as well be in another country."

"Another country," I said. "I like that idea. Maybe Australia. Or India."

"Florida's as beautiful as anywhere else," she said. "And there's a lot more culture down there than you think. Plays and music, world class. And wonderful universities. You don't need to be in California to study your Latin. Maybe there's a good program in Miami."

"I'm not moving to Florida, Mom."

"Will you come for the holidays, at least?" she said, eyes welling up before she could turn away and roll the last of the silverware in a thick wad of bubble wrap.

"Of course I will."

"If you weren't all alone out there," she said. "If you were engaged at least—"

"Bernice," my father said, sealing a box with a loud squawk of the tape gun. "Look at her. She's fine. She can take care of herself."

"Are you really okay?" my mother asked.

"I'm great," I said, and for the most part thought I meant it. It's true that I was single now, and that I spent some long nights on my own, but I knew I didn't have to be single if I didn't want to be—there was always someone who expressed an interest, and often enough the interest was mutual. But actually, I didn't think much anymore about how I was from one day to the next. I just went on with my life, reasonably content with my work and friends and domestic routines, busy enough to keep from brooding. Still, the question agitated me for the rest of the weekend, and I worked harder than I wanted to prove to my mother that indeed I was great, that she needn't worry. I smiled until my face hurt and listened to her advice cheerfully, refusing to show any irritation.

After the moving truck came and went, my parents drove me back to the airport, taking the Victory Park route – the bypass had been built shoddily and was always under repair – and I was shocked to see how much the West End had changed. The transitional housing had been turned into lofts and condos. A glass and steel high-rise had gone up on the site of the old concert hall. The boarded-up theater was back in operation, showing foreign and art house films. There was a Cuban restaurant, a Thai restaurant, a steakhouse. The park was bustling with young families, hip kids on skateboards, middle-aged shoppers. Children climbed on the statues while their parents watched, gleeful voices reaching me through the open car window. The Vietnamese man was there, still ageless, still smiling, but only two or three pigeons pecked around in front of him as he dropped bits of bread on the ground. Where was the place I'd known? How much of it had I only imagined?

"What happened to the birds?" I asked.

"What birds?" my mother said.

"The pigeons. There used to be hundreds of them."

My father shrugged. Maybe the construction had disturbed their roosts, he said. Or more likely, the city had poisoned them to keep the new park benches clean.

Only The Victory Manor looked the same, its awning sagging, the elegant script on its front faded and unreadable. The bricks were dark, the windows grimy, the brass door in need of polishing. And in the instant we passed it, the last seven years collapsed. Right in front of me, distinct as if it had all just happened, were the sleepless, worry-filled nights I'd spent here, the sound of the sewing machine overhead, the smell of the rumpled sheets as Stephen and I hid inside the wall. Every detail I'd forgotten, or wished I'd forgotten, came flooding back, along with the feeling, lost long since, that the future was open and undetermined, ripe with possibility. The sound of water rushing through pipes, the hum and creak of the elevator, the long sweet moments before the disappointing kiss, when we huddled together in the dark, hands locked, dreaming ourselves in a Cadiz of my imagination. While I described streets I'd never seen, buildings that didn't exist, I'd also secretly been bargaining. If I could only have this, I'd thought – not daring to invoke God or universe directly, but hoping someone, something was listening – I'd never ask for anything else.

My father honked at a car in front of us and cut across three lanes of traffic to make a hurried left turn. "I'll be glad when I never have to drive through this mess again," he said. "These streets are meant for horses, not people."

And then, as we rounded the square, I spotted Miss Elkin. Her knitted bag was soiled, the handles frayed. Her back was hunched, the dignified posture gone. She seemed to have more trouble than before with her bad leg, the knee nearly scraping the sidewalk as she swung it forward, the brace coming down hard. We passed close enough for me to see her face, her cheeks sunken now, her mouth open in what seemed like a grimace of pain, the stain on her teeth deepened to a greenish brown. Her hair had thinned so much it could no longer support a bun. It had been cut short, her scalp showing through, a bluish tint to it, not the healthy pink of my father's. I thought I should call to her, but of all the Miss Markowitzes she'd known, what chance was there that she'd remember me? And if she did, what chance was there that she'd want to?

I felt a sudden chill and rolled up the window. My father honked again and gunned the car through a yellow light. In a moment Miss Elkin and the West End were behind us. I fixed my eyes ahead.